PRAISE FOR

"Romantic angst powers this fast-paced novel, and readers will return to the series to learn more about the enigmatic side characters whose own stories are waiting to be told."—Publishers Weekly

"A well-written story that kept me entertained from start to finish."—Harlequin Junkie

"This story had me hooked and addicted on page one!"—Reading in the Red Room

"Made me laugh, sigh and cry a lot."—Only. Ever. Books.

"Wow! Talk about getting hooked on a story right away!"—Red Hot Blue Reads

"I loved this book; this is romance at its best, this is that perfect ending we all read romance for, this is an absolutely beautifully told love story."—Guilty Pleasures Book Reviews

"The story is amazing and the suspense is thrilling."—Just One More Chapter

"The author has an amazing and deep connection with her characters. . . . I loved every single page."—Extreme Damage Blog

"TELL ME WHEN is a heartbreaking and emotional story. Be prepared to do nothing else but read once you start this book!"—Fresh Fiction

"Six stars—Stina Lindenblatt has a skill to write heroes with some depth like few can."—Collectors of Book Boyfriends & Girlfriends

"I Need You Tonight is one of those books that you go into thinking one thing and end up getting your mind blown because you were not expecting the emotion that this made you feel. Honestly, this had to have been the best book of the series because of that."—Life of a Crazy Mom

"[Stina Lindenblatt's] writing shows superb talent and care for both the storyline and her characters. This is not a book you want to pass the chance at reading."—Ellie Is Uhm . . . A Bookworm

"There are so many, many things that I loved about this story. . . . I hadn't realized I'd been missing and I was craving the Pushing Limits boys until this one came along. And it came with a bang!" —Collectors of Book Boyfriends & Girlfriends

"I. LOVED. THIS. BOOK!!!!"—Seeking Book Boyfriend

"If you are looking for well written story that will take you on a ride of highs and lows of our human emotional states and of the good and the bad of what life is willing to offer, then I highly suggest you read this fantastic story!"—Biblio Belles Book Blog

"I love Stina's writing style. It's very emotive, and flows beautifully. I felt connected to the characters from very early on and cried several times at the pain these characters go through"—Reading Realm Blog

"...a truly unique and utterly swoon-worthy romance." —Mary Dubé at Frolic/USA Today's HEA

ONE MORE SECRET

HIDDEN SECRETS TRILOGY BOOK 1

STINA LINDENBLATT

Cover design: Stina Lindenblatt
Cover art by Stina Lindenblatt. Cover copyright © 2023
Print book interior design by Stina Lindenblatt. Heart, shells, and flower illustration from Depositphoto.
Editing: Lauren Clarke at Creating Ink
Copyediting: Flat Earth Editing (Hope)
Proofreading: Flat Earth Editing (Jessica) and Karen Hrdlicka

ISBN: 978-1-990177-33-0 (print)

ISBN: 978-1-990177-19-4 (ebook)

*To the women who have sought a new start in their lives
and to those who have helped them.*

AUTHOR'S NOTE

One More Secret is the first book in the Hidden Secrets Trilogy. The story is about hope and healing and finding yourself again after leaving an abusive relationship. It's also about surviving the loss of a loved one to suicide due to PTSD (the hero's journey) and about struggling with complex PTSD, which can happen with domestic abuse. I wanted to address some of the real-life issues that survivors of domestic abuse face. Issues often skipped over in romances where the heroine has previously escaped an abusive partner.

Prior to the beginning of the story, the heroine gave up her parental rights to her toddler daughter after she was convicted of her husband's murder. In reality, once a mother has been found guilty of murder, she is usually stripped of her parental rights. If the children do not have family they can live with, they are placed in the foster care system and available for adoption. For the sake of the story I wanted to tell, I took some creative license and made it my heroine's choice to give up her parental rights.

Another thing I took creative license with was the timeframe between the heroine's arrest and when she was found guilty by a jury for the murder of her husband. The legal system doesn't work that fast. Just the opposite. But to simplify the timeline, I treated it as if she had gone straight to the maximum-security correctional institution even though that wouldn't have been the case. I hope you can forgive me for speeding up the timeframe and for giving my heroine the choice to choose what happened to her daughter.

xoxo,

Stina

ONE MORE SECRET

ONE MORE SECRET

1

JESSICA

March, Present Day
Maple Ridge

T he vibrations of the bus under my feet do nothing to calm me. But I don't think I'll ever be truly calm again after spending five years in prison for killing my husband. My abusive husband.

I stare out the window. Blue sky peeks between gray clouds, so different from the endless blue I left in San Diego three days ago. Snow-topped mountains reach up, their sides blanketed with pine trees.

My fingers close around an imaginary camera in my hand. My old camera. And they itch to press the shutter-release button, to capture the beauty of the mountains. The freedom.

I glance at my watch, one of the few possessions I still own. If the bus is on schedule, we'll be arriving in Maple Ridge, Oregon in fifteen minutes.

A place where I can easily disappear. Start a new life. Leave my past behind.

I twirl a goldish strand of hair around my finger. I haven't gotten used to the color yet. Until three days ago, I'd spent my thirty-one years as a brunette.

From what I've read about Maple Ridge, the scenic town seems to be a haven for tourists traveling to the mountains. Someone is less likely to recognize me from all the "Wife Murders Heroic Cop" coverage than if I'd stayed in California.

The bus pulls up to the depot, which is nothing more than a tiny brick building. I wait for everyone to get off, then make my way down the aisle. My heartbeat is a series of large waves crashing against rocks during a storm, the rhythm and intensity due to fear or excitement or a combination of both.

My small suitcase is on the sidewalk when I step off the bus. I grab it, turn to the building, and see a woman looking at me through the large window of the bus depot. She's in her early fifties, wearing jeans and a navy-and-white-striped top. Has to be Anne Carstairs. My new landlord.

Her straight, chin-length blond hair is ashier than mine. The sunny streaks look like the result of a salon. She didn't grab a cheap hair color like I did while picking up bread, peanut butter, and a couple of apples at the grocery store.

I hitch up my black pants, which hang awkwardly on my body, and shiver. My short-sleeved top isn't meant for the chilly temperature. It's better suited for San Diego's cool spring nights versus Maple Ridge's brisk afternoons.

There wasn't time to go clothes shopping once I was released from the women's prison. No time to make a quick trip to the mall while Florence drove me to a motel. I didn't want to deal with the media circus my release ignited. "Abused Wife Exonerated of Husband's Murder."

The next day she took me to the bus station. "Assuming the

media doesn't discover you're in Maple Ridge, you should be able to get a new start. No one has to know about your past."

"Does Anne know anything about it?" Is she okay with a former convict—even one innocent of the crime—living in her house?

"She knows you as Jessica Smithson. She doesn't know you're Savannah Townsend. I told her something traumatic happened to you, and you need a place to heal for a few months. She is happy to help. And you don't have to worry about her asking questions. If there's anyone who respects someone's privacy, it's Anne."

I pull out of the memory and scan the bus depot. No one seems to be paying attention to me. The couple at the ticket counter is busy buying tickets. The woman with a baby is strapping the sleeping infant into its car seat. I'm just another nameless person arriving in town.

I'm safe now.

Safe. It's been a lifetime since I felt that way. A lifetime since I didn't have to constantly check over my shoulder or brace myself for another mean word or slap or kick or punch.

Anne opens the door for me, and I step into the warm brick building. The inside has a quaint, small-town feel. Clean and cozy and welcoming. Picture perfect for the tourists, and hopefully a taste of what I can expect for the rest of Maple Ridge.

"Hi, you must be Jessica." Her gaze flicks briefly to my mouth and the two-inch scar from the corner of it down to my jaw. The result of a surprise knife attack. In prison.

I fight the need to duck my head, and I will my mouth into a smile, which fails to hit the mark due to the scar. "Yes. And you must be Anne." I hold out my hand to her, the polite girl I was raised to be temporarily stepping up for the one who fears being touched. Fears, but at the same time craves the physical contact of another person. A grandmother's touch. The touch of a best friend.

Anne shakes my hand, her grip confident and friendly. She doesn't seem to recognize me from all those times my picture was flashed on the news during my trial. But why would she? Savannah Townsend was gorgeous. Unforgettable. The two words my husband called me the first time we met.

Jessica Smithson is the one with the scars on her face. The scars the media never found out about.

I'm safe now. They'll never find me.

"Did you have a pleasant trip?"

"I did, ma'am. Thank you." My voice sounds rusty to my ears, the result of years of speaking as little as possible. Of trying to be invisible. For my own safety.

She makes a funny noise. "You don't need to call me ma'am. It makes me sound old." She glances at my small suitcase and then around the waiting area. "I wonder where they put the rest of your luggage."

"This is all there is. I traveled light."

Fortunately, she doesn't question that.

Twenty minutes later, Anne steers her car into the driveway of a small two-story house.

If I were asked to describe the house in one word, haunted would take top spot. The wooden siding needs several coats of paint. White? Possibly, if the remaining bits clinging to it are anything to go by.

"I know it's not much to look at," Anne says, her tone apologetic. "The place belonged to my great-aunt."

I study the house, half expecting to see the pale form of a ghost peering down at me. I shiver. "Where is she now?"

"She died ten years ago. I'm finally at that place where I can let the house go. My husband and I plan to sell it at the end of the year."

"You and your great-aunt were close?"

"Very much so. Did Florence warn you the place needs to be fixed up? We're planning to renovate it before we put it on the

4

market. We just haven't agreed yet on what specifically we're going to do. My husband and I have very different opinions on the topic." Anne chuckles. "But I will warn you that the house is a bit of a mess inside. Not the kind of mess that begs for a roach infestation. But, well, you'll see what I mean in a few minutes."

"I'm sorry for your loss. Do you mind if I ask how your great-aunt died?" Will her restless spirit haunt me because someone murdered her in the house?

"She died of a stroke. But don't worry." Anne's smile is some-what reassuring. "My husband replaced her bed. It's brand-new."

"Thank you." I can't complain about living in a house where someone died. If not for Anne and her husband, I wouldn't have a place to stay while I figure out what I'm going to do next. I have no references under my new name. I only have a bank account—thanks to my brother-in-law, Craig. "I can definitely clean up the place while I'm staying here." It will give me something to do. Something to keep me from dwelling on the past ten years.

We climb out of her car.

"There's a bike in the garage." Anne points to the detached garage located farther back from the house. "It's old and probably a little rusty, but you're welcome to borrow it if you'd like. It has a basket attached to the front, so it's perfect for shopping. My great-aunt loved to bike whenever possible. She practically lived on her bike until she was no longer able to ride it."

"Thank you. That would be great."

"The lawn mower is also in the garage." We walk up the steps to the front stoop. "It's manual, unfortunately. There're also gardening tools in there."

"When do plants start growing around here? If it's okay with you, I'd be happy to clean up the area and plant some flowers."

Small piles of decomposing leaves lie on the grass and winter-dead garden, but the place holds so much potential.

"In a few more weeks. It's still too early to plant the annuals. I would wait for May to do that." Anne unlocks the front door. "But

I'm okay with you doing some gardening if you'd like." Anne smiles at me, and I get the sense she's going to say something else, but she just opens the door. We step inside.

The outside of the house looks sad, dejected, and the inside isn't much better. The walls had been covered with bright floral wallpaper, but the color has faded and the paper is peeling.

We enter the living room. Dust covers the furniture, which is an eclectic mix of styles and eras that somehow works.

My husband would've hated it.

He would've also hated the chest-high piles of magazines, several rows deep, spanning the length of the far wall.

"Auntie Iris liked to be well read." Anne glances around the room, embarrassment at the mess and her obvious love for her great-aunt tilting her lips, pinking her cheeks. "She enjoyed books but loved magazines and journals. Fashion, news, history, gardening. It didn't matter what they were, she would read them. This is just a small sampling." Anne nods at the collection. "The only place you won't find them is in the garage and the bathrooms."

"Any idea how far back they date?" I eye the stacks with curiosity and not the dismay Anne is probably expecting.

"My guess is six or seven decades. She didn't keep all of them, but she did keep most of her favorite issues. She had a filing system, but I never figured it out. I always figured I'd one day go through them. Check out some of the articles. Have a giggle over how much things have changed since the articles were written... or maybe not changed as much as you would've expected. But my failing eyesight makes that more difficult now. I only read large-print books, and I use large font on my devices." Anne points to three stacks of magazines in the corner, separate from the others. Each magazine in this collection is in a Ziploc bag. "Those in particular were Auntie Iris's favorites."

I check the top few magazines. Their titles and dates appear random. The *Vogue* dates back to the 1940s. The other two are more recent issues, if you can call anything published in the 1980s as recent. There's nothing to indicate why these were her favorites.

I return them to the pile.

"I'm not expecting you to live with the magazines," Anne says. "My husband figures there might be some in her collection that could be worth something on eBay. We just haven't found time to go through them. We decided it's up to you to figure out what you want to do with them."

A twinge of excitement I haven't felt in a long time stirs to life, and I run my hand over an issue of *The New Yorker* from 1951. I wouldn't be surprised if there are articles in these magazines that were written by some of the greatest journalists from several decades ago. The greats I studied in college.

Anne continues with the tour of the house, giving me insight into the woman who once lived here. "She suffered from arthritis, especially in her right hand, which she injured when she was younger. It made things more challenging as she got older. But when I was a kid, I remember her always tinkering around the house. Always trying to fix something. She was very much a hands-on type of woman."

"Was she ever married?"

"No. She never found a man she loved enough for that. She once told me if I ever fell in love—the deep-in-your-soul kind of love—I should keep him. Cherish him. She didn't want me to waste my life with someone who didn't worship me."

I follow Anne upstairs, suitcase in hand. A deep pain twinges in my back, radiating from above my left kidney. I do my best to keep it from showing on my face.

Anne opens the door to the first room on the right. Inside, the queen-sized bed, shelves, dresser, and a maze of stacked magazines pack the space. The stale, dusty smell of the house is stronger than downstairs.

Damn, when was the last time someone opened a window in here?

"Did Florence tell you my husband and I will be going to Europe in two weeks?" Anne asks. "Dan just retired, and my family is originally from England. So we figured it's time we explore that side of the ocean. We'll be gone for six weeks."

"She did mention something about you traveling soon. The trip sounds wonderful." My voice is soft with awe. I've always wanted to visit Europe. To take pictures. To tell the stories of the people who live there.

We finish off the tour and head to the front door.

"Do you still want to stay here?" Hope lifts Anne's brow, lilts her voice. "I know it's a bit of a mess. But the roof doesn't leak, and the furnace works fine. So you don't have to worry about freezing during the cold nights we'll get for another month or two."

"No, it's perfect. It has a great view of the mountains. It's the perfect place to heal." Given where I've spent the last five years, it's Bucking-freaking-ham Palace. And better yet, it doesn't look anything like the house where I spent the five years of my marriage. That place had been cold, remote. But not in the physical sense.

She hands me the keys to the house and garage. "Welcome to your new home for the next few months, Jessica. I hope you enjoy staying here."

I lock the front door after her, making sure it's secure, and walk upstairs to the bathroom. I carefully lift the hem of my top and turn to inspect in the mirror the large sterile pad on my back. Blood isn't seeping through, which is a big relief.

I reach awkwardly behind me and pull the pad and tape away from my skin, revealing the long, jagged wound above my left kidney. Where I was shanked. In prison.

The wound that almost cost me my life.

That deepened my resolve to be free of my past.

And to not repeat my previous mistakes.

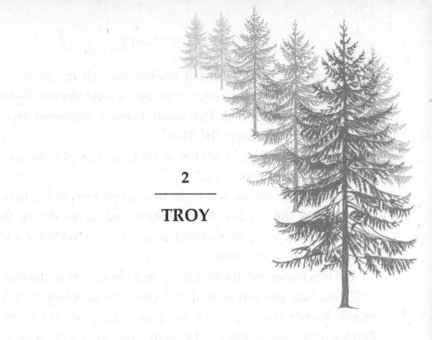

2

TROY

March, Present Day
Maple Ridge

I enter the rec room of the Veterans Center, Butterscotch trotting beside me. The scarf around his neck proclaims he's an emotional support animal. The lanyard around my neck says "Volunteer." I've been volunteering here since I retired from the Marines five years ago. The pint-sized Cavapoo has been my sidekick for the past two.

I unhook Butterscotch's leash from his collar. A table-tennis ball bounces past us, and he rushes off to retrieve it.

Jimmy laughs from the table where he and Adam are playing the game. Adam lost his leg when an IED went off. Jimmy lost his arm above the elbow when a missile hit his tank.

Butterscotch returns with the ball in his mouth and drops it at Jimmy's feet.

Jimmy crouches and pets him. "Thanks, little dude."

Katelyn steps away from the pool table next to where the guys are playing. Her blond ponytail swishes through the air as she turns to me. She has on yoga pants and a long-sleeved T-shirt that skims her tight bod. Her usual Tuesday afternoon recreational-therapist uniform. "Hi, Troy."

"Hey, sorry I'm late," I tell her, walking farther into the room. "I was held up at the worksite."

Butterscotch bounds over to the two elderly men sitting in the armchairs by the window. Both of them had served during the Vietnam War. They'd been close friends of my grandfather until he passed away several years ago.

Bill lifts Butterscotch onto his lap, and I head over to the duo.

"'Bout time you two showed up." The smile twitching on Bill's mouth lessens the impact of his grumbling tone. He strokes Butterscotch's loose curls. "Thought you were gonna stand us up."

I take the empty chair between Frank and him. "I would never do that. I was held up at work for a few minutes."

"Was that for those cabins you and your brothers are building?" Frank asks.

"Nope. We work on those on the weekends." For now, our full-time careers come first. The adventure program for military vets is our passion project. A way to give back to those who served our country. "I was delayed because the team renovating a house for one of my clients had an issue with the plumbing, which set back a shitload of things I needed to finish before coming here."

Frank shifts forward in his chair, settling his forearms on his knees. "How're those cabins coming along?"

"Good. We've finished the main building. The first half of the cabins will be ready midsummer. For the out-of-towners." Phase one of the long-term plans for the Wilderness Warriors program. A program dreamed up by my brother Lucas and our grandfather years ago. A program that started to become a reality last fall.

Frank picks up the playing cards on the coffee table and

begins shuffling them. "It's too bad your grandfather isn't here to see his dream come alive."

Bill looks up at the ceiling, still stroking Butterscotch, who happily basks in the attention. "I like to think he's watching from above and hooting you boys on." He drops his gaze to me. "He'd be proud of what you boys have accomplished. Both with your careers and the outdoor rec program. I don't suppose we'll get to sign up for it?"

"You guys are more than welcome to participate," I tell them. "My grandfather would be thrilled to know you got to enjoy his dream. It's meant for veterans of all ages and physical abilities."

"So you'll take us rock climbing?" Frank grins, his teeth white against his weathered face. Bill cracks up.

A chuckle vibrates through my chest. "Our insurance might not go for that." They definitely wouldn't approve of the two eightysomething-year-olds rock climbing.

"Damn insurance companies," Bill mutters. "What do they know anyway? We've already been put out to pasture as far as they're concerned."

Frank nods in agreement. I fight back the smile twitching on my mouth.

Katelyn comes over and stands next to his chair. "Hey, Troy." She sounds breathless, as if she was just running. "Did you want to play a game of ping-pong?"

"No, I'm good, thanks." I'm more interested in hanging out with these guys.

"All right. Let me know if you change your mind." She heads to a group of women playing cards at another table.

Frank shakes his head, the slow movement powered by either disbelief or disappointment or both. "Are you crazy, Troy?"

"The last I heard, no."

"C'mon, you telling me you don't want a piece of that?" He nods at Katelyn, and his hands mime a curvy body.

Bill snort-laughs, startling Butterscotch on his lap. "I think what he's trying to say is why don't you date her? And I have to agree with him there. She's a cheery sort of girl. Flexible too from all that yoga she does." His eyebrows dance above faded blue eyes.

I glance at the woman in question, but as much as I like her as a casual friend, my dick isn't interested. "I'm not looking to date anyone. I'm busy with work and the cabins. Plus, I've been looking into buying a house and flipping it. More specifically, buying Iris Bromfield's house. That's if Anne Carstairs will consider selling it."

Frank stops shuffling the playing cards and looks at me as though I've announced I'm painting my body purple and running down Main Street naked. "Why would you want to do that?"

"The proceeds will go to help Olivia and Nova. Colton left them a life-insurance policy, but because his death was ruled a suicide, they were screwed out of the money. Olivia's back to teaching again, but I know things are tight for her and her daughter." I'm also doing it because I'd promised Colt two years ago that I'd take care of Olivia and Nova if anything ever happened to him. As kids, we'd been The Three Musketeers. *All for one, and one for all.*

"Damn insurance companies," Bill repeats. "They failed your friend when he had PTSD, and they failed his family. It's not Olivia's and Nova's fault he killed himself. It's the insurance company for not helping him when he was struggling."

I wince. The insurance company wasn't at fault. The system failed Colton, and I failed him. I knew he'd struggled after a truck collided on the highway with a bus filled with young athletes on their way to their hockey game. Colton was a paramedic and one of the first responders at the scene. Half the passengers were already dead when he got there. I should have pushed harder to get him help. He couldn't deal with the nightmares and stress anymore, and he ended his life.

Frank resumes shuffling the cards. "There needs to be more

done to help PTSD sufferers and their families. The mental health field has come a long way since we served in Vietnam, but it's not there yet."

Butterscotch jumps off Bill's lap and walks to Frank. Frank pauses his shuffling and lifts him up. Butterscotch settles himself on the man's lap. "Like everything else, it comes down to lack of funding. Those damn politicians in Washington waste money on stupid stuff, but they don't do enough for mental illness."

It's true. Things are better than they used to be, but the system still comes up short. Especially for those individuals who can't afford therapy or medications or even health insurance.

"Someone ought to have a fundraiser to help the military vets and first responders in the area who struggle with PTSD," Bill suggests. "The money could go to assist them and their families."

"Are you volunteering to organize it?" I raise an eyebrow, even though I know where this is headed.

"Hell, no. I did the work of coming up with the idea. It's up to you young'uns to figure out the rest." Bill nods at me, and I grin, knowing I walked into that. But his idea does have merit.

"Speaking of Iris's house," Frank says, steering the conversation back to where it started. "I think you're gonna be out of luck, Troy, if you're hoping to buy it. I saw a woman with Anne at the house earlier this afternoon. She had a suitcase. Maybe Anne decided to rent the place."

Shit. "Are you sure about that?"

"The only thing I know for certain is the girl was pretty."

Bill leans in, his face brightening and giving me a glimpse of his younger self. "Was she a looker like Iris?"

Frank chuckles, the sound papery thin with age. "Definitely. From the photos I've seen of Iris back in the day. Remember Old Man Winters? He kept asking her out, and she kept brushing him off. She was only interested in being his friend."

"Maybe that's 'cause she wasn't interested in dating an old man?" I point out.

"He wasn't old for Iris. But he was much older than us." Frank nods at Bill.

Bill points at the cards in Frank's hand, indicating for him to keep shuffling or to deal them. "I can't believe Anne managed to rent the place out. The exterior is quite the eyesore, especially compared to the infills going up in the area."

Some of which my construction company built.

"Maybe she hired the woman to clear the house out. From what I'd heard, the place was also a mess inside. If the Carstairs are serious about selling the house, they would need to deal with that first."

And if that's the case, I still have a chance to buy the property and flip it. I still have a chance to earn some extra money to help Olivia and Nova. Still have a chance to honor the pact I made with Colton. The pact where I promised to be there for Olivia should something happen to him. Because even though Colton is no longer with us, Olivia and I are still the Three Musketeers. We're still the same friends we were twenty-five years ago.

I make a mental note to call Anne tonight to get things rolling with my plan.

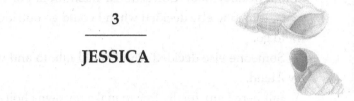

3

JESICA

March, Present Day
Maple Ridge

I sit on the bed in my new bedroom. The window is open, letting in the cold air and driving out the dusty smell.

My bedroom. A room I'm not forced to share. And a comfy queen-sized bed.

I lie back, arms to the side, a wide grin on my face. A *very* comfy queen-sized bed.

I stay like that for a minute, then sit up and glance around. The room is similar to downstairs with an eclectic mix of furniture. The floral wallpaper still clings to the walls. It's peeling and faded, but it's obvious the wallpaper in here, with the white background and the delicate yellow flowers, was once pretty.

"Okay, Jessica." My voice is louder than necessary, and relief cartwheels through me that for once no one is shouting obscenities at me for using it. No one is tearing me down for whatever I said. "You can't stay in here all day."

I need to bike to the grocery store. I can't hide in this house forever, even if part of me wishes I could.

For the past ten years, I've been bumped from one prison to another, first with my husband, followed by the correctional institution. Beckley State Correctional Institution. For eight of those years, someone else decided when I could go outside and where I could go.

Someone else decided who I could talk to and who could be my friend.

But here I am, finally free to make my own choices, and I can't pry myself off the bed and walk out the front door.

I sigh, rally my battered self-confidence, and push to my feet. *Baby steps.* I've come so far in the past few days. Ever since new evidence turned up while I was recovering in the hospital. Evidence that proved I didn't kill my husband. That someone else pulled the trigger and framed me.

The tightness in my muscles loosens and I release a long breath, my new reality fully sinking in. Ever since I learned I was being released from prison, I'd been positive it was just a dream.

I run my hand over the comforter, proving once again that it isn't a dream. I really am free.

Downstairs, I search through the utility drawer in the kitchen and find sticky tape and a cosmetic bag containing sewing supplies.

I remove the white thread and small scissors and cut an inch-long piece of tape. I stick it across the bottom of the front door, forming a bridge between it and the doorframe. If anyone opens the door while I'm gone, I'll know.

It was a trick my grandmother taught me when I was a kid. Although back then, it was because we were pretending to be spies and having secret missions in her house. Now, it's a makeshift security system.

I do the same trick to all the windows.

Once I'm finished, I return the tape to the drawer and cut off a two-inch piece of thread. I grab my purse and keys from the kitchen table. The purse is one of the items Florence gave me, along with a few items of clothing from Target. The black faux-leather bag is big and practical and perfect. It doesn't scream, *Pay attention to me.*

I go out the kitchen door and lock it. I crouch and fit the thread in the narrow gap between the door and the frame. It's enough for me to notice if the door's been opened while I'm away.

I enter the garage using the side door. The late afternoon sunlight streams through the windows and cobwebs fill the dimly lit space. Before I met my husband, spiders terrified me. Granny tried to convince me they wanted to be our friends and served a great purpose in life. She wondered how I could be scared of anything that created artwork that sparkled in the morning dew like diamonds.

I've since learned that scarier monsters exist. The eight-legged creatures don't bother me. It's the two-legged ones I fear.

I flick on the light. The sorry light bulb doesn't do much to wash out the shadows, but it does let me take inventory of the garage. The building is large enough for a single car but is currently used for storage. A cabinet stands next to the far wall. An assortment of tools—wrenches, hammers, saws, screwdrivers—are fastened to the wall above it.

I walk past the lawn mower, rakes, shovels, and an old work-bench. I open the cabinet. It's empty other than a metal toolbox, clay pots, and several gardening tools. None of the tools appear to be new, but they do look well cared for.

I close the door and straighten. Iris's old bike is parked against the main garage door. I walk over and inspect the frame. I don't know much about bikes, but this one resembles an older model, designed for cycling around town, shopping, or visiting friends.

The red paint has faded, spots of rust mar the frame, and the tires are flat. I pull open the drawer of the nightstand next to the bike and discover more tools. I close the drawer and open the door underneath it. A small hand pump sits on the top shelf. Perfect.

I inflate both tires. They should hopefully hold out while I bike to the store, but I will need to get some new inner tubes soon. Who knows how old these ones are? The tires also need replacing, the treads well-worn, almost smooth.

I pedal toward the grocery store, the wind blowing through my hair. And for a moment, the quaintness of the street, the trees lining it and the small cozy houses, lulls me into feeling safe. Even the newer homes have retained that quaint small-town feel I imagined on the bus ride to Maple Ridge.

But the feeling quickly shifts to one that's more familiar, the one ingrained in me. I'm on high alert, cataloguing anything that could hide a potential threat or be one. A tree. A tall bush. A parked car. A man walking along the sidewalk. My heart is racing, but not in the way it did when I was a kid. Back then, I'd felt free and alive pedaling alongside my best friend.

I am free and alive. No matter what my husband and the inmates and prison guards did to me in the past, they can't hurt me anymore.

But even though I can remind myself of that a billion times, I still have a hard time believing it.

I lock the bike in front of the store and go in through the sliding doors. I pick up a basket and pause, all the smells fighting for dominance—the citrusy fruits, the fresh herbs, the just-out-of-the-oven bread. I can't remember the last time I went shopping without my husband. He always came with me. Always made sure I couldn't escape.

During those final years, he made sure I had no phone, no car, no money, no dignity.

I might not have a phone or a car even now, but thanks to Granny's will, I at least have savings.

I put a tomato in my basket. And a banana. And then three more bananas. Why not? It's been forever since I last cooked for just me. Forever since I cooked what *I* wanted to eat.

Food had been fuel for my husband's body. The body he spent long hours honing in the gym. His body was his temple, the weapon he used against me. And only healthy food was permitted in our home.

I grab a box of sugary cereal and a package of gingersnap cookies with chocolate on the bottom. The kind Granny used to give me when I was a kid.

On the way to the self-serve checkout, I select a small bouquet of spring flowers. The symbol of hope and new beginnings. If I could, I'd fill my house with them. They're so pretty, a rainbow of uplifting colors. I pay for everything and load it all into the basket on the front of Iris's bike.

A woman walks up to me, wearing a thick jacket that's better suited for the cool spring temperature than my sweater. She smiles, the curve of her mouth warm and friendly. "Hi. Can you tell me how to get to Picnic and Treats Café?"

I shake my head, working toward finding my voice again. "I'm-I'm sorry. I'm new in town."

Air rushes from her like a leaky bike tire. "That's what I get for not charging my phone this morning. I can't even google it. I don't suppose you can google it for me?" Her smile turns hopeful.

"Sorry. I forgot my phone." I lift my shoulders in a quick shrug, not wanting to explain why I don't have one. It's not as if anyone will be contacting me. Granny's dead, and all my premarriage friends disappeared from my life soon after my wedding.

I climb on my bike and pedal away before anyone else asks me a question I can't—or don't want to—answer.

At home, I put the bike in the garage and walk through the wooden gate in the hedge surrounding the backyard. The leaf buds have yet to appear on the branches, and the hedge's lack of foliage leaves me feeling exposed.

I check the status of the thread I tucked in between the back door and the jamb. It hasn't been disturbed. I unlock the door and go into the house. A hollow silence eerily greets me. I should be thrilled it's so quiet. Even the quiet in prison was punctured with the occasional noise. Coughing. Snoring. Whispering. Yelling.

Now the silence reminds me of how alone I am.

I put the food away and remove a vase from under the sink. I turn on the water. Nothing comes out. I turn it off and try again. This time the water explodes from the faucet. Icy droplets hit me in the face, soak through my top, and I let out a startled giggle-shriek.

I attempt to turn the water off, but now that it's discovered freedom, it isn't interested in being contained. Water continues to spray everywhere. *Well, fuckers.*

I try jiggling the faucet off. That eventually seems to work. The water slows down with a little more jiggling and then stops. *Hmm.*

I slowly twist the faucet in the other direction, but not all the way this time. The water comes out in a steady narrow stream. I fill the vase and place it on the counter. It takes me a few attempts, but I manage to turn off the water, jiggling the faucet as I twist it.

I put the flowers in the vase. They don't do much to fill the silence or to make me feel less lonely, but none of that diminishes their beauty.

I search the living room and stumble across an old record player built into the top of what I thought was a wooden cabinet. I press the power button. Nothing.

I hunt for the power cord and find it on the floor behind the cabinet. I push it into the electric socket. "All right, Iris. Please tell me this works." I press the button once more. The red light turns on. *Well, that's a start.*

I flip through her record collection, but they're mostly early

Frank Sinatra, Doris Day, Billie Holiday, Ella Fitzgerald, and Bing Crosby. Couldn't she have at least listened to Elvis Presley, the Beatles, or The Rolling Stones?

Or maybe Anne took those albums.

Granny and I loved watching *White Christmas* together, so I put on a Bing Crosby record. Music blasts through the speaker, rattling the windows. I quickly turn down the volume. No need to piss off my neighbors.

My gaze shifts from the record player to the stack of magazines. As much as I appreciate the lifetime of reading material, the majority of them need to go.

I remove a Ziploc bag with a magazine inside. *Vogue, September 1, 1943*. The headline reads: "Take a Job! Release a Man to Fight!" Despite the protective covering, the magazine isn't in pristine condition.

I sit on the couch, flip through the magazine, and read the article about narrow skirts and the editorials. I return the magazine to the bag and put it on the floor, creating a new pile.

An hour later, I've gone through four other magazines, but none of them gave me insight as to why they made it to the important-to-Iris pile. Their contents are as varied as the dates on the covers.

I switch the album to Billie Holiday and eat the small baguette, fruit, and cheese I bought for dinner. Compared to the food I've been eating for the past five years, it's a meal akin to a royal banquet.

The sky is turning pale blue, and the thinning clouds promise a spectacular sunset. Anne told me how to get to the nearby lake. If I'm lucky, no one else will be there.

I pedal along the street. The air is colder now, and it nips at my skin through my sweater.

A woman walking her dog glances at me. I keep my head down, avoiding eye contact. Praying she doesn't see through my cheap disguise of blond hair coloring and nondescript clothing.

I'm safe. The media doesn't know where to find me. No one knows I'm here, other than Florence, and maybe my brother-in-law, Craig, and his wife.

At the lake, I leave the bike in the empty stand and walk down the embankment to the water. No one else is here, but unlike at the house, I don't feel so alone. I don't actually know what I feel. Until recently, I'd bubble-wrapped myself in numbness. It was easier that way.

I remove my sneakers and socks, drop them onto the sand, and walk to the water. Dry granules push between my toes.

The surface of the lake is nearly smooth, the breeze creating small waves. So different from the ocean. The ocean is never calm. It's dangerous, always changing. Challenging. It let me know who was the boss. Brought me gifts. Sea glass and shells. Swept me off my feet. Left me unsteady.

Left me floundering.

I close my eyes and wiggle my toes. Memories leak in. Of a toddler crouched near the water, pointing at a half-buried shell in the sand. I'd kneeled next to her, and my fingers dug at the prize. The cold tide rushed up the beach, taking us by surprise.

And my daughter—my reason for living, for surviving my real-life monster, my dangerous ocean—giggled and smiled and splashed the water.

My daughter...who I'll never see again.

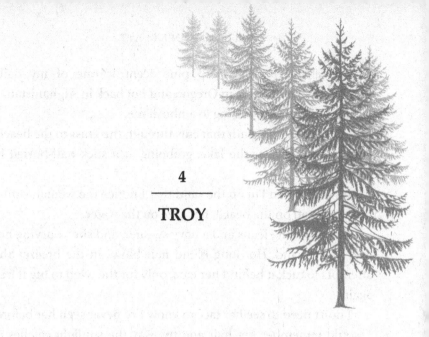

4

TROY

March, Present Day
Maple Ridge

I pull into the small parking lot near the lake, frustration simmering because I might have missed the chance to buy Iris's house.

I kill the truck's engine, climb out, and open the rear door. Butterscotch hops down and bounds over to the grassy bank separating the parking lot from the beach. It's early evening, and my truck is the only vehicle here.

He disappears into the long wild grass that's dry and bent over from the winter snow that once weighed it down.

I survey the area, something that's second nature after serving with the Marines. The sloped embankment leading to the beach. A potential hiding spot for a sniper. The tangled undergrowth, bare and a challenge to vanish behind. Unless you're skilled at camouflage.

I fill my lungs with the cool, pine-scented mountain air and slowly release it. The crisp pine scent is one of my daily reminders that I'm here in Oregon and not back in Afghanistan.

The enemy isn't waiting to ambush me.

I walk along the path that cuts through the grass to the beach. Butterscotch is near the lake, grabbing at a stick half-buried in the sand.

It's only when I'm on the sand that I notice the woman sitting farther ahead on the beach, her gaze on the water.

She's wearing jeans and a navy sweater, and she's burying her toes in the sand. Her long blond hair blows in the breeze. She attempts to tuck it behind her ears, only for the wind to tug it free again.

I don't need to see her face to know I've never seen her before. I would remember her hair and the way the sunlight catches it. She's probably a tourist passing through town.

I head toward her, curiosity driving me forward. Usually when tourists come to the beach, they aren't alone. I glance around, but there's no sign anyone's with her. "Hey, there."

She startles and scrambles to her feet, turning to face me. Her eyes are wide, and something about her expression makes me think she's on the verge of bolting.

I raise my hands. "Sorry. Didn't mean to scare you."

She stares at me with anxious eyes. Even from where I'm standing, I can see the dark shadows under them.

Butterscotch walks over to her, moving slowly enough so she can retreat if she feels threatened. There's a reason Butterscotch makes a great emotional support dog. He reads people's emotions. He knows when someone is nervous. He also knows when someone needs his type of loving.

The woman's gaze remains on me, her muscles tense. Shit, what has her so scared?

Butterscotch drops his ass near her feet and gives her a friendly bark.

The woman flicks her gaze to him and then looks back at me.

The corner of her mouth is pulled down by a scar that cuts from the corner of her mouth to her jaw. Possibly a knife wound.

It's not an old laceration. The redness suggests the scar is less than a year old.

The scar isn't the only one on her face. There's also a smaller scar on her right cheek. What has this woman been through? It's no wonder she's scared—especially if they are the result of her being attacked at some point.

I take a cautious step forward. "His name is Butterscotch. He volunteers as an emotional support dog at Maple Ridge Veterans Center."

She crouches and slowly reaches out to him, offering her hand for him to sniff. Butterscotch closes the distance, and she strokes his small body. The tension in her shoulders lessens.

I take another step. When she doesn't balk, I walk closer. But I don't push my luck. She doesn't know me. I could be a psychopath in her mind.

Her clothes swamp her body, as if they're two sizes too big, but they appear new. There's something familiar about her I can't identify. I don't mean I recognize her. It's just something about her, her reactions, that stokes the unease in my gut at just how deep her scars run.

"You're sweet." Her voice comes out stiff and rough as if she hasn't used it in a while. She continues stroking Butterscotch. She doesn't acknowledge me.

"Are you staying in Maple Ridge or just visiting?" I don't advance any closer, giving her a chance to soak up Butterscotch's therapy.

"Yes," she says, her message clear. It's none of my business.

I glance farther down the beach and spot an old-fashioned bike perched in the metal stand. It's not a mountain bike, nor is it a regular street bike. So she's probably not a tourist here to make the most of our mountain bike trails.

"Do you like ice cream?" I ask, mostly to see if she'll respond.

She doesn't look at me. Her focus is strictly on Butterscotch, but I have a feeling she's very aware of every move I make, no matter how small. "It's too cold for ice cream."

A low laugh rumbles in my chest. "You're definitely not from around here. For locals like me, it's never too cold for ice cream." I can't imagine her thin sweater is doing much to keep her warm. I shrug off my jacket and hold it out to her. "You look cold. Put this on."

Her gaze flicks up for a fraction of a second, and that's all it takes for me to become mesmerized by the honey brown of her eyes. Her attention returns to my super content, tail-wagging dog. She keeps petting him, not missing a beat. "I don't need your coat. And yes, I like ice cream."

I let my arm fall to my side, wanting her to look at me again. "Do you have a favorite flavor?"

"Does it matter if I do or not?" she asks, her words soft, almost thoughtful.

"I guess not."

She straightens, her back stiff, her eyes never leaving me as if she's worried I might attack. "It's mango."

A smile ghosts my mouth. "Good choice." There's something about her that sets off a warning in my gut and makes it hard to walk away. "Are you okay?"

"I'm fine." She hugs herself as if she's trying to keep her pieces together, to shield herself.

The unease in my gut flares. She's so distant, she's acting like my best friend Colton and my brother when they were battling PTSD.

That doesn't mean she's got the same thing, though.

Shit, what the hell happened to her? What's her story?

"You do realize that when a woman says she's fine, it usually means she isn't?" I say.

"And sometimes it means exactly that. She's fine. Good.

Happy." She smiles as if to make a point, but the scar prevents the smile from fully forming.

The smile falls away. She grabs her shoes and socks and walks toward her bike. Her bare feet sink into the loose sand, making her movements awkward, as if she's limping.

Or in pain.

"See you!" I call after her.

She doesn't reply or look back. Once she reaches the bike rack, she pulls on her shoes and pedals away.

I walk along the beach, my mind unable to let go of what might have happened to the woman and who'd possibly hurt her. Her eyes linger in my thoughts. Eyes that have seen too much. Who the hell is she? And what is she doing in Maple Ridge?

Shit. And what are those honey-brown eyes like when she's happy? Are they as spectacular as I think they'll be?

My mind flicks to the earlier conversation at the Veterans Center. About organizing a fundraiser to help the veterans and first responders with PTSD and their families. People like that woman.

I don't know the first thing about organizing a fundraiser, and I'm not going to kid myself into believing it will be easy. But what if it were a success? It could mean the difference between someone giving up on life the way Colton did—the difference between a wife losing a husband, a child losing their father—and a family remaining together and healing.

I grab my phone from my pocket and hit the speed dial for Zara. Butterscotch trots alongside me.

My brother's best friend picks up on the second ring. "Hey, Troy."

"Hey. I need your help with something..."

5

JESSICA

March, Present Day
Maple Ridge

I leave the lake but don't go far. I dismount from the bike.
The man who was talking to me is now on his phone and is walking away from me. Butterscotch trots alongside him on the sand, and my fingers crave to stroke the cute dog again. To experience the temporary reprieve from the fear, the uncertainty, the emptiness.

The emptiness that comes from my daughter no longer being in my life.

Tears kiss the corners of my eyes, and I push the memories of Amelia aside for now and focus on Butterscotch. He's not the type of dog I'd expect someone like that man to own. Maybe Butterscotch belongs to his girlfriend.

Thoughts of the man's smile slip in unguarded. His smile was friendly. Seemed genuine. Nothing like my husband's. My husband's smile had a hint of darkness, easily missed unless you were on the wrong side of it.

I bury the memory of the man I was married to and turn to the pastel-colored clouds. Purple, lavender, orange, pink. Together, they're startling and stunning. It's been a long time since I've last seen a sunset. I'd forgotten how incredible they are. The peaceful beauty makes standing in the cold worth it.

Movement in my periphery catches my attention, and I turn to it. The man throws a ball and Butterscotch chases it. I watch the duo play for a moment, then watch the sunset until the colors are no longer spectacular and the cooling temperature becomes too much.

I pedal home slowly, careful not to twist my body and aggravate the area where I was stabbed. The windows in my new neighborhood are lit with welcoming lights. What would the homeowners think if they knew an ex-con was living on their street? Would they see me as someone who fell in love with the wrong man? Would they see me as someone getting her life back on track? Or would they see me as undesirable, despicable, and dangerous because I spent five years in prison?

Five years is a long time to be locked up with violent criminals. A long time to survive without my psyche being damaged and demolished. A long time for the system to not change me for the worse.

I lock my bike in the garage and check the thread I placed on the back door when I left earlier. It hasn't been disturbed. I go into the house and make sure the same is true for the front door and the windows.

I put Fred Astaire on the record player, and his voice fills the living room. I dust and vacuum while he sings the songs Grandpa used to dance to with Granny when she was in the kitchen cooking dinner. It's one of my favorite memories of them together.

By the time I'm finished, exhaustion crashes down on me. But no way am I going to bed yet. The nightmares. The memories. Prison. Fear. It all conspires against me.

I grab a twenty-year-old issue of *Pacific Northwest Life* from one of the stacks of magazines, sit on the couch, and flip through the issue. I rip out all the interesting pictures I admire and place them on the coffee table.

The rest of the magazine goes in the pile for recycling.

I keep doing this—grab, flip, rip, repeat—until I can barely see. I've hardly made a dent in Iris's collection, but at least I've distracted myself.

I drag my weary body upstairs to my bedroom and unzip my suitcase. The clothes Florence bought me are neatly folded. She had no idea what I would like, so it's mostly long-sleeved T-shirts, the colors muted. Not the height of fashion, but better than prison-issued blue jumpsuits.

It's been a while since I've bought clothes. But since I'm starting over, I get to reinvent myself. I get to be anyone I want to be.

Too bad I have no idea who that is.

An old shoebox lies next to the clothes. I sit on the bed and open the box. A white envelope rests on top of the contents. Underneath it is a baby shoe. Amelia's shoe. So small and perfect. Just like my daughter back then.

A pain stabs my heart so deep, so sharp, so visceral, it feels real.

I put the envelope beside me on the bed, grab the shoe, and hold it to my chest. And all of a sudden I'm humming the lullaby I used to sing to my baby.

Hush-a-bye baby, my sweet little one.
Fall asleep, my love,
And dream of the stars and the sun.
Unicorn wishes and rainbow dreams,
Fairy-tale princesses and butterfly wings.
Hush-a-bye baby, my sweet little one.

I will protect you while you slumber on.

And I'm rocking and crying and I almost can't bear the pain.

Once I'm finally all cried out, I trace the tiny pink flowers painted on the white canvas. I haven't let myself cry since the day the cops arrested me. Since they took Amelia from my arms and handed her to Child Protective Services.

I didn't let myself cry the day I was sentenced to life in prison for murdering my husband. I didn't even let myself cry the day I signed away my rights as Amelia's mother. I wanted her to grow up in a home full of happiness and love. I didn't want her to grow up resenting me, believing I'd murdered her father. Her father who had been considered a hero to everyone but me.

I set the shoe aside and go through the other items in the box. Her birth announcement. A teensy-tiny sleeper from Granny with cute pink hearts all over it. Amelia wore it home from the hospital.

The only reason I have the box is because I'd kept it at Granny's house. My husband would've destroyed it. Destroying my things was one of the ways he'd kept me in line.

I put everything back in the box, open the envelope, and take out the two photos.

My baby. My beautiful baby.

My heart splits in half all over again, the endless ache bleeding into my body. "I love you. And I miss you so much." My voice sounds rough and raw, the words pushed past a too-tight throat. I sniff and close my eyes against the pain.

I don't even know what she looks like now. All I have are the two photos. The two photos I didn't dare look at while in prison. It would have hurt too much.

I open my eyes. In the first picture, Amelia is sitting on a blanket outside, smiling and drooling on her pretty pink dress. I put the picture down next to me.

She's a toddler in the second photo. She was grinning at the camera and showing me her stuffed doggy when I took the photo. It joins the other one on the bed.

I go over to my purse on the dresser and pull out the sealed envelope Florence gave me when I was released from prison. I tear it open and remove the photo of five-year-old Amelia. She's drawing with crayons and making a silly face for the camera. Her adoptive parents—my brother-in-law and my sister-in-law—must have taken it.

It's not even a recent photo. It's two years old.

I stroke her beautiful golden-brown waves, so much like mine before I became a blond. The new hair color is just one more thing separating me from my daughter. One more thing to show she's not mine.

I know I'll never see my daughter again. Wouldn't dare to try.

I don't know how I could see her without dying even further on the inside. To not hear her call me Mommy, but to hear her say the term to another woman.

I don't even know if her adoptive parents would be okay with me seeing her. They might be afraid I would tell her that I am her real mother.

I would never do that.

But maybe...maybe Craig and Grace will let me see her. As a friend of the family.

But first, I need to change my life around.

I need a job and I need to prove prison didn't change me.

I need to prove under the broken shell of the woman my husband and the prison system left behind, I am the same girl I was before my life took a wrong turn. A girl with dreams and goals and stars in her eyes.

I JOLT AWAKE, MY HEART RATE SPEEDING. IT TAKES ME A FEW seconds to remember where I am. The house creaks in the wind that has picked up since I fell asleep. But the sound isn't what woke me.

Tears dampen my face and pillow and sweat covers my body, the details of the nightmare a foggy memory.

I climb out of the bed and walk to the window. The cold air prickles my bare arms and legs, and I shiver.

I pull on a sweater and peek through the gap in the curtains. The world outside is blanketed in the glow of the full moon. *I'm okay.* The monsters that haunt my nightmares are locked away or buried deep in the ground.

I grab five magazines from the nearest stack, knowing I won't be able to fall back asleep just yet. I don't pay attention to the magazine covers or their titles.

I turn on the bedside lamp, climb into the bed, and spread out the magazines. It's only then I realize they aren't all in English. Two are in German. The *Vogue* magazine is in French. The other two magazines—gardening magazines—are in English.

I took high school Spanish, so the German and French magazines are a lost cause. But that doesn't stop me from flipping through the French *Vogue*. The magazine is dated March 1975.

Once I'm finished checking it out, I put it on what will become a new pile. There's bound to be someone interested in old editions of the French magazine. Maybe someone who is into the history of fashion.

Next up is the German magazine. This one is from 2001 and appears to be some sort of women's magazine. The recipes look delicious. Too bad I don't know a word of German. It goes into a different pile. The German-language pile. The second German magazine quickly joins its companion.

The gardening magazines are more interesting, with photos ranging from cozy cottage flowerbeds to the cultivated gardens my husband preferred. He thought they spoke of wealth. Power.

The adrenaline that pumped through my body from the nightmare has faded. Staying awake is no longer an option. My thoughts drift to Butterscotch and how stroking him eased my panic attack at the lake when his owner approached me. But that's not the last image that slips in as sleep pulls me under its spell.

That would be his owner's smile.

6

TROY

March, Present Day
Maple Ridge

Olivia removes Nova from her car seat and puts her on the sidewalk. The red Honda Civic is parked on the street in front of the house my crew and I are renovating. We've currently stopped for lunch and are sitting on the low brick wall in front of the house.

The toddler charges across the dead grass to where I'm sitting, her puffy yellow jacket bright in the sunshine. I push to my feet, ready to catch her.

She stops and her little arms reach for me. "Up!"

I scoop up the giggling two-year-old and swing her into the air. "Hey, sweetheart."

She giggles some more.

Olivia walks up the path, carrying a picnic basket. "She's been excited to see you all morning. I told her we were bringing you lunch, and she wouldn't stop bouncing."

Nova's bright-blue eyes peer up at me, so much like her father's. For the longest time after his death, it hurt to see so much of Colton in her little features. "Butterscotch?"

Butterscotch scrambles to his feet from where he'd been snoozing in a patch of sunlight and rushes over to my leg. I kiss Nova's forehead and put her down.

She attempts to pat Butterscotch's head, but he jumps back and bounds over to his ball. He returns with it in his mouth and drops the ball at her feet.

She grabs the ball and tosses her arms up. The ball lands a foot away, and my crew chuckles.

Butterscotch doesn't seem to care he doesn't have to go anywhere to retrieve it. He's just happy to play with her. He picks the ball up and drops it again at her feet.

"I made this for you, Troy." Olivia holds up the picnic basket and sets it on the ground in front of where I'd been sitting.

"I hope you baked us some of your world-famous brownies, Livi." Lance flashes her a goofy grin.

She rolls her eyes. He knows better than to use that name. The three of us went to school together, back when she only responded to the name Livi. But somewhere during the past decade, she decided to only answer to her legal name—a fact Lance likes to ignore.

"Of course I brought y'all brownies." She opens the basket, removes a plastic container, and hands it to him. "God knows you'd never give me a moment of peace if I didn't."

"And this is why we love you." He flutters his eyelashes at her. The other men on the crew laugh.

Olivia sits on the wall. I sit next to her. The men resume their previous conversations. And we all keep an eye on Nova and Butterscotch.

"How're you doing?" It's been my standard question for Olivia since Colton committed suicide. In the beginning, she was so devastated, she could hardly talk. Colton had been the love of her life. My mom and Olivia's mom had taken turns looking after Nova. It had taken Colton's mother months before she could look at her granddaughter without bursting into tears. "No school today?" I ask.

"Nope. So we thought we'd bring you and your crew some lunch. Then Nova and I are going to the lake to visit the ducks."

Her mention of the lake brings with it memories of the woman I saw there the other evening. I've thought about her off and on for the past two days, trying to figure out what could've happened to her to make her so jumpy. And that made me think more and more about the fundraiser Bill had suggested someone organize to help people with PTSD and their families.

Olivia hands me a sandwich. "Did you hear? A woman is now living in Iris Bromfield's house. Can you believe someone *wants* to rent that haunted old place?"

Shit, I was hoping Frank had been wrong about that. "I don't think there are actual ghosts living there."

"You can't be sure about that."

A snort-laugh pushes past my lips. "The place needs work. That doesn't mean it's haunted."

"Iris was always looking over her shoulder as if she expected the boogeyman to be there..."

"Again, that doesn't mean her house is haunted." Iris hadn't always been like that. But the hypervigilance had been more noticeable during the last decade of her life.

It was the same for my brother, Lucas, after he left the Marines and was struggling with PTSD. In his case, he had good reason for constantly looking over his shoulder. It hadn't been the same for Colton. His problem wasn't the fear of being attacked.

"She was old," I remind Olivia. "You can't blame her for that. Who knows what was going through her mind at that point? Anyway, how do you know her great-niece has rented out the house?"

"My neighbor was playing bridge at a house down the street,

and her friend told her a woman our age moved in. She assumed the woman is just renting the place and didn't buy it. That's all I know."

I need to talk to Anne and see what's going on. I'd planned to do that on Tuesday, but then I got busy and haven't had a chance yet. If she's just renting the house to the woman for the short term, I could talk to Anne about my offer to buy the house.

I don't mention this to Olivia. She has no idea what I'm up to.

Butterscotch flops onto his side in front of Nova. She giggles and does a cute little dance for my dog's benefit. I bite into my sandwich. "This is delicious. If you weren't such a great elementary school teacher, I'd tell you to open a café."

Olivia's lips spread into a grin, and amusement lightens her eyes. "Zara's café is the most popular spot in town. Not sure I'd ever be delusional enough to try to compete with her."

I laugh. "Good point." I remove my wallet from my back pocket and hand Olivia a fifty.

She looks at me, her forehead pinching into a frown. "What's that for?"

"Café or not, Aramis, I'm still a paying customer." I don't want her to spend what little money she makes from teaching on the food she occasionally brings for my crew and me. She and Nova need it more.

Her frown deepens, but I know it's not because I used The Three Musketeer nickname. "You're not a customer, Athos." Her voice is low, her tone stiff, and the pride I know her for burns bright.

"I'd still feel better if you'd take the money. It's sweet that you bring us food, but you shouldn't be the one paying for it." I shove the bill at her, keeping my hand down so no one else can see the cash. Olivia can be plain stubborn at times, especially when it comes to her pride.

"Is that why you think I'm here? To feed you guys?"

"Not entirely. Nova loves visiting Butterscotch."

Olivia mutters something under her breath I don't catch.

"What was that?" I ask.

She doesn't respond beyond rolling her eyes and shaking her head. I've known Olivia long enough to recognize the expression that says I'm an idiot.

I might be an idiot, but I also know when to keep my mouth shut. I fill it with the sandwich.

The guys chuckle, their attention on Nova.

"Nova, you're a great dancer, like your momma." Amusement soars in Lance's voice, and his gaze shines with affection.

She grins at him and runs over to Olivia. Her mother picks her up, and Nova throws her arms around Olivia's neck. With Olivia distracted, I slip the fifty into her basket.

She kisses Nova's cheek. "You ready for your lunch?"

Nova nods, the movement overly enthusiastic, the way only a little kid can do.

"You want to sit on the blanket or on the wall between Troy and me?"

Nova wiggles off her mom's lap and drags the small blanket from next to the basket to where Butterscotch is sitting. She doesn't bother to straighten the fabric. She just sits her butt on it, her short legs stretched in front of her. She's not facing us. She's facing the street like we are.

Butterscotch shifts closer to her and flops next to her legs. Nova strokes him on the head. And I smile at how cute they are together.

Olivia removes two smaller plastic containers from the basket and takes them over to Nova. She opens one and produces a wipe, which she uses to clean her daughter's hands. She then removes the lid from the other container and puts the plastic box next to Nova.

"And no trying to eat her lunch this time," Olivia sternly tells Butterscotch, even though it wasn't technically his fault. Nova was the one who fed him the small sandwich. Butterscotch was just too polite to decline it.

My mind flicks back to Tuesday night again and the woman at the lake. She wasn't there last night when Butterscotch and I went for our usual evening walk. I'd hoped to see her. No idea why. The woman clearly wanted nothing to do with me.

But something about her has left me off-balance. It's a twisting in my gut I haven't felt in a while. A twisting that surfaced right before I lost my best friend.

But I ignore it.

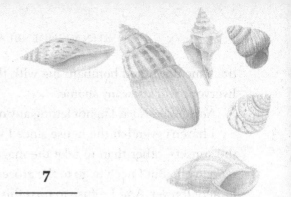

7

JESSICA

March, Present Day
Maple Ridge

Billie Holiday plays through the speaker in the living room as I spend Thursday morning going through Iris's magazines. Just like I've been going through them for the past three days.

The recycle bin is full from yesterday's discarded pile. I've still got a long way to go with the periodicals, but at least I'm getting somewhere.

The doorbell rings, sending my heart rate scrambling. *Fuckers and damn.*

I push myself to my feet and rub my hands on my thighs, smudging dust from the magazines onto my jeans. This is the first time someone has rung the doorbell or knocked on the door since I moved in.

So far, I've avoided my neighbors. Someone might recognize me and out me on social media, making it easier for the media to track me down and bombard me with their relentless questions. Everyone will know my shame.

Nope. Nope. Nope. I'm not letting any of that happen.

I haven't even left the house since I went to the lake to watch the sunset—other than to take the magazines to the garage and recycle bin. But I need to go to the grocery store soon. I can't hide in here forever. And I refuse to turn this house into another type of prison.

My heart pounding, I walk to the front door and peer through the peephole. Anne?

Cold fear clutches me in its fist. Has she changed her mind about me staying in her house? Is she tossing me out because she figured out the truth about me?

Dreading her next words, I unlock the door and open it.

Anne smiles, and some of the tension loosens its grip. "Hi, Jessica."

"Hi, Anne. C'mon in." I step back from the doorway. "How are you doing?"

She walks into the house. "Good, thanks. And you? I thought that since you don't have a phone yet, I'd drop by to check if you need anything."

The remaining tendrils of fear vanish. "I've been busy going through the magazines. I didn't realize your great-aunt spoke French and German. I found a collection of magazines in those languages."

"That's right. My great-grandfather worked in the British embassies in Paris and Vienna when my grandmother and Auntie Iris were younger." Anne smiles nostalgically as she glances at the diminishing piles of magazines and the decades-old furniture and couch.

"Can you speak French or German?"

"Not really. Auntie Iris taught me some French and German when I was a kid, but I took Spanish in high school with my friends."

42

I show Anne the progress I've made in the living room with the magazines.

Shock widens her eyes. "Wow. I'd forgotten what the place looks like without so many magazines. It looks so much bigger than I remembered." She chuckles and flashes me a sheepish grin. "The house hasn't always been overrun with them. In the beginning, she kept them in the attic. When her last TV died, Dan and I were going to get her a new one, but she said she didn't need it. She was happy reading her magazines."

"Would it be okay if I decorate the place once I've cleared them out?" I've been thinking about it since yesterday. The place doesn't feel like mine, the way the house I lived in with my husband never felt like my home. I wasn't the wife, the lady of the house. I was the housekeeper, the punching bag, the thing he raped and demeaned.

But now...now I want to make a home while I figure out what to do next.

"Go ahead. Like I said the other day, I'm planning to put the house on the market at the end of the year. And a fresh coat of paint will certainly help. Let me know what colors you're thinking of. Dan can bring them over, along with the supplies you'll need."

"Do you know your asking price yet? For the house?" The questions roll out without a second thought, and hope grows in me like a daffodil bulb pushing through the cold earth.

Anne lists a number. It's a decent price considering the age of the house and the amount of renovations required. I would remove the dated wallpaper and paint the walls a light beige. And remove the wall between the kitchen and living room to open up the space. Make downstairs feel airy and light and warm...

"I would like to buy it," I say before I can change my mind. "I have the money. So I can pay you in cash."

Anne's expression tumbles through a series of emotions—

surprise, disbelief, relief, uncertainty, happiness—all in a matter of seconds.

"My grandmother willed me her house," I hastily add. "I sold it a few years ago." When I thought I'd be spending the next twenty-five or so years in prison with no chance of parole.

"Are you sure you want to buy it?" Anne's expression settles somewhere between relieved and hopeful.

I nod, maybe a little too eagerly. "It will be the perfect new start for me. I recently got out of a bad relationship." Might as well keep somewhat to the truth. "A new town. A new home. It's the perfect new start."

"Most women just get their hair cut after something like that."

I smile, despite how close she came to the truth. "Sometimes you need more than a haircut"—*or hair color*—"for a new start."

The voice of reason—or possibly self-doubt—begins an argument in my head. Questioning the wisdom of my plan.

But I only allow the self-doubt a voice for a second. Then I arm myself with the reasons I'm doing the right thing. Because yes. Yes, it is a good idea. A scary idea with a number of potential roadblocks, but it's still a good idea.

My husband stole five years of my life. His killer stole another five. I've lost so much of who I was because of the mistakes I've made over the past eleven years, beginning from the moment I met my future husband. I don't know who I am anymore. But I can't fix what he broke, can't find myself again, if I'm always running.

"I'm positive I want to buy it," I say. "I mean, unless you think it will fall apart as soon as I sign the deed."

Anne laughs a heartfelt chuckle. "No, I think you're okay there. The house is a fixer-upper, but as long as you realize that, and you're willing to renovate the place, you should be fine. Will you be able to renovate it enough to make the neighbors happy?" Her eyebrows lift in question.

I nod even though I'm not sure if I can, but I want to try. I won't abandon the house the way my mother abandoned me when I was little. The way my father walked out of my life when he found out my mother was pregnant with me.

I'll be like my grandparents, who showered me with the love and compassion my parents failed to provide. I'll love this house —my house—if Anne lets me buy it.

"Okay, in that case, I don't see a reason not to sell it to you." She glances around the living room. "Gosh, I never thought I'd get to the point where I was ready to part with this house. But it feels right, this, selling it to you." She smiles at me, an almost embarrassed tilt to her mouth. "It feels like Auntie Iris is finally giving me her blessing to sell the place. That probably sounds weird to you."

"Not at all. I completely understand." And I do.

"Alright, then. I'll contact a lawyer, and we'll get the process started. There are a few pieces of furniture I want to keep. But everything else is up for negotiation."

"What about your great-aunt's bike?" Right now, it's my only mode of transportation.

"You can keep that, too, if you'd like. Or you can get rid of it. It's up to you. You can also keep the tools in the garage. Dan already took what he wanted. Consider them part of the house." Anne glances around the room once more, a mix of emotions on her face. Sadness? Relief?

"Thank you so much." The tools will come in handy for gardening and renovating the place.

I come up with a mental list of things I'll need to do, like checking my finances to make sure I have enough to renovate the house. I might not be able to do it all right away, but I can swing the top-priority tasks.

Finding a job will also be vital since I won't be able to live off the money I've saved. Not if I'm buying and renovating the house. Plus, I'll have to let Florence know what I'm doing so my ID can be updated with my permanent address.

Permanent address. My address. A wave of dizziness washes through me. Everything's changing so quickly. My feet are planted on the ground, but at any moment the undertow could yank them out from under me.

Am I making a mistake?

No, this is what I want. I'm making the choice, for better or for worse. Me—and only me. Until a week ago, all my choices had been taken from me. Taken from me for the past ten years.

I grin, despite feeling a little overwhelmed by everything. Choices. I have choices. I can paint this house any color I want, and it will be my choice. No one else's.

"If you want," Anne says, "I can give you a list of contractors in the county who do renovations. I've heard great things about Troy Carson. His brother, Garrett Carson, is a *New York Times* bestselling thriller author. Dan loves his books."

"Thank you. A list would be great." Not that I'm planning to hire a contractor. I'm going to do this myself. It's something my husband wouldn't have considered me capable of doing. In his mind, I wasn't capable of anything.

But he was wrong. I've done plenty of things right. He was the one who refused to acknowledge them.

Anne and I talk a little longer. I've spent the past ten years practically alone, so it feels odd having someone treat me like a person with feelings and dreams and ambitions. I'm not a number or a cop killer or someone to attack or bully. Her warm attitude is a blanket in the empty void. A promise. A flicker of hope.

"I should go now. I'll contact a lawyer about the sale," she tells me, "and then contact you so we can arrange for the transfer of funds."

"Sounds good. Thank you!" *Thank you for helping me start my life over.*

Anne leaves, and I retrieve the bike from the garage. I need to get some more groceries since there is only so much I can fit in the basket, and it's about time I check out downtown Maple Ridge. The town that will soon be my permanent home.

I climb on my bike and head toward Main Street.

At the library, a single-story brick building on the edge of downtown, I lock up my bike and walk along the sidewalk. I still don't feel like a resident. I'm more like a tourist who's constantly looking over her shoulder.

The two-story buildings on either side of Main Street are quaint. Like chalets. An excited hum vibrates inside me. While Maple Ridge might not be San Diego, the city I loved so much, the small town is beautiful with the gorgeous mountain backdrop.

And it's now going to be my home.

I go into a store that sells clothes, but the items are overpriced and meant for tourists. What do most residents do when they need clothes? Drive to Eugene? Order them online?

I don't have a car, so the first option is out. And I don't have a computer or phone, so buying them online also isn't an option. I guess along with clothes, I'll need to get a phone soon.

The next store, Little Wonders, has a *Help Wanted* sign in the window. Antique cribs and cute dresses and stuffed animals decorate the window display, and the pang of emptiness and loss sucker-punches me in the solar plexus.

The Amelia I knew would have loved this place with the cute cuddly animals. Would seven-year-old Amelia love it?

I pull open the door and walk to the front counter. I could see myself working here. Sure, it's not what I imagined when I was studying for my journalism degree, but I need a job, and there are worse things I could be doing.

"Hi, there." The woman on the other side of the counter must be in her late fifties and is all smiles. "Is there something I can help you with?"

"Yes, please. I saw that you're hiring."

"That's right. Do you have a résumé?"

I inwardly cringe. I haven't gotten around to creating one yet. Hell, I don't even have a computer I can write one on.

I smile back, fastening on what I hope comes off as a confident smile. "I don't have one on me right now. I can drop it off, though." Maybe I can use a computer at the local library and print my résumé off there. Except...I haven't worked in ten years —other than in prison. And that's not something I wish to highlight on my résumé.

"Do you have any retail experience?" The friendly curve of her mouth doesn't falter even a fraction of an inch.

"I-I don't. But I'm a fast learner." The words stumble from me, trying to find their footing. It's been over twelve years since my last job interview.

"Hmm. I really wanted retail experience." The corners of her mouth dip slightly, but it's nothing too discouraging. "How about references?"

My stomach sinks, shame and disappointment weighing it down. "I-I don't have any." I never asked my brother-in-law or sister-in-law if they would be a reference. They had already helped me find a place to stay after I was released from Beckley. It felt like too much to also ask for references—especially when they didn't know me all that well.

"I'm sorry, dear. I do have someone else in mind for the position. But if you leave your résumé with me the next time you're in the store, I'll be sure to keep it on file." Her smile no longer seems quite as genuine as it did a moment ago.

"I will. Thank you." I flash her the most optimistic smile that I can muster and head for the entrance, stopping long enough to check out a few items as if I'm considering buying them.

Several people are walking on the sidewalk when I leave the store. No one is paying attention to me, and I make a detour to the florist. The early afternoon sunlight brightens the flowers on display. Especially the red roses, their petals the shade of spilled blood.

A memory seeps in of cold concrete pressed against my face and of blood—my blood—spreading across the gray floor. My first thought after I was stabbed, when I registered the blood, was how beautiful it looked. Like rose petals.

My second thought was how I'd survived an abusive husband only for an inmate to kill me. During the years of living in fear, wondering if the next strike of my husband's fist would be the one that finally killed me, not once had I imagined my life ending in this way.

And as my life drained away on the concrete prison floor and my vision darkened, fear, anger, sadness—none of them visited me. Instead, I'd been relieved.

Relieved the last thing I saw in a world of hatred and rage and distrust was a thing of beauty.

I turn away from the roses.

And accidentally bump someone with my shoulder. *What the...?*

My vision blurs. My muscles tense. The edge of a shank spears through me, the blade slicing through my back like my husband's sharp words, cutting into vital organs.

But I won't just stand here, letting it try to steal my life from me.

Not this time.

8

TROY

March, Present Day
Maple Ridge

Olivia and Nova leave the worksite, but my crew and I work for a few more hours before calling it a day. Tomorrow night is my turn to host Game Night with my brothers, my sister-in-law, and our friends, so I need to pick up some beer and vodka coolers.

I park my truck near Picnic & Treats and head to the grocery store. Butterscotch trots alongside me. As I walk, I call Anne, but I'm sent straight to her voice mail.

"Hi, Anne. It's Troy Carson. I hope you're doing well. Could you give me a call when you have a chance? I'd like to talk to you about your great-aunt Iris's house. Thanks." I end the call.

The blond I saw at the lake the other day is ahead of me and is constantly checking over her shoulder, surveying her surroundings. Her actions are familiar. They were part of my military training. Always vigilant. Never resting. Because the second your guard slips, the enemy attacks.

I walk toward her, my instinct to protect driving me forward. Her sweater and jeans are dark as if she's trying to be invisible, but her hair glows in the sunlight.

She stops to check out the flowers in front of the florist. Her body goes stiff as if something has scared her. A spider? She wouldn't be the first woman I've seen react that way. She turns and takes a step, accidentally bumping into a man.

She goes rigid once more. Then her arms flail as if she's fighting off an assailant only she can see.

Her palm drags over the sharp corner of the wooden display holding the various buckets of flowers. The contact jostles the contents. Nothing falls over, but a thin line of blood appears on her hand.

Panicked glances are directed her way, but mostly, people hurry past, pretending not to see her. A bloated silence crowds the sidewalk, only interrupted by several passing vehicles.

I approach her with caution, worried about making things worse. Butterscotch remains by my side. Neither of us is a rookie when it comes to this kind of thing. We've witnessed similar scenes a number of times at the Veterans Center.

I get close to her, but not too close. Fear widens her eyes, drops her mouth open in a soundless scream. Shit, I wish I knew her name. "You're safe." My voice is calm and even, hopefully not loud enough to startle her. "Whoever hurt you isn't here." I don't attempt to touch her. "You're safe. You're in Maple Ridge, Oregon. Whoever hurt you isn't here."

My words don't bring her comfort. Her expression doesn't change, and she doesn't make eye contact. For all I know, whoever was responsible for her flashback is also in town. Maybe the person was also responsible for the scars on her face.

"You're safe. You're in Maple Ridge, Oregon." I keep repeating the words until she finally lowers her arms to her side. She flinches as if I appeared out of nowhere. Which in her mind is probably true.

She lifts her hand. Blood drips from the cut across her palm and splashes onto the sidewalk.

"Your cut doesn't look like it needs stitches," I tell her, "but you might need a tetanus shot. Depending on when you last had one."

Her forehead crinkles, her gaze on her hand. "How-how did I get cut?" She yanks several tissues from her purse, presses them on her palm, and looks around us.

A few individuals are watching us from a safe distance, but most people have moved on. Embarrassment curves her spine, slumps her shoulders. I throw a dark scowl at the unwanted audience. They get the hint and hurry on.

The florist walks out of the store, her worried eyes assessing the area. They land on the woman from the beach. "What happened?"

"It's okay," I say, giving her a quick nod. "I'm handling it."

Butterscotch whimpers by the blond woman's feet.

"He senses you're upset and wants to help you feel better," I tell her.

She glances at him. "I remember you. You're such a sweet boy." Her voice is soft, hoarse, as if she just survived a desert storm, her mouth now dry.

"The medical clinic is just down the street. Butterscotch and I can walk you there." I notice in my periphery the florist duck back into the store.

"No, that's okay. I don't need a tetanus shot."

"That might be the case, but you still need to get cleaned up and bandaged. Are you staying nearby?"

Her gaze cuts away from me and switches again to hypervigilance.

"Did you bike here?" I ask, remembering her biking from the lake. "I have a first aid kit in my truck. Or I can walk you to my friend's café around the corner. Zara will have a first aid kit there."

The woman's eyes return to me, her expression weary and wary. "Wh-why do you want to help me?"

"Because I'm a nice guy who doesn't like seeing women bleed to death." I thought maybe she'd laugh at the exaggeration, but her face goes pale. "We'll go to my friend's café. You'll feel safer there. You had a flashback, didn't you?"

The fingers of her injured hand clutch the tissues against the cut. She uses the other hand to pull her purse tight to her body like a shield. "I-I don't know what you're talking about."

"Something happened to you in the past. And you just experienced a trigger that caused a flashback. My guess is this isn't the first time you've had one, is it?"

"Y-you're wrong. Th-there's nothing wrong with me." Her gaze narrows, honey-brown eyes peering from beneath thick lashes. "Let me guess, you...you have some sort of hero syndrome. Always t-trying to rescue damsels in distress who don't need rescuing?" Her tone cuts deeper than whatever sliced her hand. There's nothing flirtatious about it.

"Can't say anyone has accused me of that before. My mother raised my brothers and me to be gentlemen. But this isn't the first time I've seen this kind of thing." I wait a beat to let my words sink in. "You can't bike home like that." I point at her hand. "I can patch you up at the café, then Butterscotch and I will drive you home so your hand doesn't start bleeding again."

"I don't need a ride." Her voice isn't so harsh this time. Resignation echoes in her words. "I-I can walk."

"Alright. Let's get that wound cleaned and bandaged first. Can Butterscotch and I at least do that much? Picnic and Treats is around the corner."

"Okay."

Butterscotch and I walk with her to the café. "You know my dog's name, and I'm Troy." I wait for her to tell me her name, to take the bait, because damned if I haven't been wondering what her name is since Tuesday night. But she doesn't say anything. "This is where you tell me your name."

"Only...only if I want you to know it."

"Ahh. A woman of intrigue. That's just made you more interesting to a guy like me." A small smile flickers on my face, enough to tell her I'm trying to lighten the mood a little, nothing more.

She lifts her shoulders in a the-wall's-staying-up shrug.

"You don't say much, do you?"

"May-maybe I don't have a lot to say." The words are soft, heartbroken, as if she really believes them.

I frown, wondering if someone had told her that. There was a kid in my fourth grade class who didn't talk much. He had a lisp, and some kids made sport of tormenting him because of it.

Or they did until I caught them bullying him, and I punched the bigger bully in the face. His nose bled. My hand hurt like hell, and I got suspended for the day. But it had been worth it.

The kid they bullied soon became my best friend. Colton.

I want to ask what happened to make her believe she doesn't have a lot to say, but I also don't want to make her uncomfortable by asking too many questions. It's none of my business.

We arrive at Picnic & Treats, and I tie the leash to the bench near the entrance. "Sit."

Butterscotch dutifully does as he's told.

The woman looks at me, eyes wide in alarm. "W-we can't just leave him outside."

"He'll be fine. He has a fan club. It won't be long before someone stops to say hi to him." I open the door for her.

She enters the café, her gaze not leaving Butterscotch.

Zara is working the front counter, her many braids pulled back with a bright-purple scarf. The sounds of talking and laughing and clinking dishes fill the café. As do the delicious smells of baked goods and today's lunch specials.

"Hey, Troy." Zara says something to Tracy, who takes her place at the counter.

Zara walks over to us, and she smiles at the woman standing next to me. Curiosity gleams in her brown eyes. "Hi, welcome to Picnic and Treats."

"Hey, Zara. This woman cut her hand outside the florist," I tell her. "Is it okay if I take her to your staff room and patch her up?"

"Sure, go ahead." Zara waves toward the hallway. "No one's in there right now. I'll get the first aid kit and be right with you." She rushes off to the kitchen.

I guide the woman down the hallway that leads to the public restroom. The other door at the end of the corridor is for the staff room. I open it, and we go inside. I point to the couch.

She doesn't move. If anything, she looks ready to run.

"I'm not gonna hurt you." I keep my voice to a low, soothing rumble. "Whoever hurt you in the past, I'm not them."

"No one...no one has hurt me." Her voice is quiet, tone guarded. Another brick is being added to the wall she keeps around herself.

"You have PTSD, don't you? Post Traumatic Stress Disorder."

"There's...I'm...there's nothing wrong with me." Her tone's not defensive, not angry, but tight and anxious. She shifts her body, angling away from me. "I'm fine." She doesn't say it to me. The words are directed at a framed poster of New Orleans at night.

They're the same words Colton said to me when I was worried about his mental health.

"I never said anything is wrong with you." My tone is soft, my throat constricting just thinking about him. "My brother struggled with PTSD for a year after he left the military. And my best friend had it too. He was a paramedic and was called to the site of a traumatic accident. He wasn't the same after that." I slowly reach for her hand and cradle it in mine.

Her hand flinches at my touch but stays put, the crumb of trust fragile.

Her fingernails are chipped and uneven. She unfolds her fingers holding the tissue, revealing dry, calloused skin. I might not have sisters, but I do have four close female friends who are like sisters to me. They do whatever they can to keep their hands soft, their fingernails manicured. Even Zara, whose job involves physical labor.

Dark circles create half-moons under the woman's eyes. She has the appearance of someone who suffers through sleepless nights and nightmares. A look I recognize only too well.

But as much as I want to ask her about her hands and the dark circles, I'm not stupid enough to risk it. I don't want to give her a reason to raise her walls any higher.

The cut is no longer bleeding. I was right. It won't need stitches, but it will be sore for a day or two.

Zara walks into the room, first aid kit in one hand, a mug in the other. She puts the first aid kit on the coffee table and hands the woman the mug. A rich, chocolate smell seeps from the steam.

"By the way, I'm Zara. I hope you like hazelnut hot chocolate, but I can get you something else if you prefer."

The woman lifts the mug to her nose and sniffs. Her eyes close, the corners of her mouth flutter up, and a soft moan vibrates in her chest.

And I will my body to not give away my reaction to the sound.

Her eyes open. "Thank you. I'm-I'm Jessica."

"Ahh, so you do have a name." I keep my voice light and open the first aid kit.

A faint blush creeps up her cheeks.

Zara drops onto an armchair and glances between Jessica and me, her gaze assessing.

Jessica sips the hot chocolate and sits on the couch. "This... this is really good."

"Thanks." Zara leans back in her chair. "It's my family's secret recipe, passed down from generation to generation. My gran used to claim it had magical powers. But she also claimed she was a voodoo priestess..." Zara chuckles like she usually does when she tells that story.

Another smile arranges itself on Jessica's face, a little wider this time, but not enough to be a full-out smile. A smile I bet is spectacular once you've earned the right to see it.

I sit next to her, remove a package of alcohol antiseptic pads from the plastic box, and rip it open. I touch her hand again. It jerks away.

"Well, there's a first." Zara's head tilts as if trying to get a firmer read on Jessica. "A woman who isn't throwing herself at you, Troy, and shoving her phone number in your pocket. It's a refreshing change."

I raise a mocking eyebrow at the girl I grew up with. "Women don't throw themselves at me." I look at Jessica, who doesn't seem to know what to make of Zara's comment. Her lips are parted, her cheeks a deeper pink. "She's kidding. Zara's younger than I am, but gets a kick out of big-sistering me."

"That's because *my* brothers aren't as much fun to bug." Zara grins at Jessica, her eyes taking on a devious glint. "You notice he didn't argue the part about the phone numbers. It's been that way for him and his brothers for as long as I can remember. There probably isn't a woman in Maple Ridge who hasn't lusted over one of the Carson brothers."

I can tell the moment Jessica homes in on the one question Zara hadn't counted on, and a laugh bursts from my lungs, short and to the point. "What about you, Zara? You live in Maple Ridge. Which one of us do you lust over? Oh, wait"—I level a got-you grin at her—"that would be Garrett."

Zara huffs out a comically exasperated breath. "I don't lust over Garrett. He's my best friend. Absolutely no lusting there."

I laugh harder and recline on the couch. "What do you think, Jessica? Does Zara protest too much for someone who doesn't lust over my brother?"

"Garrett Carson? The...the *New York Times* bestselling author who writes thrillers?" Something about Jessica's voice, the curiosity, the tremor, sets me on edge.

"You're a fan of my brother's books?" Suspicion turns my tone cautious, and I exchange a worried glance with Zara.

Jessica winces and takes a sip of her hot chocolate. "I've-I've never...um...I've never actually read them." She doesn't sound nervous, more like embarrassed she hasn't read his books. "Someone I met in town mentioned him."

Tension unknots from my muscles. A woman stalked Garrett a few years ago because she was his number-one fan. That memory always puts Zara and me on edge.

But Jessica doesn't seem like the stalker type. More like prey.

9

TROY

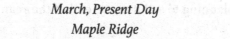

March, Present Day
Maple Ridge

"I guess me being his brother doesn't impress you, then."
Amusement tints my tone, and I dab the antiseptic pad on
Jessica's cut. A hissed breath squeezes past her teeth.

"Are you visiting someone in town?" Zara asks, sounding
genuinely interested.

"I-I just moved here." Jessica leans back an inch, putting
distance between Zara and me. And my gut tells me it's not only
men she doesn't trust. She doesn't trust. Period.

"That's great." Zara passes me a bandage from the first-aid kit.
"You'll love it here. Are you renting an apartment?"

"No, I'm..." She glances between Zara and me. "I'm in the...
the process of buying a house. In town."

Surprise kicks me in the ass. "You are?"

Jessica nods.

I don't bother asking her where. She won't tell me. I open a package with a sterile pad inside, place the pad on the cut, and wrap the bandage around her hand. I'm probably going overboard, but it's an excuse to keep talking to her.

"What made you decide to move to Maple Ridge?" Zara groans and flops against the back of the armchair. "God, if you don't already think small-town folk are up in everybody's business, you will now. I didn't mean to come off so nosy."

"As opposed to how you normally are?" My tone isn't asshole, it's ruffle-her-hair teasing.

Zara makes a cross sound, somewhere between a grunt and a huff. "I'm not nosy."

Jessica looks between us, but I can't tell if she's amused or alarmed at our teasing. "The house...the previous owner's great-niece was planning to sell it at the end of the year. So...I...I made an offer."

Great-niece? *Shiiiit.* What are the chances she means Anne? "What's her name?"

"Anne Carstairs. She doesn't live in Maple Ridge."

Fuckity-goddamn-fuck.

"I know the house you're talking about. The place needs major renovations." *Are you sure you want to be stuck with that kind of expense?*

"If you're looking for a skilled and reliable contractor," Zara says, "you're sitting next him. Troy's so good at what he does, he's big in demand."

Damn, what do I do now? Try and talk her out of buying the house? I've done that a few times when prospective homeowners were facing major renovation expenses for a house they wanted to buy.

The reason I chose Iris's house was because there isn't another house on the market that meets my requirements and would be available at such a low asking price.

"That's okay. I've...I've got it covered." Jessica stands. "I should go now. Thank you for the hot chocolate and for fixing up my hand."

I close the lid on the first aid box. "I'll drop you and your bike off at your house. I'm guessing you biked here. You're the mysterious woman who's staying there, right?" That's why her bike looked vaguely familiar the other night. Iris used to ride it around town. I remember it from when I was a kid.

"I can bike home," she says, avoiding my question.

I push to my feet. "That's not a good idea with your cut hand."

"Thanks, but I'm sure I'll survive." She edges away from the couch. "It was nice meeting you, Zara." She disappears out the door, not giving Zara a chance to respond.

I make a move to go after her, but Zara puts her hand on my arm. "Leave her for now, Troy. Something's made her jumpy. And if you're right about her having PTSD—yes, I did overhear the part where you asked her if she has it—you chasing her won't help."

"You might be right." I settle back on the couch.

Zara gasps, whips her phone from her pants pocket, and points the camera at me. "Can you repeat that, so I have it recorded for posterity? I don't remember you ever telling me I'm right about something."

"You're a brat. Has anyone ever told you that?"

She grins, lowering her arm. "Sure, my brothers have." The smile disappears from her face. "Garrett told me your plans for Iris's house. Whatcha gonna do now?"

"I have no idea. It was the perfect place for what I had planned. I wanted a challenging project to showcase my team's abilities, with the freedom to do what we want instead of doing what the homeowners are after. And the proceeds would be going to help out Olivia and Nova. But I didn't realize Anne was actually planning to put the house on the market. She wasn't sure of her plans last year when I talked to her...before I realized what a great opportunity it would be if I bought it. I was just waiting for final approval from the bank before I approached her with my offer."

"They're the reason you want to do the fundraiser, aren't they? Olivia and Nova?"

"It would be partly for them, but not only them. PTSD has impacted a number of families in the region. Not all of them get the help they need when they need it. I want to make sure no family is left behind." It's why I phoned Zara the other evening on the beach, after bumping into Jessica there. I told Zara I was thinking about organizing a fundraiser, something I have zero experience with.

"Olivia likes you, you know?" Zara stands and walks to the sideboard cabinet she painted white after buying the unit at a garage sale last year.

"I like her, too. And Nova."

She picks up a magazine. "That's not what I mean, Troy."

"Then what are you talking about?"

"God, you guys can be so dense at times."

"Are you talking about guys in general, or me and my brothers?" The corners of my mouth twitch, and I fight back a laugh.

She parks her fists on her hips, shaking her head like a disappointed mother. "I was going for you and your brothers. But I'm rethinking that and including everyone who associates with being a male. But that's beside the point. Do you like Olivia?"

"Of course I do. You know Colton, Olivia, and I were The Three Musketeers growing up. The three of us were tight." Maybe a little less so once Colt and Olivia became a couple during our junior year of high school. But I was also busy with other interests and friends.

"Right. But do you like her in the same way Olivia likes you? I've seen the way she looks at you, Troy."

"How's that?"

"Like she sees you as Colton's replacement."

My amusement at the earlier part of our conversation fades, and I scowl. "You're hallucinating, Zara. Olivia's still grieving her husband's death."

"I don't doubt that. But you've been there for her since he was found unconscious and they tried to resuscitate him. More so than before his death. You've stepped in to help whenever Colton would've been the one by her side."

"What am I supposed to do? Ignore that she needs assistance?" My tone is winter-lake cold. "I'm Nova's godfather, for Christ's sake. I'm not going to abandon them. I owe it to Colt. To Olivia." *All for one and one for all.*

Zara's expression volleys between exasperated, unruffled, and sympathetic. "No, that's not what I'm saying. But I don't want her to get hurt any more than you do, and that could happen if she feels something for you, and you don't feel that way about her. Are you sure she isn't in love with you?"

For the love of Christ. "Of course I am. She's still in love with Colt."

"But he's dead. Look, all I'm saying is I'm worried you've inadvertently taken over his role in Olivia's and Nova's life. And Olivia is expecting more from you than you're willing to give."

"What Olivia and I have is friendship. Plain and simple. She was my best friend's wife. She's still one of my closest friends. And I owe it to him—to Olivia and to Nova—to keep an eye on them since he can't." The last words come out harsh, weighed down with the guilt of failing my best friend.

Zara puts the magazine on the coffee table. "You don't owe him anything. You're doing it because you're a good friend. But you need to be sure Olivia is on the same friends-only page as you."

I nod and push to my feet. "She is."

"Okay." Zara doesn't seem convinced, but that's not my problem. My problem is deciding if I want to take on the responsibility of the PTSD fundraiser now that I can't buy Iris's house.

That, and I hope Jessica got home safely and flashback free. Especially since her home isn't within walking distance.

10

JESSICA

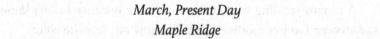

March, Present Day
Maple Ridge

The world is dark outside the living room window, the sun having set thirty minutes ago. Bing Crosby's voice sings through the speaker as I decide how to spend my evening. My hand is sore from the bike ride home, but it's better than it was when I cut it.

I still don't remember what happened, other than I was looking at the roses outside the florist and thinking about the moments after I was shanked. And then Troy was telling me I was safe and no one was going to hurt me.

I've only lived in Maple Ridge for three days, and that's the second time I've seen him. That's more than I've seen of my neighbors. But that's my fault. It's a lot harder to meet them when I'm hiding out in the house like a fugitive.

That isolation was what led to my downfall in San Diego.

I'd made things so easy for my husband. All those times I

wanted to escape, I couldn't because I had nowhere to go. I had no car. No credit card. No neighbor I could reach out to.

I have no intention of getting lost down that path again. No intention of making the mistake of giving my heart to another man. This time I want to have a life with friends. Real friends. Not the people who were acquainted with my husband and were supposed to be my friends by default.

I turn off the record player and head upstairs to the spare bedroom. I haven't been in there since Anne first showed me around the house. Curiosity and the need for a change of view has me opening the door.

I step into a world of faded-pink walls and bedding. A girl's bedroom. Amelia also loved pink when she was a toddler.

Is it still her favorite color?

A breath-stealing pain furies inside me because I don't know the answer. I'm her mother. I should know her favorite color.

I close my eyes against the pain and the tears...because... because I'm not her mother. I did what I thought was best for her. And I still believe it was the best decision—even if it doesn't feel like it at times.

I did it because I love her. Will always love her.

For a second, I let myself slip into the fantasy where Craig and Grace let Amelia visit. This could be her bedroom. The walls need repainting, and I would decorate the room so it's magical regardless of her age and interests.

The bay window area is empty, but the faded pink carpet hints that maybe a chair once sat here. How hard would it be to create a window seat with storage underneath? The perfect spot for watching the clouds and to get lost in a book.

I open my eyes and weave my way through the hip-height piles of magazines. Like in my bedroom, there's an assortment of magazines in English, German, and French. The languages make sense now that I know Iris's father was a British diplomat in Paris and Vienna.

Until my move to Maple Ridge, I'd never been out of California, never mind out of the country. I'm in awe of the woman whose house will soon be mine.

What was the world like when she lived in France and Austria? My best guess is she lived in Paris and Vienna during the 1920s or 30s. She was born in an era when a woman didn't always marry for love. She married so she would be taken care of. If the woman was lucky, she and her husband loved each other.

And yet, according to Anne, Iris had never married. She never relied on a man to look after her. She was independent.

I check out the titles on the bookshelf. *Little Women. The Lion, the Witch and the Wardrobe.* There are also books I don't recognize. A few are from Enid Blyton, an English author who died decades before I was born. I've never read any of her stories, but I do know that much about her.

The doorbell rings. I'm not expecting anyone. I don't even know anyone in Maple Ridge...other than Zara and Troy. And I'm not sure the short time I spent with them this afternoon really puts them into the category of knowing them. Did Anne forget something and drive all the way back here to get it?

I walk downstairs and peer through the peephole to find the dark silhouette of a woman standing on my stoop. But it's not Anne this time. I click on the porch light. The woman appears to be in her seventies and is holding a casserole dish.

I unlock the door and open it. "Hi?" My voice stumbles out in need of a little WD-40.

"Hi, I'm Delores. Your neighbor from across the street." She points to the house with all its lights on. "Welcome to the neighborhood. Anne mentioned you're buying the house." Delores is all wrinkled smiles.

I return the smile, but mine is more on the side of caution. "That's right."

"It's great to finally have someone move in here. The poor place has been lonely since Iris's death." Delores's face flushes, and she splutters. "I mean...not that the house has been talking to me or anything."

My smile grows a little wider, and a nervous laugh brushes over my lips. "Don't worry. I know what you mean."

"Anne said you're looking to renovate it."

"That's the plan."

"And the garden?"

"Yeah, I definitely want to do something with the garden. Make it pretty." And thanks to Iris's love for gardening magazines, I have all the advice and inspiration I could possibly want. "The renovations will be slow going, but I plan to start on the garden soon." With pretty wildflowers. Like a cozy cottage garden.

"That would be wonderful. Iris loved gardening, but when her health began to fade, gardening became too difficult for her, especially with her arthritic hand. The neighbors offered to help, but she didn't like that idea. She was very stubborn and very independent." Delores lifts the casserole dish in her hands. "This is for you. It's a little something I whipped up. I thought you might appreciate it."

I take the dish from her with a gracious and friendly smile— as friendly as the scar by my mouth will allow. I pretend to inspect the food, my usual self-consciousness rushing in on a giant wave. "Thank you. I'm Jessica, by the way."

"Anne said you aren't from Oregon."

My muscles tense at the unspoken question, one I can't truthfully answer, and my gaze darts up to Delores's face. "That's right." My tone is back to being cautious.

"So what brought you to our small town?"

I roll my bottom lip between my teeth, and Granny's sweet voice inquires in my head, *Why haven't you invited the woman in? Offered her a drink. I taught you better manners than that.*

And the voice is right. Granny had taught me better.

"Would you like to come in and have a drink?" An embarrassed heat spreads across my face. "Not that I have much to offer you by way of a drink. Just water."

A gracious smile curves Delores's lips. "Water is fine, dear."

She follows me past the living room with the numerous stacks of magazines. She whistles appreciably under her breath. "I knew Iris adored her magazines, but I didn't realize her collection had gotten that out of hand."

In the kitchen, I place the casserole dish on the counter and get us both a glass of water, taking care not to turn the faucet too quickly.

We sit at the kitchen table.

"So why Maple Ridge?" Delores asks, sounding genuinely interested.

Yes, why Maple Ridge when I don't have a job here? And if what happened earlier at the children's store is a taste of what I can expect, I might not have a job here unless I can figure out what to do about my résumé and lack of references.

Can I even ask Craig and Grace for references? It's not like they really know me. Craig was estranged from his family because he saw the monster his brother was when the rest of them refused to see the truth. I didn't even know Craig existed until after I was accused of my husband's murder.

Either way, I'll have to wait another week to contact them. They're away on vacation.

And even if they agree to be references, that still won't help me with my résumé. Changing my name to give me a new start came at a cost. I've erased who I am and everything about my past —including my job experience. My very out-of-date job experience.

"I'm here to..." To what? What won't raise suspicion? "To write a book," I tell Delores. "A thriller?" I inwardly groan at the way I turned the genre into a question. And what the heck do I know about writing thrillers?

"Wow, that's impressive. I don't know the first thing about

thrillers, but that sounds interesting. I bet there's a lot of research involved."

"There is," I say since I assume that's true. "I'm currently doing research and planning the story. But since I'll be starting the renovations soon and working on the gardening, the novel will be put on hold for a bit. I'll be too busy clearing away the magazines and preparing for the renovations."

Delores's expression brightens with wide-eyed excitement. "What are you planning to do with the magazines?"

"I haven't figured it out yet. Most of the old ones aren't in pristine condition, so collectors probably won't be interested in them."

"Oh, don't get rid of them yet, dear. I wouldn't be surprised if some people in the area would love to get their hands on some of the issues, especially the older ones. I mean, what would be cooler than getting a copy of *Vogue* that came out the month you were born?" She rubs her hands together as if formulating a plan to take over the world—or my magazine collection. "I'll talk to my friends and see what they think."

Delores and I talk for a few minutes while we drink our water. She tells me about everything Maple Ridge has to offer. Which I appreciate. She goes into more details about the town than Anne did.

Afterward, I walk her to the front door. She waves good-bye and hurries down the path to the sidewalk.

I lock the door and go back upstairs to start the process of sorting through the magazines in the extra bedroom. Maybe I'll get lucky and one of them will have an article on what to do when you're starting your life over and you want to find a job.

Or ten easy steps to writing a résumé when you don't want anyone to know the truth about your past.

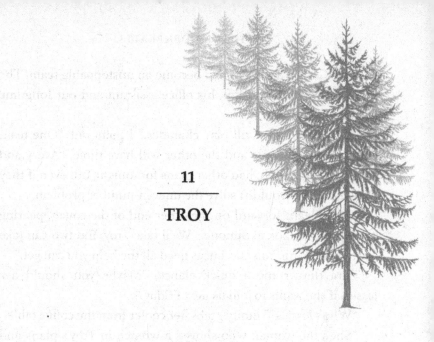

11

TROY

March, Present Day
Maple Ridge

Zara sits on the couch, wineglass in hand. "Does anyone know someone looking for a job? Debra's moving back to Portland to look after her grandmother. And I need to hire her replacement, preferably someone with kitchen experience."

My brothers, Simone, and I shake our heads.

"I'll let you know if I think of someone," Emily tells Zara. "So, what are we playing tonight?" Her questioning gaze trails over us.

Simone, my sister-in-law, smiles sweetly at me from Lucas's lap. "If you had a girlfriend, we could play charades."

"Why is it I'm the one who needs a girlfriend? Garrett and Kellan are also single." A year ago, it wouldn't have even been a question. Simone was living in Portland, having decided she was happier there than in Maple Ridge, where she had grown up. Lucas and I were the ones always teaming up on Game Night because Garrett and Zara had become an unstoppable team. The same with Kellan and Em, his office assistant and our longtime friend.

"Besides, we can still play charades," I point out. "One team will have four people and the other will have three." Avery and her boyfriend, Noah, had other plans for tonight, but even if they were here, that wouldn't solve the uneven-number problem.

Kellan leans forward on the other end of the couch, peering around Em to look at Simone. "We'll take Troy. You two can take Garrett and Zara. You and Lucas need all the help you can get."

Zara throws me a quick glance. "Maybe you should ask Jessica if she wants to join us next Friday."

"Who's Jessica?" Emily grabs her cooler from the coffee table.

"She's the woman who shoved a wrench in Troy's plans and bought Iris Bromfield's house. She's new to town and seemed kind of lonely."

Garrett winces. "Mom's always saying that the early bird gets the worm."

"Which is great if I ever go fishing and need worms," I grumble. "I know to steal them from the early birds."

The dumbass snort-laughs. "Good plan."

"And I didn't know Anne was actually looking to sell Iris's house. I had planned to talk to her once I heard back from the bank."

"So what are you gonna do now about flipping a house?" Garrett asks.

Kellan grabs a nacho from the plate, cheese stringing between it and another chip. "How are you planning to flip a house, work on the cabins we need to build this spring, *and* do your regular day job? From what I've heard, you're booked solid for the next eight months."

"That's why I missed the early worm and the robin snatched it before I could." I flash him a wry smile. "Thought I had time to buy the house so I could finish the cabins first. You know getting

Wilderness Warriors up and running is one of my top priorities." It's been that way ever since Lucas revisited the idea for it last year.

"We do know that," Lucas says. "But we also know life is short, and you need to get out there and live it instead of doing your job twenty-four seven." He pulls Simone tighter to him and kisses her temple, to prove his point...and because he can't keep his hands off his wife after what they went through last year.

"I happen to love my job. And those two projects are not my job. They just involve a skill set that I apply to my day job. Besides, I owe it to Colton to help out Olivia and Nova. If it hadn't been for him, I wouldn't be here today." He'd saved my life in college when we were in a car accident. That was when he realized he didn't want to be an accountant like his old man was pushing for. He wanted to be a paramedic.

If he'd been an accountant, he might still be alive.

"So, this Jessica person. What's she like?" Emily asks Zara.

"She seems nice. Troy brought her into the café yesterday afternoon when she cut her hand. I got to talk to her for a few minutes while he patched her up. She's not very talkative."

"How did she cut her hand?" Em's gaze jumps between Zara and me.

I lift my shoulders in a *Who-knows?* shrug. "I think she might have PTSD. She was having some sort of episode outside the florist and sliced her hand on the corner of the displays."

"You think everyone is struggling with PTSD." Lucas points to the nachos. Simone leans over and grabs him one.

"You forget I've had firsthand experience with people in my life who've struggled with it." I look pointedly at him since he was one of them. "And even if she doesn't have it, she's definitely dealing with something. The woman looked exhausted."

"Can't say I'm too surprised. She's living in the haunted house." Em fakes a dramatic shudder.

I chuckle. "The house isn't haunted."

She grins, head tilted to the side, her blond hair—lighter than Jessica's—brushing her shoulders. "You don't know that for sure."

"Well, she won't be bringing the ghost here for Game Night," I say. "Don't they usually stick with the house they're haunting?"

Em laughs. "Smart-ass. But that's a good thing, though—that ghosts can't leave the house they're haunting. Otherwise, we'd be back to the uneven-number issue again. Anyway, I vote you invite her to Game Night next Friday. If she's new to town, she might not know anyone yet. And then we'll finally have even numbers to play partner games. Unless you have someone else who you'd rather invite as your partner."

"I'll think about it." It might not be a bad idea to invite Jessica. She's new to town and would probably be open to making friends.

And if not, I could always ask Olivia or Lance if Em is that desperate for me to have a partner for Game Night. Usually, both have other plans for Friday night, but Lance has occasionally joined us. Olivia too, but she has to arrange a sitter for Nova first.

From her oversized purse, Emily removes the notepad she brings with her every Game Night. "Now that Jessica's buying Iris's house, what will you do about your plans for helping Olivia and Nova?"

"I'll have to keep my eyes open for another house that comes on the market and fits my requirements." But who knows how long that will take?

"I was thinking about your thoughts on organizing a fundraiser to help families who are impacted by PTSD." Zara picks up her vodka cooler, keeping us in suspense. "What about some sort of daytime event, like a festival? It might have a bigger draw for the surrounding towns. And if it's big enough, you might get media coverage, which can't hurt with raising awareness of the event and the struggles families go through."

"That's not a bad idea. But I have no idea how to organize something like that."

"I can ask Delores," Simone says. "She used to do a lot of planning for big events. I bet she'd be happy to give you some pointers."

Emily sits up straighter, like that kid in class who's dying to answer the teacher's question. "And I can help too."

"I'll take you up on that." I run a successful construction business, but Em's organizational skills put mine to shame.

Simone shifts on Lucas's lap, almost bouncing, her face bright. "You'll need a theme. Something that will draw in the crowds. Avery and I can help you with the branding and marketing side of things."

"Would a musical act work?" I just pulled that suggestion out of my ass, but it doesn't sound like a bad idea. If we get the right act.

"Sure, if you know any who are big enough to draw in the crowds. The county already has the Strawberry Festival, so you don't want to try to replicate that. It needs to be something different. We can all brainstorm some ideas over the next few days and decide which are the most feasible. But I think we can all agree it needs to be family friendly. That will bring in more people. When are you looking at having it?"

"I don't know. But the sooner the better."

Too many families need the help.

Too many people like Jess need the help now.

12
JESICA

March, Present Day
Maple Ridge

A week after I offered to buy Iris's house, Anne beams at me from the other side of the lawyer's conference table, her reading glasses sitting on the bridge of her nose. "Well, congratulations, Jessica. You're officially the new owner of my great-aunt's house."

"Thank you." A smile tugs on my face, excitement and nerves twisting and pulling it into place.

I. Bought. A. House.

Sure, it's a fixer-upper. But so am I. We're caterpillars just waiting to come out of our cocoons. But a lot of work needs to be done before we're ready for that. Work I'm willing to do.

We leave the office and head to Anne's car. The light spring breeze ruffles my hair, and the warm sunlight kisses my face. Eugene, the city where the law office is located, is an hour from the mountains and slightly warmer than Maple Ridge, but I still prefer the small town I now officially call home.

Anne unlocks the car doors with her key fob. "Is there anywhere else you'd like to go in Eugene while we're here? I figured I'd ask because you don't have a vehicle. And I still need to pick up a few things before Dan and I leave for our trip tomorrow."

Her question, her kindness, is a flicker of warmth in my chest. "Are you sure?"

"Absolutely. I took the afternoon off work to come here, and I'm not against the idea of shopping."

An avalanche of joy buries the nervousness that comes with buying a house, and the smile that stretches across my face is wider than before. "I wouldn't mind getting some soil and seeds for the garden. And I need to buy new inner tubes and tires for Iris's bike." Luckily, I checked last night what sizes I need for the tires. "And even though I've been reading through your great-aunt's magazines, I wouldn't mind checking out a bookstore." And I really should get a phone.

Plus, I need an outfit I can wear during a job interview. Once I land a job interview.

At the mall, we wander through the shops. No one seems to pay attention to me or recognize me. I'm just another shopper.

I allow myself to relax a little more. The sounds, sights, and smells of the mall are overwhelming to someone like me, to someone who hasn't experienced them in quite some time. But I don't mind. They're a welcome difference from those that were part of my life a month ago.

I manage to get a phone and a cheap plan, and I purchase bike tires and inner tubes, underwear, bras, socks, and some more clothes. Mostly a cheap pair of jeans for working around the house, a few pretty blouses and T-shirts, a simple skirt that would work for a job interview, a couple of cardigans, including one with a delicate knit. Clothes that don't scream, "Look at me," but make me feel feminine and a tiny bit more confident, even with the ugly scars on my face.

"This would look gorgeous on you." Anne holds up a dainty floral sundress. "It's still cool in Maple Ridge, but it does get warmer in the summer."

I flinch at the sight of it. "It is pretty. But I don't have any occasions to wear it." That's the truth. It's also the kind of dress my husband expected me to wear when we were together in public.

It was one of the mean games he liked to play.

"You're nothing but a cheap whore," he'd said one night after we went out with some of his friends. He was the one who'd demanded I wear the dress. Who'd demanded I go with him.

I didn't say anything. There was nothing I could say to prevent what would come next.

He hit me across the cheek so hard, my ears rang for the next few minutes. I knew then...knew I wouldn't be allowed to leave the house until the bruises healed.

"All you did tonight was flirt with my friends," he'd accused, venom in his tone. "Right under my fucking nose. And don't deny it, Savannah. I saw how they were looking at you."

The clinking of metal against metal behind me brings me back to the present. I uncurl my fingers, my nails digging half-moons into my palms at the memory. *He's dead. He's dead. He's dead.* I can wear a sundress and it's my choice. It has nothing to do with him.

Relief rides the long breath gliding over my lips.

Anne is still inspecting the dress. She adds it to the clothes draped over her arm and goes to pay for her small collection. I keep looking around the store while I wait for her.

Once she's finished, we leave our bags in her car and walk to the bookstore. I almost weep at the selection. This place is heaven. Heaven compared to the prison library.

Anne heads to the biography section. I don't even know where to start. I wander through the store, touching the spines of various books as if they're made of precious jewels. People in the aisles don't give me a second glance.

Maple Ridge has a small library, but I couldn't register for a card because I didn't have proof of my address. I can now. In the meantime, it wouldn't hurt to pick up a book or two while I'm here.

I walk, almost sprint, past the romance section. After everything I've been through, that's one genre I can't be bothered with. A few aisles later, I find myself staring at the self-help books. Books about improving your life, dealing with life after a trauma, time management, finding your creative self in a busy world, and other motivational topics.

The authors smile brightly on the covers, silent promises on their faces, but none of the titles call to me.

I stumble across a book on job hunting and résumé writing that looks promising.

Shame squirms inside me at what Anne would think if she sees the book. We haven't talked about my past or what I plan to do now with my life. But she does know I'm recovering from a traumatic event, I recently left a bad relationship, and I'm starting my life over. She must realize that at some point I'll need to look for a job.

I start walking past the kids' section but stop at the display table stacked with picture books. New books I've never seen before and the ones by authors whose stories I used to read to Amelia. I run my fingertips over the cute cover with a bear and woodland critters on it. I pick up the book and read the story about a bear who can't sleep.

A little girl zooms a tiny toy car on the floor while making engine noises, reminding me I don't belong in this section.

I return the book to the table, longing for those days when I used to read to my daughter, and continue on to the general fiction aisle. There, I find a novel about a woman starting her life over again after a tragic loss. Maybe it will inadvertently have some pointers, even though our situations aren't the same. I add it to my growing pile.

I head to the front of the store to pay for my collection. On the way, I stop at the table with new releases and scan the suspense and thriller titles.

One of Garrett Carson's novels is on the table. I check out the blurb. It sounds good. The book is a political thriller. Not a genre I read, but neither is the other novel I'm buying.

I join the short line of customers to pay for my books.

A toy truck slips from the hand of the five-year-old boy in front of me and lands on the floor with a soft *thud*. He bends to pick it up. When he straightens, his eyes go to the ugliest scar on my face, and he stares at it, his body unmoving.

And I pretend to study the cover of Garrett's book.

"She don't look so pretty now."

"Hey, pretty girl."

Those were the kinder comments following the attack that resulted in the worst of the scars on my face. But even the harshest of inmate insults paled in comparison to my husband's mean words when he was in one of his moods.

The memory of the insults stoops my shoulders and strangles my self-esteem. It threatens to light a match to my self-worth, to burn it down.

The words shouldn't matter anymore. They shouldn't have power over me. They can't cut or eviscerate.

Words can hurt, no matter what the sticks-and-stones children's rhyme may claim. But the words my husband hurled at me can no longer destroy me like they once did. Not unless I give them the power to do so.

I gather my inner strength, the strength that kept me alive for the past ten years. That kept my lungs filling with oxygen, kept my heart pumping blood. And I use it to curve my lips into a gentle smile.

The little boy grins and waves his chubby hand. I wave back.

He presses his face into his mother's leg, much like Amelia used to do when she was being shy with strangers.

A burst of pain hits me square in the chest at the memory. I push it aside. This isn't the time or place to let that pain fester.

I pay for my books soon after and join Anne, who's waiting for me near the door, reading the back of a book from the nonfiction table. She looks up at me and shows me the cover. "My book club wants to read this. It's supposed to be really good. Have you read it?"

It doesn't look familiar. I shake my head. "What's it about?"

"Virginia Hall. She was an American spy in occupied France during the Second World War."

That gets my interest. "Some of the magazines your great-aunt saved had articles about the war. And there were also a few commemorative issues."

"Auntie Iris believed the more you know about the world and about past events, the less ignorant you are. She kept telling me while I was growing up that ignorance leads to hatred. Knowledge leads to understanding and love. It was why she read so much and why she became an advocate for reading. When I was in elementary school, my mother wasn't able to volunteer there even though she wanted to. So, Auntie Iris went in her place. She helped with the school's reading program."

"How old was she when she died?"

Anne tells me. Based on my calculations, Iris would have been in her late twenties during World War II.

"Did she talk much about the Second World War?" I ask as we head back to Anne's car.

"No. I asked her about it once because we were learning about the war in school. She told me she didn't want to talk about it. All I know is she and her sister were living in England at the time."

"What about your other grandparents? Were they living in England at the time, or here in the U.S.?"

"My grandparents on my father's side lived in Portland. I

never met my mother's parents. They lived in England but died when she was a little girl. Auntie Iris raised her. What about your family? Where do they live?"

I inwardly groan. My curiosity to learn more about Iris caused me to forget I was opening myself up to questions I don't want to think about. "They're dead. Heart disease, cancer, car accidents. It all catches up with you eventually." I wince at how cold that sounded. I don't even know if any of that's true. For all I know, I still have a father and another set of grandparents somewhere.

The only family I loved were my grandparents on my mother's side. It's hard to love parents who gave up on you before you were even born. At least Amelia won't feel that way. Unless her adoptive parents tell her the truth—that she's adopted—there's no reason for her to ever believe her biological mother never loved her.

"I'm sorry." The sad tilt of Anne's mouth seems genuine.

Even though she's saying she's sorry I have no family, I pretend she's telling me how sorry she is my own family—other than Granny and Grandpa—treated me that way.

"It's okay. It's been a while. I've made my peace with the loss." I give Anne my standard crooked smile, but my self-consciousness about the scars slithers in again, and I let my smile slip away.

Anne drives me to a gardening center next. I purchase soil, seeds, and tiny containers for growing the seedlings. It's almost 6:00 p.m. by the time she drops me off at home. I invite her to stay for dinner, but she declines. She has to finish packing for her trip.

"I have something for you, Jess." She reaches behind her car seat and pulls out a small bag from one of the clothing stores we visited. "This is for you."

She hands me the bag, and I open it. Inside is the pretty floral sundress.

"Th-thank you," I managed to say past the knot of emotions clogging my throat. "You didn't have to do that." I can't even tell her how much her gesture means to me, not unless I want to reveal the truth about my past.

Anne's eyes search my face. I don't know what she finds there, but her expression softens some more. And I know...I know on some rudimental level, she does understand how much the dress means to me.

"I know I didn't have to buy it for you," she says, smiling, "but I'm glad I did."

13

JESSICA

March, Present Day
Maple Ridge

I pour a can of corn chowder into a pan and set it on the stove. Fred Astaire sings "Steppin' Out with My Baby" from the record player in the living room. The Iris in my head sings along while she fixes her dinner.

The doorbell rings, and a rush of adrenaline kicks into action. My heart clambers into my throat and a tremor grips my body. Like it does every time someone rings the doorbell.

Fuckers. Will it always be this way? Will I always fear that whoever's on the other side of the door is here to expose my secret? To let everyone know my shame?

It's okay. It's probably Dolores checking on me again.

The doorbell rings once more, and this time I manage to move my feet. After spending five years in a maximum-security prison, I thought I'd be a hard-ass. A fortress. Cold and unfeeling.

But I'm just as scared of my shadow now as I was before I'd been incarcerated.

I check through the peephole. A tall man is standing on the stoop, his features obscured in the dark shadow. But even then I recognize him. *Troy? What the fuckers?*

I click on the outside light and unlock the front door. "Hi?" An urge to study my feet nudges me so he can't see the scar by my mouth.

"Hey. I came to see how your hand's doing." A friendly, easy-going smile stretches across Troy's face.

"It's much better, thanks. You didn't need to come by. It wasn't that big of a deal. It was only a tiny scratch." I don't invite him in. But I move back a half step into the shadows so my face is less noticeable. Not that it matters. He's already seen the scars. But I don't need him quizzing me on how I got them.

The smile is still on Troy's face. "It was more than a tiny scratch."

"I survived, so no biggie." I lift my hand so he can see for himself the cut on my palm from a week ago is healed.

He leans against the railing, which is hopefully sturdier than it looks. "You're right. It is looking good. And how're you doing?"

"I'm fine, thanks." I start to shut the door. He puts his hand on it, preventing me from closing it all the way. My heart beats louder and faster in my chest, and my guard hunkers down for a battle.

My gaze darts to his hand.

He takes his hand away from the door, his expression not apologetic. "One more thing. My brothers, some friends, and I get together pretty much every Friday for our regular game night. I thought maybe you'd like to join us tomorrow. Zara will be there."

"I don't play cards." The words come out flatter than a deflated bike tire.

"That's okay. We don't always play poker. Last week we played charades."

I almost laugh. Troy doesn't look like the kind of guy who plays charades on a Friday night. He looks more like the kind of man who would take out gorgeous women.

"I have plans." Plans that involve working on my résumé, a stack of magazines, the bathroom grout, and one of the novels I bought today.

They're the same plans I have for tonight.

"Maybe another night."

"Yeah, maybe." I start to close the door, but Troy stops me again. My guard rears up, claws drawn. "Would you quit doing that?"

He moves his hand, but my words roll off him, as if he's able to repel them. He responds with a soft, humorless laugh and leans against the doorframe like he's settling in. "Are you okay? You look exhausted. You having trouble sleeping?" His gaze searches my face, searches my wary eyes.

Dammit. Does he have to be so observant? What else has he noticed about me? Even Anne didn't comment today on my obvious lack of sleep.

"I'm sleeping fine." For a few hours a night, when the nightmares give me a reprieve.

"You sure? You look like you haven't had a good night's sleep in a couple of weeks."

Way to sweep a girl off her feet. "That's because I've been tidying the house in preparation for the renovations. And I've been staying up late reading too. I've got a really good book." That sounds convincing enough.

"Have you hired a contractor yet?"

"No, I'm doing the renovations myself. Except when I'll need to hire professionals, like for the electrical work. I might be crazy-ambitious taking on a project like this old house, but I'm not deluded about what I can do on my own." I didn't mean to say that much. Sleep deprivation is dulling my resolve to say as little as possible. Putting me at risk of being ridiculed—like my husband used to do.

"Do you have experience with home renovations?"

"I'm all for learning as I go." The truth is, I can't afford to spend all my money on turning this place into a beautiful haven.

Troy laughs. It's a nice laugh, deep and nothing like my husband's. But when I first began dating him, I'd thought he had a nice laugh too. It was only later that I recognized it for what it was. An illusion.

"Home renovations aren't as easy as the HGTV shows make them out to be." Troy moves away from the doorframe and pulls on his expert-opinion face. "They use professionals. And for an old house like this, you'll need someone who knows what they're doing. For starters, you could be facing asbestos in the insulation. Incredibly dangerous. It needs to be removed carefully. The workers have to wear hazmat gear."

Oh, damn. I hadn't thought of all that. "Thanks. I'll keep that in mind."

"Or you could hire me, and you won't have to worry about any of it." He smiles the smile that no doubt has women drooling and tripping and losing their hearts. Like Zara said happens all the time.

"I'll think about it." When donkeys learn to fly. There's no way I can hire him. Not if it means spending time with him. So far, he seems to be the kind of guy who'd be easy to drop your guard around. And I can't risk that happening.

This time when I shut the door, Troy doesn't try to stop me. But I still hear him say, "Pick you up tomorrow night at six thirty."

AFTER DINNER, I HEAD UPSTAIRS TO THE EXTRA BEDROOM. I'VE already made a dent when it comes to the stacks of magazines in here, but the closet is still packed with them, and they're preventing me from shutting the closet door.

An hour and a half later, the situation is reversed. I've sorted through the magazines in the closet, and most of them are now downstairs in the living room. The closet is empty except for a squat, built-in bookshelf. But it isn't flush with the wall like it should be. One side sticks out. The other side is slightly receded into the wall.

When I was younger, I used to pretend my grandparents' house had secret passages, some behind their bookshelves. There weren't any, but it was a fun game to play on rainy days.

I slide my fingers through the narrow gap and pull the book-shelf toward me. It reluctantly budges a fraction of an inch at first but then gives way to my insistent tugging. The healing injury on my back protests. I ignore it. The journalistic curiosity that served me well in school wants to play after being locked away for so long.

Once the gap is wide enough for me to slip through, I duck my head inside, but the space is too dark to see anything. I already know the closet light doesn't work, either because the bulb has burned out or because there's an electrical issue.

I rush downstairs, grab my phone from the kitchen table, and race upstairs. I turn the phone flashlight on and crawl into the space behind the bookshelf. The hardwood floor is dusty, and there are cobwebs in the corners. But other than that and a card-board box, the space is empty. There's not even a single magazine in here.

I shine the light around the area. The ceiling appears to be the same height as in the closet and the bedroom. A single mattress could fit in here, but not much else. And the door can be shut from the inside with the handle that's attached to the back of it.

I open the flaps on the box and shine the light inside. The bright beam glints off a bronze cross. Some sort of medal? It's sitting on top of what looks like a pile of journals.

I take the medal out and inspect it. A female head is engraved in the round center, but I can't quite make out the words. The second word is *Française*. Two swords intersect behind the cross, which is attached to a red-and-green-striped ribbon. It's an old medal but nothing I recognize.

I put it back in the box and push the box through the opening between the wall and the bookshelf. I stand, hoisting the heavy box up. The healing injury protests again, but it's outvoted. Journalistic curiosity for the win. It hums through my body like electrical currents during a storm.

I carry the box to the bed and lower it onto the mattress. I remove the medal and put it on the bed. Next, I take out a delicate chain, the clasp broken. A small gold heart dangles from the chain, intricate leaf patterns etched in the tarnished metal. An heirloom?

I set it down next to the medal. Once Anne and Dan return from their European vacation, I'll call her and tell her what I found.

I wipe the first journal clean with my sweater and open the cover to the first page. The only things on it are the faded handwritten words:

Angelique D'Aboville
Book One

I turn the page to find the elegant if not shaky penmanship of whoever wrote in the journals. I read the first lines. Surprise and intrigue widen my eyes.

The curiosity humming in me has me practically running downstairs carrying the journal. I make myself comfy on the couch and begin reading...

14

ANGELIQUE

April 1943
France

The Parisian sidewalk is busy, but it's not as busy as I would prefer.

Before the Nazis invaded France, these streets were vibrant with life. Now, I'm wearing a drab dress and drab coat, and my dark-blond hair is tied back under a beige fedora. To the individuals who do not know otherwise, I'm just another Parisian trying to be inconspicuous, trying to survive under the stench of oppression.

The chilly April breeze nips at my bare legs, reminding me of one of the inconveniences brought on by the war. But the lack of available stockings is minor compared to the constant fear and hunger that plagues France. Plagues this country unless you are one of *them*.

I keep the speed of my footsteps slow enough not to gain attention, yet I'm light on my feet, ready to run if need be. My gaze is trained ahead of me, but I'm still aware of my surroundings. The cough behind my back, smothered with a hand. The rumbling of an engine, belonging to one of them, no doubt. The murmur of quiet conversation, paranoia buried in the words. The two German soldiers on the corner of the street, watching, waiting.

Their presence sends my heart thumping faster and louder than a round of ammo from an MG 42.

I push past the never-ending fear and glance to the fourth floor of the building ahead of me. The fourth floor and the second-to-last window on the left.

A white vase sits on the right side of the windowsill. The lace curtains are closed, but I catch their slight movement as though a light breeze has ruffled them.

I enter the building. My heartbeat seems to echo off the dingy walls and stone stairs. The foyer is dim and empty and silent. A few light bulbs have burned out since the last time I was here.

I listen for footsteps or voices on the spiral staircase. There's nothing, nothing but quiet. No fearsome pounding on a door, no dreaded shouts from the French Milice or German Gestapo.

I climb the stairs, heedful of the sounds and smells around me. My soles are almost soundless on the polished steps.

On the top floor, I walk along the hallway and knock on the last door on the left. The rapping is quiet so not to draw the attention of anyone in the building other than my "cousin" and his wife. You never know who might be a collaborator. You never know who might be willing to sell their soul to gain a reward, to gain favour with the Gestapo.

The door opens, and I'm met by a pair of cautious blue eyes set in a pretty face.

The smile that spreads across my expression is genuine and full of relief. "*Bonjour*. It is a beautiful day for a stroll. Is my cousin home?" My French flows easily, as though it were my native tongue.

"Even better for a waltz in the park" is Élise's reply. The phrase is the code for "It's safe to meet."

Élise opens the door wider, and I step through the entrance to the flat. She peers down the hallway I came from, ensuring I wasn't followed, and shuts the door behind me. Tension drains from her narrow shoulders, and her lips curve into a delighted grin. "You are doing well, Carmen, *oui*?"

"I am. And you?"

"As well as can be expected."

We kiss each other's cheeks and go into the tiny drawing room. Allaire is at the window, gazing down at the street I just travelled. The lace curtains are pushed aside barely an inch so he can check to see if I was tailed. Check without anyone being wise to his surveillance.

He nods at me and releases the curtains. Allaire and I sit at the small dining table while Élise goes to the kitchen to fetch us drinks, giving us a moment to talk business.

"How are things going?" Allaire asks in English, complete with his native Yorkshire accent.

"Please tell me we're getting a wireless operator soon. It would save time when it comes to communicating with Baker Street." Then the courier in my region would not have to make the frequent train trips to Paris, to deliver messages for Allaire's operator to transmit to the Special Operations Executive's headquarters in London.

"You need to recruit more couriers."

I bristle at his non-reply to my operator concern, but I keep it from showing on my face. "I'm working on finding more couriers. But Baker Street does need to send us more operators."

"I told them the network needs three more. They can't train them fast enough to meet our demands." The weight of his words looms heavy in the air.

Being a wireless operator tends to mean you have a low life

expectancy. The Germans have become more skilled at flushing them out, and it's certain death once an operator is caught.

"Can you also tell Baker Street to stop giving us the wrong count for how many packages they're dropping?" I say. "We wasted two hours last week searching for a package that didn't exist."

Allaire winces. "Better they overestimate than underestimate."

"Both mistakes put the reception committees at risk," I remind him. "We don't need to make it any easier for the Germans to stumble across our drop zones."

He nods, clearly knowing I'm right. We've heard the rumour that the same error cost members of another reception party their lives. "All right, I'll tell Baker Street to do a better job with their count. How are the reception committees doing?"

Élise returns to the drawing room, carrying two glasses of water. She sets them in front of her new husband and me and takes a seat at the table.

"They're tired," I tell Allaire. "Morale is taking a beating."

He releases a sharp breath and clenches his hands together on the table, shoulders stiff. Being the leader of the *Cashmere* network hasn't been easy, but the SOE's Baker Street headquarters was sensible when they assigned him to the position. "We are all tired, Carmen. I don't remember the last time I slept through the night."

"Once this fucking bloody war is over, I'm sleeping for the next ten years."

His mouth twitches. I am sure the smile has more to do with my use of a swear word than my plans for an extra-long nap once the war is over.

His mouth straightens, his face slipping into his previous sombre expression. "Baker Street wants you to recruit more safe houses. And they want more parachute drop zones and airplane landing strips in your region."

"I'll let my contact know, and we'll coordinate our activities."

We discuss several other dire topics that relate to Baker Street's goal of ending the war. Ending the war and getting rid of the Jerries. Topics that are too difficult or cumbersome to relay via the usual method of drop boxes, cut-outs, and couriers.

"Jolly good," Allaire says once we're finished. "Now, how about we take a stroll to the park? There is someone I want to introduce you to." He nods at his wife, who speaks some English but not enough to follow most of our conversation. "He will be my second-in-command should I be summoned back to London for a short visit. And he might have some need of you at a future date should his regular girls be unable to assist him."

I nod in understanding. His "regular girls" means I could be an escort or a spy or a contact person. Someone the Germans don't suspect because I am a woman.

While I was in Allaire and Élise's flat, the early afternoon sun slipped past the clouds and is providing a little warmth to the otherwise cold city.

We walk to the park. Allaire feigns a slight limp. The limp is to prevent questions as to why he isn't in a German prison camp like the rest of the French men who tried to defend their country against occupation. The feigned limp also helps keep him from being deported to the Nazi work camps.

He and I easily slip into French as we walk. No one would suspect only moments ago, the leader of the *Cashmere* network and I were talking about Baker Street's plans for the Bourgogne region. Now, we're chatting about the recent theatre production he and Élise saw. No one would doubt that they are newlyweds. Her arm is wrapped around his, and they look utterly in love.

They might be talking about the costumes and set design and production, but they weren't at the theatre to enjoy the show. Allaire attended the production to gain new intelligence to relay back to London. The slip of a tongue. A boastful comment. Any tiny morsel is desirable if it helps bring an end to the war. With the Allies the winner.

I smile while they regale me with stories about their delightful evening. Smile while I pretend everything in the world is all right.

Élise points to the large pond, and we head towards it.

A man walks in our direction. He's tall and handsome, but the strain of war mars his expression as it does for everyone else in the park. He catches sight of us, and his face breaks into a welcoming grin. To an onlooker, it appears as though he wasn't expecting to run into his friend here.

"Élise, it's always a pleasure to see you." His tone is all Parisian charm, and his French sounds natural. I can't tell if he grew up speaking the language because one of his parents is fluent in it, or if perhaps he really was born in France.

Élise gives him an easy-going smile.

"And this is my cousin Carmen," Allaire tells him. "Carmen, this is Christian."

Christian is his code name. For the sake of security, we don't know each other's aliases. I offer Christian my hand to shake.

"*Enchanté, mademoiselle.*" He lifts my hand to his mouth and plants a soft kiss on it.

I release a delighted giggle. His hazel eyes belay a warmth and humour that seem out of place during these days of uncertainty and despair.

His white dress shirt, black trousers, and black shoes would have been in better shape prewar, but that does not diminish his striking good looks. His clothing only serves to enhance them.

This man's role isn't to blend in, to become invisible. His job with the SOE is to associate with powerful individuals, to be noticed, to charm both men and women alike, to glean from the enemy the intelligence Baker Street will salivate over.

When it comes to women, how far will he go to gain the information? One of the guidelines our training imparted on us is sleeping with the enemy to gain secrets is frowned upon. But I am certain Baker Street would not condemn him for his actions if it meant ending this war sooner.

Christian releases my hand. "And how are you enjoying our fair city?"

"It's beautiful. I wish I could travel here more often. But with everyone gone because of the war, I need to help my father with the work around the house and the vineyard."

"Well, I hope you're able to visit your cousin more often. I would enjoy showing you all the delights the city has to offer."

I bite back a laugh and smile graciously. I am certain he speaks this way to all women. I can almost imagine the fifty-five-year-old widowed courier blushing at his words, and she is not one to easily fall for a man's cheap flattery. "I'll keep that in mind for the next time I visit."

The four of us exchange words for a few minutes, and Christian bids us goodbye. We need to keep to the cover that we just happened to come across him while walking in the park.

Allaire and Élise return to their flat. I head for the train station.

I'm barely out of the park when I spy a family in thread-worn clothing and wearing the recognizable black armband with the yellow star on it.

The two little boys are huddled against their mother's legs. An SS officer shoves their father to a truck filled with other men. The man climbs in, the stoop of his shoulders resigned. Another officer pushes the mother and her sons towards a different truck.

Anger coils hotly in my muscles, and I have to rein in the urge to run across the street and grab the family from the Nazis. To hide them away. To spit in the officer's scowling face.

Or better yet, to knife him the way I've been trained to do.

But I cannot do any of those things.

It won't help the family. It might make things worse. As much as I hate it, I must stick to my task, even though my heart tells me that is not the right thing to do.

I curl my fingernails into my palms and hurry forwards before the Nazis' attention is diverted my way.

I don't go directly to the train station. I walk along a relatively empty street, pause to look in a shop window, then casually glance in the direction I came from. No one is following me.

At the station, I head for the correct track and board my train. I take an empty seat in the middle of the car and slip on my mask of indifference.

Two Wehrmacht soldiers enter the train car, and my near relief that no one is after me stumbles and falls, sending my heartbeat into a mad scramble.

"Papers," one of them barks in French, his harsh German accent twisting the word into something ugly.

They proceed down the aisle, checking everyone's *carte d'identité*.

A dangerous silence fills the space, choking us with its oppression. Even if your papers are genuine, there is still an ingrained fear the Gestapo, Milice, or a German soldier will find fault with them.

But when your *carte d'identité* is fake—no matter how good a forgery—it requires tremendous courage to keep the truth from your face. To keep your body from betraying you.

The officers step closer. My heart beats faster. I try swallowing my fear.

The man stops by my seat. I remove the papers from my purse, praying my hands don't tremble.

15

JESSICA

March, Present Day
Maple Ridge

The next day, I cycle to Main Street and park my bike at the grocery store. The mountain air is crisp, the midmorning sky a welcoming blue. Spring has kissed the region and is beginning to show on the trees. Birds chirp cheerfully between the promise of leaf buds.

I lock my bike and walk through the store. I pay for the food and load everything into the cloth bag I found in Iris's kitchen. Next, I go into the drugstore a few shops down and locate their small stationery section. I grab a package of pens and a thick pad of lined paper. Angelique's journal is tricky to follow at times because of the faded ink and shaky handwriting. Anne and her husband left this morning for their European vacation, so I couldn't tell her about the journals I found. Maybe she knows who Angelique is.

The investigative reporter in me, the one my husband

thought he'd buried, wants to finish reading the journals. Wants to figure out why they were hidden in the secret room.

The investigative reporter in me also senses it's important I read them.

I plan to copy the journals as I read them, writing it all word for word. When I have the chance, I'll type it out at the library. Because Anne said her eyesight is failing, I plan to give her the typed-out copy—along with the journals and everything else I found in the box—so she can read the entries without further eye strain. It's my way of saying "thank you" for everything she has done for me, starting with offering a stranger a place to stay while I figure out my life.

And, well...I really want to find out what happens next with Angelique. I *have* to keep reading the journals.

I'm about to bike to the library but have second thoughts and pedal to Picnic & Treats first. To get a dessert. Because I can. And because Granny loved making cakes to celebrate special occasions.

And what's more special than buying your first house?

I remove the bag from the bike's basket and enter the café.

Zara steps through the door behind the counter, carrying a tray of Danishes, her copper-brown skin glowing in the natural light streaming through the café windows. A smile, bright and friendly, stretches across her face. "Hi, Jessica. Give me a sec. I want to ask you something."

I nod, a flush warming my cheeks. It still feels weird having people ask me questions instead of ordering me around or raining me with insults.

I wait by the door, playing chameleon and blending into my surroundings. Trying to be invisible. Which is ridiculous. This is a small town. I bet at least half the population has heard about the scarred woman who just moved to Maple Ridge.

I feel naked, raw, my entire story printed in large headline font on my body.

"Wife of Murdered Cop Sentenced to Life in Prison."

"Wife Believed Husband Having an Affair and Killed Him."

"Wife Sentenced for Murdering Husband Declared Innocent."

"Killer of Murdered Cop Still At Large."

If they knew...if they knew the truth about my life, would they blame me for what happened? Would they blame me for not walking away when he first hit me? When he first tore me apart with his words? How could they not? I've spent the past eight years wondering how I could've been so stupid. Wondering how I'd missed the signs until it was too late.

And then I was too scared to leave. Scared no one would believe me. I couldn't even file a police report. Who would believe that one of their own, the man who was paid to protect others, who was a hero...who would believe he terrorized his wife on a daily basis?

Terrorized his wife between those stretches of time when he showered her with gifts and affection.

I knew no one would believe me. And I'd been correct. No one believed me when I went to trial for his murder.

I close my eyes against the memory of the day he found out I was pregnant. The delight on his face. Not because he was excited to be a father.

It was because he'd found a new way to manipulate me.

"Are you okay?" Zara's voice breaks through my thoughts, and I open my eyes.

I fix a smile on my face. "I'm fine, thanks. What is it you wanted to ask me?"

A woman walks past us and wishes Zara a good day without pausing a beat.

Zara responds with a quick answering wave and turns back to me. "Troy mentioned he invited you to our weekly game night."

At his name, a shudder shimmies up my spine, but I can't put a finger on the reason for it. Uncertainty? Caution? An emotion I don't want to admit to? "He did."

"I don't suppose you've changed your mind about coming. I promise you, it's a lot of fun."

I flash her an apologetic smile, my decision unswayable. "Thanks, but I've got plans." The same plans I've had every night this week, but with the addition of reading Angelique's journal.

"Are you sure? Simone, Emily, Avery, and I would love to have you join us."

"Why? You don't even know me." The words come out in a near whisper, hope and wariness flickering to life. Zara is offering something I haven't experienced in a long time—an escape from perpetual loneliness. Friendship.

But I was tricked and hurt too many times in prison. Given a glimpse of friendship only for it to be snatched away. I can't risk that happening again. I won't.

"Because I like you, and you seem like someone we'd want to be friends with." Zara shrugs as if she can't imagine any other reason. "Emily and Simone are sitting by the window. I'm taking my break now. You might as well join us. Then you can see for yourself we aren't all that scary."

"Okay." Doubt hangs from the word, and I draw it out, but Zara doesn't appear to notice.

I order a strawberry-kiwi fizzy water from the girl working the counter. Zara grabs a coffee and leads me to a table where two white women our age are sitting. She introduces them to me.

"You can call me Jess," I tell them.

Both women are pretty like Zara. Emily's blond hair brushes her shoulders and is several shades lighter than mine. The sunlight shining through the window next to Simone has turned her hair reddish brown. So different from the golden-brown hue of my natural color.

Their gazes flick to the worst of my scars. They don't wince in sympathy or pity or even seem relieved the scars don't mar their faces. But that doesn't keep my self-esteem from slapping me like cold seaweed.

Zara sits beside Emily, and I take the empty chair next to Simone. I put my shopping bag on the floor by my feet.

"So what brings you to Maple Ridge?" Simone's smile is as warm and friendly as Zara's, and the tension I didn't realize I was clinging to eases from my shoulders. "My husband told me you bought Iris Bromfield's old house."

Damn. How many people already know that?

Oh, who am I kidding? Probably everyone in Maple Ridge. Small town and all.

Hopefully, that's all they know about me.

"I recently got out of a bad relationship. So I bought the house. I figured the renovations will keep me busy for a while and be a great distraction." And if I'm lucky, I'll be so exhausted, it will keep the nightmares away. I won't wake up gasping for air. "And I'll also be looking for a job soon," I add, not wanting to admit I tried to get a job at Little Wonders last week.

Zara sits up a little straighter. "What kind of job?"

"I'm not sure. Something local." That doesn't require a car for me to get to.

"One of my employees had to quit the other day to look after her grandmother in Portland. I don't suppose you have any experience working in a kitchen, do you?"

"I do, actually." Three years of working in the prison kitchen, to be exact, but I don't want to explain that to Zara.

"Can you start Monday morning?"

I blink, waiting for her to remember to ask for references. She doesn't. And after a beat, I swaddle myself in relief. I won't need to contact my brother-in-law, Craig, after all to see if he and his wife will be references. "Monday would be perfect."

Zara seems even more relieved than I am, her smile wider than before.

Delores and two other elderly women approach the table and put their coffee mugs on it.

One of the other women leans down and kisses Simone on the cheek. Then the three older women grab chairs from the empty table next to us and move them over to our table. We scoot our chairs over to make space, and they take a seat.

"Jess. This is my grandmother, Rose." Simone nods at the woman who shares her hazel eyes. The one who'd kissed her. "And her two friends, Samantha and Delores."

Delores grins at me, deep, knowing creases forming at the corners of her eyes. "We've met. Jess is my new neighbor."

"Oh, *you're* the new neighbor," Samantha gushes, her voice cheery and crinkly with age. "We've heard all about you. You're the poor soul who has to go through all those magazines Iris held on to for too many years."

"It probably would have been worse if she hadn't waited until Lizzie got married before she started collecting them," Rose points out, and I give a silent *Thank God* to that.

"Lizzie?" I ask.

"She was Iris's niece," Rose explains. "Lizzie's parents died when she was little, and Iris became her guardian. Lizzie was Anne's mother. She died about twenty years ago."

Silence falls over the group for a beat. The chatter from the customers sitting at the other tables chips away at Rose's news.

"Jessica is writing a thriller. Isn't that exciting?" Delores says, doing a complete turn-around in topics, and ignoring how I told her last week the novel is on hold for the time being. She swivels her shoulders to me. "What's it about?"

Zara picks up her coffee mug. "You're writing a thriller? You never mentioned that the other day. And you really don't know Garrett Carson?"

"To be honest, I didn't know his name until Anne mentioned him." I already told Zara and Troy how I knew Garrett's name, but I guess if I'm writing a thriller, it must seem weird I'm not familiar with a *New York Times* bestselling author in my genre. An author whose books are placed on the table at the front of the bookstore. "I've put the novel on the back burner for a bit. I'm doing research for the story, and I'm going to be busy for a while renovating my house." Sounds like a good enough excuse. It's halfway correct, at least. "I'm not ready to talk about the story yet because...because I don't want to jinx myself."

The first part is mostly true. As for the jinxing, who knows if that's a thing when it comes to writing books. But it sounds like a good reason for not talking about the story prematurely. The story that I don't plan to write.

"Well, I can't wait to hear more about it once you can share details with us." Delores pats my hand and turns to Simone. "The girls and I"—she nods at Rose and Samantha—"have given some thought to the main attraction for Troy's charity festival idea."

"Charity festival?" I ask, my inner journalist getting the better of me.

Zara and Delores fill me in on the details. The more they tell me, the more an impressed warmth fills my chest at what Troy wants to accomplish.

"So the main attraction should be..." Delores gives a dramatic pause and looks at each of us in turn.

Her two friends eagerly nod. And I try not to giggle at how much they remind me of Granny, with their warm smiles and that sense of camaraderie—like they're all in it together. I bet she would've loved these three women.

"Well, it's more like one idea," Delores says. "They could auction off dates with hot men—"

"Of all ages," Samantha pipes in.

"Right, of all ages," Delores echoes.

Yep, Granny would have been besties with these women and called them a hoot. And she would've been all for their suggestion.

Zara and Emily exchange grinning glances and crack up

laughing. I can't contain my laughter either. And it feels good. Freeing. I can't remember the last time I laughed...or had a reason to laugh.

"You can guarantee Katelyn Bell will be all over that if Troy's part of the auction." Still grinning, Emily picks up her coffee.

"Katelyn and quite a few other women, too, no doubt," Simone says with the look of someone who has done the mental math of what it means and is impressed with the results.

Delores rubs her hands together, clearly excited about this. "Even better. The demand for him will drive up the bidding price. And it won't be any different for Lucas, Garrett, and Kellan."

That comment seems to sober Simone, Zara, and Emily, and they stop laughing. Zara and Emily stare at the contents of their coffee mugs.

Simone's eyes widen, and her mouth goes momentarily slack. "Wait, my husband's going to be auctioned off for a date with another woman?"

Samantha rolls her eyes like a girl six decades younger but with a little extra sass. "It's not like he's expected to kiss her. This is just a fun date. And Rose is okay with it if John is one of the bachelors."

Rose gives her a comical double take, her expression mirroring her granddaughter's. "You never said anything about John being auctioned off."

"I just assumed it's a given," Samantha says, the eye roll now in her tone. "We said hot men, and your boyfriend is certainly hot."

Delores's eyes gleam with mischief. "Are you worried one of the younger ladies will bid for your man?"

Rose's eyebrows disappear under white bangs. "Perhaps. What about Fred? Will he be auctioned off too?" Her question is directed to Delores.

"As much as I love my husband, I don't think he falls into the category of hot men." Delores pats Rose's hand. "You have nothing to worry about. I've seen how John looks at you. You're the sun in his sky and the oxygen he breathes."

"That's very poetic." The words stumble over my lips, a dreamy quality to my tone. "It must be nice to have a love like that." Love is for other people, but it clearly will never be for me.

"I'm sure one day you'll find the same love," Rose says. "There are plenty of nice men in Maple Ridge. Some are just a little rougher around the edges than others."

An abrupt laugh erupts from Zara. "Maybe that should be on the welcome sign when you drive into Maple Ridge. Welcome to Maple Ridge, where some of the men are a little rougher around the edges."

The other women burst out laughing. I let my lips slide into a wider smile. These women are nothing like the ones in prison. *Friendly* wasn't in the vocabulary of the inmates who constantly targeted me. They'd probably combust if they uttered the word.

"Where did you move from, Jess?" Emily asks and takes a sip of her coffee.

"Randolph, Vermont." I'd randomly picked the name before moving to Maple Ridge. I know nothing about the small town. But mentioning I'm from San Diego isn't an option.

"I've always wanted to go to Vermont. Do you ski?"

"No. I'd always planned on learning but never had the chance. I was always too busy."

They continue peppering me with questions. I do my best to evade them and redirect the questions to the others. The questions I don't evade, I answer but keep as close to the truth as possible, making it easier to keep my lies straight.

"Have you had any luck finding a photographer to replace Kim?" Simone asks Emily.

Emily shakes her head, and disappointment surfs on her sigh. "Unfortunately not. It's hard to find someone as talented as her and who shares a similar vision for wedding photography."

My gaze drops to Emily's hands around her coffee. She doesn't have on an engagement ring. "Are you getting married?"

"Oh, no. Nothing like that. I started a wedding consulting business that specializes in mountain destination weddings. It's only a side thing for now. Zara provides catering. Simone has special wedding and honeymoon subscription boxes. Kim was our photographer if you were looking for something different than your typical wedding photos." Emily taps on her phone and turns the screen to me.

The black-and-white image of a bride and groom tugs at something in me. It's gorgeous, with its light and airy, photojournalistic aesthetic.

It's the style my husband hated. He called it ugly.

But there's nothing ugly about the photo. The image is breathtaking. Spontaneous. It captures the spirit of the couple, the special bond between the bride and groom. It isn't practiced or controlled. The photographer caught the perfect expressions on their faces. The pure joy as they gaze at each other, laughing and smiling, the wind blowing her veil around both of them.

Every detail about the picture is the opposite of my wedding photos. My husband was rigid, unsmiling. He had the stiff, straight-backed appearance of someone in uniform for an official portrait, even though he wasn't wearing his uniform for the wedding. I was gazing at him, a hopeful expression on my face. He looked dangerous and arrogant. I looked like an innocent lamb oblivious to its upcoming fate.

A reflection of our truth.

Only I hadn't realized it at the time.

No photographer, no matter how talented, could have made our wedding photos as special as the one on Emily's phone.

I've never taken wedding photos, but I used to experiment with photojournalistic-style portraits. Granny and my friends were the subjects. They were the type of photos that revealed the person's personality, their strengths, their passions. I'd even won a few awards in college for them.

A deep longing weaves inside me, wraps itself around my organs. I miss experimenting with natural lighting to create different moods. I miss playing with composition to tell a story. Stories that spoke of triumph, of joy, of sadness, of hope.

It's the same craving that tugs at me every time I read an article that calls to me from one of Iris's magazines. The photos, the articles...they remind me of why I studied journalism. To tell someone's story, to share about the challenges they faced and of their courage.

To make a difference in my community, in my world.

But instead of helping me follow my dreams, my husband slowly changed my story. My goal of being a journalist—I gave it all up. Because...because it didn't fit my perfect husband's plans for a perfect marriage with his perfect wife.

I don't even have a camera anymore. He destroyed it during one of his tirades.

I smile at the image on Emily's phone, protecting the longing inside me as if it's a fragile blossom. "It's gorgeous."

A long and wistful sigh skims over Emily's lips. "Kim's photos are incredible. Unfortunately, her husband—Zara's brother—got an amazing job offer in Portland, and they moved there last fall. I mean it was fortunate for them. Most brides and grooms I've worked with so far hadn't been looking for this style of wedding photography, so it's been okay. But I'd love to have that option available with a photographer who lives in town or nearby."

The woman working at the counter approaches our table. "Em, here's your samosas order." She places a paper bag in front of Emily.

"Thanks, Tracy. I guess I should get back to work so the slave driver doesn't wonder what happened to me."

Simone and Zara snicker.

"Kellan's probably so busy with the program he's working on, he hasn't noticed you're missing." Zara shakes her head as if it's some sort of inside joke.

"You might be right about that. But I do have a ton of paperwork I need to finish before tonight." Emily pushes her chair away from the table and stands. "I'll see you two tonight. And I expect to see you tonight as well, Jessica. We need another player to even out the teams."

I open my mouth to tell her I can't make it, but then I change my mind. I'm starting a new life here. And that includes making friends. "What's the address?" Is it somewhere I can easily bike to?

The smile Zara directs at me sends relief swirling through me, confirming joining them tonight will be good for me. "I can pick you up. Then you won't need to worry about getting lost."

16

TROY

March, Present Day
Maple Ridge

My phone rings from my jeans pocket. I set the screwdriver on the granite kitchen counter and check who's calling. Zara.

The buzz of the jigsaw travels from the hallway where some of the guys are working on making the home wheelchair accessible. The comforting smell of sawdust permeates the air.

I open the back door and step onto the porch. The late afternoon sun shines through the leafless branches of the trees, creating shadows on the weathered wood.

I accept the call. "Hey, Zar. What's up?"

"Can you do me a favor?"

"Depends what it is." I glance at the clear sky, and the scent of pine triggers my craving to go hiking.

"I convinced Jess to join us tonight. But something came up, and I'll be running late. Can you pick her up?"

I don't bother to tell her that I'd already told Jessica I would pick her up. I can only guess Zara had also promised to drive her to Lucas and Simone's house. "Sure. How the hell did you convince her?" Jessica was adamant she wouldn't join us tonight when I asked.

"Em told her she had to come, and Jess relented."

That would explain it. Saying no to Em requires special powers. Powers most people don't possess. "What time is she expecting me?"

"Six thirty."

After my crew and I call it quits for the day, I go home, shower, and head to Jessica's house. Her outside light is on, as are the lights inside on the main level. I open the passenger door and let Butterscotch jump down.

Music from another era comes from the house. Music my grandparents or great-grandparents might've once listened to.

I ring the doorbell. The music stops, and the front door opens a beat later. Jessica's wearing jeans and a cream-colored top, no makeup, and a startled expression.

She leans to the side to look past me. The dark shadows under her eyes haven't changed since I last saw her, and her eyes hold a wariness as they scan the area. Her body's an overly stretched elastic band. Shit, when was the last time she was able to relax?

"Zara was held up at work and asked if I could pick you up."

Jessica nods, the wariness firmly in place, and she crouches in front of Butterscotch. "Hey, boy." She lets him sniff her hand and strokes him. Her hand shakes, but the trembling subsides after a few moments of petting him.

"I'm almost finished getting ready." She stands and steps aside. "You might as well wait for me inside."

I toe my shoes off and follow Jessica into the living room. A shitload of magazines fills the space, the numerous stacks hijacking much of the floor.

"You really like magazines, don't you?" I walk to the nearest stack and check out the top issue. *Vogue*, September 1952.

"They belonged to Iris. This is nothing compared to what it was like when I first moved in."

The individual magazines in the stack next to the coffee table are stored in plastic bags. Two books lie on the table. According to their subtitles, one is about America's greatest female spy during World War II. The other is about how breaking the Nazi code helped the Allies win the war. Both are library books.

I pick up the books and read the blurbs. "I hope these aren't Iris's, because damn, that will be some overdue fine."

The light chuckle from Jessica swirls around us like silk, sending a wave of desire through me. "I borrowed them from the library, not Iris." Jessica takes them from me and puts them back on the table.

"You're interested in the Second World War? Is it just that war or wars in general?"

"Just World War II."

"You're a history buff?"

Her gaze goes to the magazines in the plastic bags. "Not really. That time period's a new interest of mine."

The magazine on top proclaims in big bold font: *50th Anniversary of D-Day*. "Why the sudden interest in the topic?" I pick up the magazine. The next issue is also about the war.

"I saw the books in the library this morning. They looked fascinating. S-so I borrowed them."

"They do." I know a little about the war. Mostly from what I learned in school. But what I know about spies—male or female —during the war, and the Enigma machine, amounts to very little. But she's right. The books do look interesting.

"I'll be right back." Jessica disappears from the room.

I look through the magazines in the Ziploc bags while she's gone. Every one of them seems to have some connection to the Second World War, whether it's a single article or the entire magazine dedicated to the topic. I'd say Iris had more than a passing interest in the subject.

I'm flipping through the issue on the fiftieth anniversary of D-Day when Jessica returns.

"I'm ready to go," she says.

I don't glance up from the old photos of soldiers and civilians who were involved in the resistance against occupation. "Are these also Iris's magazines?"

"Yes."

"I guess it makes sense she kept them. She might have lost friends and family over there during the war."

"You're probably right about her friends and family."

I return the magazine to the Ziploc bag. "It's different for me. I fought in Afghanistan, but I have no intention of buying magazines or books on the topic. I've witnessed firsthand the pain and loss that war caused. I'm not interested in revisiting it through a journalist's eyes." Jessica doesn't offer any insight or hand me empty words, and I put the magazine back on the pile. "Okay, Butterscotch. Should we go visit Jasper now?"

Jessica grabs the bottle of wine that's sitting on the side table in the hallway. "Give me a moment. I'll meet you outside."

"Sure." Butterscotch and I go out on the porch and wait for her to come out.

She joins us a few minutes later, locks the front door behind her, and jiggles the doorknob to make sure it's locked.

"Have you given any thought to hiring me to renovate the house?" I ask.

"I'm still going to do it myself." She turns away from the door without looking at me.

"Why? If you hire me, you know I'll do a good job." We walk along the path to the driveway. "Okay, maybe you don't know that," I continue without missing a beat. "But if you want, I can take you to some of the recent projects I've worked on. It'll give you a taste of what I can do."

She releases a long, exasperated sigh. "I don't doubt you're good at your job, but I'd prefer to do the work myself and hire the individuals I can't skimp on, like an electrician."

At least she realizes the importance of tradesmen.

I stop at my truck and turn to her. "People who do renovations on their own without the necessary skills and training usually aren't thrilled with the results. Then they have to hire a professional to fix the botched job. And this puts the homeowner way over budget." This is especially true when they severely mess up the job. "If you're positive you want to do it yourself, I can recommend tradespeople who'll do a great job and will do it right the first time."

She just nods.

I still think she's making a mistake. For starters, she doesn't have the physical strength she needs for the job. I have several women on my crew, and they're a lot stronger than Jessica. She's slight, the opposite of those women.

I help Butterscotch onto the back seat and climb into the driver's seat. I turn over the engine and reverse out of the driveway.

Jessica peers over her shoulder. "Butterscotch isn't the kind of dog I'd expect a man like you to own."

"What kind of dog would you expect me to own?"

"Something big, like a German shepherd."

"Maybe not exactly a German shepherd, but you're right. I always thought that one day I'd get a large breed."

"So how come you ended up with this little cutie?" The affection in her tone is directed at Butterscotch.

"I was working on a reno project about two years ago and found him in the crawl space under the deck. Turns out his owner had been an elderly woman who recently died. Butterscotch had somehow gotten out of the house. He was scared and all alone when I found him."

In a way, he makes me think of Jessica. I know nothing about her, but I can't help thinking she's all alone. Most people have photos of loved ones in their living room. Jessica doesn't have a single picture. Maybe she has them somewhere else, but I still get that gut feeling she's alone in the world.

"It took me a while to gain his trust," I tell her. "But by the time I'd discovered the truth about his owner, he'd wiggled his way into my life. He quickly proved he was a great emotional support animal for the vets at the Veterans Center in town. And he and I became a team."

"He's your family." Jessica's voice is almost a whisper, as if her words are meant mostly for herself.

"He is."

"He's very lucky."

"He is." I look over at her, and our eyes catch. A light blush spreads across her face.

I return my gaze to the road and think for a second about a safe topic I don't have to worry about her shooting down. I want to know more about her, but I don't want to rush her until she's ready. "Do you have a favorite fruit?"

Christ, that's the best I can come up with?

"Favorite fruit?" There's almost a quiet desperation in her voice at the last part. Like she's hoping I'll fill in the silence so she doesn't have to talk. But a twinge of laughter is also buried deep in her words. "Is this like your favorite-ice-cream-flavor question?"

"Damn right. You can learn a lot about a person by their favorite fruit and ice cream flavor." The corners of my mouth twitch into a smile.

"Okay. Mango. That's my favorite fruit."

"It must be. It's also your favorite ice cream flavor."

My eyes are on the road, but I can tell she's now staring at me.

"You remembered that?" The timbre of her tone lifts up at the end in more than a question. She's genuinely surprised I remembered that small detail she'd told me the first night we met. "Do you have a photographic memory or something?"

"Isn't that just something that happens when you read?" Because hell if I know.

"I...I don't actually know."

"I wish I had it. Photographic memory. It would've made school a lot easier if I could've just read something once, and then I was good to go."

I'm rewarded with one of her sweet laughs. And damned if I don't want to hear it more often.

"I know what you mean. About the photographic memory and school. W-what's your favorite fruit?"

"Peaches. No idea why. I just happen to love them."

She's quiet for the remainder of the short trip, and I don't try to push her to talk. The silence between us isn't uncomfortable. And I sense that she needs it. It's clear that she's an introvert. An introvert who's about to be thrown into a house with nine people who aren't nearly as introverted as she is—except for maybe Kellan.

We arrive at Lucas and Simone's house. I open the rear passenger door for Butterscotch. He jumps down, bounds over to the front door of the house, and releases a little bark—his version of a doorbell. A moment later, it's met by Jasper's answering bark from the other side.

The door opens, and Kellan holds back Lucas and Simone's energetic eleven-month-old, golden Labradoodle puppy.

Butterscotch rushes in, unable to wait any longer to see his friend. He and Jasper sniff each other in greeting. I enter the house. Jessica follows.

"Jessica, this is my brother Kellan," I tell her.

A small, hesitant smile arranges itself on her face, but its lifespan is fleeting. She nods, retreating half a step. He replies with a nod of his own, and she ducks her head in that self-conscious way of hers I've noticed.

And I silently curse. My brothers and I are over six foot, our bodies shaped by our Marine days and our still regular workouts. It's probably tough enough to face one of us, but all of us at once?

I lead her into the living room and introduce her to Lucas and Garrett. Zara told me Jessica met Em and Simone this morning, so hopefully she won't be too overwhelmed. There's a fragility about her, but I also sense a strength beneath the surface. A stubbornness that prevails.

"And this is Avery and Noah." I point to them in turn.

Avery grins at Jessica. "It's nice to meet someone else who isn't from around here. I'm a Portland transplant."

Jessica smiles, but even without the scar by her mouth, I suspect the smile would come off equally as unsure. Her gaze flickers briefly to the door leading to the backyard. "What made you move to Maple Ridge?"

Avery's smile doesn't falter. "Simone. We were roomies and used to work for the same ad and marketing boutique. She moved back here last spring to focus on her subscription-box business. It took off. Big-time. She needed help to keep up with the orders." The redhead who wasn't originally a fan of Lucas spreads her arms wide. "So here I am, doing that while I solidify my career goals."

And I thank the ever-loving Christ she moved to Maple Ridge. "My brothers and I recently hired Avery. She's our office manager for the outdoor rec program for military vets we're in the process of getting up and running. Avery is the one who helped us with the branding and all that crap."

Avery laughs. "I happen to love that branding crap. That's my ultimate plan. To help small businesses grow their brand. It's what I'm helping Simone with and what I'm doing with Wilderness Warriors." She nods at me. "The Wilderness Warriors job right now is just part time while they construct the cabins and main building," Avery explains. "But things will get busier once the program starts this summer. And I'm also starting to gain a few other clients."

Noah slides his arm around Avery's waist, his large body towering over her. "And then I'll probably never get to see my girl." He grins fondly at her.

She fake-glares at him and half-heartedly smacks him in the chest. "Hey, I can't help you're often doing the night shift."

"Oh?" Jessica asks, shifting nervously on her feet. "What do you do for a living?"

"I'm a cop," Noah replies.

Jessica's face pales, and her body goes rigid. Her breathing is fast and shallow as if she's a wild rabbit that's hoping a bobcat doesn't spot her. The changes aren't huge, but they're enough for me to notice.

Shit. What the hell's going on?

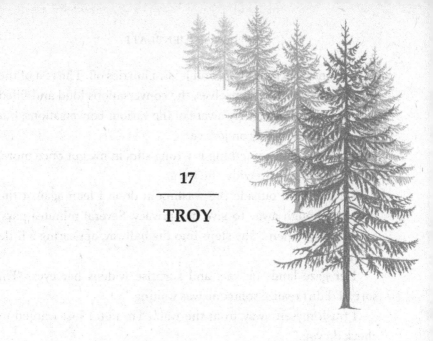

17

TROY

March, Present Day
Maple Ridge

If Noah noticed Jessica's fear toward him, his expression doesn't give anything away. Maybe her reaction had nothing to do with him. Perhaps something else triggered it.

She turns to Simone. "I brought you wine. I wasn't sure what I should bring. I've never—this is all new to me. Playing games, I mean." She holds out the bottle to Simone, her hand and voice shaky.

Smiling, Simone takes it from her. "Thank you. The girls and I never turn down a chance to drink wine. Especially during Game Night."

Jessica's gaze darts briefly again to the door leading to the backyard before returning to Simone. "Where's the washroom?" The volume of her voice drops. Her face is still pale, but her cheeks are now pink.

Simone directs her to it, and Jessica hurries off. The rest of the group chats among themselves, the conversations loud and filled with laughter. I'm vaguely aware of the various conversations, but my attention is mostly on Jessica.

The sensation something is wrong stirs in my gut once more, and I head in the direction she went.

I don't stand outside the washroom door. I lean against the wall far enough away to give her privacy. Several minutes pass, and the door opens. She steps into the hallway, appearing a little calmer.

Her gaze lands on me, and surprise widens her eyes. "I'm sorry. I didn't realize someone was waiting."

I push myself away from the wall. "I'm not. I just wanted to check on you."

"I'm fine." She glances down the hallway toward the living room.

"I don't think you are. You looked pretty freaked out when I was introducing you to everyone." More specifically, when Avery teased Noah.

"You're imagining things. I really am fine." She walks past me, and I let her. I don't buy that she's okay, but I refuse to make her more uncomfortable by pushing for answers.

I just wish I could help her.

We return to the living room. Jess pours herself a glass of soda from the table, and I grab a beer.

I keep an eye on her as she talks to the women, my attention half-focused on what my brothers are saying. It's clear she has already slipped into an easy friendship with Simone, Zara, and Emily. She smiles and laughs when talking to them, but she also startles at loud noises.

It's the men in the room she seems less certain about, especially Noah. Fear clouds her eyes when she talks to my brothers, and she keeps a distance between herself and Noah, even when Avery is with him.

But there's nothing in his expression to suggest he knows her. He's all smiles and charm and amusing stories. I mentally curse whatever was responsible for the wariness she wears.

"Hey, Garrett," Emily says, grabbing a nacho from the plate on the table. "Jessica is writing a thriller."

Jessica's face reddens. "I'm...uh...doing research for it right now. And...I'm not ready to talk about the story yet."

"You might want to get that printed on a T-shirt." A chuckle vibrates in Garrett's voice. "I can't go out without someone fishing for details on my next book."

A small smile twitches on her face. "Thanks for the warning."

Emily sets up the easel and the large dry-erase board.

I lean closer to Jessica. She smells sweet, like strawberry shampoo. "We're playing Pictionary. How're you at this game?"

She glances at everyone else, and it's obvious they're all sitting with their game partners. Her eyes dart to me, wide and uncertain. She must have just done the math.

"I've never played it before." Fear darkens her eyes, and an unmistakable tension tightens the lines of her body. "You might not want to play with me if you want to win."

"It's just a game. It doesn't matter if we win or lose. The only prize that comes with winning is bragging rights." I mean, sure, winning is great, but there are more important things in life—as serving in the Marines taught me.

True, we're a competitive bunch. Especially my brothers and me. Marines are about as competitive as you can get. But I meant what I told her. It's just a game.

A faint sigh slips past her lips, taking the stiffness in her shoulders with it. "That's good."

Everyone else takes their usual seats. I sit next to Jessica on the couch, breaking tradition as to where I usually park my ass. Butterscotch flops down next to her feet.

Emily holds out the bag with the Scrabble pieces inside. Each of the women pulls out a letter to determine who goes first.

Simone removes an A, which trumps all, and grabs the first card from the box. She reads it, picks up the erasable marker from the easel, and nods at Emily to start the timer.

She draws, and Lucas yells out answers. "Fish! Monkey!" I have no idea how he got monkey from what she's drawing. "Owl!"

Garrett cracks up laughing, and the rest of us snicker. "Dude, I have no idea how you two ended up together. Where the hell are you pulling those answers from?"

"Rose," Lucas yells, ignoring him.

Simone taps at the picture with her marker, leaving black dots on the surface.

"Flies!"

She throws him an exasperated look that leaves Zara, Avery, and Emily giggling.

"Fleas!"

She taps it again, this time with the non-marker end of the pen.

Lucas mutters a few words under his breath and jumps to his feet. "Grandmother!"

"Yes!" Simone grins at him like they've won a million dollars. She gives him a long, lingering kiss that has the rest of us groaning.

Garrett and Zara are next. "North Pole!" Garrett says after several attempts.

Zara high-fives him.

Jessica and I are after them. She reads her card, nods for Emily to start the timer, and begins drawing.

I call out a bunch of words. "Circle. Pie. Wheel. Ball."

Jessica beams and draws a cloud, which I yell out, stating the obvious. She then draws snowflakes coming from it.

"Snow."

Her smile wide, she points at the ball.

"Snowball!" I'm off the couch and on my feet.

"Yes!" And for the first time since I spotted her at the lake,

Jessica looks relaxed and happy. There's nothing self-conscious or wary or ill at ease about her. And *shit*, she's beautiful.

The game continues for several more rounds. The longer Jessica and I play as partners, the faster we are at guessing each other's words.

She draws a diagonal line.

"Mountain," I call out.

"Yes!" She bounces up and down like a cheerleader. Maybe she was one at some point.

"Seems like you're really good at this game," I say as she returns to her spot next to me on the couch.

She grins. "Maybe we just make a good team."

The game finishes with Jessica and me winning by a point.

Still looking relaxed, she pushes herself to her feet. "Excuse me." She steps past me. "I'm just going outside for a few minutes. T-to watch the sunset."

"You okay if I join you? Butterscotch might need to go for a bathroom break."

Her lips flutter up at the corners. "I wouldn't want to be the one who keeps him from his bathroom duty." She doesn't look at me, her gaze on the floor in front of her.

She heads for the front door. Butterscotch, Jasper, and I join her. I don't know if everyone else has decided to give us privacy, but we're the only ones who go outside.

The view of the sunset isn't as spectacular here as it is at the lake, but it's still pretty fantastic. I rest my folded arms against the porch railing, enjoying the relative quiet.

"I'll never get tired of seeing sunsets for as long as I live." Jessica's voice is the near-whisper it was earlier in my truck. Like she's not talking to me. She's talking out loud to herself.

The soft light from the lowering sun paints a beautiful glow on her relaxed face. Screw watching the sunset. I'd be content just watching this side of her.

"Did you always watch the sunset where you were before

moving here?" I ask, hoping she'll give a little more of herself to me.

She shakes her head but doesn't elaborate. She just watches the changing fiery colors until they finally extinguish into dusk.

I pick up after the dogs, and we all head inside. I wash up and we rejoin everyone in the living room.

"I'm up for hiking tomorrow. Anyone wanna join me?" I take a swig of beer from my bottle.

Even before I asked the question, I knew my brothers would be on board for a hike. The mountains are in our blood. It's why all four of us volunteer with Maple Ridge Search and Rescue. It's why we're creating the inclusive outdoor rec program for vets of all abilities.

Noah has the weekend shift at work, so he can't make it.

"I'm going to Portland tomorrow for a few days," Avery says. "It's my grandfather's ninety-fifth birthday on Sunday."

Emily shakes her head. "You can count me out. You guys always pick the toughest trails." She's never been the most eager hiker of the group.

"We'll pick an easier route this time," I promise her.

"Your easier or my easier?"

"Definitely yours. So, I'll count you as coming." My attention shifts to the other three women. Zara and Simone are in.

"I've never hiked before." Jessica leans down and strokes Butterscotch.

"You'll love it," Simone assures her. "It's great for just getting away, leaving your problems behind for a few hours, and being surrounded by nature. It's so peaceful."

"The dogs will be joining us," I point out in case that's an additional selling feature.

"I don't have hiking boots?" Jessica counters

Zara grabs the remaining cheesy nacho from the plate. "Do you have sneakers? That's what I wear when I hike. But I never go on the more challenging hikes with the guys."

"Are you sure you don't mind me joining you?" Jessica asks me. "I've always wanted to hike, but I've never had the chance to try it."

I don't say anything and wait for Zara, Simone, and Emily to convince her to come with us.

"You have to come." Emily smiles, the curve of her mouth generous. "It will be fun."

"We definitely want you to join us," Zara adds, equally enthusiastic about the idea. "Em's right. It will be fun."

"Okay," Jess says on a laugh. "I'll go hiking with you guys."

And maybe by the time we've finished the hike, she and I will have gotten to know each other a little more. And I will have earned a little more of her trust.

Because Jessica is an enigma I want to solve—a woman I want to get to know better.

18

ANGELIQUE

April 1943
France

I'm sitting on the train to Nancy, the train still in the Paris station, when two German soldiers enter the car. My near relief that no one followed me after my meeting with Allaire stumbles and falls, sending my heartbeat into a mad scramble.

"*Carte d'identités,*" one of them barks in French, the language turned ugly with his harsh German accent.

They proceed down the aisle, checking everyone's papers. A dangerous silence fills the space, choking us with its oppression. No one dares move or else risk the soldiers' ire.

Booted footsteps slowly make their way towards my seat. My loud and rapid heartbeats almost drown out their sound.

The footsteps halt at the middle of each row, pausing long enough for the two German soldiers to check the passengers' *carte d'identités*. Only a few more moments before I find out if my forged papers pass these officers' inspection.

One of the soldiers stops in front of me. I hand him my papers. The slight tremor in my fingers isn't enough to betray me, and I train my gaze on his insignia, and not on his face. I've already memorised his appearance. Young. Twenty-three or twenty-four years old. Oval face. Long thin nose. Straight blond hair. Narrow shoulders. Tall.

Tension vibrates through the air, squeezing my throat with its fist, freezing my lungs with cold fear. He gives my forged *carte d'identité* a cursory glance and hands it back to me.

And I stifle the urge to release the air in my lungs in a relieved sigh. That will only draw suspicion.

He moves on, but it's not until the two soldiers depart our train car that we can all breathe again. I close my eyes for a heartbeat, then shift my gaze to the countryside sliding past the window.

At Vitry-le-François, I disembark and transfer to a train travelling south. The next leg of the journey is less eventful. No German soldiers, Gestapo, or Milice board the train at any point.

The train pulls into my stop. I gather my handbag and step onto the small platform. Monsieur Beaulieu is the only other person to depart the train.

He nods and gives me a small smile, revealing tobacco-stained teeth. "*Bonjour*, Madame D'Aboville. Did you have a pleasant trip?"

I return the smile. "Very much, thank you."

"My son is with the wagon. We can give you a lift home if you'd like."

"Thank you. That would be wonderful."

Normally, I cycle when I need to go anywhere, but this time, I didn't want to risk leaving the bicycle where a German soldier might claim it for his own. As the French have learned, the Nazis and Wehrmacht soldiers have no respect for that which does not belong to them.

The one-horse wagon is waiting for Monsieur Beaulieu at the front of the station. The horse's ribs show slightly through her black-and-white dapple coat, but I know she eats better than the family.

Pierre sits on the driver's seat, a slow smile spreading across his face at seeing his father.

Pierre is a year or two younger than my twenty-eight years. By day, he farms alongside his father. At night, he's a member of the local resistance circuit. Like Allaire, he has a limp that precluded him from fighting in the war, but unlike Allaire's limp, Pierre's is not faked. But even with the limp, he's strong from working in the fields. I've witnessed that strength during the parachute drops, when he has helped carry the heavy crates of guns England sends us.

He nods at me, but there's more than just a greeting in those knowing blue eyes. It's the acknowledgmatt we have a job to do tonight. It's the full moon, and the weather is favourable for the scheduled parachute drop.

Monsieur Beaulieu assists me onto the wagon, and I settle myself between the two men. Pierre clicks his tongue and flicks the reins. The horse starts walking.

Neither man asks about my trip to Paris. They don't know I'm an English agent, but Pierre does know I'm part of the local resistance group. I was the one who recruited him after I moved to the village.

The trip to the safe house I'm staying at is short. Pierre drops me off at the end of the driveway of the farmhouse, and I hurry up the dirt path to the front door. The place looks the same as it did when I left, with no tyre marks from unwanted German visitors. So far, the unassuming village has been lucky. The Germans have pretty much ignored it. For now.

I open the front door and step into the house. "Papa," I call out, keeping to my cover that I'm his daughter. His widowed daughter.

"We have a problem," my *Papa's* weary voice says in French behind me.

I pivot on my heels and take in the austere expression of the man who is a decade older than my real father would be if he were alive. "What kind of problem?"

Jacques doesn't elaborate. He walks out of the house and heads to the large red barn several yards away. The barn that contains straw and hay for the horses, a wagon, some equipment he uses in the vineyard, and what little is left of the produce he stored over the winter.

After the Germans took their share like a swarm of locusts and moved on.

I follow him.

A tortoiseshell cat plods alongside the barn wall, heading in the opposite direction and ignoring us. Mars, one of the two barn cats living on the vineyard.

Jacques opens the small door to the barn, scans the surrounding area, and steps inside. I join him.

He closes the door behind me and walks to the several bales of straw sitting in the middle of the building. He pushes them aside, revealing the trapdoor few people know exists, and says, "*Le Hobbit.*" The code word to let whoever is in the hiding space know it is a friend not foe about to open the door.

He pulls open the door that hides the small space with a camp bed and a kerosene lamp on a crate. A man wearing a uniform similar to an RAF uniform is lying on the bed, a revolver next to him on the worn blanket.

And for a second, I see my ex-fiancé's features in the pilot. The messy light-brown hair, the rugged good looks, the inquisitive eyes. I have no idea if Charles is alive, or if his plane is missing somewhere in Europe, shot down by the enemy.

It's not something I've given much thought to, and I won't dwell on it now.

"Géraud and another man brought him here. He's injured."

"How bad is it?"

"I have no idea. They said something about his leg. And this man"—Jacques points at the man on the bed—"doesn't speak or understand French." The fermented disgust in his tone doesn't hide his concern for the downed pilot. I can see it in Jacques's eyes, in the firm set of his mouth.

A large proportion of the French don't trust the English after the Great War. Jacques's opinion has only recently softened towards those from the other side of the Channel.

"Can you boil some water so I can clean the wound?" I ask.

Jacques leaves, and I climb down the ladder leaning against the wall.

The pilot cocks his head to the side. "Hello? I don't suppose I'll get lucky and you speak English, eh?" His accent isn't British. And he's not American. Canadian, perhaps?

I smile, the tug on my mouth weary from my long day and my soon-to-be long night. "You're in luck."

"Ahhh, you're English."

"And you're not. Are you Canadian?"

He pushes himself to sit, wincing with the movement. His injured leg remains stretched in front of him. "That's right. I'm from Calgary, Canada, to be exact. My name's Lieutenant Todd Matherson."

"Nice to meet you. I'm Carmen." He doesn't need to know my real name or my alias. "And for now, your code name is Conrad. I understand your leg is injured." From the looks of his torn trouser leg, he has bled a fair amount.

"That's right. Sliced it open when I tried to evacuate my plane."

"Can I see?"

He nods, and I peel back the ragged edges of the fabric and

gently remove the bandage from his leg. A nasty opened wound cuts across his thigh. It's bad, but it could have been worse. He's fortunate to still have his leg.

The wound is no longer bleeding heavily, but blood oozes from it. I reach under the bed and pull out a small valise. The pilot isn't the first injured ally or member of the local resistance circuit to show up at the safe house.

"I have the water," Jacques calls down in French from the opening of the hiding space.

I climb up the ladder and take the small pot from him. Steam rises from the water. "*Merci.*"

"I will stand guard at the door." He walks to the closed barn door and leaves, shutting it behind him.

I cautiously climb back into the hiding space, working hard to keep the water from spilling. I kneel next to the bed. The flickering flame in the lamp creates deep shadows on the walls. "This will hurt, but I need to clean the wound. And you might need stitches."

"Can you do that?"

"No, but we have a physician in town who can."

Todd's handsome features pinch into a frown. "Is that a good idea? For him to know I'm here?"

I dip a clean dressing into the hot water. "He's part of the local resistance group. I'll fetch him once I'm finished with this." I lightly press the cloth on Todd's wound.

He releases a hiss.

"Sorry." I carefully clean the wound, taking care not to cause it to start bleeding heavily again, then place a new piece of dressing to cover the gash.

"The two men who brought me here said you can help me return to England," Todd says, questions filling his eyes.

"Yes, that will be the goal. But you need to recover first. The trip won't be easy. I'll arrange for a guide to take you over the Pyrénées Mountains, and then you'll make your way to Portugal.

You will need to remain hidden in here while you're healing. I'll make you some broth to eat once the doctor has seen to your leg."

I pack up the valise with the first-aid supplies and push it back under the bed. "I'll need to close the trapdoor while I'm gone. Will you be all right if I extinguish the lamp?"

He nods.

"You should try to sleep while I'm away." I put my hand on his chest and encourage him to lie down. He doesn't resist. I extinguish the flame, climb up the ladder, and lower the trapdoor into place.

I cover it with the bales of straw and leave the barn.

Jacques is standing outside the entrance, watching the driveway to the farmhouse.

"I need to fetch Dr. Deschamps. I won't be long." I mount the bicycle that belonged to Jacques's wife. She died five years ago, and he's letting me use it while I stay at his house.

I pedal to Dr. Deschamps's office in the village and balance the bicycle against the brick wall that separates the garden from the road. I ring the doorbell, and his wife lets me in.

"*Bonjour*, Roselina. Is your husband available? I have a patient for him." Three years ago, I would never have thought a phrase as innocent as that question could imply the local resistance circuit needs help with a task. But these days, I can conduct entire conversations in code without batting an eyelid.

"He's with his last patient of the day."

We talk while waiting for her husband to finish. At the same time, we fold the towels he needs for his practice. In this instant, we are just two women catching up on life and sharing recipes.

It feels good. Normal.

For the past three months, I've been focused on helping to end the war and keeping alive. No spare moments to be me, to reflect on how my engagement fell apart, to think about my family and friends. No spare moments to think about my job as a translator, to appreciate the latest fashions, to lament a hole in my stockings.

Dr. Deschamps and his patient step out of the exam room. The woman and I exchange greetings.

"You have a patient for me, *non*?" Dr. Deschamps inquires once she has left the house.

"*Oui*. He may be in need of stitches." My voice is whisper-quiet, even though Dr. Deschamps, Rosalina, and I are the only people in the house. "He is resting in the chicken coop."

"I'll meet you there. I have a few more things I need to complete first. I shouldn't be more than half an hour."

I smile, the stress of the day easing slightly. "*Merci*."

I return to the safe house and prepare a broth for Todd. The familiar hum of Dr. Deschamps's car engine stops in front of the kitchen window. I go outside and lead him into the barn.

I shut the door behind us, and we push aside the bales of straw covering the trapdoor.

"*Le Hobbit*," I say, loud enough for Todd to hear me, and lift the trapdoor. The weak sunlight leaking into the barn bathes Todd's pale face as he looks up at us. His expression boasts a relieved smile that speaks of so many things.

Dr. Deschamps and I climb into the space. With the two of us in here, there is not a lot of room to move.

He examines Todd's leg and tends to the wound. "You'll need plenty of rest for the next few days." He turns to me. "Your plan is for him to leave France via the Pyrénées escape route, *non*?"

"That's correct. Unless Baker Street sends a Lysander to pick him up." Which is doubtful.

And even if Baker Street agrees to it, airplane landings can only be safely done around the time of the full moon. Todd will have to wait another three or four weeks—at the earliest—before he can be flown out. Hiding him for a week or two is dangerous. Hiding him for a month or longer will put us all at tremendous risk, especially because he doesn't speak French.

"How long will it take for him to heal enough to make the trek?" I ask.

Todd looks between us, unable to comprehend what is being said. There's not enough time to translate. Dr. Deschamps will need to return home shortly.

"He's young and the wound isn't deep. I estimate approximately two weeks. Maybe less if he doesn't attempt to rush his recovery."

I nod, mentally preparing for the next steps in getting Todd back to England. "Good, I'll send word to Baker Street and start arranging his escape."

Dr. Deschamps leaves. The sound of his car engine starting up and driving away can be heard from the hiding space. The noise is barely more than a soft rumble.

"So, what's the verdict?" Todd clutches the sides of the bed as if bracing for bad news.

I kneel next to the bed. "Two weeks. If you let your leg heal and don't push your recovery, you'll be returning to England then."

He nods, but there's no relief or joy in his expression. "Have you tried crossing over the Pyrénées?"

I shake my head. "I know people who have attempted it."

"Any of them survive?" His expression tells me he doesn't want me to lie, even now when he doesn't have to think about the odds of survival yet.

"Some did." And others were intercepted by the Milice or Gestapo before the escapees made it to the mountain range.

But it wasn't just the escapees who were captured or executed.

It was also the people who helped the downed pilots move along the escape line.

People like me. I'll be the one to escort him on the next leg of his journey.

19

JESSICA

March, Present Day
Maple Ridge

I check my phone for what must be the fifth time in the past twenty-eight minutes. Troy is due soon, and I can't stop pacing the hallway. At this rate, I'll be exhausted before we even start hiking.

A yawn powers through me, reminding me I *am* exhausted. I woke once last night and again this morning from the nightmares that still torment me.

I glance at the green shag carpet in front of my feet. "Why can't you leave me the hell alone?" That's where my husband went. Hell. "You're dead. Let me finally live my life in peace."

I'm so tired. Tired of constantly being reminded of all the mistakes I made. Tired of the constant reminders of how I failed my daughter. Not that Amelia will know I let her down. She won't even remember me. As far as she's concerned, Grace is her mother and Craig is her father. I'm nobody. She doesn't even know I exist.

I'm tired of walking on eggshells, waiting for the media to expose me.

The doorbell jerks me from my memory. I walk to the door and open it. An excuse for why I can't go hiking hovers on my lips. I didn't get much sleep last night. I'm exhausted. That's a good excuse.

What I can't tell Troy is I'm shaken from finding out Avery's boyfriend is a cop. It was what sent me into a panic attack last night. It took me a few minutes in the washroom to talk myself down from the spiral I'd felt myself slipping into.

Troy is standing on the porch, Butterscotch by his feet. The dog cocks his head to the side, his cute expression impossible to resist. He whimpers and sits his butt on Iris's welcome mat as if he senses my first words, my excuse for why I have to cancel.

Troy's wearing dark-green pants, a navy T-shirt, and an ovary-exploding smile. His well-honed biceps and the edge of a tattoo peek from under his T-shirt sleeves. "Mornin'." Behind him, the sky is crisp and cloudless.

"Sorry for not calling, but I think I'll have to cancel." *Think?* That's hardly the decisive response I was aiming for. "I have a lot to do with the house before I can start the renovations."

His smile doesn't leave his face, but there's new emotion in his eyes that I recognize. Stubbornness. "Great. I'd love to hear what you're planning. You can tell me on the hike."

Yeah, can't see that happening.

"Simone, Zara, and Emily are looking forward to you joining us." Troy's tone is casually smooth and deep and half-coaxing. "They'll kill me if I don't show up with you. They'll be positive it's my fault you changed your mind." His tone switches to teasing and flirty. "Surely, you don't want them to kill me, do you?"

I know he's joking, but the word "kill" causes a chill to knife me, and a shudder rushes through my body. I can feel my face pale, the blood draining from it.

Butterscotch whimpers again. I kneel to stroke him.

Troy also crouches and reaches for my arm but then changes his mind. He lets his hand drop to his side. "Hey." His voice is whisper soft. "Whoever hurt you in the past, I'm not that person. None of my friends or my brothers is that person. Give us a chance to prove it."

Resentment churns in my stomach. It's not directed at Troy. It's for my dead husband. It's for the inmates who tried to end my life and the guards who looked the other way. I'm tired of being like a wounded animal. The one who constantly expects a tire iron to the head. No, I don't trust Troy. I don't trust anyone. But do I want to spend the rest of my life hiding in my house, constantly afraid?

Besides, Noah won't be joining us on the hike, so I won't have to worry about him possibly recognizing me. I haven't figured out what I'm going to do about him. Do I keep as much distance from him as possible—and by extension Avery?

I push to my feet, channeling some of Angelique's courage I've witnessed so far in the journal entries I've read. The journal I can't wait to get back to. "Okay. I'll come with you."

"My backpack's in the truck if you want to put anything in it."

I grab from the hall table the food and water I'm bringing, as well as the lightweight jacket I found while I was shopping with Anne on Thursday. I also grab a piece of thread hidden under the embroidered doily.

I lock the door behind us, double-checking it's secure. The rest of my traps have already been set around my house to let me know if someone breaks into my home while I'm away. I crouch, pretending to tie my sneaker lace, and set the piece of thread in place at the bottom of the door. It's only noticeable if you know to look for it.

Troy puts my supplies into the backpack sitting on the floor of his truck and lifts Butterscotch onto the rear passenger seat.

I climb into the front seat. Butterscotch scrambles between the bucket seats and looks at me, his dark eyes wide and hopeful.

"Sorry, dude," Troy says to him, "you're in the back."

"That's okay. He can sit with me." I scoop the dog onto my lap. It's only once he's there that I can relax a bit more.

It's going to be okay. I'll *be okay.* I'll spend a few hours getting to know Zara, Simone, and Emily. Spend a few hours hiking and savoring my new freedom. It really will be all right.

Troy gives his dog a long look, amusement sparkling in his eyes. An unexpected giggle bubbles inside me and loosens the tension in my muscles.

"What's so funny?" Troy asks, but it's obvious from the way he's smiling he knows why I'm laughing.

"You and Butterscotch. Your expression." Another giggle tumbles free. "It's priceless."

He chuckles, the warmth of it chasing away the last of my tension. "Glad you find us so entertaining." He turns over the engine. "We're gonna pick up Garrett and Zara at Zara's place. Simone and Lucas are picking up Emily and Kellan. And we'll meet them at the trailhead."

"I didn't realize they're all couples." Which makes Troy and I the odd duo out.

"The only real couple is Lucas and Simone, who as you know are married. Garrett and Zara have been best friends for as long as I can remember. And Kellan is Emily's boss, but they're also friends."

"So, none of them are dating?"

"Nope. Not yet, anyway. I'm positive it's coming. Eventually. Once they stop lying to themselves." His soft rumble of a laugh wraps around me like a warm blanket.

"What about you? Are you seeing anyone?" I hadn't meant for

that to come out as it sounded—like I'm interested in him. I'm just making conversation.

"No. I broke up with my last girlfriend about two years ago, and I haven't dated anyone seriously since."

"Why did you break up?" He doesn't sound upset over it, so I figure it's a safe enough question.

He reverses his truck onto the street. "We were looking for different things. She was looking to get married and have kids—"

"And you aren't," I finish for him.

"It wasn't quite like that." Troy's tone is casual, non-defensive. "I have nothing against getting married and having kids. I'm all for that happening, eventually. When I find the right person. She wasn't that person..." We share a glance, the warm depths to his eyes more noticeable in the sunlight streaming through the truck windows. "What about you? You interested in settling down one day? Maybe having a family?"

My heart twists painfully at his question. No one can replace Amelia. "No. Not at all." The words come out a little too bluntly if the way Troy looks at me is any indication.

"Not even if you find the right man?"

That's the thing. I thought I had found him, only for my husband to prove me wrong. There were warning signs. Not at first, though. At first, he was sweet and generous and affectionate. But then in time things changed. Little things at first. Easily brushed off as my imagination, my reading the situation wrong. They were buried between all the days when things were great between us.

But in time, the good days grew fewer and sparser between the long stretches of mean words and his fist.

I look out the truck window at the houses moving past us and continue to stroke Butterscotch. "It's not something I'm interested in. I prefer my freedom. So what made you decide to create your own construction company?" That seems like a safe enough topic.

"My degree's in Construction Engineering Management. As a teen, I helped my father's friend with his construction projects and enjoyed doing that. But it was after my four years in the Marines I decided to specialize in adapting homes for individuals with mobility challenges. A number of my Marine brothers ended up with injuries that cost them their limbs."

I turn to Troy and study him. Really study him. "You wouldn't have done that if you hadn't served in the Marines?"

"Probably not. Wouldn't have been on my radar. Lucas became a physical therapist for almost the same reason. He was discharged from the military because of a shoulder injury. Once he recovered from that and got help with his PTSD, he went back to school, earned his doctorate, and became a PT for military vets."

"Did Garrett and Kellan go to college, or was it just you and Lucas?"

"We all did. We also all served in the Marines. Garrett studied political science with a minor in military history. He'd planned to go to law school but changed his mind after serving our country."

"How did he end up writing political thrillers?"

"He worked for me after leaving the military and while figuring out what he wanted to do with his life. He wrote a book in his free time and queried it to agents. If you ask him, he'll claim he got lucky. Lucky or not, his debut book did great, hit the *New York Times* bestseller list. It was enough for him to keep writing. Pretty quickly, it became his full-time career."

"What about Kellan?"

"He designs computer programs. He's pretty secretive about his work. I think that partly has to do with some of his clients. I'm not sure how much even Em knows about his job, and she works for him."

I smile at Troy, the movement as real as the sun in the sky, but it's barely more than a small upturn of my lips. Troy doesn't see it.

His eyes are on the road. "So, you're all smart guys." Book smart and street smart, I would imagine.

"What about you?" Troy asks, his eyes flicking briefly to me. Making me feel seen. "Did you go to college, or did you do something else?"

"I have a journalism degree." That much is safe to tell him.

"What made you decide to move to Maple Ridge? Wouldn't Washington DC or New York City or something like that be better if you're a journalist?"

"It's hard to break into the field, and I decided it wasn't for me." That much is also true, especially after being a victim of unwanted media attention. My favorite parts were the writing and research. Those I'll miss.

"Is that why you decided to write a thriller? Because of your journalism background?"

"Pretty much. It's given me some wicked research and interview skills that come in handy." I squirm in my seat at all the lies I've been telling him and stroke Butterscotch, who is looking out the side window. "So, you only have brothers? No sisters?"

"That's right," Troy says, showing no hint of whiplash from my sudden change of topic. "I have no idea if Mom was hoping for girls and got stuck with Lucas, Garrett, and me, or if she was happy to only have boys. I'm sure there were plenty of times when she wished we'd been girls instead of four hell-raising boys." There's a snicker in his tone that makes me wonder what he and his brothers were like as kids.

My journalistic mind whirls with questions. Questions about why he didn't mention Kellan. His blue-eyed brother. Troy, Garrett, and Lucas share similar likenesses, when you go beyond the dark hair, brown eyes, and tall muscular bodies. Likenesses their blue-eyed brother doesn't share. For starters, Kellan has a reserve about him the other three don't have.

"What about Kellan?" *Crap. None of my business.*

"My parents knew what they were getting with him," Troy

says, not giving me a chance to backtrack. "He was Garrett's friend even before they adopted him. We've known Emily and Zara most of our lives. Our parents were all friends. Simone came into the picture later on, in elementary school. All three women are like sisters to me."

He steers down a street that's similar to where I live with the mix of old homes and new infill houses. Tall trees that have been here decades line both sides of the road.

"What about your family?" he asks. "Where do they live?"

For a second, I consider coming up with a wonderful fairy tale about my family. The family I'd wished for growing up. But I've already told Troy enough lies. This is one truth—a small window into my past—that I want him to know. Mostly because it recognizes the amazing woman who was the main role model in my life. "I have no idea where my family lives. I don't have any siblings. That I know of. My father abandoned me before I was born, and my mother dropped me off at my grandparents' house when I was three, and she never looked back. My grandmother raised me."

"Are you and your grandmother close?"

"We were. Very much so." Or we were until my husband prevented me from seeing her. She'd been suspicious about him from the start. Turns out she'd been right. "She died six years ago. My grandfather died when I was twelve."

Troy's gaze shifts from the road to me. "I'm sorry."

"Me too."

He pulls up to the entrance of a small apartment building. Garrett and Zara are standing at the doorway. I move to the back seat so Garrett can sit up front. Butterscotch pops through the space between the bucket seats and joins Zara and me.

It takes all but two seconds for me to appreciate Zara and Garrett joining us. They carry the bulk of the conversation, and I get to listen. The less I have to talk, the less self-conscious I feel. A lesson my husband taught me.

"You should have seen Troy," Zara says, trying not to burst out laughing. "It took three days for the blue marker to disappear after Nova scribbled on his face."

"That's what I get for not checking first that it was a washable marker."

I stare at Troy, disbelief and a rush of tenderness surging through me. I imagine Troy with blue marker scribbled on his face and laugh. Maybe not as loudly as Garrett and Zara, but it's definitely a real laugh.

Simone has her arms around Lucas's waist when we arrive at the hiking trail. They're gazing at each other with so much love and tenderness, my heart doesn't know if it should ache or wish for the same one day.

I study the mountain in front of us, jutting up from the forest of tall pine, and gulp down my uncertainty. Medically speaking, am I even allowed to hike that? My stab wound is healing on the outside, but what about the internal damage? I was supposed to see a physician after I was released from prison. It didn't exactly fit in with my plan to escape the media and my former life in San Diego.

When it comes to clearing away Iris's magazines, I've been taking things easy and carrying smaller loads to the garage. I've been biking, but not all that hard. And my lungs have started to acclimatize to the altitude. All of that must count for something.

"You all right?" Troy asks. I didn't even notice him approach.

I nod, still staring at the mountain. *I. Can. Do. This.* I want to do this. It's not Mount Everest. It's survivable.

Savannah Townsend would never have hiked a mountain—mostly because her husband wouldn't have let her. But Jessica Smithson wouldn't think twice about scaling it. "I'm fine, thanks. I just don't want to slow you down."

That's the truth.

Troy gently hooks my chin with his finger, and I flinch.

"I'm sorry," he murmurs, dropping his hand away.

"It's okay. I promise I'll try not to react that way if you touch me like that again." A smile ghosts my lips. "How about we rewind time and have a do-over." I turn my face back to the mountain I was just staring at. "I'm fine, thanks. I just don't want to slow you down, Troy."

Troy hooks my chin with his finger once more and turns my face to his. I don't flinch. My fight-or-flight instinct doesn't kick in. A shiver travels up my spine. It's not a shiver of disgust or fear or shame. Just the opposite. It's a shiver of want. Desire. Desire to be touched like I matter.

His gaze searches my eyes. "Don't worry about me, Jess. This is about you having a good time. Don't push yourself too hard, respect your limits, and everything will be fine."

Right. I can do that. *Hopefully.*

20

TROY

March, Present Day
Maple Ridge

Every hiking season, Maple Ridge's search and rescue team locates missing hikers who didn't respect the landscape, the weather, their limits, or a combination of all three. Some hikers don't even make it out alive.

I don't want Jessica to make the same mistake. "Tell me if you need to slow down, or if you need to take a break. It's not a race to see who can get to the top first."

She nods, her attention on the mountain ahead of us. "I will."

The group walks along the trail. I purposely picked the easier one for Jessica's benefit. I want her to enjoy the hike. It helps when you're struggling with PTSD to do activities that relax you. And I can't think of anything more relaxing than being out here. In the mountains. It's so peaceful.

The path is wide enough for two people to walk side by side. Simone and Lucas are together. Zara and Emily are busy chatting about a wedding Emily is helping organize. Garrett and Kellan are in front of Jessica and me. None of my brothers are talking. Like me, they're paying attention to our surroundings. Being vigilant.

Much like what Jess is doing. She's constantly scanning the area as if expecting a bear to charge us.

"You haven't served in the military, have you?" I ask her.

"No. Why?" A stick snaps somewhere to the left of us, and her head jerks in that direction.

Shit, this was supposed to be relaxing.

"You're constantly checking our surroundings. Like they're doing." I point to Garrett and Kellan. Kellan's attention is on the trail ahead of us. Garrett is doing a shoulder check, his muscles taut as if ready to react to danger. "They can't switch off the ingrained instinct that came from our Marine training. But what about you? Why are you constantly looking over your shoulder like you're expecting someone to sneak up on you?"

She turns her face away from me, but not before I catch her slip her bottom lip between her teeth. She's silent for a beat, then turns back to me. "A...a friend of mine in college was stalked. She was always checking over her shoulder. I guess it must have rubbed off on me."

"I'd say it did more than just rub off on you." If anything, I'd say she was the one who'd dealt with the stalker, not her friend.

An affirming silence settles between us, and I let it sit there like an unexploded land mine.

We're here to have fun and relax. For today, anyway.

I lock away what she just told me, to be reexamined another day.

We've been hiking for more than an hour when Jessica's steps start to slow. Her pace isn't as fast as it was in the beginning, and her breathing is coming in harder. We're at a higher altitude now and the incline is steep. We're all breathing heavier, but she's struggling the most.

"How about we take a break here?" I call to the group, not wanting to single her out.

We find a spot to the side of the trail, overlooking the valley. The women sit on the boulders to catch their breaths and drink water.

Fir trees blanket the mountains and spread deep into the valley, an endless forest for as far as the eye can see. The only break in the trees is the lake, the blue sky reflecting off the surface.

"It's breathtaking." The awe in Jessica's voice makes me smile. For once, she's appreciating what's in front of her instead of searching for signs of danger.

My gut tells me she's hiding from someone. But who? And why? Zara hired her to work at Picnic & Treats, so that means she didn't already have a job when she moved to Maple Ridge. She doesn't have friends or family in the area. She's not an avid outdoor person who was lured here by the mountains. Maple Ridge is the kind of place where it's easy to disappear from the rest of the world.

For the most part.

"How are the cabins you guys are building doing?" Zara lifts her water bottle to her mouth.

I sit on the boulder next to Jessica's. "Good," I reply. "We're on schedule. The first bunch will be ready for early July."

Jessica turns her head to me. "Where are the cabins located? In the mountains?"

"No, they're on a plot of land just outside of town."

"What exactly is the program?" She shifts her body to face me.

I explain all the ins and outs of the outdoor program for vets that my brothers and I created. Who it will benefit and how it will work. "We've ordered specialized equipment so vets with disabilities can participate in the outdoor activities. Our program is about inclusivity."

Jessica claimed journalism ended up not being the right career for her, but her expression says the opposite. She leans forward, absorbing everything I tell her, curiosity gleaming in her eyes. "And you're building cabins for this?"

"Yes. It won't be a huge operation. We'll still have our regular jobs, and for the most part it'll be nonprofit. As it grows, we'll hire additional trained staff who can help with the various programs. It's our way of giving back to those who have served our country."

Jessica's mouth curves into a smile so big and beautiful, it's as if her opinion of me has shifted on its axis. And for a second, I'm the one who's breathless. I don't want this moment to end. I don't want her to stop smiling. "You're doing this and the PTSD fundraiser? You sure are a caring guy. I think that's really sweet and amazing of you."

"Thanks. I'm not sure about the sweet and amazing part, but the program and fundraiser are important to me."

We take a five-minute break, and then the women are on their feet, ready to get moving again.

Jessica resumes her position at the rear of the group with me. Asking her to join us was a good idea. She seems more relaxed now than she was at the start of the hike. Whatever ghosts she's been dealing with have left her alone out here. Her eyes are brighter and she's smiling more.

"I want to do the majority of the renovations on the house myself," she says with no preamble, as if voicing the thoughts in her head midway through. "I *need* to do them but...but I would like to hire you to help me. Except...now that I'm working for Zara starting Monday, I won't be..." She leaves the sentence unfinished.

"We can work on it part time if you want. But you're not hiring me, Jess. I'm helping you as a friend." That hadn't been my original plan, but now that she's giving me a chance to be her friend, I'd rather help her out as one. That will give me a chance to get to know her better. Give me the time I need to gain her trust. Fully gain it. That's the only way she'll let me help her to deal with her demons. And I do want to help her. I'm not going to let her struggle. I'm not going to fail her like I failed Colton.

"You can't do that," she says, her stubbornness coming out to play.

"Sure, I can. It's the same thing I'd do for any of my friends. We can work on it a couple of evenings a week."

"But you're already working during the day and building the cabins on the weekends. Surely you want your evenings off to do other things."

"I enjoy what I do. And I'm always happy to help out a friend."

"You think of me as a friend?" Her voice lifts at the end, as if she's genuinely surprised.

"Why wouldn't I?"

"You don't know me."

"I know enough to want to be your friend, Jessica. You can never have too many of those."

She nods, but uncertainty clouds her expression. Strands of hair have slipped from her ponytail, and a light gust of wind blows them in her face.

I curl my fingers into a loose fist, fighting back the urge to tuck the strands behind her ear, to touch her cheek. "We'll take things slow."

"Okay."

"Is that okay, we're friends? Okay, we can take things slow? Or okay, I can help with the renovations in the evenings?"

"All of that." She says it with great determination and no second thoughts.

I don't ask her to clarify what "taking things slow" means for her. Getting her to agree to being my friend and letting me help her with the renovations is a big enough step. For now.

"How about I order pizza after the hike, and we go back to your house? You can show me what you're thinking of doing to the place, and we can discuss the options." It's the perfect excuse for spending more time with her after we're finished hiking.

She hesitates for a second, clearly thinking my suggestion through, and nods. "All right. We can do that."

"It might take a few meetings to hammer things out, and then we can determine our plan of action. Do you know what kind of budget you're looking at?"

She states a reasonable number for the amount of renovations the place will need.

But that might change if there's asbestos in the house.

And if there is—which I suspect is the case—Jessica will need to stay somewhere for a few days or a week while it's dealt with.

Possibly my place. If she has no other options.

Why pay for accommodations when she can stay in my extra bedroom for free?

My body will just have to get over the fact she's off-limits.

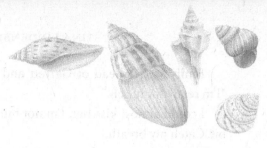

21

JESSICA

March, Present Day
Maple Ridge

I 've always loved San Diego, with the blue skies and the sand and the sea. But as much as I loved those things, this area, with the pine trees on either side of the hiking trail, and the clean fresh scent of nature, is quickly becoming a new favorite location.

Which is why the hike is more enjoyable than I'd expected.

The only thing that isn't enjoyable is the growing ache in my back over my wound. I'm not worried I'm inflicting more damage to the healing injury. I won't bleed out. But it's clear I haven't fully recovered from it and the lifesaving surgery.

I fix my face into a pain-free, peaceful expression. I don't want the hiking to end prematurely. But I have a feeling that's what will happen if Troy believes I'm struggling. I've noticed him glancing at me numerous times, even though he doesn't voice his concern.

Emily stops ahead of Garrett and Kellan and spins around. "I'm ready for lunch."

I could almost kiss her. I'm not hungry. I just need to sit for a bit. Catch my breath.

"We're almost at the top." Kellan's voice is loud enough to carry to me. "We can stop there to eat."

She turns sticks her tongue out at him. "God, you're so bossy." Her grin suggests otherwise.

I don't want to ask how much farther because I don't want to disappoint anyone. And I don't want to give away that I'm finding this a challenge.

"It's only about five more minutes," Troy tells me as if reading my mind. "I can give you a piggyback ride if that helps." He winks at me in the flirty protective way I'm starting to recognize as his trademark when he's with me. It's more about putting me at ease than anything else.

My lips tug into a genuine smile at his comment. A smile I hope looks more real than it feels. I shake my head. Even the effort to do that seems too much.

"I've got you." Troy weaves his fingers with mine, startling me, but I can't find the will to pull my hand away. He gives them a squeeze. "But if this is too much, let me know."

I'm unsure if he's referring to him holding my hand or the hike to the top of the mountain, and I don't bother to ask him to clarify.

His skin is rough and calloused from his job, much like mine is from working in the prison kitchen. The touch feels intimate, foreign. But at the same time, it feels like he's sharing his strength, sharing his drive to keep going.

Holding Troy's hand gives me the boost of energy I need. That might also be because he's half pulling me up the mountain.

We step beyond the tree line into an open area that's mostly rocks and wild grass. A strong wind nudges me sideward.

I let go of his hand. I don't want to give his friends the wrong idea. And they don't need to know I was struggling near the end.

We walk to a group of boulders that provide shelter from the wind and sit on the ground. Troy sits next to me, and Butterscotch lies by our feet. My back still aches, but less so than it did when we were hiking. I look out at the stunning view of the lake, the surface painted with various shades of green and blue reflecting the trees and the sky. This...the view. It's perfect.

Perfect and worth every ache and pain I'll feel tomorrow.

A different ache fills me, a longing, and my fingers twitch for the weight of a camera in my hand again. I mentally compose the various photos I'd shoot if I had my camera. If my husband hadn't smashed it.

I would try taking photos with my phone, but what if they aren't any good? I used to win awards with my photojournalistic pictures. Nothing major. Mostly college-level awards. But...but that was with fancy equipment and lenses. It wasn't with a phone camera.

I bury the urge to try to capture the scene in front of me.

Photography was my past. Savannah's past. It's not part of Jessica's future.

Zara unloads Garrett's backpack and passes out white paper bags with her café's logo on the front. "Yesterday's leftovers," she says by way of explanation.

Simone hands two to me. I pass Troy the bag with his name on it and open mine. My stomach rumbles at the spicy, sweet scent.

The group starts talking and eating. I don't say anything. I just savor the delicious food and listen to their conversations. Answer the occasional questions I'm comfortable answering.

And enjoy the taste of normalcy I've been denied for so long.

THE RETURN HIKE IS CHALLENGING BUT FOR A DIFFERENT REASON compared to going up. Gravity wants me to run down the steep slope and risk tripping over the rocks and the roots. But even if I had tripped, it wouldn't have changed my opinion about today. I loved everything about it: the hike, the scenery, hanging out with Troy and his friends.

Troy drops Garrett and Zara off at her apartment and drives to his house to shower.

As soon as we step inside, he pulls out his phone, asks what I'd like on the pizza, and calls the restaurant. He places the order, and we go into the kitchen. He fills two glasses with water and hands one to me.

"Thanks." I take a sip and scan the room. Everything is placed in straight lines, not a single item deviating by so much as a fraction of an inch. And that includes the tea towels hanging from the oven door, their edges even with each other.

I don't have to check the rest of the house to know I'll find the same terrifying rigidity in all the rooms.

A tremor takes over my body, and the hand holding the glass jerks. Water sloshes over the rim. I place the glass on the counter and hug myself, hiding the effect Troy's kitchen has on me.

"You okay?"

I startle, my mind spiraling back to a kitchen that was once in a similarly kept order. "I'm good." My voice trembles, my own control fraying.

Now it's Troy's gaze that studies the kitchen, a confused frown pinching his brow.

"Why don't you have your shower now?" I try to make the words sound carefree. My mouth is dry, and the words come out scratchy.

"Can you tell me what happened to you? Why are you suddenly so jumpy?" Concern and tenderness fill Troy's eyes, but it's not enough to soothe the fear churning inside me.

"Nothing has happened." My words still come out scratchy and hoarse. I cough, hoping he'll think I have something stuck in my throat.

"We both know that's not true." Troy's voice is gentle, free of judgment. "Your friend who was stalked, that was really you, wasn't it?"

I wince but manage to keep it off my face. Troy's a smart man. Of course he would think *your friend* is synonymous with me.

"No, I wasn't the one who was stalked." Not a complete lie. I told him my friend was stalked in college. That's not when my husband began stalking me. "Nothing bad like that has happened." It's a good thing he can't hear my heartbeat. He'd know for sure I'm lying. Why can't he drop it? Why does he have to be like a dog with his favorite bone?

"Okay." It's obvious he doesn't believe me. His eyes and the way he's looking at me tell me that much. "I won't be long in the shower."

He leaves, and I gulp down the water he gave me. I empty the glass, walk to the towels hanging on the oven door, and adjust them so the bottoms are uneven.

I grab Troy's empty glass from the counter, wash and dry our glasses, and put them in the cupboard. The other glasses are arranged in tidy rows. I put the two glasses on the shelf, purpose-fully making them uneven with the others, and shut the door.

Butterscotch peers up at me, his head cocked to the side. I lower myself to the floor next to him and stroke him. His soft hair against my palm slowly begins to soothe me.

The tremor subsides after a few minutes, and I can breathe again. I'm tempted to leave, to not wait for Troy. But what if Troy's extreme tidiness is the result of being in the military? What if it isn't a warning sign of a dangerous man who needs to be in control all the time?

I think about when we took a break during the hike and he

touched my chin. I'd flinched, and he apologized and let me take the lead when it came to him touching me. He hasn't tried to do anything to control me or make me feel uncomfortable.

But neither had my husband in the beginning.

Troy returns wearing jeans and a clean T-shirt, his hair messy and damp. He walks past the towels without giving them a second glance. My husband couldn't have done that. He would have stopped, straightened them, and made sure I knew he was displeased with my sloppiness.

"You'll need to stay here while I go to Jessica's house," Troy tells Butterscotch.

"He can come too."

"Are you sure? His breed doesn't shed a ton, but he does still shed. It drives the woman who cleans my house crazy."

"Someone cleans your house?" The timbre of my voice rises to a dry squeak.

Troy laughs, and the rich deep sound vibrates through my body and eases my fear. "My house isn't normally this tidy. I'm not a slob, but I also don't have much time for housework. So I hired a woman from down the street to come here weekly. She's kind of a neat freak. Probably puts some of my anally-neat-freakish COs to shame. She doesn't usually work on Saturdays, but something came up this week, so she came over today."

All the fear and tension leaves me in a *whoosh*, taking the rest of the tremor with it. "I'm not a neat freak either. And I'm fine with Butterscotch getting his hair all over my house."

"All right. As long as you're sure."

We drive to the restaurant to pick up the pizza and head to my house.

Troy and Butterscotch stay in the living room while I go upstairs for a quick shower.

In the bathroom, I pull my hair up in a loose ponytail and strip out of my dirty clothes. My body is a tangle of scars, some visible, others invisible to the naked eye. Some were the result of my time in prison. The rest are from a different hell.

In one light, they make me look weak, a victim. Easily broken. In another light, I look kick-ass, strong. A fighter. Not easily taken down. It all depends on the story told, and the backstory people choose to believe.

I spin around and look over my shoulder, inspecting the wound on my back. I haven't needed to cover it during the past week. The stitches have dissolved, and the wound is now a healing red scar.

I turn the shower on and step under the hot water. Heat sinks under my skin, chases away the residual tension. I grab the soap and lather my body. A sweet strawberry scent mingles with the steam.

I close my eyes and inhale the soothing fragrance. An image of Troy stepping into the shower slips unexpectedly into my thoughts. Drops of water sliding down his tanned skin, kissing those golden muscles. My heart rate spikes and my breathing quickens. Why couldn't this be the image that appears in my dreams instead of the usual nightmares that slither in?

I open my eyes and the image of Troy vanishes. I'm broken. Damaged. Troy's only interested in me because he's trying to help me. Being protective—it's part of his DNA. He wouldn't be inter-ested in me that way if he saw the scars on my soul.

I finish in the shower and dry myself off. The foggy mirror hides my reflection, but I don't need to see it to know I'm ugly. My husband married me because I was beautiful. Together, we were the picture of perfection.

I swiftly change into a pair of sweatpants and a long-sleeved T-shirt and head downstairs to find Troy inspecting my kitchen. He turns on the faucet before I can warn him not to twist it too fast.

A disgruntled groan comes from the pipe, and a blast of water that would make Old Faithful proud erupts over Troy. The force of it causes him to take a step back, and a giggle explodes from me.

"S-sorry. I...I should have...warned you," I manage to get out between giggles.

He turns, and my hand flies to my mouth, trying to smother the laughter. Water drips from his hair and his soaked T-shirt clings to his well-formed chest and ab muscles. Even when the faucet exploded on me the first day, I didn't end up this wet.

I duck around him and do my well-practiced trick of jiggling the water off. "Ta-dah!" Pride curves my mouth into a grin.

Okay, I didn't permanently fix the problem. But I did learn how to avoid it and how to turn the water off. I'd say that's progress.

Troy chuckles. "You're very talented."

"Right? It's my new superpower." I grab a tea towel and toss it at him. "I'll be right back with something bigger." I rush upstairs, remove two freshly-washed bath towels from the linen closet, and hurry downstairs.

His T-shirt is no longer clinging to his body. I take a second to drink in his defined muscles before I hand him the towels. Water droplets drip from his hair and trickle down his exposed skin.

He towel-dries his hair and his body.

I remove two plates from the cupboard and place them next to the pizza box. "The kitchen definitely needs work."

"You could say that." Troy removes a slice of pizza and takes a bite. He leans back on the counter.

I grab a pizza slice and take a tentative bite. It's a habit of mine, ingrained from being in prison. You can never be too careful about food prepared by other inmates. Especially with inmates who have something against you.

The moment the cheesy taste of heaven touches my tongue, I groan. "God, this is sooooo good." I know it's been a long time since I last had pizza, but I don't remember it ever tasting this delicious.

"Infinity is renowned for its pizza. People drive to Maple Ridge just for it." Troy takes another bite of his slice.

I nod, finishing what's in my mouth. "I'm not surprised."

"You telling me you didn't move to Maple Ridge because of the pizza?" The corner of Troy's mouth quirks up and sends an unexpected warmth shimmering up my spine.

I laugh, the sound slightly off-kilter because I'm also moaning from eating another bite of the pizza. "If I had known about it, there would've been no question about me coming here."

I pull my seat out from under the table with my foot and sit. Troy joins me on the chair next to mine.

We polish off another two slices of pizza. Troy tells me what it was like growing up in a small town. He gives me room to reciprocate and tell him about my childhood. I don't.

"Did you dream of playing in the NHL?" I ask after he tells me how his parents used to drive him and his brothers long distances for their hockey games.

"What hockey-loving kid doesn't dream of playing in the NHL? I loved playing the game, but I eventually realized I would never be good enough for the league. Fortunately, I was even better at math."

"Do you still play? In an adult league or something?"

"Yes. When I can. It's the same for Lucas, Garrett, and Kellan. And we enjoy playing street hockey during the off-season. Do you play any sports?"

"No. I'm not athletically inclined. I was that kid no one wanted on their team." The words flow from me on a soft laugh, unrepentant and unafraid. Troy's so easy to talk to.

We finish our slices and I put the dishes in the sink to be washed after he leaves.

"I'll be right back." Troy walks out of the kitchen. The front door clicks open, and a minute later, he strolls into the kitchen, carrying a large metal toolbox. "I'm going to fix your faucet so it doesn't explode on you again."

"You don't have to do that."

The look he slants me says he does.

I help him remove everything from under the sink. Mostly it's just old cleaning products that expired over a decade ago. He lies down to get a better look at what he's dealing with. And a few minutes later, I have a faucet that doesn't require any special feats to turn it on and off.

I grin at him, not caring for the first time about the pull of skin at my mouth because of the scar. "Thank you! That's much better."

"You're welcome. Why don't you give me a quick tour of the house first? Then we can get together soon to start planning the renovations. It's gonna take a few days for us to nail it down and to come up with a schedule."

"That sounds like a plan." I lead him out of the kitchen. Butterscotch follows us.

"You have any ideas of how you want the place to look? Any particular style of interior?"

"Iris had a lot of home-decorating magazines. Many were out-of-date, but from the most recent ones I looked at, I was drawn to the farmhouse and quaint cottage styles." The opposite of the clean modern lines of the house I last lived in. That house never felt like me. The quaint cottage style, now that's more like me.

"Those are definitely doable. But I suggest we look at some more current designs as well." His gaze takes in the living room, and he walks over to the wall between the living room and the kitchen. A few days ago, he wouldn't have been able to reach the wall due to the magazines. He knocks on it. "There're options we can explore that weren't available even a few years ago. And given your limitations with the space, I suggest we make the most of what you have and do what we can to increase your storage space."

I give him the quick-and-dirty guided tour. This isn't about us discussing my visions for the place. He just wants to see the rooms.

We step into the second bedroom. The door to the secret room in the closet is closed. Unless you know what you're looking for, there's no way to know it's there.

"There are plenty of things the two of us can do," Troy says, "and my brothers can help out when we need extra hands. I suggest we start downstairs and focus on the living room and kitchen first. I'll contact the company I use for testing for asbestos, but it's usually present in these old houses. We'll want to get that removed before we begin work on the place."

"Can I work on the garden in the meantime?" The sooner I begin that, the more time I'll have for creating my dream garden this summer.

"Yes, but I wouldn't do anything yet with the flowerbeds next to the house, other than remove the dead plants. We'll need to replace the roof tiles, and there are other issues with the exterior that need to be dealt with. Are you free Tuesday night?"

My lips curve into a grin, and for the first time in too long, the seed of hope becomes fully rooted. "I'm available then."

Excitement surges through me, deep as an ocean. I'm going to have my dream house. A house decorated my way, with my vision. Something I couldn't have imagined a year ago. Or even last month.

The excitement is too much to contain. It needs an outlet. So I hug Troy—surprising myself. Probably surprising him too, especially because he's still shirtless. "Thank you!"

It's not a big hug. Or romantic. Most people wouldn't consider the hug I'm giving him to be significant. But for someone who has feared being touched for so long, who didn't think she'd ever be capable of hugging again, who was starved of affection for quite some time, this hug, the idea of it, is huge. Monumental.

Scary.

Troy's arms wrap around me but avoid squeezing too tight.

My skin tingles and my heartbeat thumpity-thumps against his chest. And I feel...safe. Warm. Protected.

"You're welcome." Troy's voice is rough, his tone gentle. And I can hear a smile in the words as if he also gets how monumental this is for me.

22

ANGELIQUE

April 1943
France

The full moon looms bright in the sky, preventing the ground from vanishing in a huge black shadow.

I pedal along the empty dirt road. Tangled thickets of trees and undergrowth taunt me from either side. Anyone could be hiding in them. Hiding in fear or hiding to ambush me. Friend or foe.

It's well past curfew, and German soldiers could be nearby, hunting for the location of the Allied parachute drop. Only Baker Street, the pilot, and the reception party know the exact coordinates. Coordinates that change every month.

Fear of being discovered pulses through me with each rapid beat of my heart. *Don't get caught, don't get caught, don't get caught.*

Up ahead, the trees disappear, replaced by the open stretch of flat farmland and the lake that is less than half a mile to the right of me. The water reflects the light of the moon and will guide the pilot to the drop zone.

I dismount, hide the bike in the thicket, and walk the last mile. My ears and eyes and nose are alert for signs of danger.

The reception party, a group of six men including Pierre, are already gathered when I arrive. We get into position on the field and sit and wait for the low hum of the Lysander.

The sweet smell of grass tugs back memories of sitting in a field when I was a little girl. The sun was high in the sky and clouds floated lazily across the ocean of blue.

My sister and I loved pointing out the different shapes the clouds created. Some were common like bunnies and flowers. Others bordered on magical—like dragons.

The hum of an airplane engine drags me from the long-forgotten memory. I turn on my torch. Three other men do the same. My light is red, representing the dash in Morse code. The other three lights are white.

Dot. Dot. Dash. Dot.

F. The signal that it's safe to drop the load.

Three parachutes descend from the low-flying Lysander as it continues south along the route. We turn off our torches.

As soon as the first long wooden box hits the ground, we run towards it, quickly pry open the lid, and check the contents. I detach the parachute and dig a small grave for it in the soft ground.

While I'm hiding the parachute, the men carry the box to the waiting lorry parked out of view and unload the weapons Baker Street sent us. They return with the empty container, and four of the men carry it to the lake to be submerged deep under the surface.

The remaining members of the party search for the two other containers. We work in silence, focused on our task, conscious that at any second we could be facing the wrong end of a gun. Talking is a distraction, a luxury none of us can afford.

It takes several minutes to locate the second box. The men carry it away, and I bury the parachute. Exhaustion settles inside me, heavier than the weapon-filled containers. The same exhaustion that makes up every red blood cell, every organ, every nerve. The same exhaustion that's been a familiar part of me since I landed in France three months ago.

The burst of energy because of the danger we face is the only thing that keeps me going.

I finish my task and stand, stretching out the aching muscles in my lower back.

Pierre approaches, moonlight gleaming off his blond hair, shadows carving strong angles in his face. "I found the final container."

I open my mouth to reply, but a yawn overpowers the words. We've had to be here for the past five nights, waiting to see if the parachute drop would happen. Then a few hours later, we've had to go about our daily routines so as not to draw suspicion.

"*Halt!*" The sharp voice slices through the air with the intent to kill. My body turns cold. Cold like the lake in January, freezing my heart and my lungs and my thoughts.

Bloody hell. How did I not hear the Germans advance on us? What happened to the man who was supposed to keep watch?

I don't know how many of them there are. The voice came from behind me.

Pierre grabs my hand. "Do you trust me?" His fear-hitched words are quiet and cracked.

And then...he's kissing me.

For a second, I remain frozen, too stunned to know what to do, too stunned to speak. But I do trust Pierre. Trust him more than I trust my ex-fiancé. More than I trust my sister.

Shock and fear and dread collide and combust into anger. Anger at this soldier. Anger at those who betrayed France. Anger at those who betrayed my heart. The heat thaws me, brings me to my senses, and I return the kiss.

Return the kiss because our lives depend on it.

Pierre's plan might save us, might be our chance to escape.

Or it might get us executed.

My hands rest on his shoulders. His arms go around my waist. My back is still to the soldiers. Only Pierre can see them. His body trembles slightly beneath my touch.

"What are you doing out here?" The words spoken in German are stiff, but I can also hear the exhaustion in them.

Pierre and I jerk apart as though embarrassed to be caught kissing and turn to the soldier. Pierre doesn't understand German, and he isn't aware I am fluent in the language. It was my fluency in both French and German that made me desirable to the SOE.

Two German soldiers are standing several yards away, pistols aimed at us. The young soldier looks to be Pierre's age and is tall and skinny. The other one is several years older and looks as if he plays sports in his free time.

A tiny wave of relief pumps through my body that they aren't SS. We'd have no chance if they were.

"*Pardon?*" I say, feigning a lack of understanding for German, my voice shaky, my tone respectful.

The younger soldier laughs. The cruel sound assaults the night air, fuelling my anger and fear. "They don't understand us. The simpletons only speak French." He snorts, his gaze still on us. "It is well past curfew. What are you doing here?" This time his words are spoken in broken French.

I bite my lower lip, looking nothing like an SOE agent and looking every part of the role I'm about to play. "You won't tell anyone you saw us here, will you?" I infuse the words with a quiet, my-papa-will-kill-me-if-he-finds-out desperation. "We know we aren't supposed to be out after curfew, but it's the only time we can be together."

I speak slowly so the soldier can understand me, but my heart rate is five times the speed of my words.

The younger soldier laughs once more, the sound as cruel as before, and he roughly translates what I said for the benefit of his comrade. I don't possess the vocabulary for some of his foul words, but I do comprehend the general gist. My cheeks heat, and I glance down, hoping neither soldier notices.

Somewhere behind us, the final container lies exposed, and the other members of the reception party are loading the weapons into the lorry. Have the Germans stumbled across those men as well?

Or have the men escaped, leaving Pierre and me to fend for ourselves?

It's the risk we all were willing to take when we signed on to defeat the Germans. We know each mission we go on might be our last.

I allow a small amount of hope to float to the surface, pray the German soldiers believe my pleas, pray they think Pierre and I are lovers, pray they let us go.

Pray they don't rape me.

The older soldier drags his leering gaze over my body, and my chest tightens, my stomach churns. "Don't let us see you out after curfew again." The harsh-growl command in his tone sends a shudder through me.

I look at the younger soldier, waiting for the translation I don't need.

"You can go. But you won't be so lucky next time if you ignore curfew again."

"Thank you. We won't." My voice trembles, but I don't know how much of that is real and how much is for show.

If this had been daytime, I have no doubt they would have dragged us in to be interrogated. If they had seen the Lysander or witnessed the parachutes, we would not be leaving this field alive or without escorts.

The soldiers wait for us to start walking and follow a few

yards behind us. We lead them in the opposite direction from where the rest of the reception party took the boxes.

I let out a shaky breath and whisper, "Bloody fucking hell, that was too close. Thank you, for reacting so quickly."

One side of Pierre's mouth kicks up a fraction of an inch, as it normally does when I swear in such an unladylike manner. "Thank you for not slapping me and getting us killed, Carmen."

The soft laugh that slips out, too quiet to be heard by the soldiers, is genuine. "You're welcome. Let's hope no more bloody Germans show up while we lead these two away."

Let's hope these two don't change their mind about letting us go free.

23

JESSICA

March, Present Day
Maple Ridge

Monday morning, I arrive at Picnic & Treats at 6:00 a.m. There was a time when I couldn't imagine getting up so early, but marriage to a monster and prison changed that. But this morning, when I got up, dread didn't fill me at the prospect of the day and what I'd be facing. I woke up excited. And a little nervous.

Today is the first day of my new job.

I lock up my bike and hurry down the alley to the rear of the building. The alley is clean and empty, other than the dumpsters, but there's still something creepy about the place. My eyes and ears and gut are alert to anything that shouldn't be here. But there's nothing. Not even the squeak of a scampering mouse or the purr of a prowling cat.

I knock on the back door that belongs to the café.

The door swings open a few seconds later, and I'm met by a

young woman's smiling face. Keshia. She's just as Zara described, squeezing a few inches past five foot. Her black hair is cut short, the textured curls framing her face and her warm brown skin.

Her gaze briefly drops to the scar on my face, and I can imagine all the scenarios as to how I got it now crowding her thoughts. "You must be Jessica."

I return her smile. "Call me Jess."

She opens the door wider and lets me in. "Zara told me you have some experience in the kitchen."

"I do. Mostly prep work."

"That's great. The daily menu offers a variety of international foods, and the recipes require a crapload of chopped veggies." She widens her eyes in emphasis of crapload. "So that will be your job. Chopping."

Keshia takes me to the staff room, hands me the paperwork I need to fill in for Zara, and shows me how to clock in. She hands me a white T-shirt with the café's name and logo on it, purple pants and a hairnet, and points where the restroom is located so I can change.

I lock my purse and street clothes in the spare locker in the staff room. My hair's pulled up in a ponytail, and I cover it with the hairnet.

My first task is chopping the onions. Keshia shows me how fine they need to be. While I work on them, she makes a batch of muffins.

Memories of Saturday night, of when I hugged Troy, seep in as I chop. I can't stop thinking about it. Can't stop thinking about how good it felt to hug him and to be hugged. Granny had raised me to show I care about a person through an embracing touch. She told me love and hugs made the world a better place, and if more people embraced, there'd be fewer wars.

"What time do you start?" I ask Keshia without pausing a beat from my onion chopping. Showtunes from her playlist pipe through the Bluetooth speaker, loud enough to be a distraction, but not too loud we can't talk if we want.

"Four-thirty."

"This morning?" The pitch of my voice rises in a disbelieving squeak.

Keshia's laughter fills the room. "It's not all that bad. I'm used to getting up early. And it just means my day will be finished that much sooner, and I have time to do more fun things in life. That's the best thing about this job. While everyone else is working, we won't be. We'll be done for the day."

She's right. My shift finishes at two, which leaves me with the rest of the afternoon to clear the mess of dead plants in my front yard.

Keshia sings, her Jennifer Hudson voice echoing off the walls. By the second song, she has me singing along with her. I can sing. But nothing like Keshia.

When Zara enters the kitchen an hour later, I've already finished chopping the massive pile of onions, and I'm working my way through the huge bag of carrots. It's a mindless task, but Keshia's playlist makes it more fun than it was when I worked in the prison kitchen.

"How's it going so far?" Zara's voice isn't cold. Her tone isn't demanding. Her words are spoken with a casual, friendly ease I never experienced in Beckley.

"Good," I tell her, the hint of a relieved smile on my face.

"Have you recovered from the hike?"

"I have. But I haven't gotten over how incredible the view was from the top." It made up for the lack of the ocean I miss.

"Does that mean you'll come with us the next time we go?"

I grin, joy bubbling inside me at how different my life has become since I left Beckley. So different than how I'd imagined it would be when Florence drove from the prison gates. "I would like that. I had fun."

"I'm glad to hear that." Zara leans back on the counter. "And are you joining us for Game Night on Friday?"

The bubbles fizzle and burst. I had fun on Friday, but sitting in the same room as a man who wears an identical uniform to my dead husband is too much. "I'm...I'm not sure yet."

Zara picks up one of the uncut carrots and fiddles with it. "Troy seems to like you." Her casually friendly tone has turned curious, her words almost a question. Keshia is working on the other side of the kitchen and can't hear us.

"He seems like a nice guy." I focus on chopping the carrot so I don't have to see her reaction to my reply.

"Troy's wonderful. You can't have a better male friend than him. I mean, other than Garrett. Troy's like a brother to me. I've known him most of my life. And I can't remember the last time he dated anyone. Well, not since his girlfriend two years ago."

I have no idea where she's going with this. I keep chopping.

She puts the carrot she was playing with on the cutting board. "Do you like him?"

"Sure. Like I said, he seems like a nice guy."

"That's not what I'm asking." Her voice is caramel smooth and just as sweet. "I know you recently got out of a bad relationship, Jess. But just so you know, it wouldn't be a bad relationship if you were with Troy."

An unexpected laugh erupts from my lungs. This is not a conversation I ever imagined having with Zara or any of Troy's friends. I look up from the cutting board. "Are you trying to set me up with him?"

She chuckles, maybe at the disbelief on my face. "No. Not at all. I'm no Cupid. Just ask Em. She learned that lesson the hard way last year. But do you know how many women Troy has invited to join us for Game Night or to come hiking with us?"

"Five?"

"Zero."

Not even his girlfriend when they were dating? "And you're telling me this because...?"

The loud tinny sound of metal hitting tile clatters behind me, startling me. My heart thumps painfully in my chest. My breath gets caught in my lungs. And I'm dragged back to another time. In another kitchen.

Dark and cold and deadly.

24

TROY

March, Present Day
Maple Ridge

Monday morning, Kellan and I meet for coffee at Picnic & Treats. We arrive at the same time and enter the café.

My phone rings from my jeans pocket. I pull it out and check who's calling. Zara?

I hit Accept. "Hey, what's up?"

"Where are you?" Her tone isn't friendly like I expected. It's urgent and panicked.

"At the counter, getting ready to order coffee. Why? Where are you?"

The line goes dead. A second later, the kitchen door flies open. Zara rushes out, heading straight for us. She grabs my arm and drags me past the counter and toward the kitchen door. Kellan follows us.

What the hell? "What's going on, Zara?"

"It's Jessica." The panic hasn't left her voice. If anything, it seems greater than before.

We step through the doorway. Jessica isn't in the kitchen. Keshia is standing near the wall, her eyes wide, and she's looking at something behind the workbench in the center of the room.

Zara rounds the bench with me in tow. It's only once we've cleared it that I discover what Keshia is looking at.

Jess is on the floor in the corner, her back pressed against the wall. Her knees are pulled to her chest, one arm wrapped tightly around them. She's staring into space and her body is trembling. A knife is clutched in her hand, held up as if to protect herself from an attacker.

Oh, fuck.

Zara lets go of my arm. "I was talking to her when a pan fell on the floor. She was chopping carrots and had the knife in her hand. Keshia and I have tried talking to her from a safe distance, but it's like we're not even here."

"How long has she been like this?"

"Two or three minutes."

Christ. I can't imagine what Jess is going through.

I keep my eyes on her, but my next question is still for Zara. "Do you have a small blanket or something?"

"I do. In the staff room." Zara rushes off, the soles of her shoes squeaking on the tile floor.

"Hey, Jess." The words are spoken with the level of calm one uses when defusing a land mine. I maintain my distance, more for her benefit than mine. Kellan stands next to Keshia.

Jess doesn't look up. She doesn't even acknowledge my presence.

"It's Troy. Everything's going to be okay. You're safe, Jessica. No one is going to hurt you." I keep repeating myself, not knowing how much of my words or voice she's registering.

Zara returns and hands me a wrap. "Should I call nine-one-one?"

"Not yet." I'm concerned what will happen if the cops see Jess holding a knife. Things might not go well if we end up with a twitchy officer.

It's not uncommon for war vets to experience a flashback after hearing a loud bang. Is that what happened to her? At some point someone shot at her? Is that her traumatic event?

I step closer, crouch beside her, and gently put my hand on her arm, praying I'm not about to make things worse. The wrap is ready in case I need to immobilize her arm and the knife. I don't believe for a second she intends to use it, but I also don't want to be on the receiving end of the knife if things go wrong.

Adrenaline courses through my body the way it did when I was on a mission. My reflexes are well-honed from years of playing hockey and the military.

I glance behind me, ensuring Kellan has my back. Everything will be okay. We're both trained to take down the enemy. Neither of us wants to hurt Jessica, but we'll do what we have to in order to protect her, ourselves, Keshia, and Zara.

"Can you describe the room, Jess?" I ask.

She blinks and looks at me with unfocused eyes. "Troy? Why am I on the floor?" Her gaze lowers to the knife in her hand, and she drops it as if it burned her. The knife blade clatters on the tile floor.

I pull the knife toward me along the floor and flick it behind me for Kellan to retrieve. "We were hoping you could tell us that."

"Did I hurt anyone?" Her eyes shift from Zara, Keshia, Kellan, and to me again.

"No," I tell her, my voice still low and calm. As if this scenario happens to me all the time. Like going to the grocery store.

She closes her eyes and bounces the back of her head against the wall. "Oh God," she mutters. "Oh God, oh God, oh God." The words are faint, probably only heard by me.

I swivel to Zara. "Is it okay if I take her somewhere else? She won't be back for the rest of her shift."

"No," Jess blurts and makes a move to stand but doesn't get that far. Her legs don't seem too willing to support her. "I can't leave. This is my first day on the job."

Zara studies me with appraising eyes. She's warring with herself if she should fire Jess or give her a second chance. A chance that could have dire consequences if the same thing should happen again. "No, you should go with Troy. Maybe he knows something that will help you." Zara's eyes plead, *Please tell me you have an idea.*

I don't answer because I don't know if my plan will help. I'm hoping it will.

I wrap the blanket over Jess's shoulders and help her to her feet.

She looks at the two women, her expression flickering between nervousness and shame. She chews on her bottom lip, eyes shiny, body trembling. "I'm so sorry. I have no idea what happened."

I can only imagine what she's thinking. She doesn't know us any more than we know her. She doesn't understand I'm not the type to turn my back on someone in need.

Zara retrieves Jess's stuff from the staff room. Neither of them brings up the topic of Jess returning to her job tomorrow. I'll talk to Zara later about it. But I won't try to convince her to give Jess a second chance if Zara's uncomfortable with her working here.

I lead Jess to the rear exit. Kellan doesn't follow us.

"I biked here," Jess says as we walk down the alley to the street.

"You won't need your bike where we're going. I'll put it in the bed of my truck and drop it off at your house. You'll want to change into other clothes."

"Where are we going?" An unexpected curiosity seeps into her tone. Journalistic curiosity if I were to hazard a guess.

"You'll find out soon enough."

Jessica's head turns away from me, the movement jerky, and she looks over her shoulder at the near empty alley. "I guess I need to search for a new job." She says that more to herself than to me.

I glance up, instinctively identifying locations where a sniper could hide. Building rooftops. Two windows overlooking the alley. Both closed. "Can you tell me what happened? Why you get flashbacks?" Because I'm positive that's what she experienced back there.

Jess shakes her head, her shoulders curved inwardly.

"It might help."

"It might, but it doesn't matter. I still can't tell you." A slight edge shapes her tone. It's not a keep-out-of-my-business edge. It's a fearful, resigned one.

We round the corner. Butterscotch is waiting patiently where I left him tied to the bench. Jess practically runs to my dog.

She crouches next to him and pets him. Butterscotch seems as happy to see Jess as she is to see him. And the more she strokes him, the more the fear and shame and uncertainty fade from her face.

I hold my hand out to her. "Bike-lock key?"

She rifles in her purse and hands me a key chain. I untie Butterscotch's leash and hand it to Jess, then I unlock her bike. We head to my truck with me wheeling her bike alongside me.

I load her bike into the bed of my truck, and the three of us climb into the cab. Butterscotch joins Jess on the front passenger seat, his ass on her lap, his front paws on the door.

I drive to her house, unload the bike, and wait for her to unlock the garage. This is the first time I've seen inside the garage. The place is cobweb and dust free. And crowded with all kinds of abandoned furniture, tools, gardening supplies, and old magazines.

In the house, Jess goes upstairs to change. While she's gone, I make a call to the client I was supposed to meet with this afternoon. I tell Dylan an emergency came up and ask if it's okay if we reschedule. Dylan, his wife Jenny, and I went to school together.

"That's fine," he says. "We're just happy you're doing our renovations."

That makes two of us. As clients go, they're easygoing. "I'll give you a call later once I've checked my calendar. Plus, there's something I need to talk to Jenny about."

Faint puppy barks come from Dylan's end of the line. I smile at the sound of the golden retriever puppies who are no doubt chasing a ball for playtime.

I'm just finishing the call when Jess returns wearing jeans and a long-sleeved top. Her hair is no longer in a ponytail. The silky waves hang loose over her shoulders. I want to run my fingers through the strands, to feel them against my skin.

I startle at the thought, at the realization my interest in her stretches beyond friendship. In the short time I've known her, I've gone from wanting to help her to being attracted to her. But that's not what today is about, so I get my head back in the mission.

"Is this outfit okay for whatever you have planned?" She turns, giving me a great view of her gorgeous ass.

"It's perfect." I push aside my thoughts of what I'd like to do with that gorgeous ass.

"You really won't tell me where we're going?"

"You'll find out soon enough." Once we get to my house. "We just have to go to my place first to pick up something."

"WE NEED A CANOE FOR THIS ADVENTURE?" JESSICA STARES skeptically at the canoe in the truck bed.

"That's right."

Butterscotch barks, excited at what this means. He's a big fan of canoeing.

I go into the garage again and come out with three life jackets, including a small one for Butterscotch. I toss them into the truck bed with the rest of the gear.

Only a handful of vehicles are in the lake parking lot when we arrive. It's the last days of March, so anyone here will be walking their dogs, running, or going on a short hike around the lake. It's too early in the season for most people to be out on the water.

I grab the life jackets from the truck bed. "You can carry these." I hand them to Jess. "I'll carry the canoe."

She hugs the life jackets to her body like a shield. "Why are we playing hooky and going canoeing?"

"I'm far from an expert on PTSD, but I do know that relaxation is an important part of the healing process. You might not want to tell me what happened, but that doesn't mean I can't help you relax." I spread my arms wide. "And what's more relaxing than canoeing on a day like this?"

The weather is sunny and warm for an early spring day. It's not unexpected for Maple Ridge to experience a snow flurry at this time of year. Or heavy rain. Thankfully, that's not the case today. The area is peaceful. Calm. Small birds chirp from the nearby trees. I couldn't have asked for a better day for this.

I pass Jess the two paddles and hoist the canoe above my head. We carry everything to the water, Butterscotch trotting between us. I lower the canoe so it's half in the water, half on the sand.

Butterscotch barks next to the canoe as if telling me to move faster.

I laugh. "Getting a little impatient are you, buddy?"

"I take it he loves canoeing?" Jess's gaze surveys the trees skirting our side of the lake. To enjoy the view? Or because she's hypervigilant?

"That's an understatement. Plus, this is the first time we've been able to go since the fall." I take the paddles from her and place them in the canoe.

She hands me Butterscotch's life jacket. He waits patiently while I put it on him. Then Jessica and I slip on our life jackets and fasten them.

I lift Butterscotch into the canoe. He makes his way to the bow and jumps onto the small seat I made for him. I help Jess into the boat.

"Where do you want me to sit?" she asks.

"On the bench behind Butterscotch." I steady the canoe as she makes her way toward him, keeping her body weight low. She moves with the ease of someone familiar with being on a small boat.

Once she's seated, I slide the canoe farther into the water and climb in. I sit in the stern and push the canoe away from the shore with the paddle.

Jessica starts paddling. I don't even have to tell her what to do. She performs the J-stroke perfectly.

"You've canoed before?"

She lifts her shoulders but doesn't look back at me. "A few times."

She lived in Vermont prior to coming here. They have plenty of lakes and rivers there, so it makes sense this isn't the first time she's been in a canoe.

We paddle in sync as if we've been canoeing together for quite some time. I steer, keeping to the shoreline. The gentle splash of water as we paddle is the only noticeable sound. If the soothing movement of the canoe through water, the surrounding stillness, and the effortless silence between us doesn't relax her, I don't know what will.

This isn't the first time I've taken a woman canoeing. Garrett once joked canoeing is my test to determine if a woman is right for me. If that were true, more than a few women have failed the test. They didn't want to get wet or didn't enjoy paddling (or were hopeless at it) or spent the entire time talking nonstop.

The last woman I took canoeing I came close to tossing over the side because she wouldn't shut up about the benefits of gel nails versus acrylics.

Even Butterscotch is quiet, enjoying the view and occasionally looking over the side to spot a fish.

All the possible reasons for why Jess reacted the way she did at Picnic & Treats scroll through my head. I failed my best friend. I don't want to make the same mistake with Jess.

But if she won't tell me what happened, will she at least open up to a therapist? If she can't do that, it'll be difficult for her to process her painful memories and eventually heal.

If Colton hadn't kept brushing off the therapist he was supposed to see, he would've realized he wasn't responsible for the death of the hockey players, the coach, and the support staff on the bus that tragic day. His guilt of not being able to save them would've been resolved, and he would still be alive.

And Olivia would still have her husband, and Nova would still have a father.

Jessica tilts her face skyward. The rhythmic rising and lowering of her shoulders, in time with her breathing, is slow and easy. My plan has worked. For now, anyway.

We eventually paddle back to the beach and climb out of the canoe.

Jessica yawns. It's not the first time she's yawned since we left Picnic & Treats. She's clearly not getting enough sleep. She resembles Colton during his final days, the same dark circles under the eyes.

"When was the last time you slept through the night?" I casually ask, examining her face for other signs of exhaustion.

"I sleep through the night all the time." The defensiveness in her voice has returned, replacing some of the bricks I'd torn down from her wall.

I don't exactly believe her. I wouldn't be surprised if the lack of sleep was part of the reason for the flashback this morning.

I check the time on my phone. "All right. Let's get going. There're some people I want you to meet."

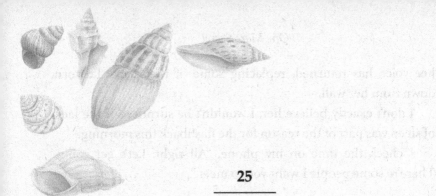

25

JESSICA

March, Present Day
Maple Ridge

T roy drives us back to town and parks in a visitor stall at the Maple Ridge Veterans Center.

"What are we doing here?" I stare at the building as several people enter through the glass doors.

"Like I said, there're some people I want you to meet."

My palms grow clammy at the idea, and I squirm on the passenger seat. "I'd rather not."

Troy smiles. His warm, knowing eyes crinkle at the corners, and something inside me stirs. "I promise you, Jess, you're safe. These men and women are on your side." He gives my hand a small squeeze, and the tension in my body eases a tiny bit. "Nothing bad will happen to you in there."

I nod, but I'm not sure if I'm nodding because I believe him or because I'm agreeing to go in with him.

We climb out of the truck. Troy puts a scarf on Butterscotch that proclaims he's an emotional support dog, and we walk through the building entrance. Troy signs me in as a visitor and leads me to a sunny rec room.

Two women in their forties are playing what looks like a heated match of table tennis. The blond has an above-the-elbow amputation and whacks the ball over the net. The brunette doesn't reach the ball in time, and the blond woman scores a point.

She hoots and raises her arm in victory. "And the reigning champion wins again!" She puts the paddle on the table.

Cheers and laughter rise from a group of individuals sitting near them, and the woman she was playing against laughs and high-fives her.

"This way." Troy takes me to a small table where two elderly men are sitting, studying the fanned-out cards in their hands.

A man with shaved-short white hair looks up from his cards. "Hey, Butterscotch. You want to help me beat Frank's sorry ass?"

Troy bends down and unhooks Butterscotch's leash. The dog walks over to the man.

A woman my age with dark-blond hair and a scar-free face joins us and smiles at Troy. Her pale skin turns luminous. "I didn't realize you're volunteering today, Troy."

"I'm not," he says. "We just dropped by for a few minutes to talk to Bill and Frank."

I glance around the room. I'm not the only person here with visible scars. One man has burn marks on his cheek and jaw that look several years old. Others have what could be shrapnel scars on their faces or arms. And those are just the scars I can see.

For all I know, Troy also has scars on his body from being in the Marines.

"Troy, are you going to introduce us to your beautiful woman?" Frank grins at him. A scar bisects one of his bushy white eyebrows.

"This is Jessica," Troy explains, surprising me. I thought the man meant the woman who'd said hi to Troy. "She just moved to town. She's the one who bought Iris's house."

Both men wince.

Huh? Is that not a good thing? Do they know something about the house I don't? Something Troy and the house report failed to mention?

"I take it you're still looking for a property to flip then," the man with Butterscotch on his lap asks, his voice a grumble of either disapproval or disappointment.

"Flip?" Troy was interested in Iris's house? *My* house?

"It's nothing," Troy tells me like he's half-heartedly swatting away an annoying mosquito.

The man with Butterscotch huffs. "It's not nothing. He was planning to renovate the house and sell it. And give the profit to his best friend's widow and her two-year-old daughter." The man studies me, and I suddenly feel naked, as if he's stripping away my layers, determining if I'm worthy of Troy's attention.

I stare at Troy, waiting for him to fill in the blanks.

Troy sighs, the sound heavily resigned. "I told you my best friend lost his life to his battle with PTSD. He committed suicide, leaving his wife and daughter to go on without him."

"And because he killed himself," the man with Butterscotch says, "his life insurance was void."

Oh. I turn to Troy. "And my buying Iris's house prevented you from helping them?"

That's why he was so eager to help me. Is he going to tell me the house isn't salvageable and try to convince me to sell it to him? So he can flip it?

Fuckers. I retreat a step.

"It's okay." Troy's brow creases, and a silent plea glints in his eyes. "There'll be other places. Anyway, that's not why I brought you here. Jess, this is Bill, Frank, and Katelyn." The men wave at me in turn. Katelyn regards me with disinterest. "Katelyn's one of the center's recreational therapists," Troy explains.

My lips tilt into a wonky smile, partly because of the scar, and partly because of Bill's news about Troy's plan for Iris's house. Has he really given up that easily on the house? I don't know what to believe.

"You must be the new woman in Troy's life that Delores mentioned." Frank flashes a toothy grin that's stained with age, but it's as cocky as it probably was when he was younger.

"Oh, no. Nothing like that. More like his pet project." The words rush from me like water hurtling down a hundred-foot drop. I hadn't meant to say that, but it definitely got everyone's interest.

Frank and Bill lean forward, slow smiles spreading across their faces.

Troy's eyebrows are raised, his body still.

Sure, he came over to my house twice last week, and now Delores is getting things all wrong about what's going on between him and me. Or maybe she just meant I'm friends with Troy, and Frank is the one who misunderstood her.

"Explain." Frank looks between Troy and me.

"Troy thinks I have PTSD—which I don't—and is out to try to save me." I don't roll my eyes, but I can hear what resembles an eye roll in my tone.

Katelyn's unsettled expression flips between relief and worry. She clearly likes Troy. A lot. Hopefully, she hasn't misread the situation between us. He and I are just...friends.

Friends. I sound the word out in my head. Is that really what Troy is to me? A friend? It's been such a long time since I had any, the concept seems foreign.

No, he's not a friend. Not if he plans to manipulate me out of my new home. That's why he's been so kind to me. Now it all makes sense. He doesn't actually plan to come over tomorrow night to discuss my renovation ideas. Maybe he's coming over to persuade me to sell my house to him.

Troy makes a funny noise that's a cross between a snort and a grunt. "I don't think of you as a pet project. You're my friend. And from what I've seen so far, you do show signs of having PTSD."

"No. I don't." I fix a smile on my face so I don't come off quite so defensive. "I bet if you spend more time with Katelyn, you'll start believing she also has PTSD." I'm assuming she doesn't. Plus, I have no clue how much time they spend together. Maybe it's a lot more than I realize. Sooooo, probably a bad example.

Troy shrugs, but not in acquiescence. I haven't won this battle. But my marriage and my time in prison have left me splintered, chipped, cracked. I don't need anyone else to see me that way. I don't need to be reminded of how big a broken mess I am. I just need to look in the mirror for that reminder.

Frank waves at the chair between him and Bill, indicating for me to sit down. I glance at Bill. He nods. Troy sits in the chair opposite mine.

I drop my butt onto the empty seat. Katelyn doesn't seem too fazed that she's the only one standing.

"There's nothing shameful about admitting that you have PTSD," Frank says. "I was in denial for years after the Vietnam War. It destroyed my family. I drank heavily because that was the only thing keeping the nightmares away. It wasn't until I hit rock bottom that I finally found the strength to get help and turn things around."

"I convinced myself I had everything under control," Bill adds. "If I just kept those bad memories and nightmares locked away, everything would be all right. But it's not only the bad memories that get locked away. The good ones do too. All the things that bring you joy are no longer within reach."

He leans forward, accidentally flashing his cards to everyone at the table. They're too busy looking at me to notice. "Don't let whatever happened to you win, Jess. Make sure at the end of the day, you're the one who wins."

"It won't be easy." Frank's gruff voice has the same pain and understanding as Bill's. "But the reward in the end will be worth it. Maybe you're right and you don't have PTSD. The only way to know for sure is to talk to a counselor or therapist. They'll determine if you fit the diagnosis criteria, and then they can discuss treatment options."

"Having a support system is a good idea," Bill says. "Friends and family who will be there for you."

At the murmur of female voices behind me, I turn to see a dark-haired woman take a seat between two women in their late fifties. She looks over her shoulder toward the door, her body stiff with anxiety. It's a feeling I know only too well.

"Do you, Jess?" Bill asks. "Do you have a support system?"

I swivel back to him. "My grandmother was the one who raised me." Along with my grandfather before he died. "She's my only family, but she's dead."

"How 'bout friends you can talk to?"

I want to brush Bill off with a lie. To tell him I have friends and an incredible support system. I want to walk out the door and never again have to face the two men's compassionate and probing glances.

I want to, but I can't seem to make myself say the words. "I haven't had a chance to make friends yet." After what happened in Picnic & Treats with the knife, I can't imagine Zara wants to be my friend. And this means Simone, Emily, and Avery might not want to hang out with me either. I'm in no better position than when I was married or in prison. I thought I finally had a chance to have friends, but instead, I screwed it up.

I try to swallow the pain, but it gets caught on the camera-sized lump in my throat.

"I'm your friend." Troy's determined tone dares me to claim otherwise, warns me he'll have a thing or two to say about it if I do.

But how can I really trust him?

What if he's just using me to try to get something he wants—my house?

Troy doesn't waste time claiming his brothers, Simone, Zara, Avery, and Emily are also my friends. I appreciate that. I don't need false hope. I've had more than a lifetime of that. Even when I was told new evidence proved I was innocent of my husband's death, I expected someone to laugh and tell me they were joking. Or tell me he'd been alive all this time.

"I can also recommend a good support group," Frank says, interrupting my mental freak-out. "Being able to talk to people who have gone through similar situations and knowing you aren't alone makes a difference."

I can't imagine there's a support group in Maple Ridge for victims of domestic abuse who were also abused while serving time for a crime they didn't commit. But since I can't mention that, I simply nod.

"Hi, Violet." Frank's cheerful voice calls out to someone behind me. I turn to see who he's talking to. A blond woman smiles at him, but there's something off about her smile. It's as if she doesn't have the energy to smooth it onto her face. I can relate.

Frank places his cards facedown. "Have you come for that pool game you promised me last week?"

"Yes. But I can only stay for a few minutes."

A puzzled frown dents his brow. "Isn't today when you usually volunteer here?"

"It is, but I can't volunteer anymore."

"How come?"

She looks away, but not before I catch regret and sadness flickering in her features. "I need to stay home with Sophie."

Frank seems to deflate at the news, shoulders drooping. "You'll be missed." He straightens. "How's the kiddo doing?"

Violet's face brightens. "She's good. She took her first steps the other day."

There's a rush of excited comments from everyone at the table.

Everyone but me. I fight back the memory of when Amelia took her first steps. I can't bear thinking about it and risk releasing the dam of emotions. I hate myself for failing her. I don't need these people to know how badly I messed things up.

To know that because of my mistakes, my daughter doesn't remember me.

Violet shows the group the latest photo of her daughter—an adorable young toddler sitting on a man's lap.

Frank inspects the picture closer. "Sophie looks like her father."

"I think she looks more like her mother," Katelyn pipes in. I have to agree with her there.

Frank pushes his chair away from the table and stands. "Violet, have you met Jess yet? She just moved to Maple Ridge."

I smile, self-conscious. Violet's skin is flawless, other than the smudge of dark circles under her eyes, which isn't unexpected when you have a young toddler. "Hi."

She returns my smile. "It's nice to meet you."

"All right, ladies. Violet and I have a pool date. And I plan to make good on that promise now." Frank holds out his arm to Violet. She accepts it, and they walk over to the empty pool table.

"I'll see you tomorrow." Troy nods at Bill and Katelyn and attaches Butterscotch's leash to his collar. We say our good-byes to the pair and leave.

"Were those the people you wanted me to meet?" I ask as we walk down the hallway.

"I thought hearing from people who had at one point struggled with PTSD might be of interest to you. And I wanted you to hear how much therapy helped them."

"Thanks. I'll keep that under advisement." But in the end, it doesn't matter if I accept I might have PTSD. I can't afford to see a counselor. I don't have health insurance. Not anymore. Not after what happened at Picnic & Treats.

I'm quiet on the way to Troy's truck, my mind spinning

through my options for finding a new job now that I'm surely unemployed again. I have a journalism degree. And I once was a writer who received praise from her instructors, praise from the women's rights organization I volunteered with in college.

I scan my surroundings, my attention razor-focused on the vehicles in the parking lot. Anyone could be hiding behind a parked car. Anyone could be watching me from the building windows overlooking the area.

The different possibilities ambush my thoughts. My skin prickles, and my heart rate picks up with a resounding *boom, boom, boom.*

"What are you up to tonight?" Troy asks, startling me.

"I'm going to sort through some more of Iris's magazines." And read more of Angelique's journal.

He was planning to renovate the house and sell it. And give the profit to his best friend's widow and her two-year-old daughter. The friend who killed himself because his PTSD became too much for him to manage.

"Why didn't you tell me you wanted to buy Iris's house and flip it?" The words pour out in a rush of hot lava, even though I know I don't have the right to be angry. His rationale for flipping the house was incredibly sweet.

"Because I didn't think it was important." Troy's voice is deep and annoyingly even and doesn't give away what he's really thinking. "You'd already bought the house. There was nothing I could do about that."

"So you weren't planning to convince me I'm making a mistake?" The lava continues flowing around my words, but with a little less heat this time. "You weren't planning to convince me to sell the house to you?"

He winces. It's a tiny wince, sneaking past his schooled expression. But it's enough to tell me the thought had crossed his mind.

"So what made you decide not to?" I demand, stepping away

from him, creating a crevasse between us. "Why volunteer to help me do the renovations?"

"Because I want to. It might not be what I'd originally planned, but I did want to help you. Still do. And in the meantime, I'll keep my eyes open for another project I can flip. I mean it, Jess. I want to help you with the house. I'm not trying to take your home from you." He unlocks the truck doors with his key fob.

I open the passenger door and climb in.

Troy helps Butterscotch into the back seat and slides into the driver's seat. "Are you gonna be all right tonight?"

"Sure. Why wouldn't I be?" The bite in my voice isn't as strong as before, but the essence of it is there. "You think I'm going to spend the night upset because you were planning to buy the house?"

A harsh laugh vibrates low in his chest. "No. I was referring to your reaction when someone dropped a metallic pan on the floor. People tend not to curl up in a corner with a knife held in a defensive position when they hear a pan hit the ground. I want to make sure when I drop you off at your house, you'll be okay."

Right. I'd temporarily forgotten about that. I release an equally harsh sigh. "I overreacted, that's all. I was cutting vegetables when it happened. And that's why I was holding the knife when I had the panic attack."

A cavernous silence accompanies us back to my house, other than the country song playing through the speaker.

Troy pulls into my driveway and shifts the truck into park. "Promise me you'll call me if you need anything tonight. Or tomorrow. I'm volunteering at the Vet Center after work, but I'm always available on the phone. And I'll see you after that."

"Sure," I say, not really meaning it.

He puts his hand gently on my arm. My muscles instinctively tighten under his touch. *He's not my dead husband. He's not my dead husband. He's not my dead husband.*

I will my muscles to unravel.

Troy moves his hand away. "I meant what I said about being your friend, Jess. If you need someone to talk to, I'm here. I won't judge you. Fuck, I'm a Marine. There are things I can't discuss with anyone because I was part of secret operations. I've had to do things you don't want to hear about. Trust me on that."

"Isn't that the definition of hypocritical?" I stare out the windshield so I don't glare at him. "You want me to tell you things I'm not comfortable sharing with anyone, yet you can't discuss your past missions with me." I know where he's coming from. In the government's opinion, they aren't the same. But I still can't risk telling him the truth.

Can't risk the information getting out and everyone learning about my shameful past. They'll judge me for who I am and for who I've been. They'll wonder why I didn't try hard enough to get away from my husband. Why I didn't try harder to get Amelia out sooner?

And I can't risk my neighbors turning on me because they don't want an ex-con living in their community.

I hop down from the truck. "Thank you for taking me canoeing. I had fun. See you tomorrow night." I shut the door, not giving him a chance to respond, and I quickly put an end to our discussion.

26

ANGELIQUE

May 1943
France

I hand Lieutenant Todd Matherson the bowl of food and sit next to him on the bale of straw in the barn. I am situated between him and the small hole in the wall, my body blocking him from view, even though it's unlikely anyone is on Jacques's property who shouldn't be. The midday sunlight streams through the high window, bathing Todd in its spotlight.

"I have some good news," I tell him.

Todd's mouth slips into the grin I have come to recognise as his playful, swoony smile. It's his way of coping with the oppression and fear Hitler has placed on our shoulders. "Good news? You've agreed to marry me?"

"Even better. I've received word that we're ready to get you out of France and back to England." And eventually he will make his way to Canada.

It's been almost two weeks since the lieutenant was brought to the vineyard with an injured leg. Once his leg was healed enough to bear his weight, he began walking in the barn, preparing for his upcoming journey into Spain. But he has also been resting as much as possible. The journey promises to be gruelling.

There are no guarantees he'll make it that far. The escape route between here and the Pyrénées Mountains is laden with danger. Walking through a pit of angry vipers is safer than travelling to the mountain range. And a deadly snake bite is preferable over being caught by the Milice or Gestapo or SS, all who are hungry to capture anyone siding with the Allies.

And once he crosses into Spain, his next worry will be the Spanish guards. If they capture him, they'll hand him over to the Germans.

All any of us can do is take precautions and pray for the best.

A series of emotions flicker and flare on Todd's face. Relief. Anticipation. Anxiety. We've discussed in detail the dangers he'll be facing on the French and Spanish sides of the border. "That is good news. As much as I've enjoyed your company, Carmen, I'm ready to go back to ridding us of Hitler."

He flashes me his charming, one-sided grin that I'll miss once he is gone. But the sooner I get him away from here, the safer Todd and Jacques and I will be.

"I'll take you to the train station and travel with you to Dijon. From there, your guide will escort you on the next part of the journey. We'll leave tomorrow morning."

"What about my identification?"

"I have forged papers for you. But your inability to speak French beyond the few words and phrases I have taught you might be troublesome." His atrocious French accent won't fool anyone. "As long as the French-speaking Germans don't try to engage with you, you should be safe. Remember, neither myself nor the other escape-line guides will sit with you while you're on public transportation. We also won't acknowledge you. And you should avoid watching us. We cannot risk being seen with you if something should go wrong."

"I understand." He lifts the spoon to his mouth. I procured some additional food for him from the black market. It's not much more than a few scraps of meat in his soup and some bread. But it's more than most people get to eat.

"Do your best not to look suspicious, and everything will be all right." It's an empty promise. We both know that.

Todd finishes his food and climbs back down the ladder into the hiding space. I close the trapdoor, throwing him into darkness, and push the straw bales on top of it.

I go outside. The warm midday sun paints patterns on the ground through the young leaves on the nearby trees. I cycle into the village, leave the bicycle outside the bookshop, and go in. The bell above the door rings, the sound sweet and crisp and welcoming. The shop is empty of people other than the owner, a short, balding man in his late fifties with glasses and a hooked nose and a ready smile.

I return his smile, pretending for a moment a war isn't raging outside the quiet confines of the walls. "*Bonjour*, Monsieur Joubert. Do you have a book you recommend for today?"

He nods, and his gaze darts to the large window that overlooks the village square. "Yes. I have a poetry book you might enjoy." He tells me the title, even though the name doesn't matter.

"Thank you." My smile this time is shared with a secretive nod, a message that goes beyond the simple act of gratitude.

I walk down the aisle to the poetry section and remove a book of verses from the shelf. Then I walk to the next section, pull out a thick book, and flip open the cover. The carved-out compartment contains a folded piece of paper.

I remove the paper and return the book to the shelf. The aisle isn't in view of the shop window, so I unfold the paper and read the message. To the casual reader, the message contains nothing of value, other than some idle female gossip.

I refold the paper, making it narrower than it was when I found it, and slip it into the tiny opening in the hem of my skirt.

I take the book of verses to the counter and purchase it. Monsieur Joubert asks about Jacques as if I really am his child. He knows better. He knows Jacques only had the one daughter. The daughter who died several years ago.

"Thank you for everything," I whisper so he knows what I am talking about.

"You're welcome, Angelique. I just wish I could do more."

The shop door opens, and Madame Lavigne enters, her grey hair twisted back in an elegant bun. Her expression is wary and worn. The same expression most people wear these days. It's hard to know whom to trust. But her distrust seems to dial up a few notches every time she sees me.

And I have yet to determine where her loyalties lie when faced with the benefits of the Gestapo's blood money.

"Say hello to your father," Monsieur Joubert says, giving me a quick out.

I tell him I will, nod my greeting to Madame Lavigne, and hurry out of the shop.

Jacques is still in the vineyard, tending to the grapevines, when I arrive at the safe house. I go inside and walk up the creaky wooden steps to my bedroom. The bedroom that once belonged to his real daughter.

I shut the door and pry the coded message out of the slit in my hem. Then I carefully pull up a small portion of floorboard under the rug, revealing a long and narrow hiding spot that's about the length of my arm, from elbow to fingertip.

The first thing I do is check that the large amount of money—money Jacques doesn't know about—is still there. The SOE gave it to me to help fund my work in the *Cashmere* network. The gold compact Major Maurice Buckmaster gave me the day I departed from England is also there. All his agents receive something valuable to remind us there will always be a link back in London, ready to help us in our difficulties. And the gift is something we can pawn on the black market if necessary.

I remove the supplies used for decoding messages and carry them and the half-melted candle from the bedside table to the desk. The next twenty minutes are spent deciphering the message from the bookshop. And the relief at what the message says is a welcome lightness in my chest.

Baker Street is finally sending us a wireless operator.

The relief isn't enough to chase away all my concerns; it's not enough to end the war. But the wireless operator will make a difference to our side of the battle. The SOE agents will be able to quickly send intelligence to Baker Street. We won't have to waste time sending it to Paris to be wired from there and risk it being intercepted *en route* by the Nazis.

I light the candle and hold the paper in the flame. It greedily consumes each incriminating word, and the letters disintegrate at my touch.

I open the window and toss the ashes into the breeze. Next, I hide everything linked to my real purpose in France under the floorboard and head outside.

I retrieve the trowel and basket from the shed at the back of the house and set to work on the garden. Jacques's wife planted the small plot of land to provide food for their family. I weed the carrot beds, enjoying the normalcy of the chore. Memories of my mother and my sister and me gardening together float in like leaves on the wind.

I was six years old at the time; Hazel was eight. It was six months before my father's diplomat career took us to Paris for four years, followed by Vienna for another four. Mum had loved gardening. Hazel and I had loved watching the butterflies flutter around the flowers.

Once upon a time, butterflies would have fluttered in this garden. Now, it's as if even they resent the Germans' intrusion and have disappeared to somewhere more pleasant.

"WHY DID YOU DECIDE TO DO THIS JOB?" TODD ASKS. HE'S SITTING on the bed in his hiding space, a soup bowl in his hands. I'm next to him, having finished supper a short while ago. The only light in the space comes from the lantern on the crate. "Surely there's a boyfriend or husband at home who isn't thrilled you're here, eh?"

"I'm not married, and I don't have a boyfriend. I don't even have a family anymore." Or rather, I don't have a family who counts, especially after my sister's betrayal.

Todd's expression gives away what he's thinking. I don't bother to correct him. My family didn't die during the blitz. My sister was very much alive when I left England to come here. And our parents died long before the war, the result of two different causes: cancer and a failed heart.

"You must have known the job would be dangerous," Todd says. "What made you decide to risk your life to be here?" He lifts the spoon to his mouth.

"The same reason you did. I don't want Hitler to win. I've seen what his oppression has done to this country. I want it to end. I want to prevent his power and hatred from spreading like a deadly mould to the rest of the world." And I don't want the Nazis to invade my homeland.

What I didn't tell Vera Atkins when I interviewed for the position was I needed something to distract me. Distract me from everything that had blown up around me at home. Metaphorically speaking. Coming home early from work one day. Finding my fiancé and sister in bed together. The lies. And the tears. Mostly Hazel's tears.

I was too stunned to do much more than bloody stare at them as if I had never seen two naked people before.

They married the following month.

"Let's hope we can wipe out his form of mould sooner rather than later." Todd lifts his coffee cup as if to toast his words and frowns at the watery brown contents. "I can't wait for this war to be over so we can have real coffee."

My mouth twitches. "I agree with you on both accounts. Ground walnut shells aren't much of a substitute for the real thing." It tastes fucking awful and lacks the kick of energy to help me survive the day. The kick required to keep me alert so I can do this job without getting killed.

Todd's easy-going smile returns to his face. "What do you plan to do once the war is over?"

"Sleep."

His smile widens, and he chuckles. "And after that?"

"I'm not sure. I was a legal secretary before coming here, and my job involved some translating, which I enjoyed. So maybe I will resume doing that."

He wants to ask more about my previous job, I can see it in his eyes, on his face, but I've already shared more than I should. It does feel nice, though, to drop the charade of being Angelique D'Aboville for a minute and have a taste of being Iris Bromfield again.

"Is there a fellow back home you have your eye set on, perhaps?"

I shake my head because it's true. War isn't the best time to fall in love. I know women who have lost a loved one because of this war. The bloke either served in the military or was the tragedy of a bomb raid. "What about you? Is there a special woman who has your heart?"

Someone whose heart might be shattered if you don't survive your perilous journey?

"Yes, there is someone I like. A lot." A faint blush reddens his pale cheeks, and I can't help but grin. This is the first time I've seen the lieutenant embarrassed. And given I'm the one who has been cleaning his chamber pot for the past two weeks, that's saying a lot.

"Does she know you like her?"

"She does. But we haven't gone out on a date yet, if that's what you're asking."

"Why not?"

He points to the cellar walls, referring to the war outside them.

"As soon as you return home, you should ask her out. And treat her like she is the most important woman in the world."

"You think so?"

"I do."

I return to the farmhouse. Jacques is reading at the kitchen table. "Is he ready?" He keeps his voice low, and there's an emotion on his face I cannot decipher.

"As ready as he will ever be. I don't think anyone is truly ready for what he'll have to endure."

"Have you made the trip over the mountains?"

I sit at the table. "No, but I've heard of what it will entail. It won't be easy."

Jacques nods and resumes reading. Then looks up again. "Will you be gone long tomorrow?"

"No. I'll be back before supper." Assuming nothing goes wrong. A million things could go awry. Most of them I don't want to think about.

"But you will be returning here, *oui*?" Hope shifts onto his lips. The movement is small, but it's noticeable and heartwarming. And dangerous.

"You've become like a daughter to me." His warm gruff voice yanks on something deep in my chest. The man who was prickly when I first arrived on his doorstep appears at a loss for what to say next.

"And you've become like a father to me." My voice is a cracked whisper.

"Take care tomorrow." Jacques's troubled gaze peers at me beneath thick, grey eyebrows. "Don't let them take you like they've taken everything else from me."

27

TROY

March, Present Day
Maple Ridge

The passenger door of my truck bangs shut, and I wait for Jess to enter her house. The lights click on inside the front entrance, and I wonder if I should have ensured that the house was secure before she went inside.

Would she even want me to do that? Especially after what just happened. I have no idea why she overreacted when she found out about my original plans to flip Iris's home. Jess bought the house. And I have no intention of trying to convince her to sell it to me...now.

The Marine in me says I can't drive away without checking the place. Just to be sure her demons haven't followed her to Maple Ridge.

I kill the engine. "I'll be right back," I tell Butterscotch. I climb out of my truck, jog to Jess's front door, and ring the doorbell.

The door opens, revealing the frown on Jess's face. "Yes?" Her voice is as wary as her expression, her tone a long sigh.

"Do you want me to check that your house is secure?"

My question is met with a nearly blank expression and an unspoken *Huh?*

"I know something happened to you and left you skittish. As much as you want to deny it. But if you're in danger, I should check no one broke in while you were gone for the day. If there's anyone trained to do that, it would be me."

Her face pales, and I silently curse myself for how I put it.

"No one has broken in," Jess says. "And no one is hiding in the house."

"How do you know?" If someone doesn't want her to know they're in the house, they would've hidden all signs that could indicate they were inside.

"I set up traps whenever I leave. If someone breaks in, they'll disturb the traps, and I'll be alerted to the danger when I return. But I can't imagine why anyone would want to try to break in. I don't have anything of value."

Her answer surprises me. The traps...that's what I would do too. "Where did you learn to do that? To set traps?"

"I read it in a book."

"Okay, if you're sure you don't need me to secure the place, I'll go now."

"I'm sure. But...but thanks for checking on me, Troy." She doesn't smile, but she also doesn't toss me out on my ass, so I count that as a win.

While she might not smile, I do. "You're welcome. Have a good night, Jess." I walk away, but it's not until I get to my truck that I hear her front door click shut.

As soon as I step into my house, I call Zara.

"How's Jess doing?" she asks. The banging of pots echoes through the line, which means she's still at Treats.

I hang my keys on the hook by the garage door in the laundry room. "She's doing better now. I think she's more embarrassed than anything."

"Any idea what caused her to react like that? I get it, the pan dropping on the floor set her off, but why?"

I walk to the kitchen. Butterscotch follows me. "She wouldn't say."

"She might not have said anything, but your gut reaction is telling you something. Am I right?"

"You're right. My gut's telling me something happened to her, and that's why she's hypervigilant and jumpy. It's like she's constantly looking over her shoulder, expecting to see whoever hurt her in the past."

"You think she has a stalker? Maybe that's why she moved to Maple Ridge. She's trying to get away from him."

"It's possible." I open my fridge and pull out a beer. "She said a friend of hers was stalked in college, and that's what made Jess super cautious. But I'm wondering if she was the victim, and not her friend. It's also possible the stalking was more recent."

"But what could've happened to make her react that way when the pan fell on the floor?"

"It could be anything. I've seen guys react to a car backfiring, but in their minds it was a gunshot. The mind likes to play tricks on us."

Unless Jess tells me what happened in the past, I won't know for sure what caused her to react that way. I can only speculate.

I put my phone on the counter and open the beer bottle.

"So, let me guess," Zara says softly, "you're phoning to ask if she still has a job? Or are you calling to ask me to give her another chance?"

"It's your call, Zar. It's your business. I'm just your friend. I can't tell you what to do."

Silence stretches through the phone line, heavy with uncertainty and hope. My hope. "I don't know. What if next time she hurts someone or hurts herself? She was holding a knife, Troy."

Zara's voice is low, keeping the conversation between us, even though she's probably in the staff room by now.

"I know." My words are steady and unwavering.

"And what if next time you aren't here to help out?"

"I know." That's the big risk. One I can't ask Zara to take. She's the one who must make the decision.

Zara groans, the sound barely heard from my end, and I imagine her on the couch, staring at the ceiling as if the answer is there. "Does she even want to come back after what happened?"

"I never asked. She assumed that she was fired."

Zara is silent for another beat. "She's not fired. If she wants to try again, I'm fine with that. But she should really see a therapist."

"I know, and I'm working on that." I lean back against the granite kitchen counter and take a quick draw of the beer.

"What do you mean?"

"I took her to the Vet Center to talk to some of the guys there. About their experiences with PTSD. They all agreed that therapy helped them." There's a but in my tone, a lingering doubt that their comments made a difference. "Whatever happened in the past, it's something she doesn't want to talk about. And that might make it tougher for her to open up to a therapist. If they don't know specifically what happened to her, it'll be harder to help her."

The cost might also be a factor. Does she even have health insurance? Or resources to pay for therapy?

"Maybe she'll be more willing to open up to a therapist than she is with us," Zara says. "But either way, if she experiences a repeat of what happened today, I will have to let her go. I won't have a choice. I can't risk any of my staff getting hurt."

"I understand."

"I'll call her once I finish here."

"Thanks, Zara."

A low huff echoes through the line. "I'm not doing this for you, Troy. I'm doing it for Jess."

I laugh, a near-quiet sound deep in my throat, and push away from the counter. "I realize that. But thank you anyway." I open a cabinet door, the dark-gray wood contrasting with the cream counter. Both I installed last year. I grab a glass and fill it with water from the tap.

"Can I ask you something?" she asks.

I don't have to see Zara to know her gaze is narrowed. I can hear it in her tone. "Depends on what it is."

"You like her, don't you?"

A chuckle rumbles in my chest, and I walk over to the table in the living room. "Seriously, Zar? First you ask about me and Olivia, and now you're asking about me and Jess?" I shake my head in disbelief, even though she can't see me. "If you're asking if Jess is my friend, the answer is yes."

"That's not what I'm asking."

"Yes, I'm attracted to her. No, I'm not doing anything about it. Not yet, anyway. I don't know what happened to her, but it's not hard to figure out she's got trust issues." I pour the water onto the potted sage in the center of the table.

Zara doesn't respond right away, the beat stretching for a long moment, but I know there's more coming. "Troy, I love you like a brother and I know you wouldn't intentionally hurt anyone, but I don't think it's a good idea for you to be with her that way. Be her friend. Be the man who helps her renovate her home. But don't be the man who might break her heart."

What the fuck? "Why do you think I'm gonna break her heart?"

What sounds like another long-weighted sigh comes from Zara's end. "It won't be intentional. But how many long-term relationships have you had?"

I frown. "What does that have to do with anything?" My words come out harsher than planned. *Stand down, soldier.*

"I'm just saying your relationships tend to last only a few

weeks, with one exception. And that's when you actually do date."

"I don't have time to date. I'm running a business. And I don't see you settling down with anyone. When was the last time you dated, Zara? Two years ago? Three?"

"*Touché*. But that's my point. Our businesses come first. Neither of us has time for romance."

"Maybe I'm ready to settle down. I'm not against having a family one day soon. But that's beside the point." Just because I'm not actively searching for a future wife, it doesn't mean I don't want to get married and have kids. Eventually. But living in a small town does limit the possibilities.

"And what point is that?" Zara asks.

"That I'm helping Jess out as a friend. She's new in town and doesn't have many friends yet. She admitted that at the Vet Center this afternoon. And I get the feeling she's not sure where any of us fit on the friendship spectrum."

"As far as I'm concerned, I'm her friend. And as her friend, I'm warning you not to break her heart."

"I promise, I won't. Right now, my goal is to be her friend and to help her in whatever way she needs." Plus in a few other ways that I'm not telling Zara about.

One related to the call I'm making next.

28

JESSICA

March, Present Day
Maple Ridge

My phone rings on the coffee table. I put the magazine I was reading next to me on the couch and grab the phone, Zara. I guess she's phoning to tell me I no longer have the job.

My husband's ranted words slither into my head. "You can't fucking do anything right." He'd said it right before he punched me in the stomach. Amelia was sick, and I hadn't had time to make dinner.

Maybe he was correct that I can't do anything right. If I'd done a better job standing up for myself in prison, maybe I wouldn't have been attacked. And then I wouldn't have reacted the way I did in Picnic & Treats.

I wouldn't now be unemployed.

I accept Zara's call, an apology on my lips. My hand trembles just thinking about what happened this morning and how it must have looked. "Hi, Zara." The words come out dry and cracked.

"Hey, Jess." Her voice sounds cheery—not at all what I was expecting. "How're you doing?" Mary Poppins claimed a spoonful of sugar helps the medicine go down. Maybe Zara thinks a spoonful of cheery makes being fired easier to swallow.

"Better, thanks. I'm so sorry for what happened. I know that doesn't change anything, but I really am sorry. There's no excuse for what I did." I close my eyes.

Don't cry. Don't let them see what they're doing to you.

I repeat in my head what became my mantra in prison. It hardened my shell on the outside but didn't have the same effect on my soft, bruised insides.

The dull ache where the shank dug into my back returns. I don't know how much of the pain is real versus psychological—a constant reminder of what I've endured. I should probably get it checked out, but I'd rather avoid that if I can. I will, though, if it doesn't get better.

"It's okay. No one was hurt," Zara says. "That's the main thing. But what happened to you to make you so jumpy? And I don't mean the part about the pan falling on the floor."

I open my eyes. "It's nothing I can talk about." Or want to talk about.

"Do you think it could happen again?"

God, I hope not. "I don't know. Possibly?" My tone isn't cautious—it's downright dejected. All I wanted was to start my life over. To make up for all those years I was locked up in two separate hells.

"Have you thought about seeing someone?" Zara asks. "Like a therapist?"

I don't respond. She's beginning to sound like Troy.

She clears her throat, and her discomfort with this conversation is felt in my bones. "You're still planning to come in tomorrow, right? To work?" Nothing about her tone suggests she's about to fire me.

I jerk up straighter on the couch, hopeful I haven't misheard her. Optimism flickers in my chest, the flame too small to create any real warmth, but all it takes is a spark and the right kindle to create a fire, to warm a room. "Are you sure you want me back?"

"I thought we could try again. Let's see what happens. If you don't feel comfortable with coming back, I understand. But I'm hoping we can still be friends." Zara sounds like she genuinely means it.

"I would like that too. Both parts." Even though working in Picnic & Treats isn't ultimately my career goal, I enjoyed the physical aspect of chopping the vegetables. The repetitive motion was soothing, and it kept me from focusing on my past. Or it did until the metal-pan incident.

But if given the choice between working at the café and having Zara as my friend, it's a no-brainer. More than anything, I want to have friends like her, Simone, Emily, and Avery in my life. I used to have friends like them. Friends I could tell anything and they wouldn't judge me.

"So I'll see you tomorrow at six a.m.?" Zara asks.

"Yes. Thank you!"

We end the call, and for a second I'm tempted to phone Troy to tell him the good news. But I have a feeling he already knows. He was likely instrumental in Zara phoning and telling me I still have the job if I want it.

Part of me screams to step away. The last thing I want is for another man to have that much control over me, that much control over my life. The other part of me views things another way. Troy wants me to see a therapist.

My husband would never have wanted that.

He relished the power he had over me. He would never have handed me the tools to escape him.

29

TROY

March, Present Day
Maple Ridge

Tuesday morning, I enter Robyn Lawson's office in the mental health clinic that's part of the Veterans Center. She's sitting at her computer in her Army-green uniform, looking at the screen, her fingers not typing. Her office isn't set up in the typical way. Her desk is against the wall. It's not being used as a barricade between herself and her clients when they sit on the couch or love seat.

Robyn's gaze shifts to me, and she smiles. "So, what's this mysterious thing you want to talk to me about, Troy?" She tucks her chin-length auburn hair behind her ear.

I shut the door and take a seat on the couch. She swivels in her chair to face me.

"I have a friend who I'm positive is dealing with PTSD." I explain my reasons for that conclusion, the symptoms I've witnessed that set off sirens. "I have no idea what happened to her. She doesn't want to tell me, but she needs to talk to someone."

"And you're hoping she'll talk to me?"

I nod. That's exactly what I'm hoping. "I don't think she has health insurance, so that might be a barrier for her to get help. She's not military, but I have no idea who else to ask. I can pay for her therapy, but I'd rather she doesn't know I'm doing that." I know Jess will never accept my help, but she can't keep living this way.

I don't want her to keep living this way.

"Is she interested in being helped?"

Good question. "I'm working on that."

Robyn picks up a pen from her desk behind her. "Has she acknowledged the fact she might have PTSD?"

"She was in denial when I first mentioned it. But after what happened yesterday morning, she might be more willing to accept the diagnosis. I brought her here afterward to talk to some of the vets about their struggles with PTSD."

Hopefully that helped enough for the next part of my plan.

"I can check with the clinic's director to see if it's okay for me to talk to her after my regular work hours since she isn't military," Robyn says. "But your friend has to be willing to talk to me and to be open. It can't just be your idea, Troy."

I nod in understanding.

"You do realize it won't be a quick fix? You could be committing to months or years of paying for her therapy."

"I'm fine with that."

"If you don't want her to know you're paying for the sessions, what are you planning to tell her when she asks about the cost?"

"I'll say the state's providing it." I shrug. It was all I could come up with.

A small smile quirks Robyn's mouth. "You really think she'll believe that?" The question receives another shrug from me.

Robyn's smile flatlines, and her green eyes turn more serious. "I'm sorry, Troy, but I'm not comfortable with lying to her."

I'm not either. But I don't have any other choice. "I know. But I'm worried if she finds out I'm paying for it, she'll refuse therapy. And if she's forced to pay for it out of her own pocket, I'm not sure she'll get the help she needs. If she has another episode in Picnic and Treats like she did yesterday, she'll lose her job. I don't know how much longer she can handle the stress. It's clearly tearing her apart."

Robyn taps her fingers against her thigh, lips pressed into a line, and is silent for a beat. "Alright. But you do realize anything your friend and I talk about will be between her and me? I can't under any circumstance share the information with you."

"I understand."

"Okay, I'll talk to the clinic's director this morning and let you know what he says." Robyn's smile returns, a little more hopeful this time.

"Thanks. I appreciate it."

She leans back in her chair, and her smile widens. "Rumor has it you're organizing a festival to raise money for PTSD awareness."

Christ, I knew rumors in this town spread faster than a wildfire in a stiff wind, but I only mentioned the idea to my friends two weeks ago. I wasn't expecting it to be gossip material quite yet. "I'm thinking about it. I need to organize several committees first to help get the ball rolling." Which I need to get going on if I plan to turn the festival into a reality.

"Let me know what kind of committees you need help with. I'm sure we'll be able to find volunteers at this center. And I'll sign up to help out too."

SEVERAL HOURS LATER, I RECEIVE A CALL FROM ROBYN WHILE hammering the new handrail on the porch at a job site on the outskirts of town. I answer the call.

"Good news," she says. "I've been given the green light to help your friend, as long as the sessions occur after I'm finished with my regular clients for the day, and your friend agrees to therapy. But before we can schedule any therapy sessions, I need to talk to her first to determine if she falls within the DSM-Five Diagnostic Guidelines."

Thank the ever-loving Christ for that. "I'll talk to her tonight and let you know how that goes?"

An eleven-year-old boy rides past the house on his bike and waves at me. Smiling, I wave back. He's one of the kids Kellan coaches in hockey.

"Are you sure you want to do this, Troy? I mean, it's great you want to help her. But is this a girlfriend, or someone who you're hoping will be a girlfriend, or is she really just a friend?"

"She's a friend." Who I happen to be insanely attracted to, but that's not why I want to help her.

Okay, it partly is. But that's also why I don't want Jess to know I'm paying for her therapy. If things eventually progress from us being friends to something more, I don't want her to feel like she owes me.

At least now Jess can get the necessary therapy. But convincing Robyn to help her was the easy part.

Convincing Jess to agree to it won't be so simple.

30

ANGELIQUE

May 1943
France

I hand Todd his papers and a ration card. We're in the barn, waiting for Pierre to arrive so we can commence the first leg of Todd's perilous journey back to Canada. "Those are your *carte d'identité* and the latest ration card. Baker Street needs the card so they can update the ones they're sending with the new agents."

What I don't say, but Todd must be thinking, is by the time he arrives in England, the ration card he's holding might be obsolete.

The clip-clopping of horseshoes on gravel and the rattle of a wagon outside the barn door signal it's time.

I step out of the barn. Pierre stops the horse in front of me, and I give Todd the all-clear signal. The barn door opens, and he joins us.

Pierre and I haven't discussed the kiss that possibly saved our lives when the German soldiers found us during the parachute drop. He hasn't tried to kiss me again, and that is probably for the best.

I like Pierre. He's a sweet and caring and respectful man. But he doesn't cause my heart to flutter.

This means what we're about to do will be less awkward. We don't have the kiss hanging over us.

Todd and I climb into the wagon and sit with Pierre. There's no turning back now. We just have to pray everything goes according to plan.

I don't bother introducing the two men. The less they know about each other the better for all concerned.

The morning sky is blue with white clouds brushed across it. I pray this is a good sign.

At the train station, I purchase two tickets and inconspicuously hand one to Todd as he walks past me. He continues to the platform. I head to the loo. Six other individuals are waiting for the train. None are wearing a uniform.

I go into the ladies' toilet and take a minute to go over the plan in my head for the first leg of Todd's journey. I don't need to use the loo, but I do need to give Todd some space so no one grows suspicious that we're travelling together.

The train is pulling into the station when I step out.

Todd boards the middle car. I board the same one but through the door at the opposite end. Since I prefer to be next to the aisle in case we need to quickly disembark, I sit beside a man two decades older than me. Todd picks a seat so he's facing me, his seatmate a young woman.

The train lurches forwards, and I release a relieved breath that no German soldiers or Gestapo agents have boarded the train with us. The train is slow moving, which means it's less prone to inspections. And that is what I was counting on when I purchased the tickets.

The train travels through the war-weary countryside, and I

half watch out the window and half pay attention to my surroundings inside the train car. Even with the absence of the enemy on the train, tension looms over us.

Growing up, Hazel and I loved travelling on the train. We would press our faces to the windows and watch the scenery pass. I miss those days. The simplicity of it, the joy I had with my sister, my constant through the regular upheavals that came with having a diplomat father.

All of that is now lost to me.

The train slows as we approach the next station. We have several more stops to go before we arrive in Dijon. My body is coiled tighter than an overwound rubber band, and my heart beats louder than the never-ending shots from a machine gun. I try to think of happier times to keep the fear from my expression.

I dare a glance at Todd. He must have sensed my turmoil. Our gazes cross, and I can see my fear mirrored back at me. It only takes a second to understand why.

"Tickets and papers." The German voice barks in French from behind me.

I make a show of removing my ticket and *carte d'identité* from my handbag so Todd understands what the soldier wants. And I pray with every ounce of me the enemy doesn't ask him questions.

Todd starts to turn his head as if calculating if he can escape before the train begins moving. I give an almost imperceptible shake of my head, ignoring the rule of pretending not to know him. Todd won't stand a chance if he gives the German soldier reason to believe he's about to flee.

The soldier approaching from behind me steps into view. Without looking at his face, I hand him my ticket and forged papers.

He examines them and hands them back. I almost close my eyes in relief, but it's too soon to feel any sense of the emotion.

The soldier approaching from the other direction is almost level with Todd's seat.

Other than the sharp-commanding voices of the two soldiers, a heart-thumping silence has fallen over the train car. I lower my gaze to my hands in my lap. They weren't shaky when I handed my papers to the soldier, but now a slight tremor grips them as I wait to see what happens with Todd's *carte d'identité*. The Gestapo recently captured the person who forged the papers in my part of the network. This is the first time we will see if his replacement's work stands up to scrutiny.

What if the papers don't appear authentic to the soldier? What if Todd does something to raise suspicion, or worse yet, cast it on me?

I'm not the person who usually escorts fallen pilots along the escape route. The only time my safety is dependent on the actions of another person is when I attend parachute drops. And that...and that is nothing like what I am now facing.

"Papers!" The soldier's German accent drips with arsenic arrogance and sends a shudder clamouring up my spine.

My gaze flicks to Todd. He hands the soldier his *carte d'identité* and his ticket. His expression is calm, no hint his papers should require thorough inspection. No hint his actions require deeper reflection. His expression is that of someone who has done this a hundred times and has nothing to hide.

And for the first time since Todd arrived on Jacques's doorstep, hope flickers to life that he'll make it back to London alive.

Seconds tick by. The soldier keeps inspecting Todd's papers. Fuck. Fear and anger swell in me that the new forger's skills might be subpar. Or that the soldier is taking longer than necessary because, maybe, Todd appears *too* calm.

Shouts rise from the platform outside the window. I whip my head towards the ruckus. A valise lies open on the ground. An officer is removing garments from it and tossing them to the side.

A whistle shrills from farther up the platform. The soldier holding Todd's *carte d'identité* and ticket shoves them at him, and the two soldiers rapidly depart the train.

For a heartbeat, it feels like everyone in the train car takes a collective breath, the strain of the soldiers on the train being too much.

A small amount of tension that had coiled inside me when the soldiers boarded the train eases. And I allow myself a long exhalation, even though we're not safe until the train starts moving. Starts moving without the soldiers on it.

The train eventually lurches onwards. The remainder of the journey to Dijon is free of drama, and we arrive there without further delay.

We depart the train, and I indicate with the slight nod where we must go. The only way out of the station is through the inspection line. There is no way to avoid it.

Todd walks to the queue. I follow him, keeping several people between us. An unearthly silence has settled over the station, except for the hiss of the train, the slap of spit-shined boots against stone, and the bark of impatient commands. It's quiet enough to hear the *death-death-death* pounding of my pulse in my ears.

One soldier at the front of the line searches through valises while the other one inspects travellers' documents. With each second that Todd and I stand in the queue, my body becomes colder.

We shuffle forwards like cows at milking time. A soldier asks for Todd's papers, but it's clear the soldier doesn't normally speak French. He's just repeating the memorised command.

Todd hands them to him.

The soldier scans the documents, passes them back to Todd, and waves him on.

An older man and two women are ahead of me in the queue. The soldier checks their papers and lets them through. I hand him mine. The *death-death-death* of my pulse is now louder than a bass drum.

I keep my gaze on his insignia. There's a time to pay attention to someone's face, to memorise it. This isn't one of those times.

He nods me through, but it's not enough to quieten the pounding in my chest, to warm up my body. That will only happen once I'm safely back at the vineyard.

Todd continues to the exit. I stop, pretending to read the German propaganda stapled to the bulletin board.

I have to bury the urge to rip the poster off the wall and toss it into the rubbish. The station could be swarming with collaborators ready to turn on anyone they view as a threat to the Reich.

I leave the station and head for the outskirts of town. We walk about a hundred yards with Todd ahead of me, but then he stops outside a bakery and looks at the display of empty bread baskets. His shoulders stoop with feigned disappointment. The intentional pause is so I can lead the way without acknowledging him.

The entire time we walk, I'm vigilant of our surroundings. I stop every few minutes so I can check that no one other than Todd is following me.

I eventually pause long enough for him to catch up. "It's not much farther." I take hold of his hand and tug him through the opening in the hedge skirting the road.

Two teenagers are on the other side. Heidi is seventeen, pretty, with her blond hair tied up in two long plaits. She's leaning back against the thick trunk of an oak, gazing at her companion. Christopher's hand is on the bark above her head, his back to us.

Heidi says something quietly to him and straightens. Christopher casually turns and scowls at us as if we're intruding.

"Hello, I'm Carmen. And this is Conrad." I release Todd's hand.

"You're late." Christopher's sharp tone is aimed to puncture but not wound. His scowl deepens.

"German soldiers stopped the train and checked everyone's papers." My words are spoken softly so as not to draw attention should anyone be on the other side of the hedge.

Todd looks between us, not understanding a single word spoken, a concerned frown on his face.

"He doesn't speak French, does he?" Christopher's tone is not one of disgust or distrust, but it is resigned that their job has become more challenging and dangerous.

I shake my head, the movement more of an apology than a reply.

"I can speak a little English," Heidi tells Todd, her English heavy with a French accent. "But I will only use it if absolutely necessary and if no one is around to hear me."

"I understand," he replies.

I hand her a small package. She doesn't ask what is in it. She knows. It's money to pay for Todd's journey to Portugal, especially for crossing the Pyrénées Mountains. The mountain guides charge a fortune for their services and expertise.

I thank the two teens and wish Todd luck on his journey. That's all we have time to say.

The three of them run across the field. I don't wait for them to disappear into the tree line before I turn and head back to the train station.

I don't take the same route I used to travel to Dijon. I board a train that goes in a different direction.

It's late afternoon by the time I arrive at the vineyard. I change into the dress I wear for doing chores around the farmhouse, tuck my always-with-me ID card into the pocket, and I fetch the gardening tools from the shed.

Gardening is the only way I can calm my nerves after coming face-to-face with the enemy. It's been hours since I was in the presence of German soldiers, but my muscles are still knotted with tension.

I'm busy weeding the root vegetables when the crunch of

gravel under moving tyres alerts me to an approaching vehicle. A Jeep. With German soldiers.

My chest tightens. My heart rate picks up. And cold dread spills through my body. There's not enough time for me to push to my feet and sprint to the fields to warn Jacques.

The Jeep rumbles to a stop in front of the farmhouse and the two soldiers climb out.

Bloody hell, why are they here? It's too early in the season to demand we give them the limited food we grow, and Jacques doesn't breed animals. He only has the two older horses, and they aren't much use to the Germans—unless they plan to eat them.

I remain crouched, weighing the possibility of using the trowel to protect myself. According to my SOE training, anything can be turned into a weapon. But attacking two soldiers with a single trowel seems foolhardy.

The soldiers march towards me. I don't recognise them. They aren't the same soldiers who witnessed Pierre kiss me during the last parachute drop.

It's only as the soldiers draw closer that I straighten to my full height. Both men are taller than me, but one of them has a few extra inches advantage. Both are better fed than most people in these parts. Both are blond. Both are soldiers with the Wehrmacht.

"Papers," the shorter soldier demands, his body stiffer than an oak.

The other soldier peers at Jacques's house. If he were from any country other than Germany, he would be considered handsome. I wait a beat for the familiar sneer to appear that I've witnessed on so many of his comrades. His expression remains as neutral as Switzerland.

I remove my *carte d'identité* from my skirt pocket and hand it to the first soldier. The shorter soldier's gaze travels over me. He doesn't leer at me in the way I've come to expect from those of his ilk, but he's still appraising me the same way they all do. It's enough to make me want to climb into Jacques's pond and scrub my skin raw.

The other soldier gives me a brief glance, barely acknowledging me, and his eyes shift to the barn. The same barn that housed Todd for the past two weeks.

They know.

They know Todd was hiding here. Did they capture him while he was escaping? Are they here to punish Jacques and me for our part in harbouring an Allied pilot?

My mind grinds into action, praying there's no evidence of Todd's stay. Praying they don't find the hiding space in the barn.

The first soldier is inspecting my *carte d'identité* when Jacques arrives at the house, his work clothes covered in dried dirt. He doesn't wait for the soldier to demand his papers. He fishes his *carte d'identité* from his trouser pocket and hands it to the soldier.

"Why do your surnames not match?" the shorter soldier asks in broken French.

"Angelique is my widowed daughter," Jacques explains, keeping to the cover, his voice splintered and gruff. "She came to help me after her husband died."

The soldier nods. It isn't clear if he understood what Jacques told him, but his answer seems to be enough.

The soldier reverses a step, and the taller soldier moves forwards. "I am Captain Johann Schmidt." His French skills appear to be better than his comrade's. "I will be billeting with you for the foreseeable future." He hands Jacques a piece of paper, and my stomach sinks to my dusty, worn-out shoes.

The devil has moved into the henhouse, making it bloody impossible for me to do my job.

Making it impossible for me to defeat his kind.

31

JESSICA

March, Present Day
Maple Ridge

I leave through the back door leading to Picnic & Treats and walk along the alley to the front of the building where my bike is locked up. The early afternoon breeze is cool against my skin. Relief swells in me that I made it through my shift without a flashback, without an incident that would leave Zara doubting her decision to hire me.

I pull on my lightweight jacket and let the wound-up tension ease its grip on me. Even though I spent the entire shift flashback free, I couldn't shake the fear that at any moment a sound or touch or smell could set one off.

Not quite ready to go home yet, I head to the library and put several nonfiction books on hold. Books dealing with the Second World War. I've already finished the book I borrowed about Virginia Hall, the American spy in occupied France.

Since I don't have Wi-Fi yet in my house—it will be set up on

Friday—I use the library computer to pull up the website for a national news network. Without a TV, I've been sheltered from what's going on in the world, other than the headlines I briefly glance at in the grocery store.

I skim through the top stories. Nothing has changed during the five years I was locked away. The world is still at conflict. The environment is a growing concern. Politicians are constantly bickering. School shootings are still happening. These stories aren't the ones I was interested in when I was studying journalism. I wanted to focus on the special-interest stories. The stories about women making a difference and their impact on the next generation of girls. The unsung heroes. The women who aren't doing it for power or recognition, but who are applying their passion to make the world brighter.

I do a search on my husband's name, forcing my fingers to type it. A name I prefer not to think about. A list of articles shows up on the screen, articles confirming what I still have trouble believing. He's dead. The monster hasn't crawled out of the grave or the urn or wherever his family put him.

Maybe if I had been allowed to go to his funeral, if I'd seen his dead body in the coffin, I would absolutely positively believe he can no longer find me and kill me. I could finally say with confidence he's my late husband.

I had hoped by now news of his death had faded and his murder was nothing more than a cold case. Or his murderer was behind bars.

And maybe the news of his murder would've been forgotten if my husband had been someone else. But he was a cop. And somewhere out there, a cop killer is still roaming loose.

I scan the articles, and my skin grows itchy. The media's had trouble letting go of the news I was released. It's not so much my innocence they like to focus on. It's how I simply vanished—as if there were an ulterior motive for my disappearance.

There's some speculation I really was responsible for my

husband's death, even if I hadn't been the one who pulled the trigger. I hired someone. The murderer was my lover, and we plotted together. There's also speculation whoever killed him is responsible for my disappearance.

A shudder skids up my spine at the possibility of his killer trying to track me down. But it's also highly unlikely. What would they have to gain? I have no idea who it was—otherwise, I wouldn't have wasted five years behind bars. If anything, they would keep as far away from me as possible. Reduce the risk of them being linked to his murder.

No one accepts that maybe I just needed to get away from my past and go where no one knows me. To piece my life back together without feeling like I'm sitting under a microscope. To go where the media won't be hounding me. To go where my late husband isn't shadowing my life.

One article has a rare photo of me from when I was married. My face is tilted in a way that makes the woman in the picture look less like the one reading the article, especially when you add in our difference in our hair color and the scars now on my face.

I delete the search history, log out of the computer, and bike to the grocery store.

I'm in the produce section when I spot Violet, the woman I met yesterday at the Maple Ridge Veterans Center. She's pushing a shopping cart, her thirteen-month-old daughter in the seat.

Sophie looks so much like my daughter did at that age. The only difference is, Sophie's hair is blond and Amelia's hair is brown. Sophie's hugging a cuddly lamb, and my heart aches. Amelia's favorite toy was her floppy puppy. She wouldn't go anywhere without it.

The shadows under Violet's eyes from yesterday are still there. Shadows similar to the ones under my eyes. She notices me and smiles.

I return her smile and approach them.

"Hi," Violet says. "You're Jessica, right?"

"You can call me Jess. You're Violet, and this sweetheart must be Sophie." I crouch to her level. "Aren't you a little cutie?"

"Mama!" Sophie replies with a toothy grin, and my heart aches some more. I can barely breathe, remembering when Amelia had first called me that.

I straighten and try to think of something to say that won't sound awkward. My ability to socialize and make friends is as rusty as my bike.

"How are you enjoying living in Maple Ridge?" Violet's words eagerly roll out, her tone sweet and welcoming.

"So far, I'm really liking it. The mountains are so close, and I love living within biking distance of a lake." It might not be the ocean, but it's still water. "It's so peaceful there."

"It is. Do you do yoga? I find that's also peaceful. Or it is when I manage to practice without my daughter trying to climb me like a piece of playground equipment." She laughs softly, almost a chuckle, and kisses the top of Sophie's head.

"No, but I've always wanted to try it." It wasn't something that was offered in prison. "Is there a yoga studio around here?" I haven't seen one, but I haven't looked all that hard either.

"Yes and no. It's not an official studio. It's run out of the instructor's home, but the classes are good. I usually go to the Wednesday night session." She pulls out a notepad and pen from her purse, writes down a name, phone number, and address, and hands it to me. "The level I'm in is good for beginners and those with yoga experience."

Her phone plays a tune from her purse. She sighs, fishes the phone out, and answers it. "Hello." The greeting comes out flat, and she winces. "I'm at the store now..." Her voice is soft, almost timid. It's nothing like her tone a moment ago when she was talking to me. "Yes. Yes. I know....I will. I should be home in fifteen minutes....Bye." She ends the call, and an uncertain smile flickers on her face. "I need to get going, but I hope I see you at yoga tomorrow."

Before I can respond, Violet hurriedly pushes the shopping cart away, stopping only long enough to grab a bunch of bananas.

I buy a few items to last me the next couple of days. It's hard to stock up when you don't have a car. But it's not like I have anyone to invite over. Things, though, will be more challenging come winter. How easy will it be for me to bike to the store when the roads are covered in snow?

I pedal home, thinking about Violet and her invitation to join her at yoga. I really would like to. The more friends I have, the better. Friends who aren't necessarily linked to one man. And who won't show him loyalty over me because their boyfriend or husband is his friend.

I park my bike in the garage and walk to the back door of the house. A note is taped to the window. I pull it off and read it. Or try to. It starts with my name and it's from Troy, but the rest of the note is a strange combination of dashes, dots, spaces, and slashes.

Morse code? Maybe. Or it could be some other code I know nothing about.

I check that the thread on the door hasn't been disturbed, unlock the door, and go inside. I place the groceries and note on the kitchen table. Then I rush around the house, checking the rest of my security measures.

Back in the kitchen, I turn on my cellular data, google a Morse code chart, screenshot it, and turn off my data.

I grab a pencil and notepad from the bits-and-bobs drawer, sit at the table, and slowly decode the message:

Are we still on for tonight? There is something I need to talk to you about.

A grin spreads across my face at the effort Troy went through to write the message. All because he noticed my interest in World War II.

I check the time. He's at the Veterans Center, volunteering.

Me: Got your message. Yes. We're still on
for tonight

Troy responds a few minutes later.

Troy: Glad you figured it out

Me: I loved it

Troy: Thought you might. I'll be over in
an hour

Figuring he might be hungry by then, I make dinner for two. The casserole is nothing fancy. While it's baking, I call the number Violet gave me and sign up for the Wednesday night yoga class. I mean, why not? Part of my goal of starting my life over is to also have friends. And I would like to be Violet's friend.

I'M TAKING THE CASSEROLE OUT OF THE OVEN WHEN THE FRONT doorbell rings. I put the dish on the hot pad in the center of the table, walk down the hallway to the front door, and peer through the peephole. The sun is low in the sky, creating a halo around Troy's hair. But even though his features aren't lit, I can tell it's him. Butterscotch is by his side.

I unlock the door and step aside to let them in. I kneel next to Butterscotch and stroke him. It's funny how something as simple as stroking a cute dog can leave me feeling more grounded.

"I made a casserole for dinner," I say, still fussing over Butterscotch. "I mean, unless you've already eaten. It's nothing fancy. I thought we could eat first and then start figuring out the renovation plans."

"I haven't eaten. Thanks."

I straighten to find Troy watching me with a smile. My heart picks up its pace. While I was in prison, I would hear other inmates bemoan how much they missed sex. I swear, some of them were counting the days until they got out to get laid again.

That hadn't been my problem. I figured my husband had broken me so badly, I was beyond repair. But the effect Troy has on me makes me wonder if I was wrong. Maybe I'm not quite as broken as I believed. Not all my bits were smashed into a million tiny pieces and discarded.

And that's...that's kind of a relief. Not that I'm in any rush for that. Not yet.

I lead Troy and Butterscotch into the kitchen. The table has already been set, and I take a seat. Troy follows suit. Butterscotch sits dutifully on the floor by his feet.

"He's welcome to hang out in the living room," I tell Troy and pass him the serving spoon. "The carpet has to be more comfortable than the cold linoleum."

A chuckle rumbles from deep in Troy's chest. A laugh I never get tired of hearing. "You might be right about that." He scoops some casserole onto his plate and hands the spoon back to me. "Have you ever owned a dog?"

"My grandmother had one when I was growing up. A Yorkie. She was really sweet and friendly. Butterscotch would've loved her." I move the casserole dish closer to me and spoon some of it onto my plate.

"I spoke to a therapist at the Veterans Center this morning." His words are spoken with caution, as if he's afraid he's about to step on a land mine. He might have avoided the land mine, but that doesn't stop the warning siren in my head.

"I don't suppose you were talking to them because *you* have issues you want help resolving?" I ask with a faux casualness.

Troy raises his eyebrow in a *What-do-you-think?* gesture.

I respond with a sorry-not-happening shake of my head. "I told you I can't go to therapy. Therapy means you have to tell the person all your secrets. I can't do that."

"Why not?"

"Because there's a reason they're called secrets."

A fractured silence floats in the space between us, a tug-of-war between freedom and impossibility.

"Do you trust me?" he asks.

"I don't know you well enough to trust you."

"Fair enough. Robyn won't share with anyone what you tell her, and that includes me. The only reason she'd have to tell anything to the authorities is if she's concerned you're a risk to yourself or someone else." He looks me squarely in the eyes, and it feels like he's ripping off my layers and staring at my naked truth. "Are you a risk to yourself or someone else?"

It's a rhetorical question, but I shake my head anyway. "No. I'm not."

"You don't have to tell me what happened to you, Jess. But you do deserve to get your life back from whoever or whatever tried to steal it from you. All you have to do is meet with Robyn and see if she'll be a good fit. And for her to determine if you do have PTSD. If you still feel uncomfortable about seeing her after that, I'll drop it."

I push the casserole around with my fork. "And how long will I have to see her for?" I don't bother to look up.

"For however long it takes. Until you no longer have flashbacks and nightmares and any other PTSD-related symptoms."

For all I know, that could take months. Or years. I can't afford that.

I open my mouth to tell him no.

"The state will cover the expense," Troy says, his rebuttal faster than my refusal.

"Really?" That was the last thing I expected—that the state will pay for it.

He nods. "So you don't have to worry about that. You just have to focus on healing."

"Okay." It still seems odd the state will pay for it. Maybe it's an

Oregon thing. "I'll talk to her and then decide if I want to keep seeing her." What can it hurt to meet with her once? Especially if Troy finally lets this therapy thing go.

"That's all I'm asking. I promise, it will make a difference. If you don't believe me, you can talk to Lucas. I'm sure he'd be happy to talk to you about it."

My gaze drops to my food, and I stare at the casserole without seeing it.

Maybe he's right about the therapy. I've hung out with Lucas twice already, and I would never have guessed he has a traumatic past. He and Simone appear so happy, so in love. Would it even be possible for me to feel that way again?

No, because Lucas fought an enemy he didn't know. The man I loved ended up hurting and manipulating me.

But how long do I plan to let him have this hold over me? Don't I deserve to get my life back? A life without nightmares and flashbacks and feeling like I'm trapped in a windowless room with no hope of escape?

I've taken steps to start over, but how much of a new life will I have if I'm still chained to my past?

"No. That's okay." My gaze flicks up to Troy. "I don't need to talk to Lucas. So, when am I supposed to meet with the therapist?"

"I'll call Robyn tomorrow morning and let her know it's a go. I'll get back to you about the day and time. Because you aren't a military vet, she can only see you after she's finished with her clients for the day. That's usually around four p.m."

"I can do that." Then I won't miss any time at work.

Troy smiles, seeming relieved to be finished with this conversation. "How did work go today?"

"It was good. I didn't have a flashback, always a bonus. But you already know that. Zara told you." A small grin plays at the corners of my mouth.

He has the decency to look sheepish.

"How's the planning for the festival going?" I ask, happy to change the direction of the conversation. And because I am interested to hear more about it.

"I need to create several committees. The project's too big for one person to take on. If I can get enough people to help out, it's a go."

"I'll help. I would love to be part of it. I think it's great what you're planning to do." I studied journalism to make a difference, and I still want to make a difference, somehow.

"Are you sure? Given everything you're dealing with, maybe helping with this isn't good for your mental health."

I shake my head. "You're wrong. It's exactly what my mental health needs. But if it makes you feel better, I'll ask Robyn what she thinks. Okay?"

"That would make me feel better. I don't want to set back your recovery because I asked too much of you."

I stab my pasta with my fork, hungry now that I have a purpose, something to feel good about beyond fixing up this house. "What committee am I on, and when do we meet?"

Troy shakes his head, his expression ping-ponging between amusement and exasperation. "Get Robyn's approval first, and then we'll discuss what committee you want to be on."

I grin, enjoying this game between us and hold out my hand for him to shake. "Alright, Mr. Carson, you have yourself a deal. I bet Robyn will be begging you to let me on a committee."

Troy's expression shifts firmly to the amused side of the fence, and he shakes my hand. His brown eyes sparkle warmly in the kitchen light. "Oh, she will, will she? Any particular committee?"

I nod, more enthusiastically than I have in a while. "Anything where writing is involved." The only writing I've done lately is copying out Iris's journals. I still can't believe Iris was Angelique.

I live in a house that once belonged to a freaking SOE agent.

32

TROY

March, Present Day
Maple Ridge

I help carry the dishes to the sink, and Jess fills it with soapy water. The repairs I made to the faucet the other day have held, but the plumbing will need to be updated when we redo the kitchen.

I grab a tea towel. "What are you thinking of changing in here?"

She washes a plate, hands it to me, and looks at the small room. A whiff of her sweet strawberry scent catches me off guard, and I have a sudden need to adjust myself.

She walks to the fridge, which is not quite bordering on being an antique, but it's still several decades old. The rest of the kitchen resembles something from the 1970s, with its avocado-green cabinetry and green floral wallpaper.

"Everything?" She lifts her shoulders in a shrug. "It just looks so old and sad."

"So new cabinets, counters, and appliances?"

"Yes to all of that. And that wall." She points to the one in question that separates the kitchen from the living room. "Would it be possible to knock it down? I'd love to open up the two rooms, so the house feels more spacious."

"Assuming the wall isn't supporting the house, yes, it would be feasible. But you'd be sacrificing cabinet space if you did that." Other than that, it's not a bad idea. "We can always select cabinets that maximize storage space and compensate for the loss of those." I nod at the cabinets on the wall she wishes to demolish. "Which is what I recommend anyway for this kitchen. That way you won't have dead storage space you can't easily access. I can show you what I mean once we've gone through the house."

"That would be great. Thank you."

We finish washing the dishes.

"Do you want a dishwasher?" I ask. There's not really much room for one.

"It's not a big deal. I like washing dishes. It's oddly relaxing. And I'd rather not give up what little storage space I have for a dishwasher. Otherwise, I'll end up using it for storage instead of for washing dishes."

"Got it." I open a cabinet door. There isn't much inside. Only a few boxes of food since there's only so much she can fit in the basket on her bike.

I inspect the labels on the two cereal boxes, and a huge-ass grin spreads across my face. "I take it you like sugary cereals?"

Her shoulders lift with a tiny jerk, and she seems to almost curl in on herself, as if ashamed. I silently curse whatever caused that reaction. She has nothing to be ashamed of.

"I swear my mother thinks she failed me because I still prefer sugary cereals over the healthy crap she thinks I should be eating," I say with a self-deprecating chuckle.

Jess's eyes brighten, and her mouth twitches into a wide smile. "My grandmother loved her sugary cereals. She said that there were very few real pleasures in life, and that was one she was never gonna give up."

"Your grandmother was a wise woman."

Jess laughs, the sound as sweet as the cereal she loves. "She was."

I put the boxes back in the cabinet. "Why don't you show me around the house again and tell me what you're thinking of doing with the place. We'll take measurements and talk options. Like I said on Saturday, it will probably take us several days of planning before we're good to go."

She dries her hands on a tea towel hanging on the oven door. "Okay. Where do you want to start with the tour?"

"How about upstairs? Then we can work our way down."

We walk upstairs and into the tiny bathroom. "I think we can do a lot better than this," I tell her.

The bathroom isn't any different than I remember from the few times I saw it when I visited Iris's house as a kid. It's mostly a sink, toilet, and bathtub. Iris added a tall shelving unit in the corner for storage, and the small round mirror has tarnished with time.

"We can replace everything and add a sink with a counter and storage," I say, mentally visualizing the possibilities. "And add some more shelves for storage and decoration. Make the room as functional and appealing as possible."

Jess nods, seeming to take in everything I tell her. "That sounds like a good idea. This room and the powder room downstairs are the only bathrooms in the house, so I want them both to look nice."

I open up my notepad and sketch the room, noting the location of the sink, toilet, bathtub, door, and the window. I pull out my laser tape measure and with Jess's help, we measure the space. I can do this on my own, and with any other homeowner, I would've asked them to step out of the bathroom.

There isn't a lot of room for two people in here at the same time. But hell if I'm asking Jess to leave when the enclosed space gives me an excuse to be closer to her.

My arm accidentally, not so accidentally, brushes hers. She stiffens for a microsecond but doesn't jerk away. If anything, she seems to linger, leaning in a fraction.

The warmth from her body stokes mine, and I take a moment to inhale her scent again.

It all happens in a heartbeat, but it's enough for me to know what I feel for Jess is beyond simple friendship. It's the desire for something more. I'm just not sure what more we're talking about.

The one thing I do know is whatever this thing is, I need to take my time. No rushing things. Jess needs to be the one in control. To make the first move.

If I'm right and she does have PTSD, I need to give her as much control as possible, and that includes the renovations.

We collect all the information I'll need, and I take photos to remind me of what we're dealing with.

We go into the room that once belonged to Anne's mother. The walls are still pink, faded and dingy with time. The floral bedding looks several decades old and was probably until recently thick with dust.

"I would love to add a window seat." Jess's voice is soft and dreamy, the smile on her face matching it. "Turn it into the kind of place a girl can read and watch the squirrels scamper in the trees."

"Girl? You have someone in mind? Or are you talking about yourself?"

Jess walks to the window and looks down on the street. "No, no one in particular. I...I just...it was just a thought."

"A window seat is a good idea. It would be a great way to add additional storage." I survey what else I'm dealing with in the room. "Are you looking at converting the room into a library? Or do you want it to be a guest room?"

Jess rolls her bottom lip between her teeth. "A guest room.

Something...suitable for a child to stay in. But not only for a little girl. It needs to be good for any age range." The more she talks, the more flustered she becomes, a slight flush creeping up her face.

None of what she's saying makes a lot of sense. Unless...

"Are you thinking of becoming a foster parent?"

My parents did that with Kellan before becoming his legal adoptive parents.

"No, nothing like that. Never mind. It's a really dumb idea." She turns her head away.

I catch her chin with my fingers and guide her face back to me. "Hey, it's not a dumb idea. It's a great idea. We can do whatever you want. What do you want to do about the carpet?" Like everything else, it's got to be at least four decades old.

"Tear it up. I would love to have hardwood flooring. If it's already there. Otherwise, replace the carpet with laminate wood flooring. The same for the rest of the house."

"We can do that." I walk into the closet and pull on the light. Nothing happens.

"I think the bulb is burned out. I haven't had a chance to buy new ones yet."

There's enough sunlight shining through the doorway from the window for me to assess the space. "The bookshelf in there's a good idea. Did you want to have more bookshelves in the room? We could build some in the window nook."

Her eyes brighten. "I love that idea."

"I'll show you downstairs what I'm thinking of once we're done up here."

We continue next with Jess's bedroom, then head down to the living room. Jess tells me some of the ideas she has for the various spaces. We measure the necessary information, and I sketch each room, marking down the windows and doors and anything else I need to keep in mind with the final designs.

Her face glows as she shares her visions for the house. She

doesn't go overboard. She's not trying to turn the house into something it will never be—unless we demolish it and start from scratch.

In the living room, we sit next to each other on the couch, and I pull up a photo on my iPad. "This is what I was talking about for the reading nook in the guest room." I hand the device to her. The image is of a window seat that has bookshelves on either side of it that face each other.

"Oh, Troy, that's perfect." She traces her finger over the shelves and the cushions. "It's even better than what I had in mind. Yes, I want to make that for...for the guest room." If there was a competition between the sun and Jess as to who glows more right now, Jess would be the clear winner.

Just seeing that expression makes me want to do whatever it takes to see it on her face more often. "I'm glad you're happy with it."

"Very happy." She doesn't look at me when she says it. She continues staring at the picture, the dreamy smile back on her face. It's as if that window seat is the most important thing in the world. As if it's the one thing capable of bringing her the most joy.

She was excited about the other changes I had suggested for the rest of the house, but that was nothing compared to her reaction to this photo.

And that makes me even more curious about the woman sitting next to me.

33

JESSICA

April, Present Day
Maple Ridge

L ate Wednesday afternoon, I walk into the waiting area
for the mental health clinic in Maple Ridge Veterans
Center. A visitor's pass hangs from the hem of my long-
sleeved top.

My body is still overly wound-up from my shift at Picnic &
Treats. I feel like I'm going to snap in two after spending hours
worried I'd have a flashback.

The only thing that kept me from snapping like a frayed
elastic was thinking about the picture Troy showed me last night.
The picture of the window seat in Amelia's room, with the built-
in bookshelf inside the reading nook.

The rest of Troy's suggestions for the house were also great.
But it's the window seat that has me the most excited.

I can almost imagine my...I can almost imagine Amelia sitting
there, reading a book.

The receptionist looks like she's getting ready to leave for the day, standing at her desk, and searching through her purse.

"Hi. I'm Jessica Smithson. I have an appointment with Robyn Lawson."

The receptionist glances up from her purse, and a smile crosses her face. "I'll let her know you're here." She picks up her phone and, a moment later, ushers me into Robyn's office.

Robyn's desk is pushed against the wall near the door of the small room, and a couch and love seat take up space along the other two walls. A decorative metal-and-glass bookshelf in the corner next to the love seat, as well as house plants and a ficus, make the room feel less clinical.

The woman stands up from her desk chair, wearing a green military uniform and a friendly professional smile. "Hi, Jessica. I'm Robyn. Take a seat. Whichever one you'd like."

I sit on the light-blue couch. She sits back in her desk chair and swivels it to face me, her desk now behind her. "I thought we could talk a little first and see how I can help you. And remember, whatever you and I discuss will remain between just the two of us, unless I feel that you are a danger to yourself or others. If that's the case, I'm required to report my concerns to the authorities and no one else. Do you have any questions?"

I shift on the couch, unease and caution sitting next to me. "How much will I be required to tell you about my past?"

"The more you tell me about what happened, the better I'll be able to help you, Jessica. I know it's not easy. It never is when dealing with PTSD. If we decide to go forward with your treatment, we'll need to address things you would rather not discuss or remember. But if we both do the work here, by remembering them and putting them in the proper context, you'll eventually be able to move on and not be overwhelmed by your past trauma. And you can once again enjoy the good memories you've been repressing because of it. Is that something you are interested in?"

"Yes." I'm tired of not remembering all the good times I had with Amelia. My memories of her are like ghosts. There, but not quite.

"Good. Can you tell me what happened that might have resulted in the symptoms of PTSD?"

My palms turn clammy, but I bottle down the urge to rub them on my jeans. "You won't tell anyone?"

"What you tell me is held in strict confidence, unless if fits the criteria I mentioned." Her tone is gentle, nonjudgmental.

I suck in a shaky breath and rub my palms on my jeans.

I can change my mind, tell her this isn't going to work, and go home. I can tell her the partial truth and withhold details I'm not comfortable sharing. Or I can tell her everything, all the twisted, painful secrets.

I draw in another shaky breath. "I'm a widow." I can't even look at her as I tell her the rest. I stare at the cream-colored textured rug in front of me. "My husband, a cop, abused me. He seemed like a wonderful man in the beginning." I swallow down the demons of my past, trying to get the rest of my words out. "My husband's abuse didn't start until after we married. He then made sure I couldn't escape him." I skip the part about having a daughter, the real weapon he used to ensure my compliance.

"I was raped. I was demeaned. I was destroyed. I don't know if he had enemies or what happened, but over five years ago, he was murdered in our home. I was there, unconscious at the time. The police found drugs in my system and called it murder-slash-attempted suicide. I woke up shortly before the cops arrived." And went to find Amelia, who was crying in her crib. "At the time, the DA had enough evidence to convict me. I was found guilty, even though I was positive I hadn't killed my husband. Was positive I hadn't purposely ingested drugs." I pick at imaginary lint on my knees, deliberating if that's enough detail for Robyn to get the picture.

Silent seconds tick past while she waits for me to continue.

"But you're not in prison now," she says when it's clear I'm not going to elaborate. "Can you tell me what happened?"

A shudder travels through me just thinking about the rest of the story. As if the first part wasn't bad enough. "About a month ago, new evidence surfaced that proved I wasn't guilty of my husband's death. Someone else pulled the trigger and made sure I was covered in gunpowder residue and blood splatter. So I was released. The cops still don't know who killed him. Whoever it was is still out there."

Out there, and hopefully not giving me a second thought.

"The scars on your face? Did your late husband cause them?"

My fingers instinctively move to the scar by my mouth. "I was attacked while in prison. The guards had a tendency of looking the other way. No one was ever caught."

"I can imagine it's hard to trust after something like that and after your husband abused you."

A dry, sorrowful laugh spills past my lips. "You could say something like that. I had one friend in prison for a short time. But she was attacked. Everyone made sure to avoid me after that. I was bad luck." I finally look up at Robyn. "Shortly before I was released, I was working in the kitchen. Someone came up behind me and shanked me. I almost died. I was found bleeding out on the kitchen floor."

"And now you're constantly looking over your shoulder." It's not a question. Troy has told her that part of my story. The only part he does know.

I nod. "The only difference between my marriage, prison, and now is I'm free now."

Robyn studies me, and it feels like she's trying to peel back my layers and expose my tender insides. "Are you? Are you really free?"

"I can come and go as I please. No one is physically abusing me or playing mind games with me. So yes, I believe I'm free."

She writes something on her notepad. "Troy said you get flashbacks. What can you tell me about them?"

"Nothing, really." I run my palms over my knees. "I don't remember what happens during them."

"How do you feel afterward?"

"Confused. On Monday, I had one at Picnic and Treats." I tell her what happened both before and after I blacked out. "I don't even remember how I ended up on the floor with the knife in my hand. I only remember chopping carrots, and I heard a loud crash."

Robyn shifts the notepad on her lap and leans forward in her chair. "How does it make you feel knowing the killer is still out there?"

"Angry. Frustrated." I close my eyes and release a slow, shaky breath. "Scared." The word comes out as a small rusty squeak.

"Why scared?" Again, no judgment in her tone. Her voice is soft and coaxing.

"Because maybe deep, deep down, there's a part of me that's afraid the killer will track me down and kill me too. Which is irrational, because why bother? Why risk getting caught?"

"You have every reason to be scared, Jessica, after everything you've been through. But you also have the right to feel safe. You might want to file a report with the Maple Ridge Police Department so they're alerted to what happened."

My heart rate picks up at the suggestion. "That won't be possible. I don't trust the police." Here or anywhere.

"After everything you've told me, I can see why. But just think about it." She shifts in her seat. "Now, tell me what you do to relax."

"Relax?" I sink farther back on the couch. "I guess I read. When I moved into the house I'm living in, it was filled with magazines dating back several decades. I've been sorting through them and reading the articles."

"Why are you doing that?"

"Curiosity, mostly. I have a journalism degree. The magazines are like research—the evolution of journalism over the years. I even found articles written by some of the individuals I idolized in college." That's probably not what she was thinking when she asked what I do to relax. But it does relax me...or at least takes my mind off the events of the past ten years.

"Did you do anything with the degree once you graduated?"

"I had great plans for what I wanted to do with it. But then I fell in love. My husband didn't support my career goals, and I eventually gave in to his demands, believing he was right." It was just one brick in the tower of mistakes I've made over the years.

"Do you have any hobbies?"

I laugh, the sound part giggle, part self-deprecating. "I've only been out of prison for two and a half weeks. I haven't had time for a hobby."

"Did you have any hobbies while you were married?"

Yes, because my husband would've loved that. "I wasn't allowed to have hobbies. Not later on, anyway. There wasn't even time for them. Being his wife"—and the mother to our daughter—"was my full-time job."

"What about before you were married? Did you have any hobbies or interests then?"

"I loved photography, especially photojournalism."

"What did you love about it?"

I think about her question for a second. It's been a long time since I've allowed myself to dwell on my love of photography, other than when Emily showed me the wedding photos last week. "I love how the right image can tell a powerful story. It can reveal things in a way words can't. And when you combine the two, it takes storytelling to a new dimension. I love the creativity involved in the process, and I love capturing the contrast between the strength and beauty of the moment."

Just saying the words causes a spark of anticipation for that instant when everything comes beautifully together.

"If you could photograph anything in the world, Jessica, what would you photograph right now?"

Amelia. "Flowers."

"Have you thought of pursuing your love of photography again?"

I shake my head, not daring to think about that possibility.

"Even though you used to love it?"

"My husband took away a lot of things I loved. He smashed my camera because he thought I was having an affair. That was my punishment."

"Tell me about your parents."

I shift once more on the couch, suddenly having trouble getting comfortable, and I tell her about my mother and father and how they abandoned me.

Robyn continues to ask more questions. Some I can answer. Others leave me squirming. She continues jotting notes as we talk.

"Based on the DSM-Five Diagnostic Guidelines," she says after we've been talking for what feels like almost an hour, "I agree that you do have Post Traumatic Stress Disorder. But I don't believe it only stems from the last time you were attacked in prison. It's not due to a single event, which is the definition of traditional PTSD. The years of abuse you faced from both your husband and what happened in prison led to what is now referred to as complex PTSD.

"I believe I can help you, Jessica. It won't be easy. At times it might be emotionally painful, but you won't be doing it alone. We can start with one-on-one sessions every two weeks." She leans back in her chair. "If you get to a point where you're comfortable enough to join a group session, I highly recommend you do. But I do understand your reasons for not wanting to open up to other people about what happened. So, what do you think? Would you like to continue seeing me, so I can help you move forward and reclaim the person you used to be?"

Do I? Yes, I want to reclaim who I was prior to meeting my husband.

But do I want to continue seeing Robyn when I know I'll have to be honest with her and myself?

I chew my lip, contemplating the pros and cons. But in the end, one benefit outweighs all the negatives. This might be the thing that helps me return to being in my daughter's life. "I would like that. Very much."

She smiles, the curve of her lips still professional and kind. "Can you meet the same time next week since today was so I could assess if you have PTSD? After that, we'll meet every two weeks."

"Yes, that will work."

"Good, and in the meantime, I have two assignments for you. The first one is to make a list of all those things you enjoy doing to relax, or maybe they're things you might think you'll find relaxing and want to try out.

"The second assignment is to make a list of the things you used to enjoy doing before you met your husband, and you would like to start doing again. It might turn out you aren't as interested in them as you once were. That's okay. We all grow and change when it comes to our interests. But that's a starting point, at least. Can you do those two things for next Wednesday?"

"Yes, I can." I'm starting yoga tonight, so hopefully I can add that to my list.

"Remember, the interests can be whatever you would like. They can be something as simple as going for a walk. Writing. Photography. Sex. Building cars. Gardening. Anything. Some things might work for one or the other list. And some might work for both. It's up to you. And they don't have to be activities you plan to do next week or next month. It might take many months or a year before you're comfortable to try some of them."

Out of everything she said, my thoughts home in on one word: sex.

In the beginning of my marriage, the sex had been great. It was also great during those times when my husband was loving and affectionate, when I'd thought things were improving and he really was sorry for what he'd said or done.

When I'd thought he was trying to do better.

But then it got to the point where I dreaded it when he came home because I knew what he wanted even if I didn't.

I had once loved sex. Can I really add it to my lists?

Should I add sex to my lists?

34

JESSICA

April, Present Day
Maple Ridge

After dinner, I bike to yoga class, a twenty-minute ride from my house. The sky will be dark by the time the class finishes, but I don't have a choice if I want to do this. And I definitely want to give yoga a try.

"Jess?" Violet walks toward me on the sidewalk, a rolled-up yoga mat under her arm. I dismount my bike and jump the front wheel onto the curb.

"Did you bike here?" Her gaze trails over my rusty transportation.

"I don't have a car. And...and it's a nice night." Heat flushes my cheeks, even though I shouldn't be embarrassed by the state of my bike. The bike is surprisingly sturdy, and it still works.

"Where do you live?" Violet asks. I tell her the street address. "I can easily pick you up on my way here and drop you off after class if you decide to come again. I don't live far from you."

"Are you sure?"

"Absolutely. It'll give me a chance to get in some adult conversation. I don't get out much. Between yoga, grocery shopping, and seeing my neighbor when I drop Sophie off to come here, I hardly see any adults these days. I mean, other than my husband and his friends." Her tone turns timid at the last part. It's possible her husband's friends intimidate her the way my husband's friends had unintentionally intimidated me.

We walk up the path leading to the house. "What does your husband do?" I ask.

"He's the town's chief of police." Violet's voice is barely a whisper.

Prickles of fear throb up my spine, and I slip on a mask with a polite smile painted on. "That's nice."

Violet continues up the path to the house and waits for me at the front door. I steer my bike along a path to the shadowed side of the house, hide the bike where it can't be easily seen from the street, and join Violet.

She knocks on the door. A woman in her late forties opens it, wearing yoga pants and a cropped top.

The woman smiles, giving off a Zen vibe. "Hi, Violet. And you must be Jessica. I'm Shania."

Unlike the smile I gave Violet after learning about her husband's job, the one I direct at Shania is real. "That's right."

"I'm so glad you could join us." She opens the door wider to let us in.

Violet and I step into the house and remove our shoes. Shania takes us into a room just a few feet away with a hardwood floor and no furniture. Delores, Rose, Samantha, and Katelyn are sitting on their yoga mats and chatting.

Rose grins at me, her sparkling hazel eyes so much like Simone's. "Oooh, new blood. I know we've met," she says to me, "but I'm awful with names."

"Jessica. And you're Rose, Simone's grandmother."

"That's right." Her face brightens some more. "I heard you went hiking on Saturday with my granddaughter and her friends —including those very handsome Carson brothers." She giggles, the sound soft and weathered at the edges.

Delores shares the giggle, her eyes glinting with mischief. "That's not surprising. A certain hottie has been visiting her house more than once in the past week."

"Which one?" Rose asks, seeming a little too excited at the news. "Garrett, Kellan, or Troy? All three of them are super sweet. But don't tell them I said that. Those hard-asses probably don't want to be known as sweet."

Delores and Samantha giggle.

"It was Troy," Delores helpfully points out.

Katelyn's lips purse as if she's sucked on an unripe lemon doused with vinegar.

"He's just a friend," I hurriedly tell them. "He's helping me renovate the house."

"For now, maybe," Rose says. "But you just give him time, dear. I'm sure if you're the right woman for him, he'll feel differently." She looks at Delores and Samantha for confirmation, and they eagerly nod at me.

"I'm not looking to have a boyfriend. We really are just friends." Surprisingly, it doesn't feel strange saying that. I didn't have a lot of male friends growing up, but with Troy, it feels right.

Shania hands me a yoga mat, and I roll it out next to Violet's.

The doorbell rings, and Shania leaves to answer it. She returns with a woman my age and introduces Amy to me.

Amy smiles, her gaze dropping for a nanosecond to the scar by my mouth. "Glad you can join us." She goes over to Katelyn, rolls out her mat, and sits.

Katelyn leans close to her and tells her something I can't hear. Amy glances at me with wide-eyed astonishment, and my self-consciousness increases two notches.

Shania begins the lesson soon after, and it doesn't take long before yoga is the first item on the list of activities that relax me. It's the only item on the list, but it's a start.

We end the session with meditation, which involves clearing the mind. But clearing the mind is as easy to do as swimming in the ocean during a hurricane. My thoughts race all over the place. To my time in Beckley. To my marriage.

To Troy.

To the assignments Robyn gave me. To work.

And back to Troy.

To Angelique's journal. To the Morse code message Troy left me.

And that circles me back to Troy. So much for meditating with an empty mind.

After class, Violet walks me to my bike. "Let me give you my number, and I can pick you up next week."

"Are you sure that's okay with you? I don't want you to go out of your way if it's any trouble."

"Honestly, it's no trouble at all."

"Thank you." I tug a smile on my face again. I want to spend more time with Violet and get to know her better. But the thought of her husband being Maple Ridge's chief of police makes my stomach churn and burn.

Hopefully I never have to meet him. I don't care if he ends up being a nice guy. Just. No.

THURSDAY AFTER WORK, I SIT ON THE COUCH AND CONTINUE WHERE I left off last night with Robyn's assignment. I began brainstorming the lists after I got home from yoga. Combined, the two lists contain only six items.

I type on my phone the word that's been buzzing in my head for the past few hours.

Photography.

It's been over seven years since I last held a camera. Is it like riding a bike? You never forget?

I turn on my phone's cell data—thankful my Wi-Fi will be set up tomorrow—and google prices for the Canon camera body similar to the one I once owned. The camera, the sturdy tripod, and the lens I'll need add up to well over two thousand dollars.

Ouch.

I'm not all that surprised. I'd worked two part-time jobs to earn enough for the gear while I was in college.

Two years. That's how long it took me to save for the camera and gear. Two years of working two jobs, of sacrificing time spent with friends, of balancing work and school. But it had been worth it.

It took me two years to buy everything I needed to produce beautiful, award-worthy photos.

It had taken my husband ten seconds to destroy it.

I delete *photography* and come up with a few more items, including canoeing and hiking, before putting the assignment aside.

Troy called three hours ago to see if I was free later this afternoon. He told me he was driving me somewhere but wouldn't tell me where. According to him, it's a surprise.

Hopefully, it's a better surprise than the one for the cost of the camera and gear.

One bad surprise is more than enough.

35

ANGELIQUE

May 1943
France

Jacques reads the document Captain Schmidt handed him that states Schmidt will now be residing in the farmhouse. The paper trembles in Jacques's hand. "It says all current occupants are required to vacate the premise."

So, the captain misspoke when he said he would be billeting with us. He meant he would be confiscating Jacques's home for his own use.

And now Jacques will be homeless. Scalding heat pulses through my veins, but there is nothing I can do. The captain is the occupier. We're just the pests he's been given the rights to get rid of.

The shorter soldier's brow crunches into a frown, and he glances at Schmidt. Schmidt translates in German more or less what Jacques stated.

"There is no need for you to leave," Schmidt tells Jacques in

French. "But if you are unable to reside in the same household as me, yes, you will be required to vacate the premise."

Jacques's gaze returns to the shorter soldier. "You are staying here, too, *non*?"

"No, it will only be me," Schmidt replies, answering for the other soldier. "First Lieutenant Fischer will reside in the village while our regiment is stationed in the area."

Dread and contempt roil in my stomach at what Schmidt's presence means. I need to find another safe house in the region so I can keep doing my job, but what will happen to Jacques? I'm here under the pretext that I'm helping my papa after losing my husband. How will it look if I leave?

"I take it she isn't too impressed with you staying here," Fischer says in German. Amusement curls his lips. It's not a sardonic smile. It's the smile schoolboys give their best mates.

And that accent.

I know that accent.

Lieutenant Fischer isn't German born. He's from Austria, or he spent a good portion of his childhood there, making the accent more permanent. And since the men's accents are identical, Schmidt is from the same place.

"Can you blame her for not being too impressed?" Schmidt responds. "Do you think Anja would be thrilled to have the enemy living under her roof?" He presses his lips into a fine line as if the thought of that angers him.

"I assume you wouldn't want the enemy living with her either. But these two do not have a choice. Not unless you've changed your mind about residing here."

"No, that hasn't changed." Schmidt's reply is abrupt. His tone is no longer angry. It's determined.

Frowning, Jacques watches the two men. He doesn't understand what they're saying, nor does he realise they are from Austria. But it doesn't matter if they were born in Germany or Austria or East Prussia; they are still Wehrmacht soldiers.

They are still the enemy.

The enemy who will make my job more difficult.

And Jacques and I can no longer listen to the BBC French news. The news about what is really going on in the world. The news Hitler doesn't want people to hear. The news that relays coded messages from London to those of us fighting underground in France.

It's illegal to own a radio in France, never mind listen to it.

"I'll show Captain Schmidt to his room," I tell them, slipping easily into French. I can only hope the man won't demand to exchange rooms with me, especially given what I have hidden under my floorboard.

If those items are found, it will result in my execution or have me sent to prison.

Fischer says a few words of farewell, then climbs into the Jeep. The driver starts the engine, and they depart, leaving Schmidt, a duffel bag, and a cloud of dust behind.

I move closer to Schmidt with the caution of someone approaching a rabid dog. "I can show you to your room now if you wish, Captain Schmidt."

Jacques turns around and heads for the vineyards without a single word spared for Schmidt or me. My heart goes out to him and the latest injustice he has to endure.

"Thank you, Madame D'Aboville. You may call me Johann."

The offer for me to use his familiar name startles me, and my eyebrows draw together ever so slightly. It would make more sense for him to enforce that I use his military rank and surname. A reminder we aren't on the same level. That he is, in the Germans' eyes, superior to me. Suggesting I use his familiar name removes some of the inequality between us.

His request makes me trust him even less. But the lack of trust goes both ways, and perhaps I can use this situation to my advantage. "You may call me Angelique."

He smiles. It's a pleasant smile. The kind of smile that no

doubt has women flocking and flirting and floozying with him. Women who like a man in uniform. In German uniform.

He picks up his duffel bag from the ground and follows me into the house. Upstairs, I lead him to the small room at the end of the hallway, the room situated next to mine.

"I hope this room is suitable for you?" I open the door to a room that once belonged to Jacques's son. The room was dusty when I first came here, but I tidied it up as a way to say "thank you" to him for turning his home into a safe house.

Safe house. That's the last thing you can call the farmhouse with a German officer staying here.

Anger pours into my veins like molten metal, burning and consuming me. Jacques's son is missing, presumed in a German prison camp. And now a German officer will be staying in his old room.

I push down the pain I feel for Jacques and pick up a box of old toys I left on the desk when I was searching for hiding spots. "If you can give me a few minutes, I will clean the room and change the bedding." I use a tone that has never had much exercise. The tone of a meek housewife.

I expect Schmidt to demand to see the other bedrooms, to throw his rank of captain in my face. Instead, he removes the box from my arms. "Let me help you with this. Where do you want me to put it?"

"It can go in the attic."

I grab a box filled with sewing supplies that once belonged to Jacques's wife. It feels disrespectful to Jacques and his family's memory to put their things in the attic. But it's better to put their possessions up there than to have Captain Schmidt burn them or demand I give them away.

Schmidt helps me move the boxes into the attic. We don't talk. I get the sense he is mentally somewhere else, somewhere far from here. If only that was also true when it came to his body.

I open the bedroom window, dust, sweep, and make up the

bed, all while silently hurling colourful curse words at him. In several languages.

Schmidt is downstairs in the drawing room, reading, when I enter to tell him his room is ready. "Thank you, Angelique." He closes the book and sets it on his lap. I recognise it. The classic French novel belongs to Jacques.

"Will you be staying for dinner, Captain Schmidt?"

"Johann. Yes, if that isn't an imposition on such short notice."

It is, but I don't expect that will make a difference. "We don't have much food. The butcher was out of meat rations for the week."

"That's fine. I'll ensure from now on there is more food made available to you. I plan to invite some of the officers for dinner tomorrow evening. Will that be all right with you? There will be seven in total."

My stomach turns at being in close proximity with that many Nazis. It's bad enough to be near them when I'm outside these walls. "I'm not familiar with how to cook your German foods."

I lived in Austria as a teen, but I wasn't involved in preparing our meals. We had a housekeeper who did that. And all the cookbooks in the farmhouse are for French cuisine. French cuisine that wasn't designed for our meagre war rations.

Schmidt smiles, but this time he has the same amused mischief in his eyes that Mark Willmott had in Year Two when he put a tadpole on Miss Noble's chair. "That's fine. If Germany insists on us being here, they had better get used to the local fare."

I nod. He doesn't want to be here? That makes two of us. I don't want him here either. "What time do you want dinner served?"

"We'll eat tomorrow at twenty-one-hundred hours."

"And what about this evening? Do you wish to dine at the same time?"

He gives me a peculiar glance that says he thinks I'm being daft. "I'll eat when you and your father eat."

I almost choke on my own tongue. "You plan to eat with us?"

"Yes, if that is all right with you." He flashes me another of his smiles that at one time would have had me blushing and giggling.

But betrayal and war harden you. Change your priorities.

I nod once more because it's not as if I can say no. "Well, I'll leave you to..." To do whatever evil does at this time of day.

"I'm going for a walk."

"Well, I hope you enjoy your walk," I say without so much as a smile.

I slip into my room and move the ceramic vase to the left side of my windowsill, signalling to the local resistance group the farmhouse is no longer safe.

I watch as Schmidt steps out of the house and crosses the gravel driveway. He heads for the barn.

My insides tighten and knot and pray. Pray he doesn't go inside. That he'll walk past it. Because what if he goes inside and finds the hiding space? With the bed and lamp there, it's impossible to miss what the storage cellar was being used for.

He opens the side door and steps into the barn. I wait for him to leave, my hands gripping the windowsill. Venus, the vineyard's other barn cat, black like a shadow, disappears around the corner, but there's still no sign of Johann.

And I wait...and I wait...and I wait.

Is he searching the barn, looking for contraband? He won't find the radio there. It's hidden where he can't find it in the house. But the hiding space in the barn will be incriminating enough.

After several more minutes and still no sign of him, I hurry downstairs, slip on my shoes, and leave the house.

My foot touches the dirt ground as Schmidt steps out of the barn. His expression appears neutral. It's not the expression of a

German officer who's just found something the Nazis would frown upon. Or more specifically, would execute someone for.

Relief rushes from me in a soft breath, and I walk towards him. "I'm going to feed the horses," I say as though I owe him an explanation for leaving the house.

"Is it all right if I come with you?"

"There is nothing stopping you from doing that." My tone comes out more splenetic than expected, and I wince.

Be careful. He might not be an SS officer or Gestapo, but that doesn't mean I can afford to be disrespectful.

Schmidt releases a long, frustrated sigh. "I know I'm not a welcome guest here, Angelique."

"You're not a guest." This time my voice lacks the previous bite to it. The tone is soft, deferent. The opposite to how I feel. "Under German rule, as long as you're staying here, this is your house." And Jacques and I are the unpaid staff.

"My house is in Vienna. That is my home. This house"—he points at the brick building—"belongs to you and your father."

I'm positive others of his rank would believe otherwise. And that makes me wonder why he is so different from the rest of them.

I go into the barn and bend to pick up some hay to load into the wheelbarrow.

Before I get that far, Schmidt scoops the hay up, puts it into the wheelbarrow, and grabs the handles. "Lead the way."

We head to the small field where the two Breton horses live. Their light-brown sturdy bodies and their cream-coloured manes and tails are a soothing sight after my stressful day.

Esprit spots me and plods to the fence. She leans over and nuzzles my face.

"Hello, beautiful," I say softly to her. I hug her sun-warmed neck and breathe in her scent. I would whisper to her about my day like I normally do, but with Schmidt standing behind me, that isn't a good idea.

I release her and take a small step back.

"She's beautiful." Schmidt gently strokes the other side of her neck. She doesn't jerk her head away. She just nickers.

And I stare at Schmidt as if he has transformed into woodland fairy folk.

"What?" he asks, sounding slightly perplexed.

"She usually doesn't let strangers touch her." It took me a while to gain her trust.

"I grew up around horses," Schmidt says by way of an explanation.

"Are you responsible for the Army animals? Are you a veterinarian?"

He pats her neck. "I love animals, but I wasn't interested in being a veterinarian. I'm a mechanical engineer."

So, he's intelligent. I inwardly let out a hard breath. His intelligence will make things more challenging and dangerous for me when it comes to my job. "Your family has horses?"

"No, friends of my family have horses. Or they did before the war. I haven't seen them in several years."

"You haven't been home all this time?" I thought German soldiers got to go home every so often to see their families. But maybe that leave of absence doesn't apply to soldiers from Austria. They have farther to travel.

"I have returned to Vienna once or twice since I was...how do you say? Conscripted. But that was not where my family lived."

An emotion flickers so quickly on his face, I barely have a chance to grasp hold of it. Pain? Regret? Grief? Possibly something else?

"Lived? Where are they living now?"

"It doesn't matter." He strokes Esprit again, his rough tone implying the conversation has ended.

The rest of the feeding of the horses falls into silence. It is not exactly an uncomfortable silence, but it is one that reminds us we are on separate sides of the war.

TENSION HOVERS OVER THE TABLE AS SCHMIDT, JACQUES, AND I SIT for our evening meal in the kitchen. The tension is more pronounced with Jacques and myself, our bodies refusing to relax. Schmidt acts like he's joining us for a friendly family supper.

He eats a spoonful of the stew I prepared. It is not what he is used to eating. The stew is mostly watery vegetable broth. "Thank you, Angelique, for the fine food."

Jacques doesn't look up from his bowl, but no one at the table can miss his quiet snort of derision.

I do my best not to grin at my stew at his reaction. A response like Jacques's in the presence of any other German soldier or Milice or Gestapo would not end well. They relish any excuse to remind us of who is in power. But Schmidt doesn't respond that way. He seems to squirm in his chair and continues eating.

"Captain Schmidt will have some officers visiting for dinner tomorrow," I say, more as a warning for Jacques than to inform him of the plan.

Jacques scowls at Schmidt. The captain doesn't see it. He's busy fishing a piece of carrot from his bowl.

"I'll be in the barn, repairing tools." Jacques's words are muttered, the anger in them simmering beneath the surface. He stands, leaving me to wonder if he means he'll be repairing the tools now or tomorrow when the enemy will be prowling in his house.

Jacques storms out of the kitchen, and a moment later, the front door slams shut. A harsh silence settles over Schmidt and me and stretches like a run in a stocking.

We focus on finishing what's left of our food. Once the bowls are empty, I carry them to the sink and proceed to wash the dishes.

Schmidt is examining the faded photos on the side cabinet in the drawing room when I go in a short while later.

"Who is this?" He shows me the framed photo in his hand.

The young woman in the picture has long dark hair and delicate features. She looks nothing like me.

"She's my sister. She died several years ago in childbirth." Most of that is true. She is, though, Jacques's real daughter.

Schmidt scans the room. "Are there no pictures of you?"

"My papa and I had a falling out when I fell in love with a man my family didn't approve of. But I am back now, and my relationship with my papa is better."

Better at least with my fictitious father. My real father was happy I was gifted with the ability to easily pick up new languages. But he always viewed my sister as the perfect daughter. The daughter who would never rock the bloody rowboat the way I would.

I doubt, if he were alive, he would approve of what I'm doing in France. Not because he would have supported the Nazis. He wouldn't have. It's because I'm a woman, and a woman is incapable of doing a man's job. In his mind.

It's the same sentiment shared by the male agents the SOE section F recruited. Sexist buffoons, the lot of them.

"Did you love him?" Schmidt asks.

"My husband?"

He nods.

"Very much." My voice sounds croaky like I've swallowed a pond full of frogs. I did love Charles when we got engaged. I had envisioned us one day having two children—a girl and a boy—and being a happy family. "What about you? Do you have a wife back home?"

Perhaps the mysterious Anja I heard you talking to Lieutenant Fischer about?

A dark look of foreboding looms in Schmidt's expression. "Please do not ask me any more on that topic."

36

TROY

April, Present Day
Maple Ridge

"So how come you need me to tag along with you to your friends' house?" Jessica asks from the passenger seat of my truck. Butterscotch is sitting on her lap, looking out the side window as we leave Maple Ridge. The weather is perfect for the drive along the highway. Cloudy, but with no rain or snow in the forecast.

We're on the way to Dylan and Jenny's ranch house so I can discuss their renovation plans with them.

"Because you, Butterscotch, and I are also going to visit their golden retriever puppies."

"Puppies?" Jess practically squeals the word. "Why didn't you say so before? That's just what Robyn ordered."

"Robyn ordered you to visit puppies?"

"No, not in so many words. She gave me two assignments yesterday. One is to come up with a list of hobbies—past hobbies

266

and new ones I might like to try. The other is to create a list of things that relax me. And what's more relaxing than visiting adorable puppies?"

I take my eyes off the road long enough to briefly stare at her. That's gotta be the most Jess has ever said to me when I've asked her a question or tried to get her to open up. Usually, she doesn't say much beyond the minimal. The only exception was when we talked about her renovations. "Have you started your lists yet?"

"I have."

"Can you tell me what's on them? Or is that a secret?"

She laughs the sweet sound that's a treat to hear. The sweet sound I'm becoming addicted to. "I don't think they qualify as a state secret. So far, I only have a few items. The lists are a work in progress. I went to yoga last night. I enjoyed it, so that's now on my relaxation list."

"That sounds like a good start. What else?"

"When it comes to hobbies, I've got writing, which isn't so much a hobby as an old career plan. But I was thinking if you need someone with strong writing skills to help bring awareness to your festival, I could do that. Maybe I could write some special-interest articles for local newspapers."

I give Jess a double take, wondering what happened to the quiet woman I met two weeks ago. This woman is vibrant and smiling. It isn't because of one session with Robyn. It takes a helluva lot more than that for someone to cope better with PTSD. Plus, the change started before that, but it was too subtle to notice at first. Whatever the reason, I love seeing Jess like this.

"Are you volunteering to be part of the PR and marketing committee?" I ask. Because that doesn't sound like a bad idea—as long as Robyn doesn't see an issue with it. Jess mentioned on Tuesday that she would love to do something involving writing. The PR committee would be perfect for her.

"I don't have much experience in either of those areas, but sure, I can help with that committee. Maybe I can interview individuals who were diagnosed with PTSD and their families who benefited from assistance. Then I can show what it meant for them and how the festival will benefit so many people."

"That sounds like a great idea. Did Robyn say it would be okay for you to help with the event planning?" I didn't bring it up when I talked to her this morning, when she called to tell me Jess had agreed to see her on a regular basis.

My question is met with silence. "Did you ask her?" I prompt Jess again.

"I forgot." The pitch of Jess's voice drops to a whisper. "I'm so sorry." I turn in time to catch her shoulders curl in on themselves as if bracing against a storm.

What the hell?

My eyes go back to the road. "Hey, that's okay. You can ask her next time. Your first priority is you and your mental health. The rest can wait. What else is on your hobby list?"

"I was flipping through some of Iris's magazines and came up with knitting, making jewelry, and calligraphy."

"You don't sound too excited about them." Underwhelmed would be a better description.

A rush of air pushes past her lips in what sounds like a slow leaking tire. "Like I said, it's a work in progress."

"That's okay. What about your relaxation list? Any luck with that?"

"That one is easier. Yoga. Hiking. Watching the sunset. Biking. Reading. Listening to music." She mumbles something at the end I don't catch.

"What was the last one?"

"Nothing you need to worry about. I'm still working on the list. What do you like to do to relax?"

A chuckle rumbles deep in my throat, and my gaze flicks to her again. "Are you trying to steal some of my ideas for your own?"

Her shoulders lift in a shrug, and she grins. "Maybe."

"For me, it's hiking, watching sunsets, biking, walking and playing with Butterscotch. But hammering relaxes me as well, especially when I get into the rhythm. And sex. That's definitely relaxing."

She snort-laughs. An adorable flush spreads across her face.

"What?"

"Nothing." She chews on her bottom lip and strokes Butterscotch. "I'm guessing you get to do that often."

"Have sex? Not really. I haven't had sex in several months." A red car turns onto the road ahead of us, and I ease on the gas. Other than that, the highway is relatively quiet when it comes to traffic. "What about you? When was the last time you were with a guy?" It's only after the question has left my mouth that I remember Zara told me Jess recently got out of a bad relationship.

"You mean for sex?" she asks.

"Yep. For sex."

"I don't remember. It's been a really long time."

"Define 'really long time.'" *How long ago did your relationship end?* "Are we talking months?"

"More like years."

Damn. "How many years are we talking about?" I keep my tone light. Not exactly teasing, but more along the lines of not pushing her to answer.

"Six or seven. Maybe more."

I can't quite make out the emotion in her voice. Embarrassment, guilt, shame, maybe fear? *Fuck.* Is that why she has PTSD? Was she raped?

But if that's the case, what did she mean about the bad relationship? Was her ex an insensitive asshole because she hadn't gotten over what happened to her? Did he make her life miserable because she wasn't ready to have sex yet?

I have too many questions. Questions I don't have the right to ask.

"I'm sure once you've met the right person, you'll be ready to have sex again." I flash her a quick, hopefully reassuring smile, but she doesn't see it. She's looking out the side window at the flat ranchland. The grass isn't yet green. It's just the early shoots poking through everything that is dead and brown. Two horses are galloping across the field as if racing us.

Dylan and Jenny's house is located about forty minutes outside of Maple Ridge. Jess and I spend the rest of the trip talking about little things. Nothing that gives me more insight into who she is. But she does seem more at ease when the topic isn't focused on her, so I let her take the lead.

We steer down the gravel driveway. The sprawling, two-story ranch house at the end of it has been in Dylan's family for the past three generations. I park the truck in the driveway in front of the house, and the three of us climb out of the vehicle.

I guide Jess and Butterscotch up the stone steps to the wrap-around porch and press the doorbell. A moment later, a flood of welcoming puppy barks approaches the front door. They don't sound as young as they did the last time I was here. These guys are about four months old now.

"Sit," a voice commands from the other side of the door. I assume they obey because Jenny doesn't have to repeat it.

"Quiet." Other than one protesting bark, a muffled silence descends from her side. "Stay."

The door opens, and Jess is rewarded by the sight of five puppies sitting on the floor, looking like they're dying to come over and greet us, their expressions eager. Jenny and Dylan have done a great job training them. But I already knew that. Jenny has been training psychiatric service dogs for five years.

I step inside the house. Jess follows me, and I introduce her to Jenny.

Jenny knows the real reason we're here. She also understands I don't want Jess to know about it. Not yet.

"I'm so happy you could make it," Jenny tells us. "You can pet them if you'd like," she says to Jess, who looks like she's barely restraining herself from doing just that. Butterscotch sits next to my feet, knowing the drill when we come here. But I also know he's itching to play with the larger-than-him puppies.

Jess kneels and extends her hand for the puppies to sniff. All look at Jenny for guidance. She nods at them, and they approach Jess, tails wagging, unable to hold back any longer. Jess laughs softly at just how eager they are for her attention, and I watch the strain that always hovers in her lessen. Like it does when she interacts with Butterscotch.

Jenny watches Jess with the dogs, an approving smile on her face. She nods at me, and I understand what she's saying. She can tell Jess is the perfect candidate for one of their dogs. "How 'bout we go into the living room so we can talk?" she suggests.

We walk through the house and step into the sprawling living room that has a spectacular view of the ranch and the mountains in the near distance. The puppies and Butterscotch come with us.

Jess sinks to the floor and strokes the puppy next to her with a light-pink collar. The puppy is bigger and four months older than the others. Bailey.

Dylan enters the room through the kitchen door. Some of the puppies tumble over to him, happy to absorb his affection too. He scratches each golden retriever behind the ear.

Bailey presses her body into Jess's side. The puppies aren't ready yet to be psychiatric service dogs. They need to complete their basic training before they're eligible for the advanced PSD training. But after talking to Jenny, who conducts the training with the dog owners, she felt this might work. Unlike some of the people Jenny has worked with, Jess can at least leave her house.

Jess stops stroking Bailey. Her eyes scan the area, and I recognize the sudden stiffness in her body and her alert gaze. Her hand is frozen midair, her face pale.

"Jess?" I ask since I'm not a hundred percent positive she's having a flashback.

She doesn't respond.

I survey the room, using all five senses, and search for potential threats or a trigger. It's not only about what is visible. But without knowing what happened to Jess, it's impossible for me to know what set her off.

Dylan walks toward us. Jess's hand trembles violently, her breathing fast and shallow.

I raise my hand to stop his advance, my gaze remaining on Jess. She's not even looking at him, but I'm positive something about Dylan has triggered a flashback or some other reaction.

Understanding what I'm getting at, Dylan retreats several slow steps but doesn't leave the room.

I crouch in front of her. "Jess," I say, careful to keep my voice low and calm. "You're having a flashback. You're safe. We're in Jenny and Dylan's house, and we're visiting their golden retriever puppies. Can you describe the living room for me?"

Butterscotch whimpers and licks her hand. Bailey barks, and Jess blinks herself back to the here and now, her hands still shaking.

I want to gather her in my arms and soothe her, but I know better than to do that right now. I don't need to make things worse for her. "Jess, try taking slow, deep breaths."

She nods, her face still pale, and inhales and exhales slowly for several beats.

"Can you describe the living room?" I repeat. It's a grounding exercise I once read about that's supposed to help someone experiencing a PTSD episode.

She glances around. "The sectional couch is dark gray, like a storm cloud. The furniture is a dark-red wood. It's very nice furniture, by the way." The last part is directed at Jenny.

Jess strokes Bailey.

"Do you remember why we're here?" I ask.

She nods, the color slowly returning to her face. "You're doing renovations to their house, and we're here so you can discuss the plans. And so I can meet their adorable puppies." She continues stroking Bailey.

"That's correct. They are adorable. And they'll eventually become psychiatric service dogs. But before they go through the advanced training, they're fostered out to puppy raisers. And that's the other reason we're here."

"The younger puppies are going to their new foster parents soon," Jenny explains. "The person who was going to be Bailey's foster parent had to back out of the program. Troy thought you might be interested. She's older than the other puppies, but she's also more advanced in her regular training."

Most of what Jenny is saying is true. But she also agreed Jess is a good candidate for a psychiatric service dog based on what I told her. Because it was hard enough to get Jess to agree to therapy, I can't tell her the goal is for her to become Bailey's adoptive parent.

Jess looks wistfully at Bailey. "But...but I don't know anything about raising service dogs."

Jenny lowers herself to the floor near where Jess is sitting. "You clearly love dogs. And Troy told me you grew up with a dog. If you're interested in being Bailey's foster parent, I'll teach you everything else you'll need to know. We'll do one-on-one training sessions together. We can do a fair amount of them online to make things easier for you. Bailey likes you, so you're the perfect match." In more ways than Jess realizes.

Jess looks briefly at me, emotions warring in her eyes. Uncertainty. Longing. Worry. Her gaze returns to Bailey and then Jenny. "Won't she have to go everywhere with me? For her training?"

"That's right."

Jess shakes her head, her shoulders drooping. "I work in the kitchen of a café. She won't be allowed to be with me there. I'm sure it would violate the health department regulations."

"How's the job going so far?" I ask. Zara told me Jess hasn't had any more flashbacks at work since Monday, but she's been tense and jumpy all week. As if waiting for another flashback to hit, desperately trying to fight it before that can happen.

"Good?" Her answer stumbles out and is coated in doubt.

"Maybe it's not the right job for you, Jess. You need one where you're not so tense all the time."

"I'm not tense all the time." Her tone isn't defensive—more like defeated.

I raise an eyebrow. She shrugs, clearly knowing Zara has kept me updated.

"Ideally, Bailey should be with you at all times," Jenny says, "like she would be for someone who needs a service dog." She exchanges a quick questioning glance with me. "But I'm sure you'll figure something out."

"I get around a lot on my bike since I don't have a car. That's probably not safe, especially since she's a puppy."

I've anticipated Jess's concern. "I have access to a trailer that two young kids used to ride in whenever their father went biking. We can train Bailey to ride in it."

"And once she's older," Jenny says, "you can train her to run alongside your bike. I can help you with that. I'll also give you tips on training her so she's okay with riding in the trailer."

"Raising a puppy isn't cheap. What with the food and the vet bills." Jess stares at Bailey, wiggling her bottom lip between her teeth. "I'm about to do renovations on my house and my job at Picnic and Treats isn't exactly stable." She might be saying that, but the longing to be Bailey's puppy raiser is bright in her eyes.

Dylan takes a cautious step toward us, but still maintains a distance between himself and Jess. "We do have some funding that helps to subsidize the cost."

Dylan had already explained it to me. The money comes from donations. Most puppy raisers volunteer to cover the cost themselves, but the funding is for those individuals who'd be great puppy raisers but the expense would otherwise prevent them from helping. Some of the money raised from the festival will be used for situations like Jess's. For people who struggle with PTSD and who would benefit from a psychiatric service dog but need some financial assistance for that.

Jess smiles at Bailey, the movement a small tilt of the lips. "What do you think, Bailey? Do you want me to be your foster mommy?" Her voice catches on the last word.

Bailey places her paw on Jess's lap, and Jess's smile widens. "I take it that's a yes."

37

JESSICA

April, Present Day
Maple Ridge

Nine days after I became Bailey's foster parent, Bailey and I are standing on Simone and Lucas's sidewalk, watching Troy, Lucas, Garrett, and Kellan play street hockey. Simone, Zara, and Emily are with us, helping to cheer the guys on.

Avery is also here, but Noah is at work. Much to my relief.

The four brothers aren't the only ones playing the game. Six kids under the age of ten have joined them, not at all bothered by the late morning chill.

Bailey is sitting next to me, wearing her red *Service Dog in Training* vest. I give her another treat to reward her for staying in place. She and I have been working hard together for the past ten days, focusing on her obedience training and training for public access.

A girl, wearing a hockey jersey and with cornrows tied back in a ponytail, easily steals the ball from Kellan and scores on Garrett. Simone and I jump up and down from the sidelines, cheering. "Go, Autumn!"

The nine-year-old grins at us, her warm copper skin the same color as Zara's. Her teammate, who's also her cousin, hugs her.

"She's really good," I say to the four women standing next to me. "I might not know much about hockey, but even I can see that."

"According to Kellan, who coaches her hockey team," Emily says, "she's a natural. And she's extremely driven. She has already decided she wants to one day play for the USA women's team."

I rub my hands together, trying to warm them up. "Wow, that's impressive. At nine, I had no idea what I wanted to do with my life." And I'm pretty much back to that point now that I'm starting my life over as someone else.

The two teams set up in the middle of the quiet street. Emily puts the tennis ball on the ground between the two centers, and the game resumes.

Autumn steals the ball from another player and passes it to Troy. He nails it past Garrett, who just misses it.

"Yay, Troy!" I yell, jumping up and down again—partly to warm up. I don't remember San Diego ever being this chilly in April. My sweater is warm, but not when you're standing outside this long.

But I don't care.

I'm having so much fun.

Troy high-fives his teammates, giving them each a goofy handshake I can't describe let alone replicate.

The kids on his team say good-bye to a boy with ginger hair who has to leave because his family is going out of town.

Troy talks to the boy for a moment. It's obvious the kids adore Troy, and he's so great with them.

He tosses a grin my way, and the look he gives me almost heats me up. Not that I'm about to admit that to anyone.

Carrying the extra hockey stick, Troy walks over to the five of us on the sidewalk. "You're up, Smithson." He holds the stick out to me, a challenge in his eyes.

My stomach plummets to the road. "Me?" The word comes out on a squeak. "I don't know anything about hockey." Or any sports. As a kid, I was usually the last one in gym to be picked to play on a team.

"All you have to do is get the puck into the goal Lucas is guarding. Pass it to the kids on your team as much as possible. They'll do the rest." He flashes me those smoldering eyes that would get even a nun to do his bidding. Warmth flutters in my belly.

"But I won't be very good. I don't want to let the kids down." I glance at said kids who are jumping around from side to side and watching our exchange.

"You won't let them down. They're here to play street hockey and have fun. They don't care if they win or lose. They save that for the ice. When it counts." He holds out the hockey stick to me again and gives me an extra dose of eye-smolder.

He really isn't playing fair.

"What about Bailey?" As it is, she's been eyeing the ball, wanting to chase after it.

"She can stay with Jasper and me." Simone reaches for Bailey's leash in my hand, maiming my lame excuse.

I let her have the leash and take the stick from Troy, my movement hesitant. *It's going to be fine. He's competitive, but he won't turn into an ogre if he doesn't win.*

Except, it's not Troy's team I'm playing on. I'm subbing on Kellan's and Garrett's team.

Kellan gives me a few pointers, and I attempt to absorb everything he tells me.

"I've never played hockey," I warn him.

"That's okay," he says, not giving away what he's thinking. The standard response I usually expect from him. "This isn't the Stanley Cup playoffs. Have fun. That's all that matters."

We get into position, and the game begins. I don't chase after the ball. I try to keep open so my teammates can pass to me.

Troy moves in front of me, blocking me from the ball.

My teammate knocks it my direction. Not the greatest idea. Troy's arms are longer than mine, so I duck past him with the goal of intercepting the tennis ball.

His arm loops around my waist from behind, and he pulls me against him.

A surprised giggle jerks loose from me, and I try to squirm out of his grasp. I'm pretty sure that's not allowed. I haven't seen anyone else hug a player to keep them from getting the ball.

"Cheat!" Emily calls out, laughing. "Penalty on Troy for holding. You're off to the sin bin."

I have no idea what the sin bin is, but just the use of word sin is enough to jar another giggle from me.

Autumn sweeps in and steals the ball before either of us can get to it. She runs toward Garrett and scores once more. I cheer—because, damn, that shot was impressive.

Troy chuckles. "You do realize that she's on my team, not yours?"

I flash him a grin over my shoulder. "I believe in cheering for all the kids, even if they're on your team."

An ache twinges in my chest. Does Amelia like sports? Her adoptive father wasn't into team sports, but he does like keeping in shape from what I remember from the last time I saw him.

We continue playing hockey for a while longer. I don't get any goals...not even close. Lucas doesn't even have to make an attempt to stop the ball I send his way. It flies far left of the goal.

"I'll get it," Zara calls out and runs after the ball. Bailey and Jasper strain at their leashes, eager to also chase after it.

"You're really getting the hang of this." Troy grins, barely restraining himself from laughing at me.

I playfully smack him on the chest. "I know. Before you know it, I'll be ready for the big time."

That just makes him laugh, and the sinful sound of it sets off a cascade of heat bubbling in my belly.

The game ends, and I high-five the kids. I hold back high-fiving Kellan and Garrett, mostly because I still don't have a full read on Kellan. There have been a number of times since I first met him when I've felt like he's watching me, trying to get a firm grasp on who I am.

I turn away, unwilling to give him anything.

38

TROY

April, Present Day
Maple Ridge

Jess high-fives the kids on her street hockey team. Her smile is natural and genuine and beautiful. *She's* beautiful.

Something tugs inside me, and I almost gasp at the intensity of it. I want to kiss her. To taste her. I want to show her how special she is. Show her that...

Damn. I've never felt this way about a woman. Not the part about wanting to kiss Jess or taste her. What man wouldn't want her? But that's not what this is about.

I am falling for Jess. Falling under a spell I don't think she even knows she's casting.

Even though I want to pull her to me and kiss her senseless, kiss her until everyone knows she's mine, I can't.

Because she isn't mine.

Not now. Maybe not ever.

My phone rings in my pocket. I pull it out and check who's calling. JnZ Asbestos Removal. I accept the call.

"Hello, Troy Carson speaking," I say into the phone.

A red Honda Civic pulls up in front of Lucas and Simone's house.

"Hey, Troy. It's Pete from JnZ Asbestos Removal. We have an opening on Tuesday that came up. We can fit in Jessica Smithson's house then. Or we can leave it for the currently booked date of May fifteenth."

"No, Tuesday's good." Then we can begin the renovations on her house sooner than originally planned. The asbestos is the one major hang-up that's kept us from starting them.

Rose and Delores climb out of the Honda Civic and walk over to Simone and the rest of our group.

"As you know," Pete continues, "she can't stay in her house during the removal."

"That's right." She can stay at my place. Maybe those few days are what Jess and I need for her to see me as something more than just a friend.

This is all new territory for me. I've never had issues finding women who want to have sex. And with the few relationships I've had, the women and I didn't start out as friends. We'd dived straight into the dating and sex.

I finalize the arrangements to have the asbestos removed and end the call.

"Fred and I will be leaving tomorrow," Delores is telling everyone when I join them. "Hi, Troy."

"Hey, Delores. I've got good news," I tell Jess. "The asbestos removal company had an opening come up for this Tuesday. So we won't have to wait until May to get started with your renos." We won't have to wait another month.

"Asbestos removal?" Rose's forehead crinkles. "Don't you have to be out of the house when that happens? Because of the chemicals?"

"That's right. Jess will have to stay somewhere else for a few days while they remove it." And that's my cue. To ask her to stay with me. In my guest bedroom.

Delores claps her hands, her mouth curving into a satisfied grin. "Perfect. Then you can stay at my house, Jess, while Fred and I are away. That way you can easily keep an eye on it."

"Are you sure?" Jess asks her. "What about Bailey?"

"Bailey is more than welcome to also stay at my house. Fred and I don't have animal allergies, so that won't be an issue."

Jess's smile is wider than Delores's, even with the scar tugging at the corner of her mouth. "That's great. Thank you!"

Yes, Delores. That's. Just. Great. I somehow keep from blowing out a frustrated sigh.

So much for my plan.

"You ready for this?" I take a step back. Jess is standing at the wall separating her kitchen and living room, a sledgehammer in her hand.

The asbestos was removed last week. And now it's Monday evening, and we're about to begin her renovations. A project that will take us at least five months to complete.

"I'm ready." She pushes up the rim of the hard hat I'd insisted she wear for this part of the renovations. She's also wearing safety goggles to protect her eyes from flying pieces of dust and drywall. This look, Jess as the adorably sexy construction worker, is my new favorite fantasy.

A fantasy that's still off-limits as far as I'm concerned. Off-limits until she decides she wants to take our friendship further, to step out of the friend zone we're in.

If she decides she wants to step out of the friend zone.

"You know," I say, "once you start knocking down the wall, there's no going back."

"I have no intention of changing my mind. I'm looking forward to this." She adjusts her grip on the handle, her eyes locked on the target.

"Remember to let loose when you swing the sledgehammer into the wall. Little love pats won't do it."

She gives a determined nod, her eyes not swaying from the target. She's a world-class baseball player getting ready to hit a home run. "Got it."

"The best part is, you get to channel all your frustrations at the wall." And I have a feeling she has enough of them from whatever caused the PTSD to knock down the wall without my help.

Another determined nod, and her lips curve into position. "Got it."

"Okay, Jess. Whenever you're ready." I stand back, prepared to let her have at the wall all on her own.

She lifts the sledgehammer and swings it at the wall, creating a sizable hole in the drywall.

"Does that feel good?" I ask, already knowing the answer.

"It feels fucking amazing!"

I laugh.

Grinning, she pulls the sledgehammer from the wall and swings at it again and again and again. After each hit, she bounces from side to side on her feet, wiggling her hips as if dancing.

"Let me know if you need my help." I jump my ass up onto the counter and watch Jess demolish the wall.

Watch her attack her demons.

That's my girl.

39

JESSICA

April, Present Day
Maple Ridge

I walk through the grocery store, with Bailey by my side wearing her *Service Dog in Training* vest. I draw up short at a display reminding everyone that Mother's Day is coming next month. In nineteen days, to be exact.

Nineteen days of reminders every time I come into the store of how I am no longer Amelia's mother. Not that I need a display of cards and chocolates to remind me of that.

Nineteen days of reminders I won't be celebrating the day yet again. When my husband was alive, he would give me without fail a Mother's Day card and a gift from Amelia. The last Mother's Day card had pink-crayon scribble inside. That tradition ended when he died.

Nineteen days of daily reminders to all mothers who have lost a child that their special little human isn't in their life anymore.

The card and chocolate companies hadn't factored this in when they dreamed up the idea for Mother's Day.

Nineteen days of endless heartache.

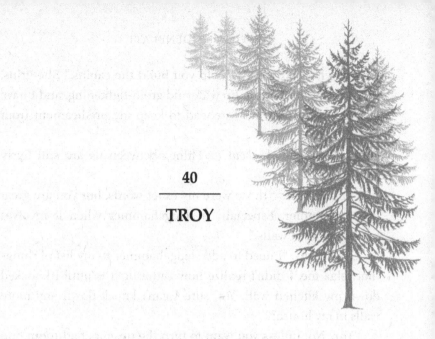

40

TROY

April, Present Day
Maple Ridge

Five days after Jess knocked down the wall between her kitchen and living room, my brothers and I are at the Wilderness Warriors cabins. It's mid-Saturday morning, and we've been working on them for the past two hours.

I'm cutting a piece of wood I need for a joint when a pair of sweatpants-clad legs steps into view. Bailey is walking alongside Jess, staring at the noisy table saw as if it's a fearsome beast.

I turn off the power and remove the protective earmuffs. "Hey, what are you doing here?" My gaze travels up Jess's body, over the large T-shirt that hides it. Her hair's in a ponytail, but I swear it looks a little blonder than it did Thursday night. Or maybe the way the sunlight shines on it makes her hair look lighter.

"We came to see how things are going. And I figured since you're helping me with my renovations and you're doing them for free, I get to return the favor. Someone told me I'm talented with

287

a hammer, so I'm here to help you build the cabins." She grins, the curve of her bottom lip wide and groin-tightening, and I have to flick my gaze to her forehead to keep my predicament from worsening.

Don't even think about it. Things between us are still fairly platonic.

"I don't believe those were my exact words, but you are great with a hammer. Especially a sledgehammer when it involves knocking down walls."

She laughs. "I need to add sledgehammer to my list of things that relax me. I didn't realize how cathartic it is until I knocked down my kitchen wall. You sure I can't knock down any more walls in my house?"

"Yup. Not unless you want to turn the upstairs bathroom into an en suite for your bedroom."

"No. I'm good. So, what would you like me to do?" Her gaze goes to the cabin behind me, where Kellan is currently hammering.

"Hey, Jess," Garrett says, walking over from the cabin he and Lucas are working on. "Did you bring Golden Girl with you?"

Jess turns her head to me, her forehead creased. "Golden Girl? Is that some sort of euphemism I don't know about?"

A laugh, short and abrupt, bursts from my lungs. For all I know, it really is a euphemism only Garrett knows about. "It's what he calls Zara. A friend of ours took photos of her in a bikini and with gold paint smeared on her body. Kim won several prestigious awards for the photo, and Garrett's been calling Zara *Golden Girl* ever since."

Amused lines crease at the corners of Jess's honey-flecked brown eyes. "Nope. Sorry to disappoint, but Zara isn't with me," Jess tells him. "I haven't seen her today."

Garrett removes a box of nails from a larger box on the ground by my workbench. "Hey, what's your excuse for not joining us last night?" he asks Jess. "Troy here"—he smacks me on the back—"could've used your help. We all whipped his sorry ass."

I step away from him. "True. But it's not like we were playing partner games. I would've still lost." I level an amused glance at Garrett, eyebrow lifted. "Unless you're insinuating Jess would have lost if she'd shown up, sparing me from that dubious distinction."

"No, I'm pretty sure she'd have also whipped your sorry ass."

Jess smiles, but there's an emotion in her eyes that's far from amusement. It's the same expression I've seen every time I've asked her to join us for Game Night since that first one. Fear. Reluctance. Longing. She always comes up with an excuse for why she can't be there.

"Maybe I'll come next time." But the way she says it tells me that's as likely to happen as a blizzard in the Amazon.

Her gaze roams the area, searching for something. "Soooo, about that hammering?"

"You can help me." Kellan's voice sneaks up on us from behind, and the three of us whip around to find him standing there, as if he's been here the entire time.

"Okay," Jess says, her smile widening. "Just tell me what needs to be done."

He grabs one of the spare hammers and a box of nails and takes her to our cabin. Bailey is by her side with the red vest on. Butterscotch follows them.

And I watch the woman who's a mystery to me walk away. The woman I can't stop thinking about. The woman I want to kiss and make her forget about her past. Forget about whatever it is that leaves shadows under her eyes.

But she still hasn't given any indication she wants what we have between us to move out of the friend zone.

I tear my gaze from her and go back to cutting the joint pieces I've been working on.

I finish them and enter the cabin Kellan and Jess are in. Bailey and Butterscotch are snoozing in the sunny spot in front of the window. Jess has removed Bailey's vest since she isn't currently working or training. Kellan and Jess are busy hammering. Neither of them is talking. Both appear at peace.

Kellan has never been much of a talker. He prefers to stay in the shadows, watching, listening. When he does talk, it's economical. He doesn't waste his words.

I watch Jess for a minute, the way she moves, the way she focuses on the hammer and nail as if nothing else in the world exists. Fuck, she's sexy as sin, even in clothes that are two sizes too big for her body.

I want to wrap her in my arms from behind. Kiss her neck, the curve of her ear, her jaw. Listen to the sweet sounds I'm positive I can elicit from her. I want to pull her into my body and see what she feels like surrendering in my arms. What she feels like when I'm protecting her from her demons.

Damn, I want to kiss her. Plan to kiss her. But not until she's ready. Not until *she's* the one asking me to kiss her.

The cabin is warm compared to outside. I remove my T-shirt and toss it onto the platform of the short stepladder.

The three of us work for the next hour until Bailey gets restless.

"You two ready for a break?" I ask Jess and Kellan. "Looks like Bailey and Butterscotch could use a walk."

Kellan glances at the dogs and then at Jess and me. "You guys go ahead. I'm going to keep doing this a little longer."

I take the hammer from Jess and place it on the workbench. "We won't be long. There's a stream not far from here I bet Bailey will love playing in."

We head out and let the dogs off leash. They run ahead of us, playing and chasing each other through the mix of dead meadow grass and young green shoots. This is when Bailey gets to be in full puppy mode and not worry about her training. If Jess has a flashback or an anxiety attack, I'm here for her.

"The area is so beautiful," Jess says. "And so peaceful."

"It is. It's the perfect place to escape, which is why we chose the spot for our program."

We continue past the tree line and along the dirt path to the stream. The dogs run into the water, leap and splash. Jess laughs, the sound so carefree. Open. Sexy.

She watches the dogs, and I watch her. The guarded expression that's been a part of her since the first time I saw her almost melts away. She talks to the dogs, her voice as carefree as her laughter.

Sunlight streams through the leaves, creating shadows on the ground, catching on strands that have fallen from her ponytail. She's like a water nymph or a fairy or a goddess or some other mythological creature who steals a man's senses.

And in this moment, watching Jess, I can't think of a better fate.

She looks over at me, smiling, her face so animated, so alive, it sends a surge of warmth through me. "Someone's enjoying the water," she says.

Bailey bounds closer to Jess and shakes her dog body. A shower of water droplets flings in all directions, hitting Jess. She giggle-shrieks, holding up her hands to protect herself from the water.

She looks so fucking adorable.

Like a man under a spell, I close the distance between us, unable to stop myself even if I wanted to. She's a siren, and her laugh is her siren's song.

We're only inches apart when I finally stop moving, when my gaze dives into those beautiful honey-brown eyes that have me mesmerized.

Her laughter dies away, and she's gazing back at me, almost panting. I want to kiss her, to plunge my tongue into that sweet mouth of hers. And she's looking at me like she's possibly thinking the same. Like she wants me as much as I want her.

She takes a tentative step forward, her eyes never leaving mine.

The snap of a twig shatters the spell, and we both turn toward the sound, always on guard, never able to let our vigilance slide. Even the dogs are watching where the noise came from, but neither appears too concerned. It's not a threat. Or they don't perceive it as one.

Jess reverses a step, putting distance between us.

Zara walks into view, wearing her Picnic & Treats uniform. Bailey bounds over to her, always happy to see Jess's boss.

"Hey, Jess. I didn't expect to see you here." Zara's thoughtful eyes dart between us. "I brought lunch for everyone and just wanted to wiggle my feet in the stream. I'm not interrupting anything, am I?"

"No, not at all," Jess says rather hurriedly. "I came to help the guys with the cabins. It was the least I can do because Troy's helping me renovate my house. And because...and because I was in the mood to hammer something."

Zara rolls her lips inwardly as if trying to hold back her amusement. "I'm sure you were. It's been a long time since I've hammered anything. I should probably get on that sometime soon."

My mouth tugs to one side. I'm barely able to restrain my own laugh. "You could always help Garrett out with his hammer."

Zara sticks her tongue out at me like she used to do when we were little kids and I teased her.

And this time I do laugh.

41

ANGELIQUE

May 1943
France

The morning after I learned Captain Schmidt will be living in Jacques's farmhouse, I ride my bicycle to the village. The sky is heavy with the threat of rain.

Exhaustion pedals alongside me. Living with a German soldier on the other side of the bedroom wall can ruin one's ability to sleep.

Captain Schmidt left at dawn, after he informed me a soldier would be dropping off food and alcohol for tonight's dinner party. I flipped through one of the old cookbooks last night that belonged to Jacques's wife and made a list of ingredients I would need. Schmidt had approved the menu.

I pedal down the cobbled street to the village square. A Nazi flag hangs ominously from the pole in front of the town hall.

The flag isn't the only thing that terrorises the populace. Nazi propaganda posters cover every available wall and window. Every shop and every building.

Several Wehrmacht soldiers stand in the square like sentries, ensuring no one forgets who's in bloody power. As if anyone could.

I should be used to this from my trips to Paris. But seeing the stain of evil in this quaint town feels like a smudge of dirt you can never be rid of, no matter how hard you scrub.

I continue past the soldiers, avoiding eye contact with them, and dismount the bicycle at the entrance to the small park. A stone figurine in a toga stands in the middle of the fountain, water pouring from her vase.

Désirée, a member of the local resistance circuit, is sitting on the fountain ledge, swirling her hand in the water. Her hair, the colour of wheat, blows about her face in the wind. I push the bicycle to where she is sitting and prop it against the back of the nearby bench.

I join her and peer into the water. Grey clouds reflect on the surface, mirroring the sombre mood of the village.

"I heard you have a new houseguest." Désirée's voice is barely heard over the splashing water in the fountain.

"A houseguest who plans to have more of them over for dinner tonight." I say the words casually, but the way her eyes widen and dart to the nearest soldier warns me it didn't come out that way.

"You don't have any—"

I shake my head. All incriminating messages are destroyed upon receiving them.

"Do you know how long he will be staying at the farmhouse?" she asks.

"He didn't say. The document only stated he'll be residing at the house, and the current occupants have to vacate it."

"You have to leave?"

"He's not making us move out. If we are unable to endure

living under the same roof as him, yes, we will have to find a new place to live."

"You're choosing to stay there?" Her voice hitches slightly, her volume still a near whisper, but it's enough to release the hounds of hell thundering through my chest.

I glance at the nearby soldiers to ensure none are paying attention to us. "For now, yes. I don't know about Jacques. The idea of a German living with him is not sitting well. But he has nowhere else to go. The memory of his wife and daughter lives within those vineyard walls. And even though he hasn't said it out loud, I know he wants to be there for when his son returns home one day."

"Has he heard from Yvon since his capture?"

"No. He's just holding on to hope that Yvon is alive."

Désirée reaches forwards, her hand still trailing in the water, as if she's trying to touch a lily pad. "Can you still locate new safe houses? With him underfoot?"

I know which him she's referring to without needing her to clarify.

"I don't know." And that's the honest truth. "He didn't mention what exactly he does for the Wehrmacht Army or if he'll be away a lot." I'm not sure I want to know what he does. Just knowing he was in the same house as me last night kept me from falling asleep. And those few times I did drift off to sleep ended with me waking from a terrifying nightmare of him leaning over my bed ready to butcher me.

"Perhaps, for now, we must assume you can no longer search for safe houses and attend parachute receptions. Does he know you're fluent in German?"

"No. As far as I am aware, he thinks the only language I know is French." Very few people in France know I speak German, and that includes within the resistance network. I thought it would be safer that way. Désirée only found out by accident.

"He might feel more at ease talking to his comrades in your

presence if he believes you don't understand him." A sly smile curls on her lips, and her eyes flick briefly to the soldiers standing like cold stone statues. "Perhaps he might even unwittingly reveal something the network will benefit from." She giggles brightly, throwing her head back in delight.

The laughter is unexpected and jarring and means only one thing.

We aren't alone.

My muscles tense for a fraction of a second, and then I follow her lead, laughing as though she's just shared the funniest joke. We've learned the Germans believe you aren't doing anything suspicious when you're having a good time. When you're sullen, it means you're about to cause trouble.

"I should return to work." Désirée stands. I do the same. We air kiss goodbye as a soldier marches past us, and I walk away, not daring to look back at either of them.

I meander through the village, pausing every so often to look over my shoulder and ensure I am not being followed.

I head to the bookshop. Monsieur Joubert is talking to a customer at the counter when I enter. Fortunately, it's not Madame Lavigne this time.

I walk down the aisle I need. After checking no one is watching me, I remove the book I'm looking for from the shelf, slip the coded message out of the hem of my skirt, and place it inside the false book.

I return the book to the shelf and make my way to the mythology section. I select a book on Greek mythologies from the lower shelf, and a twinge of pain tugs at my heart. When Hazel and I were growing up, she loved mythology and would tell me all kinds of wonderful tales.

I carry the book to the front of the shop.

"*Bonjour*, Madame D'Aboville," Madame Bassett says, taking a moment from talking to Monsieur Joubert to exchange greetings with me. "Are you having a pleasant day so far?" There's a tinge of malice in the older woman's tone, and the chill of it is felt in my bones.

"Not exactly. As you may have heard, Monsieur Gauthier's house now has vermin."

She nods, her expression softening. "I did hear that this morning. What are you planning to do about the problem?"

Madame Bassett does not know about my connection to Baker Street and the local resistance circuit. The majority of the resistance group is oblivious to my connections to London. We all subscribe to the philosophy of only knowing what you need to know. Anything more could be deadly to the local circuit.

"There's not much we can do about it," I say. "All we can hope for is the vermin soon moves on to another town. I doubt a barn cat can rid us of the problem." Mars and Venus didn't seem too obliged to rid us of Captain Schmidt last night. And if what happened with Esprit is any indication, the cats will be purring in Schmidt's presence before I know it.

Madame Bassett flattens her lips as though the German presence in the village is my doing. Jacques's house isn't the only one in the area with unwanted guests. "How is it you and Jacques can stay in his house with that—that piece of evil now living there? The German soldiers have forced everyone else from the houses the Wehrmacht confiscated."

"They have?"

She nods, the movement hard and swift. "Why is it that you don't have to leave?"

"I don't know. Captain Schmidt gave us the choice. Jacques has nowhere else to go. His family is linked to that vineyard. He won't surrender his home and his land to the Germans if he can avoid it."

Madame Bassett's gaze scans the bookshop and rests on the window. Her eyes flick back to me. "What will happen when the Germans find out you are lying? Everyone here knows you aren't Jacques's daughter." She leans in closer to me. "You are new to these parts and the Gauthiers have lived here for three genera-tions." Her tone is free of malice or accusations. Genuine concern lowers her voice.

"I don't know what will happen. Hopefully the Germans don't find out the truth." Everyone in the village believes I am the daughter of an old friend of Jacques's from the Great War.

"We can only pray the Germans don't inquire about your rela-tionship. And that neither of you gives anyone a reason to mention the truth to the Germans." She gives me a sad smile full of warning of what could happen if someone should turn on Jacques and me. Too many questions will only put us in harm's way. Too many questions will put the work I do here at risk.

And with that warning, Madame Bassett shuffles out of the bookshop with the help of her cane.

I hand Monsieur Joubert the Greek mythology book and my money.

He hands me the change with a smile that doesn't sparkle as much as it used to. "Enjoy your book, Madame D'Aboville. And I hope to see you again soon."

I thank him with an equal smile, Madame Bassett's warning burning in my gut, and leave the shop. The courier is due there this afternoon and will find the coded message in the book. Allaire needs to be appraised of the situation for numerous reasons, the number one being that Captain Schmidt impedes my ability to do my job.

A temporary solution will need to be found, and I require Allaire and Baker Street to tell me how to proceed.

"I DON'T KNOW HOW THE FRENCH SURVIVE ON THIS VILE FOOD." Arrogance slaps each of Major Müller's words. The tall lean man has the beady eyes of a cruel rat caught in the cold rain.

He hasn't bothered to speak a word of French since he came into the farmhouse. He has stuck with his native language, mocking me whenever he says something to me, almost as if to test me.

And I have stuck perfectly to my cover, glancing at Captain Schmidt every time the Major speaks. Pretending to wait for Schmidt to translate.

My real feelings towards the Major and the other officers aren't betrayed on my face. And that includes when he referred to me as a simple-minded French whore.

"I must admit that I'm rather enjoying it." Schmidt's gravelly deep voice sends an unexpected shiver up my spine. A shiver I can't explain. His voice is far more pleasant than the voices of the other individuals at the table. "I'm especially enjoying the wine." He adds the last part as I finish filling his glass. He doesn't acknowledge me, and I disappear into the background as far as they are all concerned.

"I prefer German wine, myself," the Major says. Hearty words of agreement from the other officers stroke his accolade and his ego.

The barrel-chested officer with one thick eyebrow raises his glass at Schmidt. "The food is not so bad. I don't suppose you will loan out your cook? Now I see why you decided to keep her and the old man around."

That results in a round of laughter. Only Schmidt doesn't seem amused, but none of the other officers appear to notice.

"I don't mind the food," a smaller officer responds, blond hair shaved tight to his head. "It's being stuck in this pig hole I have problems with. The Wehrmacht in Paris get to enjoy all the finest entertainment France has to offer. The theatres. The clubs. The brothels."

"Especially the brothels." The thin-nosed officer with a rough scar next to his right eye lifts his glass in toast.

"You should have seen the whore I was with last week while

on leave." The barrel-chested officer precedes to tell the other men in detail about her and some of the things they did.

Many of the details are lost on me. The words and idioms weren't part of my childhood education. Thank goodness, because if I had understood them, my red face would have given away my German skills.

Eventually, the topic changes to an upcoming local attack Germany has planned.

Discomfort flickers briefly on Schmidt's face, and I wonder the reason for that. Surely the Captain cannot be squeamish. The other men are too intent on what the Major is saying to notice Schmidt's reaction.

The more they discuss their plans, the sicker I feel, and the blood in my face drains. If anyone remembers I am here and looks my way, my reaction might betray the extent of my German.

Schmidt and Lieutenant Fischer are silent, seemingly absorbing the Major's every word, but at the same time, appearing disquieted at what he says. I, meanwhile, absorb it all so I can relay the details to Allaire and Baker Street.

"French whore!" Major Müller snaps his fingers and waves me forward. "Bring us the port."

I turn to Schmidt for his translation. He tells me what the Major requested but avoids the name calling. I serve them the port the driver dropped off earlier in the glasses he also dropped off with the food.

The evening continues with the Wehrmacht officers drinking more port. Early Allied intelligence suggested the German Army hadn't supported Hitler's rise to power. But the only truth to that here is the slight discomfort I sense emanating from Schmidt and Fischer. They do laugh at some of the tasteless jokes, but it seems somewhat forced. Neither man is drinking much.

The rest of the officers are happy with Hitler's sweeping reforms. In Germany and the occupied countries. If Churchill cannot stop Hitler before it's too late, England will also be added to that list. The country I love. My home.

The officers, with the exception of Schmidt and Fischer, eventually leave, driven back to whatever rat-infested sewer they scurried from.

I busy myself washing the dishes, but the relief I thought I would feel with them gone flounders. Schmidt's and Fischer's presence still leaves me ill at ease.

Schmidt enters the candlelit kitchen. I hear the click of his boots on the floor behind me.

"Thank you, Angelique," he says. I turn to him. "I will be leaving tomorrow for four days but look forward to more of your cooking upon my return." He nods at me in what I assume is a dismissal, and he and Fischer leave through the front door.

I open the blackout curtain a fraction of an inch and peer into the twilight-enshrouded vineyard. Fischer isn't climbing into the Jeep he drove here. He and Schmidt are walking towards the field where the pond lies.

Curiosity and duty spur me into action. I open the front door and follow the two men, my footfalls cautiously silent.

Fear sits tense in my muscles, quickens my heartbeat. But it's not enough to turn me around. I have so many questions about these two men. Questions about their reactions this evening.

42

JESSICA

May, Present Day
Maple Ridge

Mother's Day.

I sit on my couch and go through the shoebox that holds Amelia's birth announcement, heart onesie, and baby shoe. Troy and his brothers are at brunch with their mother to celebrate the day.

It's been two weeks since I came close to kissing Troy at the cabins. We haven't had another moment like that, but it doesn't mean I haven't wondered what it would be like to kiss him. Doesn't mean I haven't wondered how he tastes.

I push the thought aside and close my eyes. Instead of thinking about the kiss that didn't happen, I imagine Amelia running downstairs and hugging me and wishing me a Happy Mother's Day. Of her giving me a card she drew with crayons. A card with pink roses and the two of us holding hands.

And I would make her a special brunch with all of her favorite foods.

The image in my head shifts to Amelia doing all those things for Grace, having no clue I exist.

I open my eyes and trace over her smiling face in the photo of when she was twenty months old. "I miss you." The words come out on a croaked whisper. "I love you. Love you so very much."

An emptiness stretches endlessly inside me and smothers any joy I had. A tear drops onto the photo.

One day. One day she'll be back in my life once more. I have to keep believing that. I just need to glue the pieces of my life back together, make it shinier, brighter, and then I can talk to Grace and Craig about seeing Amelia again.

WEDNESDAY EVENING, I WHEEL MY BIKE OUT OF THE GARAGE AND pull up the flap covering the trailer. Bailey jumps in and settles herself on the canvas seat, wearing her *Service Dog in Training* vest.

It's been six weeks since I've become her foster parent. Six weeks of her fitting into my life. Six weeks of spending my weekday mornings at Picnic & Treats, and my afternoons reading Iris's magazines, and reading Angelique's journals and transcribing them. Six weeks of yoga and the occasional hike. Six weeks of therapy with Robyn. Six weeks of weekly canoe trips with Troy, Butterscotch, and Bailey. The only thing I haven't done regularly is participate in Friday Game Night.

I always have an excuse ready because I know Avery and Noah will be there.

Bailey has fitted seamlessly into my life, with one exception. She's unable to be with me when I work at Picnic & Treats. She stays in a crate in the staff room, and one of us constantly checks on her. And by us, I mean mostly me, especially when I'm anxious, which happens at least once or twice during my shift. But that's an improvement compared to when I first started seeing Robyn.

"Here's my yoga mat." I put the rolled mat next to Bailey in the trailer. Once I became Bailey's foster mommy, Violet could no longer give me a ride to yoga. Her husband didn't want a dog in her car.

The sun is still up, but May in the mountains isn't as warm as it is in San Diego. I zip up my spring jacket and pedal to Shania's house.

I keep my eyes and ears open for anything unusual as I bike down the street. I can't shake the feeling someone is watching me. My gaze darts to the bushes ahead of me. Could someone be crouched behind them? Waiting to hurt me, to steal my meager possessions?

I glance behind me and pick up the pace. *Faster, faster, faster.* My breath comes in ragged and my leg muscles burn.

Relax. No one knows the truth about me. No one knows I'm here.

No matter how many times I tell myself that, I can't shake the unsettled feeling that follows me every day. The unsettled feeling that grew after learning my husband was stalking me during the last several years of our marriage.

I arrive at Shania's home and park my bike in the shadow at the side of the house. I open the cover, unfasten Bailey's safety harness, and hug her, grounding myself again. I press my brow against her body, allowing my breath and legs to recover. "Thank you, Bailey. You're such an amazing dog."

I praise her some more and give her a treat.

My phone rings, and I answer it. "Hi, I just got to yoga."

"Hey. I might be a little late getting to your house," Troy says. "Lucas and Kellan wanted to put in some extra time on the cabins this evening. And Garrett's brainstorming a plot twist, so he's here 'cause he figures hammering nails into a wall will help with the brainstorming."

A laugh escapes me. "Do you think it will work?"

"Who knows? But it makes him happy, and it helps us build the cabins that much faster, so it works for me. But I shouldn't be too late getting to your place."

"Okay, I'll see you when you get there. Bye." I end the call and smile to myself. I never imagined I'd have a close male friend, but that's what Troy has become.

Not close like Zara and Garrett. Troy and I are friendly friends. The kind of friends you hang out with...but with whom you don't share your darkest secrets.

Violet walks up the path, and Bailey and I wait for her at the front door. Violet smiles at me, but it barely registers on her face, as if curling her lips requires too much energy.

She draws closer, and the glow from the porch light falls on her face, highlighting the faded bruise that mottles her jaw. It's only when she's standing next to me I realize it's not faded as much as covered with makeup. My unease returns but for a different reason.

A flicker of a memory crashes my thoughts, of a fist making contact with my face. One of those few times my husband hit me there. When he did hit my face, it only made him angrier, meaner. As if his actions had been my fault.

"Are you okay?" The words rush out, my voice not much more than a paper-thin whisper. "What happened?" My gaze drops to her jaw so she knows what I'm talking about.

Violet's hand jerks to her face, attempting to hide the bruise. But it's too late. I can't unsee it. "It's nothing. Sophie woke up crying. I didn't bother to turn on the light, and I walked into the doorframe."

Icicles run down my body, prickling goose bumps awake. I touch Violet's arm a beat before I realize my mistake and can stop myself.

She jerks her arm away as if my touch burned her. And I recognize her reaction for what it is. Fear.

"We should get inside," she says hurriedly. "We don't want to be late."

She rings the doorbell and rushes into the house as soon as Shania opens the door.

I can't move, every nerve in my body screaming, *What if it was her husband?*

"Jess? Are you coming?" Shania's question jars me out of my stupor. She's standing in the doorway, her head tilted to the side as if to figure out what's going on with me.

Violet, Delores, Rose, and Samantha are already in the studio when I enter it. So are Katelyn and Amy.

"There's our favorite dog." Delores smiles at Bailey but respects the sign on her vest that says *Do Not Pet.*

The group knows I'm training her to be a PSD, and they've all been supportive. Even Katelyn. But I still get the feeling she's not a fan of mine.

"How did you get that bruise?" Amy points to Violet's jaw. Violet gives her the same story she fed me, line for line. "God, that sounds like something I would do," Amy says, a chuckle leaking into her words. "I'm the most accident-prone person I know."

No one else seems to doubt Violet's excuse. Maybe I'm wrong about it, but I can't shake the feeling I'm not.

"How are the renovations going, Jess?" Rose lowers herself onto her mat, taking her time, age making her less agile.

"Troy and I have been working on the kitchen. It's slowly getting there."

"By slowly, you mean you've been too busy staring at that tight butt of his." Samantha giggles, and her eyebrows do a jig halfway up her brow. "Who can work when you've got all that shirtless handsomeness working on your kitchen counter?"

My face heats hotter than the San Diego sun in July. "I didn't say anything about him being shirtless."

"Are you telling us he's not shirtless when he works in your house?" Samantha sounds almost horrified.

"From what I've heard at bridge club," Delores says, "he's often shirtless when he works at his job sites."

I roll out my yoga mat just so they can't see the deepening blush on my face. "There's a chance he's been shirtless on occasion." On more than one occasion.

"Have you kissed him yet?" Rose's eyes are wide with the curiosity of a gossip columnist.

I shake my head a little faster than probably warranted, given I'm not trying to hide anything. We haven't kissed. In the past six weeks, Troy and I haven't come close to kissing—other than the day at the cabins when we walked the dogs to the stream. But Zara interrupted us, preventing things from getting that far.

Or maybe I imagined the near kiss. How could he possibly want to kiss someone as screwed up as me? Someone who has "kiss" on her list of things that relaxes her. But not because kissing was one of my favorite activities. It's because I want to replace the bad memories with new, positive ones.

But since I'm too messed up to be with Troy, I've deliberately avoided any situation where a kiss might end up being a possibility. "Why would I kiss him?"

"Because we're talking about Troy Carson," Delores says. "He's one of the good guys. You can't go wrong with him."

This isn't the first time the topic of kissing has come up in the past week. Robyn brought it up during therapy because it's on my list of things that might relax me.

That, and sex.

"It might take a lot longer than a few weeks or months before you're ready," Robyn explained during our last session. "But don't avoid intimacy because of what happened in the past. Consensual kissing and sex are part of being a healthy adult."

VIOLET DISAPPEARS OUT THE FRONT DOOR AS SOON AS YOGA CLASS ends, not giving me a chance to talk to her. And the sharp feeling something is wrong, that the bruise on her face was from a fist and not a doorframe, won't stop jabbing me.

Troy's truck is parked in my driveway when I arrive home. He's leaning on the driver's door, phone in hand. He looks up from his phone and smiles. "How was yoga?"

The playful upturn of his mouth causes my heart, which was already beating hard from the ride home, to pick up its pace.

I can't help but smile. "Good. If anything, I'm getting more flexible."

I unzip the trailer cover and release Bailey. She happily jumps out and stands next to me. I give her a treat and place my hand on her warm body, grounding myself once more. I inhale deeply into my belly like I've learned to do in yoga.

Troy doesn't say anything. He knows this ritual is important to me every time I bike anywhere. It helps to settle my pulse and make me feel grounded.

Once I'm ready, I lock my bike in the garage and we go inside the house.

Troy walks through the house to secure each room. Like he did as a Marine. I don't need him to do that, but it seems to make him feel better. As if it's something *he* needs to do for his own mental well-being.

I'm pushing the tiny pegs into the new kitchen cabinets for the shelves to rest on when Troy comes into the kitchen. My gaze takes inventory of Troy's hard body and the tattoo peeking from under the edge of his T-shirt sleeve. A mountain scene drawn in a maple leaf. Underneath it are two hockey sticks that cross. "You still have your T-shirt on," I blurt.

His eyebrow lifts, and damned if my ovaries didn't just incinerate. "Didn't realize I was supposed to remove it."

"Your preference of working without a shirt on was a popular topic in yoga today."

"You were talking about my nakedness?" An almost-laugh colors his tone and crinkles the corners of his eyes.

A laugh that's part snort, part giggle escapes me before I can stop it. "Hey, don't look at *me*. I wasn't the one talking about it. That would be Rose, Samantha, and Delores. They're quite enamored with you."

"Oh, really? And do *you* want me to remove my T-shirt?" His lips twitch into a smile.

Yes, please. "That's up to you."

His smile widens into a heart-stopping grin, and he tugs his T-shirt over his head.

He tosses it onto the island, his muscles flexing. And I swallow. *Damn.* He really is fine—with all that hot, firm muscle.

"And what else did they talk about when it comes to me?" His tone isn't conversational or friendly or amused. It's all smooth and seductive and teasing. Or maybe that's just my imagination.

Perhaps all that talk of kissing tonight has messed with my mind, because I can't stop staring at his lips, their soft and inviting texture. "They wondered if I've kissed you yet." My voice is low and breathy, and I can't seem to drag my eyes from his mouth.

Troy closes the distance between us. We're an arm's length apart. And still I can't stop staring at his mouth. I swallow a wave of emotion and breathe in his clean scent, a tantalizing hint of rainbows and sunshine.

"And you told them what?" he asks.

My gaze finally shifts back to his eyes. To the amusement still there. To the emotions shining in them that leave me breathless. "I told them we haven't kissed. And asked them why they thought I would have kissed you."

"What did they say?"

"That you're one of the good guys, and I can't do wrong by choosing you."

The corner of his mouth kicks up, but he doesn't widen the space between us. "I'm not so sure the enemy I once fought would agree."

"Are you saying you're not one of the good guys?" The words ride on a teasing, flirty lilt.

"Guess that depends on your definition. But I do try my best to be one."

I lean back against the counter, needing something to keep me steady. All this talk about kissing is making my legs wobbly. "From what I've seen so far, I'd have to agree that you've succeeded on that count."

Troy moves a step closer. "But that's not enough for you to kiss me."

I can't tell if he's asking a question or stating an opinion, so I accept it as the latter. "I'm not into kissing guys who don't really want to kiss me."

"Who says I don't wanna kiss you?" His voice is rough and husky. If it drops any lower, it'll be dusting the floor.

A tremor shimmers through my body, and I can barely breathe. "Why would you want to?"

"*Christ*, Jess. I've wanted to kiss you since I first saw you. But I don't want to kiss you before you're ready."

"You did? You don't?" My voice goes all breathy and high.

He releases a small laugh, and his mouth twitches into a smile. "You realize we're talking about us kissing, and you don't look like you're about to have a panic attack?" He narrows the electrically charged distance between our lips. But he also gives me enough room to move away if I need to.

"Do you want me to kiss you, Jess?" His warm breath fans across my kiss-starved lips. After everything I've been through, I shouldn't want to kiss him. But I do.

I nod, my words failing me.

"Are you sure?"

This time when I answer, it's not with words or a nod. I press my mouth against his. It's nothing more than a tentative, teasing kiss, over before it barely starts.

I pull away ever so slightly, my pulse thrumming in my ears, my lips aching for more.

And for the first time in God knows how long...I feel alive.

Troy hasn't moved even a fraction of an inch since I took the lead and kissed him. My gaze locks with his, and there's no denying my kiss affected him. His eyes are dark with lust and pleasure and need.

I nod at the unspoken question in them, the movement barely perceptible.

Troy lowers his head, and our mouths reunite.

This kiss isn't tentative like the last one, nor is it as brief. It's gentle and commanding. Teasing and guiding. Without thinking about what I'm doing, I part my lips and let Troy in.

His tongue brushes mine, and my knees almost give out from under me. I grasp my wrists behind his neck and let my body tell me what to do. I haven't had a lot of experience kissing men, but there's no doubt Troy is the King of Kisses.

He wraps his arms around me, and I don't feel vulnerable or nakedly raw. I feel safe, protected. I can't remember the last time I felt that way.

My tongue dances with his. Too many...too many emotions stir inside me. Longing. Desire. Nervousness. Relief. Panic. They all entwine and tangle and knot.

And before I can stop the dam from crumpling, tears wet my cheeks.

43

TROY

May, Present Day
Maple Ridge

The last thing I expected when I showed up at Jess's house was for her to kiss me. I've longed to kiss her for the past two months, but given her trauma, I wasn't expecting it to happen anytime soon.

Or possibly ever.

A salty wetness touches my lips. I pull away and take in Jess's tear-stained face.

Before today, I'd never kissed a woman who then started crying. If it were anyone but Jess, I wouldn't know what to make of it. But knowing she's been hurt in the past ignites something dangerous inside of me.

I pull on a mask, hiding the fire of emotions from my face, and wipe my thumbs over her cheeks. "I'm sorry. We should've waited until you're in a better place."

She shakes her head, tears still flowing. "No, it's not that. It's just...it's just you've made me feel something I haven't felt in a long time. A very long time."

I wince, guilt twisting in my gut. "I didn't mean to upset you."

She shakes her head again. "You didn't, Troy. The kiss was perfect." She smiles, eyes glittery with tears. "But don't let that go to your head." She laughs, the soft rumble twirling through my chest, hugging my heart.

I grin, the feel and taste of her lips permanently branded on mine. "I'll try not to." My grin slips away. "You sure you're okay?"

"I'm fine. It was just...it was just a lot to process. I guess I never expected anyone to want to kiss me. Not after...well, not after..." She touches the scar by her mouth and traces along the puckered skin. Whoever sewed up the laceration did a shitty job of it.

I gently pry her fingers from the scar and press my lips lightly on it. "Why wouldn't anyone want to kiss you? You're strong and beautiful and incredibly stubborn."

"Someone wants to kiss me because I'm incredibly stubborn?" Her mouth twitches, a promise of a smile that doesn't quite materialize.

"Yes. You're stubborn because you won't let me help you as much as I want. You're stubborn because you ride your bike everywhere when I could give you a lift." I move my mouth closer to hers. "And does that make me want to kiss you more? Absolutely."

Before she can contradict me, my mouth meets hers again.

This time I don't stop kissing her. Our lips joined, I hook my hands behind her thighs and lift her onto the kitchen counter.

She spreads her knees, letting me get closer. Letting her feel how turned on I am when I'm with her. My hard length presses against her core, and she gasps.

She doesn't stop kissing me. Her hands shift from my shoulders and thread through my hair. Her touch does nothing to ease how much I want her. It stokes the fire, adds more kindle to the flames.

I rest my forehead on hers and fight to regain control of my body. I don't want to rush this and risk ruining the trust I've been slowly building over the past two months. I kiss her on her forehead. "I hope that's not the last time you and I kiss."

Her eyes are slightly dazed, but not in the same way as they are when she's experiencing a flashback. This is more of a satisfied dazed, and I grin.

"I hope so too," she says. "It's on my list of things to relax me."

What the actual fuck? "Kissing men is on your list?"

"Not kissing men specifically. Just kissing. I was thinking of you when I wrote it." A flush spreads across her cheeks, and she lifts her shoulders in a small shrug. "So? Are you ready to get back to work? This kitchen and house won't renovate themselves."

"I guess not." I laugh smugly, relieved at her reply, and move away from her. "You sure you don't want to keep kissing?"

That beautiful mouth of hers curves into a wide smile. "Nope, I'm not sure at all. But kissing you won't get me the kitchen I'm looking forward to."

I don't know about that. I'm more than happy to keep kissing her and give her that dream kitchen.

She returns to setting up the shelves in the kitchen cabinets. And I tackle what's left of the ancient wallpaper clinging to the living room wall.

"I got some good news today about one of the musical acts the festival entertainment committee contacted last week..." I leave the end of the sentence hanging, building suspense. Fuck, I couldn't believe it when I got the call.

"What? Who?" The pitch of Jess's voice raises to match my level of excitement. "Please don't make me guess."

"Pushing Limits." The super-popular rock band.

"Really? They've really agreed to play?"

"Their lead singer has firsthand experience with PTSD, and because of that, they volunteered to perform a set. It's huge they've agreed to help out, especially for such a small event." And especially on such short notice. The festival is set for September nineteenth. In four months.

"That's incredible! Does this mean you're quitting your day job and becoming a festival organizer?" She flashes me a teasing grin.

A soft rumble of a laugh tickles my throat. "Christ, no. If it weren't for Delores, I wouldn't even know what I was doing. She's been coaching me." I get Jess up to speed on everything that's been arranged so far since the last meeting, minus the part where the finance committee and I are trying to raise the money needed to run the actual festival. I don't want her to worry about that.

"Which means the PR and marketing committee can step up our game now." She's positively glowing at that. "I've got some leads on individuals and their families who I can talk to about their experiences with PTSD. I was thinking I could also write an article about the work Jenny does with her service dogs. Raise awareness of how important they are for their owners with PTSD."

"What about you? Are you going to write about *your* story?" The story I want to know, but because she doesn't fully trust me yet, it's locked away in her vault. Only Robyn has access to it.

"My story's too boring to tell. But I could talk about how I'm raising a puppy who will eventually go to someone with PTSD." She glances fondly at Bailey, who's zonked out on her dog bed alongside Butterscotch. "I'm thinking of writing an article from the point of view of the more experienced PSD puppy raisers. I can talk about my experience as a newbie, but it'll be better to get pointers from the pros."

"Sounds like a great idea. Does this mean you're gonna interview people?"

She turns and reaches into the kitchen cabinet. "Yes." Even

without seeing her face, I know uncertainty is written on it. I can hear it in her voice.

I rest my hand on her arm and stroke my thumb across the soft skin of her triceps. I want to kiss her again, to show her how proud I am of her.

None of what she wants to do for the festival is easy for her.

44

JESSICA

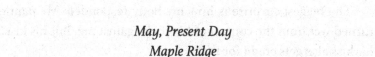

May, Present Day
Maple Ridge

For the next two hours, Troy and I work on the renovations. I help him remove the wallpaper in the living room.

The entire time Troy and I are scraping off the wallpaper, I can't help but dwell on the kiss.

Kissing Troy felt good. Better than good. Spectacular. Which had been part of the problem. And then everything collided into a big pileup of messed up emotions. It had all felt too soon...and not soon enough.

I sneak a peek at Troy. His hard-earned muscles are pieces of fine art. But it's not only that. His body isn't solely the result of working out and running. His strength and agility are innate, woven into each muscle fiber.

I run the tip of my tongue along my lower lip, allowing myself for a fraction of a second to fantasize what it would feel like to do the same to his muscles. To taste him. To tease him.

I blink, shutting down that image, not ready to go there for real.

It's getting late and we both have to get up early, so we pack up the putty knives and spray bottles and dump the torn bits of wet wallpaper into the trash.

"Can I kiss you again before I go?" Troy's warm brown eyes are filled with hope and longing. Not to mention a dose of naughty lust.

There's no doubt he wants me. I got that impression when I was on the kitchen counter, kissing him. The hard press of his length on my core gave it away.

The biggest surprise is how my body responded. My panties turned wet from the contact of his cock against me. But his kiss... his kiss also gets credit for that.

"You can kiss me before you go." I want to go to bed tonight with the memory of his lips on mine. That should chase away the nightmares that usually plague my sleep.

Troy lowers his head to mine. I meet him partway, reaching up on my toes. Our mouths touch, and the heat curled inside me from his earlier kiss unfurls, igniting lust-starved synapses. I release a small moan.

Troy deepens the kiss. Our tongues tangle and dance and tease. I feel like I've been wandering lost in the desert, dying of thirst, and Troy's the magical fountain that's appeared just as I was losing hope.

Bailey barks—at least I'm pretty sure it was Bailey and not Butterscotch.

Grinning, I glance down at the innocent-looking golden retriever. "What? Are you now my chaperone?"

Troy laughs, the sexy rumble felt throughout my body, our chests almost touching. "Hey, that's not part of your PSD training."

Bailey flashes him a puppy grin, and a giggle escapes me.

"I'll see you tomorrow." Troy brushes his lips against mine once more and leaves through the back door.

I lock the door and put Bailey's training vest on her. I click on the leash, and we go upstairs. I give her a treat as positive reinforcement and flip on the bathroom light.

A pink Post-It note clings to the upper right-hand corner of the mirror. Ever since Troy's first Morse-coded message, he's been leaving them all over my house.

And I've been leaving messages for *him* to find.

After I'm finished in the bathroom, I peel the message from the mirror, go into the spare bedroom, and retrieve the box of Angelique's things from the secret room in the closet. I go back downstairs with the journal I'm reading and my notebook. Bailey follows me.

I put the journal and notebook on the coffee table and settle on the couch. I point to where I want Bailey to lie down by my feet. After two attempts to get her to do what I requested, she follows my instructions, and I reward her.

"Should we find out what Troy's message says?" I don't even have to look at the screenshot on my phone anymore to decode it: *I figured you would be a hot kisser. And now I know I am right.*

I grab my phone and chew on my lower lip. I return the phone to the coffee table. Pick it up again. Type a text:

> I always figured you would be a hot kisser
> too. Glad to see I was right

My finger hovers over the Send button. *Crap. Crap. Crap.* I'm flirting with Troy. Not good. Not good at all. He and I are friends. Nothing more.

Is that why you kissed him?

I went through hell with my husband. I'm piecing myself back together bit by bit. But what if that isn't enough?

What if I'm still not good enough for Troy? He deserves better than the taped-together pieces of the woman I was prior to meeting my husband.

But Troy isn't your late husband. Your husband is dead, and Troy is nothing like him. Troy is patient. He doesn't expect you to heal overnight. It's Robyn's voice saying the words this time in my head.

I hit Send before I can change my mind.

His reply comes through a few minutes later:

> I'm hoping tonight won't be the last of kissing you

Me: If you play your cards right, your wish might come true

> Troy: Just to be clear, you're not talking about Game Night, are you? I believe this Friday will be charades. Not sure I can wait until poker night

I laugh even though he knows I won't be there. Noah isn't on shift at the station, which means he and Avery will be at Game Night. Robyn would probably tell me I should go, would remind me Noah isn't my husband. Would tell me not all cops are bad or abusive.

She might tell me that, but I have a hard time trusting cops or believing they're on my side when history has proved otherwise.

Me: No, you don't have to wait that long ;)

> Troy: Phew! That's a relief

Me: See you tomorrow

> Troy: Hope you have a good night

Me: After that kiss, I'm sure I'll have pleasant dreams

I bite my lower lip again, listing in my head all the reasons

Troy is nothing like my husband. Praying I'm not making a mistake in letting my wall slide down a little.

I LOWER THE LARGE BAG OF FLOUR TO THE FLOOR NEXT TO THE *industrial-sized mixer. The lights in the prison kitchen flicker off, and I'm thrown into pitch-blackness.*

I expect to hear some heavy female cursing, but there's nothing. Nothing other than the jarring silence that I feel in my bones.

I want to call out to see if anyone else is in here. But I don't. I know better.

The loud clang of metal hitting metal reverberates through the darkness and moves steadily toward me. Bang....Bang....Bang.

The sound of my breathing and heartbeat bounces off the walls and the floor, and I pray they don't give away my location. Move, my brain screams to my body. Don't let them find you.

Bang....Bang....Bang.

It's a game aimed to scare me. Goody for them; they're winning.

My brain screams its command again. Run! Run! Run! This time my body gets on board with the memo. I drop to all fours and slowly crawl across the tile floor, but I have no idea where the exit is. Fuckers, where did the sign go?

Panic rises in my chest, rattles my heart to pick up its pace.

Between the rhythmic beats of the clanging, another sound can be heard. It's slower, softer, steady. The squeak of a shoe against the tiles. The clanging stops. The sole-squeak advances in my direction. Slow and even. Squeak....Squeak....Squeak.

I have no doubt that I'm the target. No doubt that this time they want me dead.

If I make it to the door, will I even be able to escape? Or is someone waiting for me there too?

There's no point in screaming. No one will protect me. Everyone will look the other way.

Tears soak my cheeks. Don't sniff. Don't sniff and give my location away.

I hear a whimper and something wet tickles my face. I'm being licked. Doggy breath assaults my nose. Since when did Beckley have dogs?

I'm not in prison anymore. I'm not in prison. I'm safe. I'm not in prison.

I repeat it several times and then use another nightmare-escaping strategy Robyn taught me. Whoever is after me is an ice cream cone, and the heat in the room is melting them. A puddle of pistachio ice cream spreads across the floor.

"I'm not in prison anymore. I'm not in prison. I'm safe. I'm not in prison," I repeat it several more times in my dream, and slowly bring myself back to the present and my bedroom.

The room is dark, other than the glow of the nightlight. Bailey was on her bed when I went to sleep. Now she's next to me, her warm body pressed against mine.

I wiggle my arm free from where it's trapped between us, and I wrap it around her. "Thank you."

I wipe my damp face with my hand and stare at the deep shadows looming on the ceiling. I lie there for a few minutes, walking my body through several relaxation exercises. When I fail to fall asleep, I reach for the World War II nonfiction book about D-Day and flick on the lamp.

A warm light fills the room, chasing away the shadows. I check the time on my phone. 2:21 a.m.

Damn. I have to get up in a few hours for work.

PTSD plus exhaustion is an equation that never ends well.

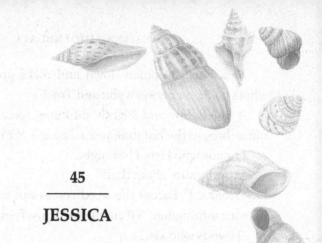

45

JESSICA

May, Present Day
Maple Ridge

I check on Bailey in the staff room and return to the kitchen. My body feels sluggish, and I can't stop yawning. The consequence of not falling asleep again after the nightmare that woke me early this morning.

I wash my hands and resume chopping the onions. Keshia is at the industrial mixer, kneading bread dough. The whirl of the motor is barely heard over Zendaya and Zac Efron singing "Rewrite the Stars."

Zara approaches my workstation. "Are you hiking Saturday?" She picks up an onion from the bag and casually examines it as if she has nothing better to do. A sly smile curves her pinkish-brown lips.

"Yes. As far as I know. I'm looking forward to it." I'm still hypervigilant while hiking, but I'm a little more at ease in the mountains than anywhere else.

Zara puts the onion down and picks up another one. "So, what's going on between you and Troy?"

A laugh, low and slightly off-kilter, forces its way out. "The same thing as the last time you asked me. We're just friends."

Friends who kissed last night.

"Are you sure about that?"

"Yeaaaah?" Except the word comes out more like a question than a confirmation. "Of course we're just friends."

"Friends who kiss?"

"He told you we kissed?" Surprise and indignation pepper my tone. I never thought of Troy as the type of guy who'd kiss and tell, but I guess I don't know him all that well.

"No. But Delores told me a few minutes ago that you and Troy are now on kissing terms."

I snort-laugh, but not for the reason Zara assumes. My living room curtains were closed when he and I kissed last night. There's no way Delores or anyone else could've seen us. "She made that up. Delores, Samantha, and Rose are in my yoga class, and they told me I should kiss him."

"So, you haven't kissed Troy?"

I focus on the onion I'm chopping. "Nope." Lying was something I'd always been uncomfortable with. That all changed with the exchanging of wedding vows. *I wasn't paying attention to where I was going and walked into the doorframe. I was carrying the laundry and missed the top step.*

"Do you want to kiss him?"

"From what I've heard, half the women in Maple Ridge want to kiss him. Isn't that what you told me, Zara? Women throw themselves at Troy and try to give him their phone number?" My tone has a singsong quality, designed to distract from the current line of questioning.

Keshia chuckles from beside the mixer. "Nice deflection."

"I'm not deflecting," I say with the equivalent of half an eye roll in my tone. "Simply stating the truth."

Zara leans forward, arms resting on my work counter, preventing me from chopping more onions. "Sooo, do you want to kiss Troy?"

"Do *you* want to kiss him?" I level my gaze at Zara and then Keshia.

Zara pushes away from the counter, maybe noticing the amused question in my eyes. "Definitely not. Troy's like a brother to me."

We both look at Keshia.

She lifts her shoulders in a nonchalant shrug. "Hey, I'm not denying I'm part of the want-to-kiss-him crowd. He looks like he'd be an amazing kisser."

Oh, he is.

"You *have* kissed him!" The exclamation powers from Zara and is aimed directly at me. "You're blushing."

"I'm not blushing." *Much.* Heat burns in my cheeks, hotter now that I've been caught in my lie.

"Oh, do tell," Keshia says, her bread-making temporarily forgotten. "Is he as good as I've heard?"

The lights flicker above our heads.

And the kitchen goes black.

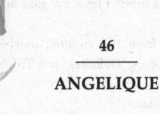

46

ANGELIQUE

May 1943
France

I keep to the shadows of the trees and follow Schmidt and Fischer as they walk towards the pond. My footfalls are soft on the grass.

An inquisitive silence blankets the area. I can't hear if they're talking, but if they are, they're keeping their voices too low to be heard. And if the latter is true, why the precautions? They don't know I speak German. They don't know I understand all the secrets I overhear. So even if they suspect I'm following them, that shouldn't make a difference.

Or perhaps...perhaps they are merely out for an evening stroll. Perhaps the war and my SOE training have made me suspicious of every action, every word.

They stop at the water's edge and pick up something from the ground by their feet.

Fischer hurls whatever is in his hand. A distant *plop* from the water breaks through the silence. Schmidt does the same and is rewarded with another *plop*. They're throwing stones?

They continue hurling the stones, each movement fuelled with what appears to be anger—or they're competing to see who can throw their stone the farthest.

And still, they don't say anything.

I hide behind a tree, the trunk wide enough to obscure their view of me.

"We have to leave." Fischer's tone is hard and cold and bruising. And I almost take a step back to avoid the force of his words.

"We can't." Schmidt's tone is not as harsh as his comrade's, but the anger or frustration remains. Anger at what exactly?

"We don't belong here. And if we don't leave soon, we could find ourselves on the Eastern Front." Panic bleeds into Fischer's words, tainting his anger with a kaleidoscope of other emotions. "God knows we won't survive that. Not against the Russkies."

"You know more than anyone why I can't leave. I can't just run away."

Fischer makes a scoffing sound. "Running away is for cowards. We are not cowards."

"They'll kill my family if I desert."

Fischer picks up another stone and throws it. "Don't be an idiot, Johann. Your family's already dead."

Schmidt grabs the front of Fischer's uniform with such force, such fury, I can barely breathe. "They're not dead!" His voice is the crack of lightning in the otherwise still air. He lets go of the lieutenant and steps back.

I shift to hide completely behind the tree and press my spine into the bark, making myself smaller. Ensuring they cannot see me.

"There's no way they escaped the Gestapo," Fischer says, his voice hovering at a near shout. "And if your mother is dead, your sister most certainly is too."

I frown. Why would Schmidt's family be trying to escape the

Gestapo? The Wehrmacht and the Gestapo are working on the same side—Hitler's side.

Silence follows once more, stretching across the darkening sky. I remain motionless, my heart pounding in my chest at the mention of the Gestapo. God, please tell me whatever they're talking about won't bring that evil banging on Jacques's door.

Another *plop* breaks the silence.

"I pray you're right about your mother and sister." Fischer's voice is quieter this time, his tone steel-plated with determination, soft-boiled with despair. "You know I want them to be alive as much as you do. But us being sent to the Eastern Front won't protect them. What will they think once this war is over and they find out you're dead? Do you really believe they will survive that?"

I don't get to hear Schmidt's reply. The two men start walking, but this time I don't follow them, even if I am left with so many unanswered questions. The absence of sufficient cover where they are headed will make it harder for me to escape notice.

THREE DAYS AFTER SCHMIDT'S DINNER PARTY WITH THE Wehrmacht officers, I walk along Rue de la Glacière in Paris.

I'd sent word to Allaire on Saturday that I needed to talk to him about what I'd overheard Friday night. There is too much intelligence for me to simply pass it through the normal network of coded messages.

The morning saw scattered rain showers, but now that the sun has pushed past the clouds, the afternoon promises to be warm. The ground is already dry as I duck into a flower shop, taking the usual precautions to ensure I'm not being followed.

Élise is inspecting a bouquet of fresh cut tulips, and I walk over to her as if I hadn't known she would be here. We kiss like the friends we've become and chat about nothing in particular. The light conversation of two companions who haven't seen each other in a few weeks.

"I'm meeting my husband at Parc Montsouris," she says, smiling as though she can't believe we bumped into each other. "You must come. He would love to see you again."

"Yes, I would love that."

We walk arm in arm to the park where I am supposed to meet Allaire. It's a dangerous game he and Élise are playing. If one of them is caught by the Gestapo or Milice, they both will pay with their lives.

And if I'm with them, my life will also be forfeited.

Allaire is standing next to the large pond, looking out at the water. His expression is contemplative. If I didn't know better, I would say he is lost in his own world. But that couldn't be further from the truth. He's an SOE agent. He's well aware of his surroundings and the people coming and going.

But there is something else in his expression beyond the exhaustion and wariness that wrenches at our seams. Wrenches at the seams of all who live under German rule.

He greets his wife and kisses my cheeks like the cousins he and I are supposed to be. Élise and I loop our arms with Allaire, and the three of us stroll along the sidewalk encircling the pond. We're smiling, three friends trying to escape the war weighing down on Europe. Or at least trying to escape it for a few precious moments.

"Your message said you have important information about an upcoming attack the Germans have planned." Allaire's voice is low so only I can hear him.

"That's correct." I relay everything Major Müller and the other officers discussed on Friday night. Élise can't overhear what I am telling her husband, but she pretends she can, laughing as if I'm telling a joke. But the few times I catch her eye, I see the fear buried deep in them.

"Is it possible they might suspect you understand German?" Allaire asks.

"I've been very careful not to give The Wolf or the other officers a reason to believe I speak a language other than French." The Wolf being code for Captain Schmidt.

"All right. I'll warn the resistance circuit leader in the area about what you told me. They must be careful with how they act on the news. We don't want to alert your new houseguest that you know more than he realises. If the captain or his fellow officers remain so *blasé* in your presence, they might inadvertently provide Baker Street with intelligence Germany would rather we didn't know." Allaire levels a smile at me. The smile of a cat about to pounce on a fattened canary.

"Your job description has just changed, Carmen. If you can still locate safe houses and be part of the reception committees, that is good. But while your houseguest is around, make the most of the situation and see what else you can learn from The Wolf and his comrades about Germany's plans. Gain his trust. Get close to him and form a relationship with him."

I laugh at the joke that Allaire didn't just share with Élise and me. "You want me to do whatever it takes to get him to reveal what he knows?" It's clear from my innuendo what I mean.

"I won't suggest that. Baker Street has rules about what we should and shouldn't do here, especially with the opposite sex. It's up to you on how you want to proceed. I trust you'll do what is right for you."

His words reassure me. The SOE's training covered plenty of topics, but seducing secrets from the enemy was not part of the curriculum.

"*Excusez-moi.*" Élise hurries off to meet a woman heading in our direction.

Allaire stops walking, causing me to do the same.

The woman is in her late forties and is wearing a blue silk dress that was the height of fashion prior to the war. She is of money, that much is obvious. At her feet are a pair of white Pomeranians.

"That's Madame Marchand," Allaire explains with a hint of frustration in his tone. "We believe she's possibly collaborating with the Germans. Or she's on our side and reports to someone else. Sometimes it's so hard to tell which is which. I have a meeting with Christian soon, but I know she'll expect me to converse with her for a minimum of ten minutes before I can slip away."

"How is Christian doing?" I'm eager for any news that maybe the war is ending soon, but I don't expect Allaire to tell me anything of significance. He can't for the sake of the *Cashmere* network's security.

The frustration from Allaire's tone slips into the sigh that escapes his lips.

"What is it?" I prompt.

"It's nothing really. Christian is leaning towards letting a group of communists be part of the network."

"Isn't that a good thing?" The Allies are working with the Soviets to end the war, so it makes sense for Christian to recruit communists to help us.

"Normally, yes. But I believe this particular group entertains a strong antisemitic rhetoric. I am trying to persuade him to not permit them to join us, but so far, he doesn't agree with me. I've managed to stall their inclusion, but that won't last much longer."

"What are you going to do?"

"I'm leaving for London next week and will see what Baker Street advises."

"How long will you be gone?"

"About a month. Less, if I can help it. Pierrot will be taking my place in command while I'm away since Christian is unable to do that this time. If you need anything, you can contact him through the usual channel." He glances over at Madame Marchand, who is busy chatting with Élise. "I guess I need to get this over with if I hope to be on time for my meeting with Christian. You'd better join me. Otherwise, Élise and I will never hear the end of it."

We walk to where the pair is standing. Madame Marchand pauses what appears to be a rather one-sided conversation. Élise introduces me to the woman, who proceeds to ask my opinion on the topic of French theatre, something I know nothing about.

"We don't get a lot of theatre of any sort where I live," I explain to Madame Marchand.

"Well, then you must be my guest the next time you are in Paris, Carmen."

Allaire eventually extricates himself from the conversation with a quick kiss on his wife's cheek. I stay a while longer, unable to escape, even if I try.

Madame Marchand seems to be nothing more than a lonely woman. If she's trying to gain information from us to share with the Germans, she's doing a horrible job of it.

"I need to go now if I hope to catch my train," I tell the two women after we've been talking for another ten minutes. If we are not careful, we'll draw the wrong kind of attention because we've been conversing too long. But I might already be too late in worrying about that. "It was nice meeting you, Madame Marchand."

"Call me Joseline," she says, smiling pleasantly, but I'm certain in another time, another place, her smile would have been brighter, more relaxed.

I catch a taxi, conscious someone could be following me from the park, and give the driver an address in the opposite direction to the train station. Once we arrive at my fake destination, I stroll along several streets, and catch another taxi to the station.

Bloody hell, if I survive the war, will I always be looking over my shoulder, waiting for the worst to happen? Will fear and para-noia be forever engrained in my body?

47

JESESSICA

May, Present Day
Maple Ridge

"Jess? It's going to be okay. You're safe." Zara's distant voice sounds like it's being carried though tumultuous ocean waves.

"Maybe we should call Troy." Keshia. Her voice is slightly less distorted.

Zara says something about Bailey training to be *my* psychiatric service dog. But she's got that all wrong. I'm just Bailey's puppy raiser.

I shake my head and blink my eyes open. My body feels as though it has been dunked in icy water. Every part of me is trembling. And I'm vaguely aware of the cold wall pressed against my back.

I'm not holding a knife this time, nor is there a knife next to me on the kitchen floor. Zara told me if anything like last time happened again, she would have to let me go. Did that mean if I was holding a knife when I had a flashback? Or if I had a flashback at Picnic & Treats, period?

I focus on my breathing, drawing air into my lungs and slowly pushing it out through pursed lips. I want to hug Bailey, to stroke her soft hair, but she isn't allowed in the kitchen.

"What happened?" My mouth is dry, my voice as shaky as my body.

"The power went out for a moment before the building's generator kicked in." Zara's words are strained with worry. "We found you on the floor, shaking."

I push to my feet, my legs unsteady. Zara stands with me. My heart pounds hard in my chest, the rapid beat vibrating in my ribs and down to my toes. "I need to check on Bailey."

"I'll come with you. Keshia, can you keep an eye on things? My cream puffs will be ready to come out of the oven in another minute or two."

"Of course."

"Gimme a sec." Zara rushes out of the kitchen and comes back with a glass of flavored fizzy water. She walks me along the hallway to the staff room. "Do you want me to call Troy?"

I follow her into the room, my heartbeat still racing. "No, that's fine. He doesn't need to know every time I have a flashback."

But I will write it in my daily journal to share with Robyn next week.

"Do you still have them fairly frequently?"

"Maybe once or twice a week." Which is an improvement since I began therapy. I've been getting better at avoiding the main trigger, which seems to be lack of sleep, but the eventual goal is for the flashbacks to no longer be an issue no matter how much sleep I get. And this will help with the other triggers, such as loud noise, that I have no control over.

I open the door to Bailey's crate. She steps out, tail wagging. I crouch next to her and stroke her. She whimpers and licks my face.

My heart rate slows to normal after a few minutes, and I remove one of her treats from my pocket and give it to her. "Thank you." I keep stroking her, lauding her with praise.

Zara crouches next to Bailey and hands me the glass. I gratefully take a long sip of the strawberry-kiwi fizzy water.

"I know you're seeing a therapist," she says, "but if you want to talk, I'm here for you. Sometimes just talking to your friends can help."

My mouth tugs into a faux smile that hopefully looks more genuine than a knock-off Chanel bag. "I'll be fine. I just needed to catch my breath. I'm ready to get back to work now." *If I still have a job.* I don't want to give Zara another reason to fire me. I enjoy working here. It gives me a sense of purpose I haven't experienced in God knows how long.

It's going to be fine. I'm going to be fine.

"If you'd rather leave early..."

I shake my head, white-hot panic rising in me, and I swallow past the samosa-sized lump in my throat. "No, it's bad enough I keep leaving to check on Bailey. I can't keep going home early every time I have a flashback."

"You've only had the two since you started here."

"I know, but I don't want to take advantage of your kindness." I turn to Bailey. "I'm sorry, girl. You need to go back in the crate." I encourage her into it and return to the kitchen.

For the rest of my shift, I avoid talking about what happened. But I can feel the weight of Zara's worried glances that she flicks my way when she thinks I don't notice.

After my shift is over, Bailey and I head to my bike and her trailer. But it's such a beautiful day, I change my mind and walk the two blocks to the library instead of biking there.

People stare at Bailey, their curiosity stoked at seeing her *Service Dog in Training* vest. Their eyes flick up to my face, and I duck my head. When I agreed to be Bailey's puppy raiser, I hadn't counted on how her vest would result in the attention I was trying to avoid.

I push the World War II nonfiction book through the library return slot, and Bailey and I head back to Picnic & Treats. A sensation someone is watching me prickles under my skin. I scan the area, searching for whatever has triggered my internal alarm. Every sound, smell, sight thrusts my nervous system into overdrive.

Will the sensation someone is stalking me ever go away? My husband is dead. He can't stalk me anymore, yet I feel like he's still following me, watching me, terrorizing me.

A police cruiser drives slowly toward me, the red and blue lights turned off.

My body transforms into cold stone, my legs cemented to the sidewalk. A flicker of a memory leaks in. Of blood seeping from my husband's body, staining the living-room carpet crimson. Of a grogginess dulling my thoughts.

Of my daughter's small, warm body being removed from my arms. Of her crying out for me. Of being roughly pushed around, read my rights, shoved into a marked vehicle. The flashing red and blue lights cutting through the cool night air.

I'm vaguely aware of my body shaking, of sweat sliding down the side of my face. I can't quit staring at the cop car.

The cruiser stops at the red light. My pulse thrums loudly in my ears, drowning out all other sounds. Drowning out all thoughts.

I hear a bark, but I can't stop staring at the police car.

The car advances and pulls into the empty spot in front of the florist. Two officers climb out of the cruiser and walk toward me. My body keeps trembling, and I can't tear my attention away from them, no matter how much I want to.

"Jess?" A man steps in front of me, his broad chest blocking my view of the cops. He's wearing a white dress shirt minus a tie.

My gaze moves up and meets Kellan's sharp blue eyes.

"Kellan?" The name stumbles over my dry lips.

A crease wrinkles between his eyebrows. Concern fills his eyes. "Are you done working for the day?"

"I-I was at the library. N-now I'm-I'm going home." To hide.

The cops walk past me. The tremor gripping my body intensifies. One glances at me but recognition doesn't cross his face.

"Change of plan," Kellan says matter-of-factly, pulling my attention back to him. His expression is neutral, an unreadable stone tablet. "We're going to the lake to talk."

"Why-why do we need to talk at the lake?"

"You'll see." His expression doesn't change. There's a hardness in it I haven't seen before. Kellan doesn't smile as much as his brothers. That much I've noticed in the short time I've known him.

Trust doesn't come easily for me. And even then, I don't fully trust Troy. I can't. Not now. Not ever.

With Kellan, I'm not sure if I should be terrified of him or give him the benefit of the doubt.

"Breathe, Jess. I'm not going to hurt you. But I do think you and I need to talk. I have a feeling I understand you better than you realize."

I only wish that were the truth. But no one can understand me. I barely can myself.

"Okay." The word is cracked but determined not to falter. It pushes past the tightness in my throat.

We don't talk as we head to his SUV, which is parked on a side street not far from the library. An effortless silence falls on us, welcome and far from constricting.

He opens the passenger door to his SUV. I encourage Bailey onto the front seat so she's sitting between my legs. She hasn't had a lot of experience being in a vehicle, other than Troy's truck, so this is good training for her.

Kellan doesn't drive to the beach where I first met Troy. He pulls into another lake entrance a little closer to town. The small gravel parking lot is empty, and there are more trees around the grassy bank than at the beach.

Kellan leads Bailey and me along the dirt path to the water. Sunlight shines between the tree leaves, painting dappled shadows on the ground.

"It's so peaceful here." Awe shimmers over my whispered words. The mountain range to the left beckons me to explore it, to escape my reality for a few hours.

Several ducks are paddling in the water near where we're standing. Bailey barks at them. They quack in reply and take off flying. She barks at them once more and looks back at me, her expression playfully hopeful.

I smile at her, even though the panic from earlier churns in my stomach. "Sorry, girl. I don't think they were interested in playing with you." I turn to Kellan, and my nerves dial up a notch. "So, what did you want to talk to me about?"

His gaze is directed out at the water. "I want to make it clear first that whatever you and I talk about will remain between us." His voice is deep and low, warm and gruff. And something else is woven into it. Disappointment? Sadness? Maybe even frustration? "I know you have no reason to trust me, Jess. Hell, you don't fully trust Troy, and you two are friends." Kellan finally glances at me. "Well, closer friends than you and I are."

"True." *Where's this going?*

He returns to staring at the lake. "What exactly have you heard about me?"

Okay, that was the last thing I expected him to ask. "That you're Troy's and Garrett's and Lucas's brother."

338

"What else?"

I give an exaggerated shrug. "Um, nothing really. I don't know if you've noticed, but I'm not exactly a social butterfly. I work in the kitchen at Picnic and Treats, which means I get to avoid the customers. Zara, Keshia, and I talk, but not about you or your brothers."

"They aren't my biological brothers. Did you know that?"

"Troy mentioned it. But he didn't say much about it." I hurriedly add the last part so Kellan doesn't think I've been prying into his life.

He nods as if he expected that much. "I have no idea who my asshole father is, and my mother was more interested in her drugs than her son. She died of an overdose when I was six. I was already friends with Garrett at the time, but even after his parents adopted me, I never felt like I truly belonged.

"After college, I served one rotation with the Marines. I became restless. Hooked up with the wrong woman, hacked into a company's computer system for her, and ended up serving three years in the slammer."

Kellan turns to face me, his gaze probing. I take a half step back, ready to build my wall higher.

"I was locked away long enough to recognize a former inmate when I see one." His words are the lightning bolt that spears my chest.

Shit. Shit. Shit. Kellan's going to tell everyone who I really am. That I'm a fraud. Someone to be disdained. I'll lose everything I've gained so far. A place to live. Friends. A job.

My body stiffens, and I sink to the grass. Grief and an overwhelming loneliness steal my breath. I hug my bent knees, trying to hide my trembling. But otherwise, my body remains rigid, more bricks adding to my wall.

Bailey lies down next to me, her body blurry through my tears.

Kellan lowers himself to the grass, giving me enough space so

I don't feel threatened. Or maybe that's the first step in separating me from his family and friends.

"I'm not going to tell anyone," he says gently. "I know you have no reason to trust me, Jess. And if what I suspect is true, I know trust won't come easily for you. Something happened to you in prison, didn't it? Is that where the PTSD comes from?"

I nod, even though that's not entirely true. Robyn believes the complex PTSD is the result of years of abuse, both at my husband's hands and the inmates who attacked me.

Kellan doesn't ask what crime I was found guilty of. He watches the ducks who have returned to the lake, but at a safer distance from Bailey this time.

"What happened to the woman you hacked the computer system for?" I ask. A speedboat cuts across the water, the distant buzz of the engine the only sound to remind us we aren't alone in the world.

"Don't have a clue. Don't really care, either. She got some fancy-ass lawyer, and the entire crime was pinned on me."

Damn. I feel sorry for the woman who falls in love with Kellan. After what he's gone through, I can't imagine she'll have much of a chance with him. "I guess I'm not the only one with trust issues when it comes to the opposite gender."

"You committed a crime because of a man?" Surprise colors his tone, but at the same time he doesn't seem overly shocked. A contradiction, just like him in many ways.

A dry laugh crosses my lips, bitterness its bedfellow. "That's the irony. I didn't commit the crime. Someone else did. By the time the justice system figured out their mistake, I'd already served five years of my twenty-five-year sentence."

"Christ," Kellan mutters under his breath. "How long have you been out for?"

I tug a blade of grass free and twirl it around my finger. "Two months."

"Fuck. No wonder you reacted the way you did when you saw

the cop car. And that's why you keep avoiding Game Night when Noah and Avery are there, isn't it? Because Noah's a cop? And you don't trust cops."

I suck in a shaky breath, nod, and unwrap the blade of grass from my finger, unwilling to spill the rest of my secret. Kellan only needs to know as much as he has guessed for himself.

"You were attacked while serving time, weren't you?"

I nod again, and Kellan curses some more under his breath.

"What happened?" The two words contain so much pain and anger, I wonder if Kellan has figured things out for himself.

"I was attacked numerous times while I was in prison. That's where the scars on my face come from. It was a reminder. Befriend me, and you'll suffer the same fate or worse." I've already told Robyn all of this, but it feels more cathartic telling Kellan. He understands it better. Given the nature of his crime, he wouldn't have been locked away with dangerous offenders like I was, but he'd still get it.

"Did it work? The warning?" he asks.

I toss the blade of grass to the side and nod. "I had a friend in the beginning, but she quickly abandoned me when she figured it wasn't safe to be my friend. She was attacked. So I spent pretty much my entire time there without anyone on my side."

Kellan reaches across the distance between us and squeezes my hand. At one time I would have yanked my hand away, afraid to let anyone touch me. Which is why I recognize how difficult that simple gesture is for Kellan. His past has scarred him much like mine has done to me. Troy's the type of guy who will give someone a friendly pat on the back. Kellan isn't.

"I'm sorry you had to go through that, Jess. Have you told Troy any of it?"

"No, and I don't plan to tell him or anyone else." The words come out in rapid fire, cold with panic and fear. I warm them up for the next part. "And I hope you keep your promise, Kellan, and do the same. I'm trying to start my life over. New town. New and improved me."

"Jessica." Kellan slowly sounds out my name as if it's fruit that doesn't taste quite right. "That isn't your real name, is it?"

"No. And I'm not a natural blond. I needed to get away because I knew the media wouldn't stop hounding me after I was released."

Kellan nods as if that makes sense. "How many people know you're here? The people who know who you really are?"

"Three." Florence, Craig, and Grace. "The person who knows Anne Carstairs told her I was recovering from a traumatic event and needed a place to stay for a few months while I recovered. But Anne has no idea I'm an ex-con." I shrink in on myself at *ex-con*, the weight of the word making it hard to breathe.

"I'd hardly call you an ex-con. Not when you were innocent of the crime." The force of Kellan's words is stronger than a Category 4 hurricane. "You're an exoneree."

"But will anyone else see it that way if they find out the truth? I was in a maximum-security penitentiary. No one will believe that it didn't change me for the worse."

"It's impossible to go through what you did and not be changed in one way or another. But it didn't change you for the worse, Jess." His gaze lowers to Bailey. "So, no one else knows you're here?"

"Not unless the bank released the information. I was dropped off at a bus station the day after I was discharged from the prison hospital. And I made my way here. I don't think anyone has recognized me." I'm sure the entire town would know by now who I am if anyone had.

"Hospital?"

"Before I found out there was new evidence proving my innocence, I was shanked."

Kellan allows what he's thinking to show on his face for

barely a fraction of a second. His expression is a mix of a frown and a grimace. "How bad?"

I reach behind me and lift the hem of my T-shirt, exposing the jagged four-inch scar. "The good news is it missed my kidney."

"Fuck, how are you even alive?"

I drop the T-shirt back into place. "Guess my guardian angel finally decided to do their job."

"You should tell Troy," Kellan says, his voice less hard this time. "About everything."

I push myself to stand and search the ground for something to hurl into the still lake. I can't let anyone know about my past. I don't want them to know how I failed my daughter. I don't want to see that look in their eyes, wondering why I didn't just leave my husband. It's easy to believe escaping an abuser is simple when you aren't the one in the abusive marriage. It's easy to believe when your boyfriend isn't manipulative and controlling.

"No. I don't want anyone to know about my past. I'm seeing a therapist. That's good enough. As it is, I have to be super careful. I can't risk my true identity being exposed. All it takes is for my picture to get out on social media and for the wrong person to see it, and my life, the life I'm trying to rebuild, will be destroyed again because of the media. I've already lost more than five years of my life. I don't want to lose any more of it."

"What about Troy? Where does he fit into all of this?"

"He's my friend." Who happens to be an amazing kisser.

"What if he wants to be more than just friends?"

I spot a stick near the water's edge and walk over to it. "I'm not looking for a boyfriend, if that's what you're asking. And I'd be the worst possible girlfriend. No one needs a partner who has gone through what I have. Who is broken and has abandonment issues. My parents were a lot like yours." I grab the stick and hurl it into the water, away from where the ducks are swimming. Bailey barks, straining on her leash to go after it.

Thankfully, Kellan doesn't bother with fake platitudes that I'm not broken or some crap along those lines.

He, more than anyone, knows what I said is true. I'm not girl-friend material.

Especially for someone like Troy.

As it is, I'll have to tell Troy we can't kiss again.

Strike that.

I'll have to tell Troy we can be nothing more than friends who occasionally kiss. I'm sure he'll be fine with that.

48

TROY

May, Present Day
Maple Ridge

My jeans pocket vibrates with an incoming call. I turn off the drill and check who's calling. Jayne, my assistant.

She wouldn't be phoning while I'm at a job site if it wasn't important. "Hey, Jayne. What's up?"

"Hi, Troy. I just found out my mom had a stroke this morning." Her voice is thick with tears.

"I'm sorry to hear that. How is she?"

"It wasn't a major stroke, which is the good news. But the doctor said it's impacted her language center, and there might be some residual damage to her motor cortex. She'll need someone to look after her for a few months. Maybe longer."

"Don't worry. Your job'll be waiting for you when you return. I can hire a temporary assistant in the meantime." Jayne's stepfather died last year. She needs to be there for Mary.

"Thanks, Troy." She takes a deep breath, the sound stuttering through the phone. "But I'm not sure if I will be returning. I'll need to convince Mom to come back with me. And she's not a big fan of the place. Too many bad memories for her here."

Can't say I blame her after the scandal that rocked our small town because her husband left Mary for another woman. That relationship didn't last.

"Well, in that case, thank you for everything you've done for Carson Construction," I say. "I've appreciated all the work you've done to make the company run so smoothly. I'm going to miss you. When are you leaving?" I make a mental note to send flowers to Jayne's mother.

"Tomorrow. I've got a flight out early afternoon."

We talk for another minute or two and end the call.

I don't have a backup plan when it comes to who I can hire. Jayne has been with me from almost day one, when I started the company. I hired her once I realized I couldn't do everything myself. Back before business picked up.

I head for the living room. Lance and Pete are pulling up the old carpeting so we can replace it with laminate flooring. "Hey, Pete. Is your sister still looking for a job?"

He looks up from the strip of carpet he's removing. "Nope, she landed one last week at the medical clinic. She's their new receptionist now that Gladys has retired."

Retired? I swear Gladys has worked at the clinic since the turn of the century. The last century. "That's great." Great for Pete's sister, but it doesn't help me.

"I'm going for a coffee run," I announce. "You guys want anything?"

I grab their orders and climb into my truck. Lance is keeping an eye on Butterscotch while I'm gone.

Zara's working the front counter when I enter Treats. "Hi, Troy," she says brightly. A little too brightly.

"Hey. Is Jess still around?" Her bike and Bailey's trailer are where she usually leaves them out front.

"Her shift ended about twenty minutes ago." Zara walks to the front of the counter. "I need to talk to you in the staff room." Her voice is low, her tone carefully neutral, but she doesn't seem overly upset. I try to take that as a good sign.

I follow her down the short hallway that leads to the public restroom and the staff room.

We walk into the staff room. No one else is here. Zara doesn't bother to sit on the couch or armchair, and neither do I.

"Did she have another flashback?" I ask.

Zara nods, worry pulling at the corners of her mouth. "It wasn't as bad as last time. The power went out for a brief moment. Keshia and I found her huddled next to the wall, shaking badly. She didn't have a knife this time, so she wasn't at risk to herself or anyone else."

"Why didn't you call me?" The words come out in quick succession, my concern for Jess squeezing the trigger.

Zara's eyes widen for a nanosecond, and a series of emotions flash on her face. Her expression finally settles on *Get over yourself, dumbass.* "Didn't realize I was supposed to, Troy. Keshia and I knew what to do this time. We didn't need you riding in on your steed and rescuing the damsel with one of your golden kisses." Her mouth jerks up in a *busted* smirk.

The concern in my chest loosens slightly, and a chuckle releases low in my throat. "She told you we kissed, huh?"

"She might've mentioned it. Or I might've guessed because it was kind of obvious from her expression. So, what are you planning to do now with all that hot chemistry between you two?"

"Sorry, that intel is need-to-know only, and you don't need to know anything about it."

Zara shakes her head the way Mom did when I was a kid and she caught me sneaking a snack before dinner. "Except Jess is my friend. And as her friend, it's my duty to make sure she's happy." Zara eases out a long-troubled breath. "So...any suggestions what to do about the flashbacks?"

"How is she otherwise here?" I suspect I know the answer, but I want to hear it from Zara.

"Things haven't changed much. She's tense most of the time, other than when she's with Bailey. She tries to pretend she's fine, but I think she's so scared of what happened her first day here, she can't relax."

My gaze drops to Bailey's crate. "I might have a solution, but it means you'll lose her as an employee."

"If you have a better solution than Jess always being on edge, I'll deal with it. Like I said, she's my friend too, and I hate seeing her struggle so much." Zara studies my face. "Any idea yet what happened to her?"

"Not a single clue. She doesn't want to talk about it. I'm just happy she agreed to see a therapist."

Zara nods, the movement slow and thoughtful. "It's a good thing the state's covering it. Seems my company insurance plan is sadly lacking in the mental health department. I need to get on that."

I inwardly winced at the first part, but it must have registered on my face a second later if the way Zara's eyes narrow is any indication. "Damn. The state isn't covering the therapy, is it? You're the one paying for it."

I shrug as if it's no big deal. As if we're talking about a simple cup of coffee and not an hour-long therapy session every two weeks. "What was I supposed to do? She couldn't keep going the way she was. She needed help."

Zara puts her hands on her hips. A series of emotions flickers on her face and lands on a frown. "And she's okay with you paying for her therapy?" The lines on her forehead deepen. "That doesn't sound like Jess. She's not exactly open when it comes to asking for or accepting help."

I don't rush to respond, and a string of silent curses flashes in Zara's eyes. "She doesn't know, does she? She actually believes the state is covering the cost. You lied to her?"

"Like I said, she needed help." A warning darkens my tone. "And if she finds out who really is paying for it, I'm worried she'll quit therapy." Because Zara's right. Jess doesn't like accepting help.

"You're right, she does need therapy. But that doesn't mean you have to pay for it. I'm sure once you told her about Robyn, Jess would've paid for it herself just to get better."

"With what exactly? She doesn't have a lot of money." That much I have figured out. "What she does have she's spending on her house." Because that house seems to mean more to Jess than anything else—other than Bailey. And I don't mean in the typical sense I see with most homeowners. The house has a deeper significance for Jess. I just haven't figured out what it is.

"You truly believe she'd put the renovations on her house above getting therapy?"

"That's exactly what I think. She would have done the renovations herself instead of hiring me or someone else. That's why I offered to help her with the renos, but as her friend. I'm not her paid contractor, and I can get the supplies at cost." And even then, it took some convincing to get Jess to agree to it.

Zara stares at me. "Let me get this straight. You're paying for her therapy, you're spending all your free time helping her renovate her house, and you arranged for her to adopt a service dog? Which, I might add, she doesn't realize is *her* dog. She thinks she's just Bailey's puppy raiser." Appraising eyes bore into mine. In a flutter of dark lashes, those same chocolate-brown eyes swirl with warmth and awareness. "Are you in love with her?"

Before I can respond, a delighted laugh powers from Zara. "Ohmigod, you *are* in love."

I frown. "I'm not in love with Jess. She and I are friends. And as her friend, it's my duty to be there for her in whatever way I can." *And that includes kissing her if it helps her relax.*

Right, because you didn't enjoy kissing her as much as she enjoyed being the recipient.

"Sure, if you'd been friends with her for longer than you have been," Zara says, looking a little too smug. "But you've only known her two months."

"You're reading way too much into this, Zara."

But is she? I push the thought away. I'm not in love with Jess. I care for her. A lot. I enjoy holding her and kissing her. A lot. And I think about what it would feel like to sink into her. A lot. But that doesn't mean I'm in love.

Except...that's not entirely true. Those aren't the only times I think about her.

I think about Jess all the time.

She's the first thing I think about when I wake up. And the last thing I think about when I go to bed. And it's not because I'm worried about her or thinking about ways I can help her. It has nothing to do with that.

I love spending time with her. Love watching her reaction to the simplest things, like the sunset and Bailey and Butterscotch playing together. I love listening to her laugh. I can never get enough of that.

I can...I can never get enough of Jess.

I'm not just falling for her.

I'm falling for her hard.

Zara drops onto an armchair and leans back to look up at me. "Alright, if you say so. Anyhow, what's your solution that will cost me an employee?"

"Jayne's mother had a stroke, and Jayne's going to Texas to be with her. She doesn't think she'll be returning to Maple Ridge, which means I need a new assistant." I sit on the couch, my forearms resting on my knees. "The job's perfect for Jess. And Bailey can be with her all the time."

"I know she worries about Bailey, which isn't helping the situation. And Bailey can't learn to be there for her if she isn't with Jess twenty-four seven." Zara levels me with a meaningful glance. "But if I were you, Troy, I'd give Jess the option of which job she wants to do. Right now, you're trying to be the white knight, fixing all her problems. But you're also not being completely honest with her."

"I'm not trying to fix all her problems. I'm helping her. And if I'm keeping the truth from her, it's for her benefit, not mine."

Zara mutters something that sounds like "Alpha men!" and shakes her head. "At least ask her which job she'd prefer to do before you sign her up for your company medical insurance."

OLIVIA AND NOVA ARE AT THE COUNTER WHEN ZARA AND I RETURN to the café. Nova is in her mother's arms. She reaches out when she sees me, and I happily accept her small body.

"Hey, Princess. What brings you and your momma here?"

She doesn't reply. She presses her small hands on my cheeks, squishing my mouth into fish lips, and giggles.

Olivia smiles, light dancing in her eyes. "Hi, Troy. We came to pick up a special dessert. I was going to call you. We're hoping you can come over for dinner tonight. You haven't been over in a few weeks."

More like three. *Shit.* How did that happen?

"I can't, unfortunately. I'm helping a friend with her renovations. Rain check, Aramis?" I blow a raspberry on Nova's cheek, and she giggles once more.

I glance at Olivia and catch the crestfallen expression on her face. The expression is just as quickly replaced with a grin, her eyes bright. "Of course, Athos."

I'm only half listening, my thoughts replaying my conversation with Zara.

My thoughts focused on how I can't wait to have Jess in my arms again.

How I can't wait to kiss her.

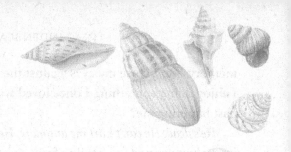

49

JESSICA

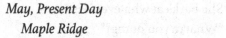

May, Present Day
Maple Ridge

I lie on my stomach in the backyard. It's been several hours since Kellan dropped me off at Picnic & Treats. Several hours since I admitted to him I spent five years in prison for a crime I didn't commit.

I compose the image on my iPhone screen, missing the flexibility I had with my DSLR camera when it came to depth of field and exposure. The last rays of sunlight strike the daffodils from behind, highlighting the soft white and yellow petals, and a rush of excitement throbs through my veins.

My husband...my *late* husband's voice screams in my head, "You don't have time for crap like that." I inadvertently flinch, bracing for the painful punch to the stomach. The kick to my side.

He's dead. He can't hurt me anymore. He's gone.

I tighten my hold on the phone, my hands clammy from the

memory, and I close my eyes against the pain. *Dammit.* Why can't I enjoy doing something I once loved without the ugliness of my past haunting me?

He's dead. He can't hurt me anymore. He's gone.

Robyn warned me healing from complex PTSD won't be easy. She also warned me the painful memories will never go away, but over time, they won't be as painful.

Healing won't be easy, but it is possible.

I study the daffodils on the screen. They're beautiful, the symbol of hope and new beginnings.

Bailey bounds past me, a blur of golden hair in my periphery minus her red vest. It's her playtime, which means she gets to be a regular puppy, exploring the backyard and probably chasing another bug.

She barks at whatever it is.

"What're you doing?"

A startled shriek bursts from my lungs, taking my heart with it. I twist around.

My butt parks on the patchy grass, my breath and heartbeat racing. Troy's standing on the other side of the closed gate, wearing jeans and a heather-gray T-shirt, and I take a second to appreciate how the cotton skims his taut chest muscles.

He opens the gate, and he and Butterscotch enter through it. Bailey immediately goes to play with Butterscotch on the grass.

Troy comes over to where I'm sitting and crouches next to me. "Sorry, didn't mean to scare you. Thought you'd heard me. I wasn't exactly being stealth."

I flash him an embarrassed smile. "I have a bad habit of slipping into the zone when I'm taking photos."

"Can I see?" Troy points to my phone. "The photos you've taken so far?" The eagerness in his eyes shines back at me, so naked, so raw. Or maybe I'm the one who feels exposed. It's been forever since I've shared my photos with anyone. Shared my passion with someone who won't use it to demean me.

I hand him the phone, and he scrolls through the various shots of Bailey. Some are obvious misses. Others capture her boundless energy and playfulness, her curiosity and innocence.

An unexpected wave of regret for showing them to him swells inside me, threatens to pull me under. "I still need to edit them," I tell him, my uncertainty building with each passing moment.

Troy continues looking at the photos but doesn't say anything. *He hates them.*

That shouldn't bother me, but it does. So far, he and my dead husband have nothing in common. I was hoping, praying, that would also be true when it came to my photography.

Troy hands my phone back to me, a wide smile on his handsome features, and my heart rate kicks up once more. "You're really talented, Jess." A sweet reverence hugs each vowel, kisses his consonants. "Why did you stop?"

I shake my head. "That falls under the category of something I can't tell you. It's enough that I did stop. But since Robyn's encouraging me to reexplore my old passions..." I leave the rest of the sentence hanging, letting him fill in the blanks.

"It's a good thing you did take it up again. I'd hate to see you give up photography when you're so good at it. It would be a waste."

I smile, the curve of my lips as wide as his, my heartbeat still fast and fluttery. "Thank you."

Troy stands and helps me up.

"There's something I wanted to discuss with you," Troy says as we head to the back door. "My assistant's mother had a stroke, so Jayne's returning to Texas to look after her, possibly indefinitely. Would you be interested in the position? It's full time. The pay and health benefits are good. And Bailey can stay by your side while you're working."

I stop walking and turn to him. "I have a job." Caution stains my words, but I don't know why. The assistant job would solve the problem about being a puppy raiser when I'm not with Bailey all the time. Guilt coats my insides like algae on an aquarium. I'm failing her when it comes to my responsibilities. Failing Bailey and the person who will eventually be her parent.

Troy rolls his shoulders as if preparing to battle. "A job that causes flashbacks and has you so tense, you're a step away from having a panic attack every time you work."

"Zara told you?" My voice is scratchy and leapfrogs an octave on the final word. *Of course she told him.*

"About the flashback? Yes."

"Did she tell you it wasn't as bad as last time?" That I wasn't holding a knife?

"She did. But you can't keep living like this, Jess. Zara told me she can find someone else to replace you."

Replace me?

The bitter taste of rejection numbs my body. Just when I think I'm safe, that no one's going to push me away, I'm proved wrong.

Warm fingers rest lightly on my arm. I flinch. "Hey, Jess, breathe. You're not losing Zara as a friend. You can still do all the things you've been doing with her, Simone, Em, and Avery. The hanging out together at Picnic and Treats. The hiking. That won't change."

Troy's hand shifts to the lower curve of my spine. The movement is cautious and this time I don't flinch or cringe or pull away. The touch is gentle and soothing. It lacks any hint of possessiveness, lacks a need to control me.

I relax into his hand and breathe deeply.

Troy kisses my brow. "It's up to you what you want to do. I'm just providing you with another option. I need a new assistant. The job's yours if you want it."

"Okay," I whisper. "As long as Zara's all right with it. I don't want to leave her short an employee and scrambling to find someone else."

The warm breeze brushes my cheeks, flicks loose strands of hair around my face that have fallen from my ponytail.

"Don't worry about Zara. She'll be fine." The reassuring smile on Troy's face somehow does its job, and I relax a little more.

The smile turns mischievous, his eyes heated. "I've been craving another kiss all day."

He's not the only one who's been thinking about last night's kisses, who still feels them on their lips, still tastes them on their tongue.

His beautiful, warm brown eyes ask the question he doesn't give voice to. I nod my reply.

He lowers his mouth to mine, igniting every cell in my body. Embers flicker and burn, smolder and heat. They incinerate regret and fear and torch my past humiliations. And then it's just Troy and me kissing. Kissing and exploring the warm, wet depths of his mouth.

Our tongues glide and dance together, and I feel...I feel like I might melt into a pool of nothingness and everythingness.

It all feels too much...and it all feels just right.

Troy pulls away, and his eyes search mine. "Jess, where do you see things going between us?" His voice is low with the roughness that could easily flash-fire my panties to ash.

"What do you mean?"

"I like you. I like you a lot. I want to take you out on dates. And I want you to be my girlfriend." He doesn't vocalize the other thing he wants, but below the belt, his body is making that request very clear.

I shake my head. "I can't, Troy."

A bird tweets from somewhere nearby, the song almost sad and bittersweet.

"Can't or don't want to?" He steps away, and his brow ridges into a frown. "Is there someone else?"

"Definitely not. We barely know each other. And now that I'm going to be your employee, dating you seems...unethical."

"We've known each other for two months. Most couples don't even know each other that long before they date."

True. My husband and I began dating shortly after I met him in a bar with my friends. I'd known nothing about him. He was a good-looking guy who bought me a drink and danced with me most of the night. I probably fell in love with him then. Before I realized he was the king of chameleons, a man who would transform into whatever you needed—until he didn't. Until the real man—not the smoke and mirrors—emerged.

Troy and I have known each other a lot longer, but it's still not enough time to know each other well. There's so much about me I can't tell him. Things even Robyn doesn't know. I'm not interested in being in a relationship that's built on a lie. I've traveled that route. And ended up abused and in prison for it.

"As for you dating the boss," Troy adds, unaware of my whirlwind of emotions, my internal debates, "no one who works for me will give a damn about that. During work hours, you'll just be my office assistant."

"I-I get that. But I need time, Troy. I'm starting to pick up the pieces of my life, thanks to Robyn. I'm not ready to have a boyfriend."

A slow breath escapes him. "Okay, I can understand and respect that. So, I guess no more kissing?" His tone isn't flirty. It isn't irritated. It's neutrally optimistic.

"No. Your kisses make me feel good. Heck, your kisses make me feel. Period."

A cocky grin lifts his mouth to one side. "Ah, so you were using me for my hot kisses?"

I have to bite my lip to keep from laughing, but I can't prevent the smile from sneaking onto my face. "I'm definitely not using you for your kisses, Troy." My expression sobers. "I like being with you. Can't that be enough without putting labels on things?"

His grin straightens to a line, and he scrubs his hand along his jaw, as if he's thinking. The smile that appears on his face after a beat sends my heart stumbling and soaring. It's sweet and supportive and a little bit devilish. "Alright. We'll do it your way.

You call the shots. When you're ready to take things to the next step, you just have to let me know. If we're moving too fast—even if we're moving slower than an arthritic tortoise—let me know."

I contemplate his words and everything I do know about Troy, all the things his friends and Delores have told me. I think about his goal with the festival and the people he's hoping to help. And I let myself smile, the wide curve of my lips generous and genuine.

I hold out my hand to him. "Okay, you have yourself a deal."

Troy doesn't shake my hand. He uses it to yank me to him. And he seals the deal with a kiss that leaves my knees quivering, my lips pleading for more.

I don't think I'll ever get enough of his kisses.

And that scares me.

FIVE DAYS LATER, I'M SITTING AT A LIBRARY COMPUTER AFTER WORK, typing the latest notes I've transcribed from Angelique's journal. Bailey is at home in her crate, taking a break from her training. It's the same routine we do twice a week so I can catch up on typing the pages I've read to eventually give to Anne.

I finish at where I stopped reading last night and log out of my Google account. It's been a week since I last looked to see if the world has finally moved on with respect to my release from Beckley. Since I last looked to see if the authorities have captured my late husband's killer.

A bunch of new articles pop up. I glance behind me, making sure no one is there to see what I'm reading. The coast is clear. I click on the first article.

So far, the murderer is still eluding the police. A picture of my late husband and me smiling for the camera unfortunately graces the article. I remember the photo. It was taken at the beach the year before Amelia was conceived, and during one of those patches when things seemed to be getting better between us—right before they shattered again.

"Hey, Troy," a male voice says from the other side of my computer screen.

I look around the monitor. Troy's a few yards away, talking to an Asian man in his sixties. *Fuckers.*

Troy nods with a smile and heads toward me.

I quickly close the browser, groaning at how there's not enough time to clear the search history first like I normally do before I leave the library. Not unless I want Troy to see what I'm doing.

"Hey." He leans down and kisses my cheek. "I didn't know you were gonna be here."

"I was just typing something. My journal. Which Robyn wanted me to keep. But I'm done now."

His brow puckers into a confused frown. "Why didn't you type it at work? You can do that, you know."

"Change of view. And I prefer not to do my personal stuff at work. Besides, Bailey needed a break from her training. So, I took her to the park for a bit and dropped her off at home before coming here."

He nods like that makes sense. I ease out a long breath. Thank God the man had said Troy's name and loud enough so I heard him; otherwise, Troy might have seen what I'd been doing and pieced together my real identity.

"I have to go to Eugene on Thursday," he says. "You want to come with me? You can look into getting a laptop. If you want."

I push the chair away from the table and grab my purse from the floor. "Really? I've been thinking about getting a secondhand laptop so I can use editing software for my photos."

And so I can sit on my patio and type out Angelique's journals while Bailey plays in the backyard.

50

TROY

June, Present Day
Maple Ridge

Five weeks after I offered Jess the job as my assistant, I steer my truck into the empty parking spot for the Ash Fall's Annual Sunshine Festival. Gravel crunches under the tires.

"So many vehicles." Jess's voice is so low, I barely hear it. But the tremor in it pivots me in my seat.

Her gaze is directed out the passenger window, her hands fidgeting on her lap. I thread my fingers with hers and give her hand a reassuring squeeze. There has been a lot of hand-holding and kissing and spending time together over the past five weeks, even though what we have between us doesn't have a label.

But during the day when she's my assistant, we're professional. No kisses. No touching. No anything that isn't part of the job description. And, like I suspected, none of my employees give a damn that I'm with her. They like Jess, and that's good enough for them.

"Don't worry; you'll be safe," I remind her. "We're just here to do research. Like a reporter."

I've been coming to the annual festival for as long as I can remember, but this will be the first time I'm attending with the intension of seeing what works and what doesn't.

"I've got this. I've got this. I've got this." Jess's words tumble out in a whispered chant.

"Hey, if you'd rather not be here, I can take you home." I was an idiot not questioning if the festival would be too much for her. She seemed fine with the idea when I initially brought it up, but now that we're here, she's clearly having second thoughts.

She turns her head to me. "No, I'm good. I want to do this. Like you said, it's research. I like research." She smiles. The tilt of her lips is small, but her eyes confirm the smile is genuine.

"Okay, but if it gets to be too much, we can leave." I'd rather not be the cause of her having another flashback. Hell, I'd rather she doesn't have any more flashbacks, period. But without knowing what happened to her, I have no idea if the festival will contain any triggers.

We climb out of the truck and, while holding hands, walk over to join my brothers, Zara, Emily, and Simone by Kellan's SUV. The dogs are at home because the festival will be too much for them, especially for Bailey since she is still undergoing training.

Lucas and Simone are acting like they haven't seen each other for several days, even though they're married. Her arms are around his neck and his are around her waist and their gaze is lovesick and horny.

A car slowly pulls past us, and Avery waves from the passenger seat. Noah's driving.

Jess stiffens, the movement almost imperceptible.

I lower my mouth to her ear. "Is something wrong?"

Jess's body melts into me, and I hold her in my arms. "I'm fine. I'm excited to be here." That's great, except she doesn't sound excited.

"Is it Noah? Has he done something?" It's the only thing I can think of. This isn't the first time she's reacted like this in his presence.

Jess's head turns to me, her eyes wide. Not with fear but surprise. Just as quickly, she shutters away the emotion, leaving nothing but uncertainty staring back at me. "He hasn't done anything. I just didn't expect them to be here."

My hand slides to the lower curve of her spine, and we wait for Avery and Noah to join us. The tension doesn't return to Jess's body, but I still get the feeling I'm missing a giant piece of the puzzle. A puzzle that *might* be tied to whatever resulted in her PTSD, but it's impossible to tell.

I watch for signs of what it could be, but she's all smiles for Noah and Avery as they approach the group. And they respond the same way to her.

"Are you okay if we check out the marketplace first?" Simone asks the women. "I'm on the lookout for some more artisans to showcase in my subscription boxes."

Everyone agrees to the plan, and we pass through the festival gates and head in that direction.

On one side of the large field, several carnival rides have been set up: a carousel, Ferris wheel, pendulum, a small roller coaster for younger kids. Screams and laughter come from that way. There won't be any rides at the With Hope Festival, so we don't bother with that section of the grounds.

Ahead of us, a large stage has been set up for the entertainment, and a local country band is playing. The gravelly male voice is singing about losing his love and finding her again. The Sunshine Festival only books small acts. Nothing popular like the rock band Pushing Limits.

Simone leads us to the area where the outdoor marketplace

booths have been set up. An array of smells fills the air from the nearby food trucks. The delicious aromas of deep-fried treats and grilling meat and popcorn dominate.

Jess checks over her shoulder. Her body stiffens, and her hand tightens around mine.

I stop walking, causing her to abruptly stop too, our fingers still entwined. I scan the area where her gaze is directed. All I see is a person dressed up as a rag doll, making balloon animals for the kids lined up for her, an ice cream truck, and the petting zoo. A father is looking at his phone and points in the direction we came from. Several other families are heading for the entrance to the petting zoo.

As far as I can tell, everything seems fine. But I can't be sure. "Is something wrong?" I ask Jess.

She tears her attention from where she was looking and turns back to me. "No, I'm fine. I just had a weird feeling someone was watching me. But I guess I was imagining things."

Something red hot turns on inside me. Because I'm pissed at whoever was responsible for making her paranoid? Or because she might be wrong to brush off her concerns? I hate that she can't escape her fears for even a few hours. "Can you think of any reason someone would be watching you?"

She shakes her head, and her shoulders loosen from their knot. A smile captures her mouth. It's the same curve of the lips, the spark in her eyes I'm seeing more of lately. The smile is enough to knock the air from my lungs—like it does every time she gifts me with it. "No. It's just my imagination working over-time. We can blame it on the suspense novels I've been reading."

"Those books about World War II spies might also have something to do with it."

She laughs. "Yeah, that too."

I glance behind us to Lucas and Kellan. Both have also stopped walking, probably because we have. Lucas is talking, but

Kellan appears to be only half listening. I recognize the expression on his face.

The rest of Kellan's attention is on our surroundings and the crowd. I have no clue what he's searching for. It could be he's expecting to bump into a friend here. Though I don't think it's that. He's in protective mode. Except that doesn't make sense either. The person he's most protective of is Emily—though I doubt he realizes that himself. But Emily is ahead of us, with the rest of the group.

He turns back to us. The guarded look vanishes, replaced with an expression that's as readable as a soggy blueprint. Even after knowing Kellan most of my life, this is one expression I can't decipher.

The others are waiting for us at the entrance to the marketplace when the four of us join them a few minutes later. Kellan leans in closer to Jess and tells her something, his voice so quiet I can't hear what he's saying. She releases my hand, and they move aside to talk in private.

An unexpected rush of jealousy surges in my veins. This isn't the first time I've noticed the subtle shift in their friendship that started last month. It's not as if Kellan wasn't friendly toward Jess before that, but he had that same restraint that holds him back with most people.

And it's not only that he's friendlier. He's protective of her too.

He shifts his body so his back is to her. If I didn't know better, I'd think he was guarding her.

We wander from booth to booth, mostly trailing the five women as they check out the different vendors. The guys and I discuss last night's final game of the Stanley Cup playoffs while we wait.

The women stop at a booth selling handmade soaps and candles. The place is busy, so we don't bother joining them. We position ourselves slightly away from the crowd and continue our hockey discussion.

A hand rests on my shoulder from behind. "Hi, Troy."

I twist around. Katelyn's smiling, her eyes wide and doe-like. "I didn't expect to see you here."

I hear Katelyn talking to me, but I don't really pay attention to what she's saying. I'm too focused on Kellan and why the hell he's acting like Jess's bodyguard. I'm her boyfriend—whether she wants to give it a label or not.

I've had the same Marine training he's had.

I should be the one protecting her—not Kellan.

51

ANGELIQUE

May 1943
France

A Jeep with a Nazi flag flapping in the breeze pulls up the gravel driveway to the farmhouse. The polished metal glints in the early evening sunlight.

And the muscles in my body turn to petrified wood.

My heart hammers against my ribs, the hollow sound echoing in my chest like a wooden xylophone. The rhythm is fast, the tune frantic.

I haven't seen the Jeep from the night of the dinner party in almost two weeks. I was hoping to never see it again.

Captain Schmidt steps out of the house.

Fischer isn't with him. Since they returned from their military operation last week, I've grown used to frequently seeing the two men together. It's clear they are close like brothers. They laugh and tease each other the way Hazel and I did growing up.

I haven't overheard any more conversations between them.

Haven't overheard anything that will aid London in this war. And I still don't know why Schmidt's mother and sister had to escape the Gestapo.

The driver gets out of the Jeep and opens the door for his passenger. The lean body of Major Müller emerges from the back seat, and I will my legs to keep moving. The idea of being in his presence makes me nauseous, makes my skin crawl like it's covered in ants.

I hurry towards the front door of the house. There are only three yards between the major and me, and I have every intention of being inside the farmhouse before he gets any closer.

The brick building, partially covered in ivy, promises me a safe haven from the man. It's an offer I hope it can live up to.

"You can stay right there, Madame D'Aboville." His clipped French sends an alarm through my body. So, the man does know French.

He marches up to Captain Schmidt, who hasn't moved since he stepped out of the farmhouse. Müller salutes him, clicking his heels together. "*Heil*, Hitler!"

Schmidt returns the greeting, and the crawling sensation on my body intensifies.

"I came to inform you that First Lieutenant Dieter Fischer is dead," Müller says in French. A chill spreads through me, bringing with it a sense of foreboding. "He was executed this afternoon for desertion."

Silence falls like a heavy weight, knocking the air from my lungs. I cannot look at Schmidt, cannot imagine what is going through his mind. I also cannot imagine why Müller would want me to hear that the Germans executed one of their own. To show me just how ruthless the German Army is?

I should feel relief the world is rid of one more German soldier. One more German who is partially responsible for the state of France and Europe and the world right now. One more German who wants to destroy all that is good and free.

But I don't.

Because Dieter was nothing like the rest of those monsters. In this moment, I cannot think of him as a German soldier, the enemy. I can only think of him as the man who lost his life to the callousness of the Nazis. The man who had shown me simple acts of kindness whenever he visited, much like Schmidt has.

Schmidt nods, all hint of emotion erased from his expression. His reaction is like a match to tinder. Anger flares in me, a bonfire burning out of control. I want to scream at him for being uncaring and emotionless like the rest of them.

But to do so could mean the death of me—and maybe it would be the death of Schmidt. Perhaps that is the real reason behind his blank expression. I look down at the grass beneath my feet so Müller and Schmidt can't see my face.

"I always knew the man was a coward." This time Müller's words are in German, his tone the cold-metal spikes of a mace. "I don't tolerate cowards. And I would hate to find out your unit is filled with cowards like the first lieutenant."

Schmidt doesn't respond. He stares ahead, not looking at the monster in uniform.

"His replacement, who I have personally selected, will be posted soon," Müller continues, his tone not defrosting even a smidgen. "The next first lieutenant will not be committing acts of desertion."

"Can I ask what act of desertion First Lieutenant Fischer committed?" Schmidt's voice remains even, his body still stiff.

"Desertion with intent to remain permanently away."

Schmidt does not react to the charge, but it comes as no surprise to him. Dieter had already warned his friend that he was planning to escape.

"Has someone contacted his family?" The muscle in Schmidt's jaw bunches, the movement barely perceptible.

Müller gives a terse nod. "It has been dealt with."

I remain motionless, my face free of any emotion that will

give away I understand their exchange. On the inside, my heart aches for Dieter's family. But at the same time, I wonder what they will think of the news. Will they be ashamed that he deserted the Army? Or will they be heartbroken to have lost a son?

Müller walks to the waiting Jeep, gravel crunching beneath his boots. The Jeep door slams shut, and the vehicle drives away, leaving silence and dust in its wake.

I stay perfectly still, waiting for the Jeep to drive out of view. Schmidt doesn't say anything. He doesn't look at me. He walks past me, his expression one I know only too well. It's the twist of emotions I experienced when I found my fiancé naked with my sister.

Anger and agony and pain and shame.

His emotions are buried beneath the surface, visible through fine cracks in his veneer. And all the anger I felt towards him fizzles, a candle flame in the rain.

He heads in the direction of the pond, where he has gone almost every evening for the past week. Sometimes Fischer was with him. Other times he was alone.

I go into the farmhouse and make supper. The front door opens a short time later while I'm preparing the food. I glance over my shoulder to see if it's Schmidt.

Jacques walks past the kitchen and goes upstairs. I finish cooking his food and carry it to his bedroom. With the exception of the first night when Schmidt moved into the farmhouse, Jacques refuses to eat with me if Schmidt will be joining us. And he refuses to eat the food that Schmidt supplies. He only eats the food he provides or what I am able to get with our ration cards.

It's the one act of defiance Schmidt knows about.

I return downstairs to an empty kitchen and still no sign of Schmidt.

I grab my worn cardigan and hurry to the pond, telling myself I'm doing this to gain war intelligence. Unlike those other times I followed him, I don't try to be quiet. I'm not going there to spy on him. But I also don't know what I plan to do once I get there.

Schmidt is sitting on the grassy bank, staring out at the water. I've never seen anyone look so lost.

An ache, so simple and pure and unexpected, fills me. And Dieter's words return from the first night they came here. If what he said is true, Schmidt might have lost his mother and sister to the Gestapo. And now he has lost his friend, a man who didn't want to be here, who risked death to allegedly desert his post with the Wehrmacht.

I walk to where Schmidt is sitting and lower myself onto the grass next to him. He doesn't react to my intrusion, doesn't remind me it's after curfew. He continues to stare out at the water.

"I'm sorry about your friend," I say after a moment. "Were you two close?" Most of the teasing and joking I overheard between them was in German, so I must be careful with how I tread.

Schmidt's handsome features in the light of the full moon are weary. His shoulders are slumped. "We've known each other since we were babies. He was a brother to me."

"Will you be all right?" As soon as the question is out of my mouth, I want to snatch it back. It's a daft question. He clearly isn't, but he won't admit to me that he's hurting. He's a soldier. To show weakness is a sign of cowardliness. Inexcusable. His commanding officer already believes Dieter was a coward. Schmidt won't want anyone else, especially me, to think the same of him.

"You had a sister. Would you have done anything to protect her, even if it meant doing something that went against who you were?"

I study his handsome features, unsure if he's referring to the sister I've overheard him talk about with Dieter, or about Dieter as his brother.

I think back to when Hazel and I were best friends. There wasn't anything I wouldn't have done for her.

I nod at Schmi—I nod at Johann's question. With him sitting here, a statue of grief for everything he has lost, possibly all at the hands of Hitler's men, I can't see him right now as the enemy. He's just a man who looks as though his own world is caving in on him in a way I hope to never understand.

I lost my sister because she betrayed me by falling in love with my fiancé and marrying him. She's still very much alive. While I might be angry at her for hurting me like that, I couldn't imagine losing her the way Johann might have lost his sister.

But if Hitler has his way, that's exactly what will happen.

If Hitler has his way, I'll know firsthand how Johann feels.

"My sister loves folklore," he says, surprising me. That was the last thing I had expected him to say. "One of her favourites involves the nixie."

"Nixie? I don't think I know that one." Hazel is the one who was once interested in English folklore. When we were little girls, she was positive fairies were real.

"They are like...water sprites who love singing and music. Their song lures humans into ponds and rivers, and once the foolish human is in the water, the nix drowns him or her. My sister would sit by the pond near our house, waiting to see one. When she was much younger, she was positive a nixie lived there, and she wanted to be friends with it." A wistful smile spreads across his face. A smile of longing for simpler days, when war was something our parents survived and we hoped never to experience.

"Wasn't she afraid the nix would lure her into the water and drown her?"

"No. My sister is two things. She is fearless and she is deaf. Even if a nixie had lived in the pond, it couldn't have lured her into the water. Anja couldn't hear its song."

I can see how that would be an advantage, if nixie did exist. "Did you believe in the folklore?"

He chuckles. "Definitely not. Or at least not at that point. My sister is five years younger than me, so by then, I thought I was wise and worldly."

"Is she in Austria?"

He looks away for a second to a tree near the water, its trunk twisted. The movement is quick, but not fast enough to hide the pain on his face. Was Dieter right about Johann's sister? Did his mother and sister know something that made them dangerous to the Gestapo? Or is there another piece of the puzzle I'm missing?

The Nazis have been rounding up Jews in Paris. Does their dislike for Jews extend to other people they consider beneath them? Like individuals with a disability? Like Johann's sister?

"What about you?" he asks, avoiding my question. "Did you or your sister ever believe in folklore?"

"My sister did. I was more of a realist. But she was older than me by almost two years and was positive the age difference meant she was right. About everything. She once sewed some tiny dresses and left them near a tree. She was certain the tree housed a family of fairies. Only she didn't leave them for the fairies. It was to convince me they were real."

Johann laughs. "Did it work?"

I flash him a sheepish grin. "Maybe a little. But then my father told me folklores were just make-believe. They were nothing more than stories that uneducated people believed in to explain the unexplainable. It just meant the individuals weren't asking the right questions."

"Yes, Monsieur Gauthier doesn't seem the kind of man who believes in fairies and folklore."

I inwardly cringe at my mistake. I'd been so focused on talking about my real sister, I'd forgotten we were talking about the sister who isn't mine.

A realisation hits me. A realisation as clear as the reflection in a polished mirror.

I miss my sister. For what must be the first time since I turned my back on her, the connection we once shared now burns bright. I miss her. I miss how close we had been. I miss how I could tell her every-thing. How she was there for me after our mother died. How she wiped away my tears. How she shared in my sorrows and my joys.

The pain of her betrayal is still there, like a scab protecting the wound beneath. But once the skin is healed, the scab falls away, revealing something stronger, something new.

I study the grass and the reeds in the pond, all so familiar, all so far away from home and my sister. "Do you miss Austria?"

"Very much so. I love Vienna, but I also miss the small town I grew up in."

"Small like where I live?"

Johann laughs once more. The sound is deep and almost musical, and it sends a shiver dancing up my spine. "Definitely not. It's much bigger than your village."

"Were you living in Vienna when the war broke out?" For some reason, I'm curious about the man Johann might have been if Hitler hadn't come into power and declared war on Europe. The man who didn't have to worry about the Gestapo arresting his mother and sister. The man whose best friend was still alive.

"Yes, I was. I had a good job in Vienna. It was my home."

"How come you're so fluent at French? You have a mechanical engineering degree, not a language degree."

"I like languages. I've always been good at them, like I'm good at maths. But I decided I enjoyed building things more."

I nod like that makes sense to a girl who grew up in a small village, married, then moved to a slightly larger town in Northern France, and lived with her husband until he passed away.

But the girl who went to university and studied languages, even though she had itched to study law, wants to know more. "How many languages do you speak?"

"German, French, and English. My mother's parents were French-speaking Swiss. I grew up speaking both French and German. And understanding English is helpful in my field. But my English isn't as good as my French. I read it more than I speak it. Even my French is pretty rusty."

If he considers his French rusty, I imagine his English is better than he gives himself credit for. But I'm not about to test him to find out how fluent he is at the language. "I'm impressed. I only speak French."

"What about your husband? Was he good at languages?"

"No. He only knew French." That couldn't be the farthest from the truth. Charles's French is awful.

"What was he like?" Johann's gaze remains on the pond.

"He was a great man. Hardworking. Sweet and loving." All the things I had once considered Charles to be.

"You loved him very much." It's not so much a question as a statement.

"I did. Still do, even though he's dead." I cross my fingers, hidden beneath my skirt, that Charles is alive. Despite everything that happened between him, Hazel, and me, I don't wish him dead. He's Hazel's husband now. And one day I'll be Auntie Iris to their children.

But that won't happen if I don't fix my broken relationship with my sister first.

I scan the dark surroundings, the country occupied by the enemy. If I survive my time in France as an SOE agent, the first thing I'll do when I return to England is to beg for Hazel's forgiveness.

Yes, she was the one who became involved with my fiancé when she knew I loved him, but I was the one who walked away from what was left of our family. Even when she tried to contact me and make amends, I refused to talk to her.

I have no intention of missing out on being an aunt to their children. An aunt who can spoil and corrupt them in a way only aunts can do. I have all those things to look forward to, as long as Charles and I survive this war.

If Dieter was correct about Johann's sister, Johann won't have that.

"What about you?" I ask. "Do you have a girlfriend or wife back home waiting for your return?"

"I had a girlfriend. But we didn't see eye to eye on a few things." There's a hardness to his tone that wasn't there before.

"So, you broke up with her?" I don't know why I'm interested in his relationships in his home country, other than it's something to talk about beyond my fictitious dead husband and Dieter and the war.

"It was for the best. She was..." He pauses as if searching for the right word in French. "She was dangerous when it came to my sister."

My eyebrows pinch together in a frown. "Why is that?"

Johann pushes himself to his feet, the movement abrupt and unexpected. "Because Hitler decided people with disabilities and those who are deaf don't deserve to live." The hatred in his voice would be enough to knock me onto my arse if I weren't already sitting.

Before his words can sink in, Johann stalks off, his body language warning me not to follow.

And I'm left gaping at him.

52

JESSICA

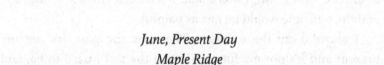

June, Present Day
Maple Ridge

"This soap smells soooo good." Emily holds up the homemade bar of soap from the festival booth for Zara, Simone, Avery, and I to sniff.

The vanilla, sage, and lavender scent sounds like an odd combination, but Em's right. The soap does smell good. They all do, as I can attest to thanks to the two bars in my hand. And that's me showing restraint.

I glance back to where we left the four brothers and Avery's boyfriend. The boyfriend I've done a good job keeping a distance from, even though he's done nothing to give me reason to fear him.

Katelyn is standing next to Troy, gazing at him like he's lost Aztec gold. Her lashes and makeup are bolder than normal. She looks nothing like me. I'm only wearing lip moisturizer and a coat of mascara.

She looks put-together, pretty, flirtatious. Her skin is smooth and perfect. She doesn't look like Frankenstein's half sister.

She's wearing a sundress that flutters in the breeze and strappy sandals. I'm wearing a T-shirt and jeans and sneakers. I don't look pretty. I look comfortable. Invisible.

At one time, I was Katelyn. But my husband wanted it that way. I was the trophy he paraded in front of his friends, his colleagues, anyone he wanted to impress.

If part of me failed to meet his high standards, I would find out about it later—with his fist to my stomach. A cigarette to my thigh.

But if I met his expectations and a good-looking man glanced at me the wrong way, I was a slut, a whore, a cheater, a disgrace, and the outcome would be just as painful.

I shove away the memory. That was the past. It's not my present and it's not my future. I'm not the girl I used to be, and I'm more than okay with that. I'm working toward a brighter, sunnier future. A future filled with all kinds of possibilities.

One day.

I turn back to the booth, pay for my soaps, and we move on to the next table.

Avery picks up a palm-sized wooden box with intricate designs carved in the dark wood. "Wow, these are incredible." She turns and shows it to Simone.

I trace my finger over the lotus carving in the lid of a box large enough to hold a pair of shoes. "It's beautiful." The whispered words slip over my lips. Beautiful and perfect.

"Thank you," the man on the other side of the table says, his smile peeking through a bushy gray beard. "Do you know what the lotus flower represents?"

"No?"

"The flower represents different things in different cultures," the man explains. "But it frequently symbolizes strength, enlightenment, rebirth. The flower grows from the murky depths of the water and raises above the surface. But the blossom is beautiful no matter how dirty the water might be."

I lift the lid and peer inside the cedar-lined box, flip the box over, and check the price. It isn't cheap, but the box is perfect for what I want it for. "I'll take it."

His smile widens. "Is this a gift?"

"You could say that." I glance over at Troy. He's still talking to Katelyn. She laughs and places her hand on his biceps.

Zara makes a huffing noise at the back of her throat. "Someone isn't being too subtle." She's also looking at the guys, so I assume she's talking about Katelyn.

"She's just being friendly." I can't believe I'm defending her. But I'm also not about to stalk over to them and make a scene because she's touching Troy.

He likes me. He kisses me.

And she's beautiful and perfect...and you're scarred and broken.

I swallow down my insecurities and turn back to the booth.

I pay for the carved box, put the soaps inside it, and Zara and I rejoin Simone, Avery, and Emily. The three women are waiting for us near the men and Katelyn.

Zara's gaze drops to the box in my arms. "Are you planning to buy something from almost every booth we visit? Because if you are, you're gonna need a pack mule." The corners of her mouth twitch in a barely suppressed laugh.

"I'm sure Jess only has to smile at Troy, Kellan, and Garrett," Simone says, "and they'll be more than happy to be the pack mules. And if they're not able to do it, I'll throw in Lucas to help out since you're my friend." She flashes me a sweet and very real smile.

A soft laugh tickles my throat. "That's very thoughtful of you."

Troy tells Katelyn something but doesn't wait for a response. He leaves her standing there and walks over to me. Her lips press together in a Victoria's-Secret pout.

"Nice box." He carefully removes it from my hands and tucks

it under his arm. He grabs my free hand and pulls me to him. His lips find mine in a God-I've-missed-you kiss.

I lean into him, my body buzzing with the need to get closer. To get inside his skin. To satisfy the growing ache throughout my body. For him.

At some point during the kiss, Katelyn disappears. Relief floats inside me that she won't be tagging along with our group.

Simone grins at Troy and me. "If you two haven't figured out yet just how adorable you are together, then look at this photo I just took of you. Sorry...I couldn't resist." She holds out her phone, the screen facing us. Troy takes it from her.

In the cropped-in-close photo, he and I are smiling at each other, having just kissed. We look like we're in our own little world. The photo is really good, the lighting perfect.

"I can send it to you, if you want," she says. "And don't worry, I won't post it on social media...unless you want me to."

My mouth goes dry. "Thank you. I don't want it on social media." Especially when Simone's Instagram account has a crazy number of followers because of her business.

Troy hands the phone back to her, his smile still on his face. "That would be great. Thanks."

The rest of the afternoon is spent with us wandering around the festival grounds, enjoying ourselves, taking notes. Kellan walks behind me the entire time, watching my back. It's been that way ever since I opened up to him about my past in prison. It's not hard to see he was once a Marine. And I feel safer knowing he's there, even though I no longer have to worry about someone attacking me when my back is turned.

Noah and Avery stop ahead of us. Two uniformed cops approach them, and my heart stumbles and trips like a drunk. Both are blond. Both aren't much older than me. Both look familiar, but at the same time I'm sure I've never seen them before. They didn't work with my husband. They never hung out at our house.

They won't recognize me. Even if they had worked with my husband—my very dead husband—they won't recognize me.

They laugh at something Noah tells them. *Too familiar. Much too familiar.*

A memory of my husband hosting a barbecue for his friends plays in my head like an old-fashioned movie. Of them laughing. Of one guy looking at me the wrong way—with a friendly smile.

A smile I paid for many times over.

And he...I dig deeper. Close my eyes. I remember...I remember he was sent to prison. A good cop turned bad. That's what my husband told me. My husband's monstrous face looms in my memory.

So smug, so satisfied, so calculating.

I gulp down the memory, squeezing it past the obstruction in my throat. *Always, always calculating.*

A steadying hand rests on my hip. Troy. I can smell his fresh outdoorsy scent.

I open my eyes, and I'm met by Troy's warm brown ones. Brown eyes that give me solace, that allow me to escape. I place my hand above his heart and walk myself through a relaxation exercise that Robyn taught me.

By the time I'm finished, I can breathe easier and the two cops have moved on.

"That's better. Those therapy sessions with Robyn are paying off." I silently thank Troy for connecting me with her. For not giving up on me.

He nods, his eyes filled with relief and something else. "That's good. Glad they're helping." His hand moves from my hip. "What's going on between you and Kellan?" The question eases over his lips like he doesn't have a care in the world, but that doesn't prevent my husband's words from slapping me. *Slut. Whore. Cheater.*

I frown, grasping at the relaxed feeling like a drowning victim grabbing a slippery floatation device. "What do you mean?"

"It's like he's become your personal bodyguard." Troy's tone contains an odd note to it. Not jealousy. Disappointment. Disappointment he wasn't given the position?

I release a small laugh that sounds shaky to my ears. "He's definitely not my bodyguard. For starters, I don't need one." Not unless the media tracks me down. And so far, I haven't seen any signs that they've succeeded there.

"Maybe you should talk to Kellan and see what he says," I tell Troy, hoping he does the opposite and drops it.

Because I'm not ready to reveal my past to Troy. Or anyone.

I'm not ready to reveal how I didn't fight harder to protect my daughter. Or how I spent five years in a maximum-security prison.

And I'm not ready for Troy to stop looking at me like he does...like I'm special.

53

JESSICA

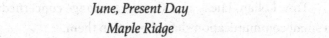

June, Present Day
Maple Ridge

After Troy and I, along with his brothers and our friends, leave the festival, we pick up pizza and Butterscotch and head to my house. All of us except for Avery and Noah. They have other plans for the night.

The moment I step through the front door, a feeling something is off blares in me. Without saying anything to the others, I check the security measures I'd set up on the living room windows. None have been disturbed. I can feel everyone watching me, no doubt wondering what I'm doing.

The room looks exactly as I left it. Not a single book has been moved. Not a single piece of furniture shifted.

I continue through to the kitchen. Footsteps trail behind me. Without looking, I can tell they belong to more than one person. More like at least four people.

I inspect the door leading to the backyard. The piece of tape I stuck across it is no longer firmly in place.

Fuckers.

"What's wrong?" Troy frowns.

"Someone broke in." I can barely push the words past my tightening throat. A tremor grips my body, and I wrap my arms around myself, trying to stop it or at least to hide it from the others.

The new-to-me laptop along with the box with the journals, medal, and heart pendant are all hidden in the secret room. But whoever broke in wouldn't have known that.

"How can you tell?" Emily asks.

"I put a piece of tape on the door so I'd know if someone opened it while I was gone." I point to the tape so they can see what I mean.

Troy, Kellan, Lucas, and Garrett exchange concerned glances; a silent communication shared between them.

Em pulls her phone from her purse. "I'll call the police."

"No! No police." The staccato words fire past my dry lips. The tremor worsens, and I'm visibly shaking now.

Everyone in the room except for Kellan stares at me in confusion. Kellan regards me with understanding and a dose of regret. Regret he's going to side with Em on this? Regret I'll have to face an institution I should trust but instead fear?

"No police," I whisper.

"Okay, no police," Kellan says softly.

Troy opens his mouth as if he's going to argue, but Kellan shakes his head once, the movement a stiff jerk. Whatever message is relayed between the two brothers is enough to silence Troy's words. His mouth snaps shut.

"Stay down here." Garrett aims his sharp-toned command at Zara, Simone, Emily, and me. "Where do you keep your valuables so we can check if anything is missing?"

I shake my head. "They wouldn't have been able to find

anything of value. It's well hidden." Maybe that's why Iris had the secret room built in the second bedroom. It was her version of a safe. Much like the secret space in Jacques's barn. "And it's not like I have much of value to begin with."

Troy and Garrett head upstairs. Lucas and Kellan search the rest of the house. I go into the laundry room and let Bailey out of her crate. She follows me into the kitchen and sits patiently while I stroke her.

Em picks up the small stack of eight-by-ten photos I'd left on the kitchen table this morning. She studies each one in turn. "These are gorgeous, Jess. Where did you get them?"

"I took them."

Emily shows Zara and Simone the top photo. In it, Troy was working at the workbench he'd set up in the backyard. He was shirtless, hammer in hand, and the low angle of the sun lit his body perfectly, emphasizing his muscles.

The image is gorgeous. Troy is gorgeous. But he's not just gorgeous on the outside. It's what's on the inside that completes the package, that makes him the man he is. And the photo somehow captures all of that.

Zara moves closer to Em to get a better look. "You really took these?"

"I studied photography as part of my journalism degree. I was playing with my phone camera when I took those." I point to the stack in Emily's hand.

The four brothers come into the kitchen. "Nothing looks disturbed upstairs," Troy says. "But you should check to make sure nothing's been stolen."

Simone's arms go around Lucas's waist. "Maybe whoever broke in realized they'd targeted the wrong house and left without taking anything."

A humorless laugh huffs past my lips. "You're probably right. They took one look at my ancient record player, saw I have no large flat-screen TV, and decided my place wasn't worth the effort."

Unless...unless the break-in had to do with my husband's murder.

A chill flash-freezes my stomach and spreads through my veins. I rub my arms, trying to generate heat in them, trying to generate heat in my body.

No one knows I'm here.

Well, no one beyond the few people whom I trust. Whom I pray I can trust.

No one in Maple Ridge has given any hint they know about my past. Surely if the rumor was circulating, one of my friends would have told me. From what I can tell, Delores is wired into the gossip grapevine. She would have told me if she'd heard anything.

Troy pulls me to him, and I lean into his long muscular length. And for the moment, I feel safe, protected.

Heat rolls off him, and my body greedily absorbs it. He kisses my temple. "You're staying at my house tonight, Jess. And we *will* be calling the cops."

I pull away and try to keep the panic from my expression. "What for? Other than the tape on the back door, there are no signs of a break-in. The police won't believe me. And maybe I'm wrong."

A long breath blows over Troy's lips, and I can tell he's contemplating the truth to my words. A crease pinches between his eyes. "You're right. They probably won't take it seriously without more substantial proof." He exchanges a quick glance with Lucas.

My gaze makes contact with Kellan's, and everything I'm thinking is mirrored on his face. He doesn't trust cops any more than I do, and he partly understands what I'm afraid of, what I refuse to tell Troy.

The SDPD didn't believe me when I tried to escape my

abusive husband. They didn't believe me when I insisted I didn't kill him. They didn't believe me when I told them I didn't know how the drugs got into my system. *Lies. Lies. Lies.* That was all they thought I was capable of.

Why should I believe Maple Ridge's police department is any different?

AFTER DINNER, EVERYONE LEAVES EXCEPT FOR TROY. "I'D FEEL better if you stayed at my house," he tells me, drying the last of the plates I just washed.

"I want to stay here." I need to stay here for reasons he can't understand. Not without me explaining why my home is important to me. I press my lips briefly to his. "But if it makes you feel better, you can stay here. With me."

He puts the plate on the counter and cups the back of my head with his hand. "Are you talking about me staying on the couch?" His mouth brushes mine. I part my lips, giving him access. His tongue sweeps inside my mouth, setting off a four-alarm fire deep in my belly.

I moan against his lips. "I was thinking more like my bed."

Troy pulls back, his gaze locked on mine. "What are you saying, Jess? I need you to spell it out for me." A million questions shine in his eyes. Questions about what has happened to me. Questions about whether I'm ready to take things further between us. Questions about if we're on the same page.

"I want you inside me, Troy. Does that clarify things?"

He nods slowly and swallows, his Adam's apple jerking up and floating down. "Definitely."

His mouth is on mine again, and all his questions and doubts and my insecurities are banished for the moment.

Troy's hands trace over my body, exploring my shoulders,

arms, ribs, breasts. His touch is so reverent, so tender, I tear up. I blink away the tears before their meaning is misunderstood, before he thinks we're moving too quickly. We're not. I'm ready.

His mouth moves along my jaw and down my neck. He gently nips my skin with his teeth. Need, desire, and want ignite deep inside me, and wetness dampens my panties.

I moan, my fingers exploring the strong muscles of his back.

"*Woof. Woof.*"

We glance down at Bailey and Butterscotch, who are gazing expectantly up at us.

"I should probably take Bailey out first and put her in her crate," I tell Troy, even though she's used to sleeping with me and not in the crate.

We take the two dogs outside. Once Bailey is in her crate and Butterscotch has settled himself in the living room, Troy takes my hand and leads me upstairs.

He flicks the bedroom light on. The sudden brightness chases away the soft shadows created in the dim twilight.

My chest tightens, and I gulp air into my lungs. My husband kept the light on when we had sex so he could see the fear on my face. See the damage he inflicted on my body. Those things...they made him more excited, harder, more dangerous.

"I need to do this in the dark." I don't fear Troy. I know he'll never hurt me. But lights mean he will see the road map of abuse on my body, and that includes the pink scar on my back where I was stabbed.

"I want to see you, Jess." Troy's tone is soft, almost cajoling. "When I make you come, I want to see your beautiful expression." His mouth caresses my lips. "I want to watch you come apart in my arms."

I shake my head with a jerk. "No. No, this has to be on my terms." My throat tightens just thinking about his reaction if he saw my body. Kellan's reaction was bad enough. It'll be so much harder for Troy.

And that will lead to questions. Questions I want to avoid.

"Okay," he says after a moment's hesitation and flicks off the light.

The room falls into shadows. There's enough glow from the streetlight to see each other, but hopefully not enough for him to see the scars.

He closes the door behind us, then takes my hand and gently pulls me to the bed. And I do my best to focus on him and not on how my room, my safe place, might have been violated.

I edge my fingers under the hem of his T-shirt. They continue their upward exploration, pushing the T-shirt up.

Troy yanks it over his head and tosses it to the side. His thumbs trace across my nipples, hidden beneath my bra. The buds tingle in response, thrilled to finally have some attention.

Needing to have skin-on-skin contact, I remove my top. A nervous sensation surges in my stomach and spreads throughout my body. I haven't been intimate with a man this way, without a gun to my head, in a long, long, long time, and it feels like I'm a virgin all over again, clueless at what to do next.

"God, you're fucking beautiful," Troy murmurs.

"How can you tell? It's dark in here." My tone is weightless with humor, tight with fear.

The low rumble of a laugh in his chest relaxes me, heightens my need for him. "It's light enough for me to see that much."

I resist looking down to see if my scars are visible. To do so will only bring his attention to them.

He reaches behind me and unhooks my bra. It's white and practical and nothing sexy. It lands on the floor, joining my T-shirt.

Troy cups my breasts in his hands and gently kneads the mounds. My nipples pucker and plead, craving so much more. As if hearing their soundless demands, Troy pops one into his mouth and sucks on it.

I arch back, and the air in my lungs whooshes out on a moan.

Troy tugs on the other nipple, which almost leads to my undoing. My body's on fire, needing so much more. I thread my fingers through his hair and pull on it hard.

"Jesus, I'm not gonna last if you keep that up." Troy's words pour over my nipple in a gravelly-rough groan, and it's like gasoline doused on a fire. My body goes up in flames. *Whoosh.*

Troy straightens and removes his wallet from his shorts pocket. He opens it, removes two condoms, and places them on the bedside table.

I slant my lips into a shy smile. "You came prepared."

He chuckles, the achingly sexy sound a low rumble. "To be honest, they've been in there for the past few weeks. I wanted to be ready, just in case."

"Thank you." I kiss him lightly, a brief brush of our lips. At least one of us was prepared for this.

Fingers trembling, I unzip my jeans and shimmy them down my legs. My panties come off next. I don't want to risk Troy spotting the scars on my upper thighs. Cigarette burns. The marks that claimed I once belonged to someone else.

By the time I straighten, Troy is gloriously naked, his length proud and rigid. A new wave of nervousness washes through me, and I bite my lip.

I can do this.

I want to do this.

I'm a long way from feeling normal again. A long way from a life free of flashbacks and nightmares.

But this—this is different.

This is about me reclaiming a small piece of myself I lost a long time ago. It's about my choices. About me having control.

I lie on the bed. Troy lies next to me and kisses me long and deep. The scent that is mountains and rain showers and hope wraps around me. Troy's scent. I feel safe. I feel respected. I feel wanted.

I focus on those things. Focus on the roughness of his

calloused hands. Focus on the beat of his heart beneath my palm, so steady, so sure, so perfect.

Troy pulls away from my mouth and plants soft kisses down my body. Every few inches, his teeth nip my skin, exciting nerve endings, igniting more flames of desire within me. My body is turning into a fireworks display, ready to burst into a billion stars, and the show is about to begin.

He reaches the junction between my legs and bends my knees, opening me up. Exposing me.

A delicious chill dances and swirls through my body. Troy kisses the inside of my knee. He's just as I imagined he would be. A considerate lover. A lover who makes my body go weak with anticipation. He continues planting kisses along my inner thigh.

He separates my seam with his fingers. Then his mouth is on the part of me that's never been touched this way. His tongue flicks along one lip, and white-hot liquid heat spreads throughout my belly.

Another flick of his tongue. And I moan, my body practically shooting off the bed.

I clutch the sheet with both hands, doing my best to keep myself from disintegrating too soon. I never expected sex to feel this good. This amazingly, addictively good.

Troy's talented tongue continues taking me higher and higher and higher. I writhe and groan with each flick, each tease, each kiss.

"I need you inside me." Gasped whispers and relief-pleading whimpers tumble from me. "Pleeeaase." I'm not sure my body can take much more.

Troy laughs softly against my super-sensitive core, the hot caresses pushing me close to falling apart. I release the sheet, and I tug on his hair.

Troy groans, pushes himself up, and removes a foil package from the nightstand. He opens it and rolls the condom along his length. "Are you sure this is what you want?" His voice is low, the want and need in it a husky moan. "We can stop now if you need."

A barely-there voice murmurs in my head, questions if maybe he's right. Maybe this is too soon. Too much.

But my body ignores it. Three months ago, I wasn't ready. But thanks to the work I've done with Robyn, I'm more ready than I've ever been.

"Oh, God, don't stop now." My words ride on a desperate groan.

Troy's mouth covers mine, and he kisses me long and hard until my body is about to combust. He positions his tip at my entrance and slowly pushes himself in, giving my body time to adjust to his glorious width.

Once fully seated, he pauses to give me another long, languid kiss. Heat builds low in my belly, igniting the final fuse. Troy begins to move, slowly at first, then faster, harder, pumping in time with my panted pleas for him to keep going.

An unfamiliar sensation, hot and heady, rushes through me. My inner muscles clench, and I explode into a shower of stars and rainbows and dancing unicorns.

Troy groans out my name, and the sound of it falling from his lips is liquid honey.

Jessica. The name of the woman I am becoming...not the woman I once was.

But the truth of that also scares me.

Because it's a reminder of how much I'm keeping from him.

Of how I'm not letting him fully in.

54

TROY

June, Present Day
Maple Ridge

My name falls from Jess's lips as I thrust inside her, her soft heat clamping my cock in its snug, wet grip. The sweet sound of my name on her lips is my ultimate undoing.

I clutch hold of my frail thread of self-control and thrust deeper, again and again. My balls tighten and I come hard, her name carrying on a worshiping groan. Her soft heat clenches my cock in endless waves, milking every last drop from me.

Once the shock waves die down, I carefully remove myself from her, plant a soft kiss on her lips, and roll off the bed. I dispose of the condom, lie back beside her, and pull her to me. I'm not sure I'll be able to move for the foreseeable future. Not after what we just shared. I'm spent. Happily sated.

Jess rests her head on my chest, and I trace lazy circles on her arm with my thumb. But even after what we just did, I don't feel any closer to her. There's still the wall between us.

And I'm not sure how I feel about that.

It's not as if I'm looking for a serious relationship. I failed my best friend by not getting him help when he needed it. Part of me fears the same thing will happen to Jess—that I won't be able to save her. That I'll fuck up.

Maybe this—us having sex—is the first step in that direction.

I pause drawing circles on her back. "You okay?"

She glances up at me, a soft smile on her face, barely visible in the low light from her window. "I am. Very much so." She starts to wiggle off the bed, the sheet around her chest.

My fingers circle her wrist. "Hey, where're you going?"

"To check on Bailey. She's not used to spending the night in her crate. She sleeps with me. Which...which she shouldn't be doing." Jess rolls her bottom lip between her teeth, and she looks...apologetic?

I release her wrist. "Why's that?"

"I'm just her puppy raiser. Eventually she'll go to her forever home. But it won't help if she's been sleeping with me instead of in her crate." Jess grabs her jeans from the floor and begins to pull them on, her body partially in the deep shadow.

"What if you are her forever home?" My words roll out, and I tread carefully, so not to step on a land mine.

"But I'm not." She slips her top on over her head without bothering to put on her bra.

I swing my legs over the side of the bed, bracing for what's bound to come next. "Technically, you are."

Her eyebrows jerk up and squeeze together, forming a divot between them. "Technically? What are you talking about?"

"This isn't how things are normally done, but Jenny and I thought you would benefit from having Bailey as your service dog, even though she still has a lot of training ahead of her."

A yawning silence stretches in the space between us, the

crevice growing wider with each passing second. *Fuck.* I shouldn't have told her yet, but I didn't want her thinking she was doing anything wrong by letting Bailey sleep in the room with her. I was right about Bailey making a difference for Jess—even if Bailey isn't fully trained as a PSD yet. The subtle changes in Jess aren't due to therapy alone. Bailey is also responsible for them.

"Why?" Jess's voice is a harsh whisper. "Why would you do that? I don't need you to give me things. I'm capable of looking after myself."

Her words slash my chest, but I keep the wince at her reaction from my face. Thank Christ she doesn't know about the arrangement I made with Robyn. Jess would eviscerate me if she found out. Now that she's on my payroll, the company's insurance plan will partially pay for her therapy. But I'm hardly bringing up either point—especially since she believes the State of Oregon is footing the bill.

"I don't need you to be my caretaker."

"I know, Jess. But there's also nothing wrong with letting your friends help you."

A grunted huff pushes past her lips, and her forehead crinkles into a stubborn frown.

"You don't believe me?" I ask.

"Maybe if you'd been honest with me…" She huffs once more, the sound no less annoyed than before.

"Would you have accepted her if I had?"

Her lack of reply confirms what I suspected. She wouldn't have. She'd have put her pride ahead of her need for help. She uses that pride as a shield against anyone who tries to breach her wall. I have no idea how to get her to put it down, but damned if I don't want to try.

"I know you've fallen in love with her, Jess. Now you don't have to worry about losing her once she's ready for her forever home. You are her forever home."

The pin-drop quiet that stretches between us this time isn't so heavy with tension. My balls might not be in as big of a risk as they were a moment ago.

Jess's lips twitch into a slight smile. But I don't kid myself into believing she'll forgive me if she finds out who's actually paying for her therapy.

She leaves the room, and I turn on the nightstand lamp. The unopened condom wrapper sits on a nonfiction library book about D-Day spies. I grab the foil square and open the nightstand drawer to stash the condom in it.

Jess's drawer is pretty much empty like mine is at home. Except, instead of a box of condoms, Jess has several photos. The top photo is of a baby wearing a pink dress and sitting on a blanket.

I remove the picture from the drawer.

The next photo is of a toddler grinning at the camera and showing the photographer her stuffed puppy. Her brown hair is tied up in two little pigtails, but her eyes are the same as Jess's. Is this Jess as a toddler? Only now she dyes her hair blond?

The same girl is about five years old in the final photo. She's drawing a picture with crayons and making a goofy face for the camera.

"What are you doing?"

I snap my head up.

Jess stares at the photos in my hand, her face pale, eyes wide with conflicting emotions.

"Sorry, I wasn't intentionally going through your things. Who is she?" I hold up the photos.

"She's...she's my niece."

"You have siblings?" Jess has never mentioned her family, other than she lived with her grandparents as a kid, and her parents abandoned her at a young age.

She nods, a single jerk of her head, but doesn't elaborate. She takes the photos from me, and her gaze drops to the picture of the girl making a funny face. Pain, deep and bleeding, cuts in Jess's expression. She returns the photos to the drawer, her fingers lingering on them.

I take her hand. She doesn't yank it away, but she also doesn't look at me.

I dip my head and try to catch her eye. "Is something wrong? Is your niece okay?"

"Why were you snooping in my stuff?" Fear flares in her eyes and in her tone.

Fuck. Fuckity. Fuck. I can already see her wall going up again. "I'm sorry, Jess. I shouldn't have looked in the drawer. I was putting the extra condom in there. I figured your drawer was empty like mine is at home."

I pull her onto my lap. She doesn't resist, but her movement is stiff, her expression guarded.

I kiss her temple. She doesn't resist that either. "I really am sorry, Jess. Do you want me to leave?"

Her silence lasts a beat, long enough for her hesitation and doubt to drill deep in my bones. "No."

"You sure?"

She's quiet for another beat. "Yes, I'm sure." Her voice is soft, but her tone is more certain this time.

She moves off my lap and sits on the bed. Her gaze locks with mine, her pain still clouding her eyes. "I want you to stay the night, Troy. If that's what you want. But please promise you won't go looking through my stuff. If I can't trust you, then this, what we have between us, is over."

I'm not exactly sure what we have between us, but I nod because whatever it is, I'm not ready for it to end.

My phone rings near my head, the sound jolting me from my sleep.

Jess's sleepy groan vibrates through my chest. "It's too early for someone to be calling."

I have to agree with her. Beams of sunlight are sneaking through the slits in the blinds. It must be around 8:00 a.m.

Normally, I'm up before sunrise, even on the weekend. But Jess and I ended up having sex a second time last night, and then she woke from a nightmare. I held her until she finally fell asleep once more.

The phone stops ringing.

"That's better." Jess's sleepy voice is a new level of sexiness.

Smiling, I lean in and gently bite the shell of her ear. "Mornin'. Why don't you sleep a little longer, and I'll walk the dogs? I'm sure they're more than ready to go outside."

I'm surprised they haven't already been demanding our attention.

My phone rings again, and this time I check who's calling. Maple Ridge's Search and Rescue dispatch. And my body goes from sleepy to alert.

I answer the phone. "What's up?" Concern coils deep in my tone.

Jess turns, and her eyebrows knot into a worried frown. My question is mirrored on her face.

"We have a report of two missing campers," Sheldon says. "A father and son. They were last heard from three days ago. The son is only nine years old."

I scramble out of bed. "Okay, I'm on my way."

He tells me where the meeting point is, and I end the call.

"I have to go," I tell Jess. She's sitting up in bed, hugging the sheet to her body. "I've been called out on a search and rescue for a missing father and son."

"How long will you be gone?" Jess scoots to the edge of the bed.

"Maybe a few hours. Maybe longer."

She knows my brothers and I are part of the search and rescue organization. This isn't the first time I've been called away for a few days because of it. But this is the first time I've been at her house when the call came in.

I phone Garrett. "Did Sheldon call you?"

"He did. I'm getting ready to leave now."

"Can you do me a favor and pick up my gear and come get me? I'm at Jess's."

"Sure." He doesn't ask why I need him to pick me up when I have my truck. It's not the first time my brothers and I have driven to a search and rescue together instead of going separately.

I end the call. "I'm leaving my truck with you," I tell Jess. "Garrett's picking me up. Can you drop Butterscotch off with my neighbor?" I text her Katherine's address. Katherine usually looks after Butterscotch whenever I get called away.

I shove my legs into my jeans and pull them up. "Maybe you should stay with Zara or Emily while I'm gone. We have no idea if someone broke into your house yesterday, and I don't feel right leaving you alone."

Jess pales, and I mentally curse whoever stole her sense of security.

"I'm sure I'll be fine. Bailey will look after me." The confidence in her voice is a tattered flag, and I wish I didn't have to leave her like this. "And I can look after Butterscotch if you want," she adds. "I'm sure Bailey would love that."

"Thank you. I'm sure Butterscotch would also love that." I want to argue her reason for not calling the cops, but she hasn't given me one, other than there was nothing missing and no signs of a break-in beyond the disturbed piece of tape on her back door. Maybe once I return, I'll talk to Noah and see what he thinks.

"I can make you some food to take with you," she says, hugging the sheet tighter to her chest.

"Unfortunately, I don't have time." I press my mouth to hers in a brief kiss. "Garrett will be here any minute. I'll call you once I'm finished. With any luck, I'll be back in a few hours." I kiss her again, this time longer and deeper.

And then I walk out the bedroom door.

55

JESSICA

June, Present Day
Maple Ridge

T roy leaves my bedroom to join the search for the missing father and son.

As soon as the front door clicks shut behind him, I remove Amelia's photos from the nightstand. I never expected Troy to find them. Never expected him to open the drawer they were in.

I sit on the bed and study Amelia's baby picture. Then close my eyes and see in my mind the blue fall sky from that day. Amelia's father was on duty, so it was just the two of us sitting in the backyard, enjoying our short freedom from his anger and mean words. She was nine months old at the time.

"I promise you," I'd told her. "I promise we'll get away from him. Far, *far* away. Somehow. Where he'll never find us. Where would you like to go? A magical kingdom? A place where fairies will protect us?" It all sounded amazing. A dream that would never become our reality.

Amelia was twenty months old in the next photo. She's holding a floppy puppy that Granny had given her when she was a baby. Amelia was happy, unaware of what would soon be coming. Neither of us had been prepared for what would happen.

The last picture is the photo I never took. Amelia looks so happy and so beautiful. It's two years old, but it's still precious to me. All three photos are precious to me.

I lay them out on the bed and touch my daughter in each image, as if that's enough to make her materialize in the room. An emptiness gnaws at me, and my chest shrinks in on itself with each ragged breath I take.

Tears sting my eyes, burn a trail on my skin.

I wish I could just hold her one more time, kiss her sweet cheek, hear her laugh, see her smile.

Hear her call me Mommy.

Even if Grace and Craig allow me into my...their daughter's life, I'll never get to hear her call me Mommy. She won't remember who I am.

Footfalls pad into the room. I glance toward the door. Both Bailey and Butterscotch have tracked me down. Butterscotch's round black eyes are questioning. Bailey jumps her paws onto the bed.

I sniff and wipe my face with the back of my hand. "I guess you two would love to go for a W-A-L-K."

But before I can take them for a walk, there's one thing I need to do first.

I retrieve the wooden box with the lotus flower carved on it from downstairs. The dogs follow me. I put the box on the bed, go to the closet, and remove the shoebox I stashed there when I moved into the house.

I transfer the contents to the wooden box and hide it in the secret space in the other bedroom. The last thing I want is for anyone to find the contents of the box, the clues to my true identity.

Bailey, Butterscotch, and I walk along the sidewalk. I didn't bother with Bailey's *Service Dog in Training* vest. This will be playtime for her.

The late June temperature is warmer than I was expecting, with puffy clouds dotting the blue sky. We turn down the street that leads to the off-leash park. Violet told me the other day she takes Sophie to the playground near there.

"We'll play ball in a few minutes," I tell the two dogs. "I want to check something first."

Several young kids are playing on the equipment when we arrive. I scan the area for signs of Violet and Sophie. I knew the chances of them being here was small, but that doesn't stop the tendrils of disappointment from spreading through me.

She wasn't at yoga last week.

Or the time before that.

She told Shania she was sick, but when I texted Violet, she told me she was too busy to attend yoga. I suggested we get together for coffee, and she agreed to the idea, but then canceled at the last minute.

Why can't I shake the feeling something's wrong?

No. I'm just being paranoid. After everything that happened to me, I'm programmed to expect the worse. Violet's fine. She has to be fine.

But no matter how many times I tell myself that, I have a hard time convincing myself it's true.

We head to the dog park, and I toss the balls for Bailey and Butterscotch to fetch. My arm is sore by the time they grow bored of the game. I click the leashes onto their collars. "We're going home, but we're walking the long way."

We arrive at Violet's house. Even though it's the middle of the day, her living room curtains are drawn. I walk along the path and knock softly on the door. I don't want to wake Sophie if she's napping.

No one answers the door. I text Violet that I'm here and knock again, but this time a little louder. Still nothing.

I look up at the second-floor windows. There's no indication anyone is home. Maybe Violet is visiting her parents in Portland.

I release a long, unsteady breath, unable to chase away the feeling something's not right. *Stop being so paranoid*. It's like with the tape on the back door. It probably came unstuck. The tape is old, the glue not as sticky as it once was. No one actually broke in. I panicked over nothing.

I give Violet's home one more concerned glance. "Okay, you two," I say to the dogs, "let's go home."

56

ANGELIQUE

June 1943
France

I n the month since I learned Johann's sister is deaf, an unlikely friendship has sprouted between Johann and me, delicate as a new shoot.

But it's not a friendship firmly rooted in trust.

For all he knows, I could be an informant, and he would be right. But I'm not an informant for the Gestapo, and none of what he told me is of interest to Baker Street.

Our relationship amounts to being polite and friendly, yet still guarded. His grief at losing his friend, someone who was a brother to him, remains.

Johann hasn't had any more dinner guests, which is both a relief and frustrating. If things don't change soon, if I don't find myself privy to information Baker Street could benefit from, the SOE will need to reassign me to a new role in the war.

I pedal around the curve in the road that passes Jacques's

vineyard. The sun is low in the horizon, peering above the tops of the grapevines, warning me it's almost curfew. Johann told me this morning he would be coming home late and not to worry about making supper for him.

Pierre comes into view on his bicycle. Once we're next to each other, the canopy of an oak tree above our heads, we stop and dismount.

"*Bonjour*, Angelique." His flushed face breaks into a welcoming smile.

"*Salut*, Pierre. What are you doing out here?" I wasn't expecting to see him today.

"I've been sent to tell you"—the volume of his voice drops, almost scraping the cracked road—"the new pianist can't keep his wireless at the safe house. The Nazis have become more vigilant in these parts. My contact thought maybe he could store it in Monsieur Gauthier's barn."

I manage to keep my surprise at his comment from my face. "Are they forgetting about the Wehrmacht captain billeted there?" Is his contact fucking barmy?

"That's why they thought the barn would be the perfect hiding spot. No one will suspect a wireless set is being hidden where a Nazi is staying."

"He's not a Nazi." The whispered words pour out harsh and waspish. The intensity of them shocks even me.

"Sure he is. He's one of *them*." Pierre's tone is equally harsh and biting, and the flush of his skin darkens.

"He's a Wehrmacht Army officer, but I get the impression he doesn't support Hitler. But it doesn't matter if he supports the monster or not; it's not a smart idea to hide the set in Jacques's barn. If the Germans find it, he and I will be executed. Or we'll be imprisoned and tortured."

"Then make sure that doesn't happen."

"And where exactly will the operator be sending messages

from? Or is your contact expecting him to also do that under Captain Schmidt's nose?"

Pierre lifts his shoulders in what is not a reassuring shrug.

"Tell your contact they need to come up with another plan. If Captain Schmidt weren't living in the farmhouse, it might be possible, but not under these conditions."

The rumble of an engine is our first warning of approaching danger. We scan the area for a place to hide. The Nazis don't like people gathering in private groups. In their opinion, even a group of two is one person too many.

And two people meeting like this, on a road where Gestapo or SS or Wehrmacht cannot spy on us, is bound to raise suspicion.

"I don't suppose if we kiss, they will ignore us?" Fear splinters Pierre's voice, a contrast to the near calm of his expression. It's a reflection to how I feel and how I'm trying to appear to the Germans who are about to stumble across us.

A military Jeep comes around the bend. My palms grow clammy against the bicycle handlebars. I tighten my grip. The Jeep has plenty of room to pass us. If it hits us, it's not due to lack of space.

The Jeep doesn't slow, but it does pass us without swerving even a fraction of an inch towards us. *Thank God for that.* I relax my grip on my bike. Johann is sitting behind the wheel. He doesn't acknowledge me. He usually greets me with a nod and a smile, but only when we are alone.

I watch the Jeep until it is out of view. It never slowed. If anything, it sped up once it drove past Pierre and me. If Johann has an issue with Pierre and I meeting away from the watchful eyes of the Nazis, he does not plan to address it here, in the open.

"Wasn't that the Nazi who's living with you?" Pierre asks, his tone suggesting he already knows the answer.

I turn back to Pierre. "Tell your contact they need to keep looking for a place to store the wireless set. If the operator stores it in Jacques's barn, there's no guarantee he can keep to his assigned communication schedule. He won't always have access to it."

I don't wait for a response. I climb on my bike and pedal to the farmhouse.

The military Jeep is parked in the driveway with no sign of Johann. I lean my bike on the barn wall and go into the farmhouse.

Jacques isn't downstairs. He would have retreated to his room as soon as he heard the Jeep. Johann is also not down here. I listen for the creaking of floorboards in his room, but silence is all I hear. He must be at the pond. He still goes there whenever he can. I have followed him a few times, but with Dieter gone, there's nothing for me to learn. Johann is always alone, and it's not as if he talks German strategy out loud to himself.

I enter the kitchen and stare at the barn through the window. The location ticks off several of the SOE's requirements for hiding a wireless transmission set. The only issue is accessibility. The operator needs to have a genuine reason to constantly be at the house.

A worker at the vineyard? The perfect cover if not for the problem that Jacques cannot afford to hire anyone. It would look suspicious if he suddenly had the money to do that—even though he wasn't actually paying the man.

The front door clicks open. The *clunk-clunk-clunk* of heavy boots walks past the kitchen and heads upstairs.

I wait to see if Johann comes back downstairs. When he doesn't, I close the black-out curtains and go upstairs, puzzled that he did not acknowledge me as he normally does.

I JERK AWAKE WITH A GASP, MY HEART POUNDING, THE NIGHTMARE of the Nazi banging on the front door fading. The nightmares are nothing new. Nor is waking up in the middle of the night because of them.

Desperately needing fresh air, I put on my robe, pick up my shoes, and tiptoe down the steps, taking care to avoid the creaky spots. Darkness enshrouds me, forcing me to navigate the journey blind.

At the bottom of the stairs, I stop and listen for signs Johann has heard me. The only sound chipping through the silence is the ticking clock on the mantel. I pull on my shoes and slip out of the house.

I gaze up at the inky-black sky. Millions of stars blink back at me. It's the same sky Hazel sees in Bristol if she steps outside.

And suddenly, I feel that much closer to her. Now that I realise how much I miss her, it's as if I cannot stop. An avalanche of emotion crashes down on me.

Memories of conversations we had under the starry sky play in my head. Conversations about school, about our futures, about boys.

"I miss you so much," I whisper. If only the stars could relay the message to her.

My gaze drops to the barn. I am positive Johann hasn't found the hidden trapdoor. If he had found the space, he would know what the bed and the lamp and the first-aid supplies are used for. And if he had found the hiding spot, he would have told his commanding officer.

I walk to the barn and reach for the door. A voice from inside —low and deep and masculine—causes my hand to freeze midmovement. I strain to make out the voice and the words. *German.* Johann? Or is someone else in the barn and Johann is still asleep in the house?

Another voice. Soft and female and high-pitched. The voice of a child.

Taking care not to make a sound, I walk to the hole in the

barn wall that is barely large enough for me to see who is inside the building.

Three adults and a little girl are standing by the open trap-door. Johann is holding a torch, a dim glow spilling from it. Whereas Johann is blond, the other three have dark hair and they look like they haven't eaten in weeks. Their clothes are worn and dirty and too big.

"Remember, you cannot trust anyone in a uniform," Johann says to the little girl, his tone tender but firm. "Those men are not like me. Do you understand?"

The girl nods, gazing at Johann like he is the sun at the center of her universe.

"I have something for you, little one." He opens his satchel and removes a stuffed bear that looks like it has been much loved by its owner. Surprise and delight widen the girl's eyes. "This bear will help you be brave while you and your *vati* and *mutti* are hiding from the bad men. But you must promise me something, Sonja."

"What is that, *Onkel* Johann?"

"You will need to be very quiet while you are hiding."

"Like a field mouse?"

"Yes, exactly like a field mouse." He presses his finger to his lips.

She nods vigorously.

And I sink to the ground, my legs unable to support me. *They're Jewish.*

Shock crashes through me, sending my thoughts spiralling in all directions. *How? When? What?* The memory of the Jewish family in Paris collides with my panicked thoughts. The SS offi-cers...they attacked the family and hauled them away.

Johann. The family in the barn. They know him. Sonja referred to him as Uncle Johann. He only mentioned he had a sister. Is that his brother or another sister he never told me about? But none of them share his features or blond hair. And he is not Jewish. Or at least I don't think he is. Surely if he were, he would not be fighting for Germany.

He would have escaped Austria with his mother and deaf sister.

I ease out a long breath, stilling my thoughts, and push to my feet. I need to sneak back into the house and figure out the ramifications of the family being here. Figure out what their presence means to my safety as well as that of Jacques and the family.

I turn.

And find myself staring at the end of a pistol pointed at my head.

Bloody hell and fuck.

57

JESSICA

June, Present Day
Maple Ridge

Butterscotch comes into the kitchen and whimpers. For once, Bailey isn't by his side. The three of us returned from Violet's house four hours ago, and they've been hanging out in the living room.

"What's wrong? Do you miss your daddy?" I pick up the dish towel and dry my wet hands. "Why don't we go for another walk?"

He barks and runs off to the living room. From where I'm standing in the kitchen, I can't see where he disappeared. But I do know that it wasn't to the front door.

He barks again, the sound almost desperate.

My stomach twists. Something's not right. I scramble in the direction of his bark. He's behind the couch, next to Bailey, who's lying down, eyes closed. Even from where I'm standing, I can tell something's seriously wrong.

I race to them and drop to my knees. Bailey is breathing, but the movement of her chest is shallow and labored. I run my hand over her body, tears stinging my eyes. She was fine a few minutes ago, and I didn't hear anything that warned me she was hurt. No strange barks or cries. Nothing like that.

"It's going to be okay, Bailey." My words tumble out, the edges roughened and cracked.

Butterscotch whimpers again and barks but doesn't leave his friend's side.

"Don't worry. We'll take her to the vet. She'll be fine." *She's gotta be fine.* My heart pounds hard and fast, and my pulse echoes the chaotic rhythm in my ears.

I grab Troy's keys from the hallway table and scoop up Bailey's warm body. "Hold on, girl. Everything's gonna be all right."

Whatever you do, don't fall apart now. Bailey needs you.

Just like I need her.

I carry Bailey to Troy's truck. Butterscotch trots beside me. I press on the key fob, unlocking the doors, and open the rear passenger door. The movement is awkward, with both my arms supporting Bailey's weight. I gently lower her onto the back seat. "Please be okay. Please be okay. Please be okay." My voice is a shaky whisper, a prayer, a plea.

I strap her in with the seat belt and shut the door. Then I lift Butterscotch onto the front passenger seat, sprint to the house, grab my purse, the dogs' leashes, my keys. I lock the front door and race to the truck, not bothering to set up the makeshift alarms in my house. No time.

I climb into the driver's seat, turn over the engine, and reverse onto the street. This isn't the first time I've driven a truck, but it is the first time I've driven Troy's.

The drive to the vet clinic is only a few minutes, but it feels like hours before I'm hoisting Bailey off the back seat. My sweet puppy whimpers at the movement, her breathing still labored.

The tears I've been restraining finally shatter the dam and wet my cheeks. "Please hold on, Bailey. I love you so, so much. Please be okay."

I can't lose her. I've already lost so much. She's the one thing that makes it easier for me to breathe. And thanks to Troy and Jenny, I won't lose her once her training is over. I won't lose her then, and I have no intention of losing her now.

I close the door with my shoulder and rush toward the clinic, practically dragging Butterscotch behind me on his leash.

I approach the glass door. A man is leaving and sees my arms are full, my load heavy. He opens the door wider.

"Do you need help?" Sympathy colors his eyes. His young German shepherd attempts to sniff Butterscotch.

"Thank you. I'm fine." My voice splinters, and I hurry to the front desk in the clinic.

The blond, white woman behind the computer looks up, smiling. The smile is quickly replaced with concern. She pivots to the Black woman with a cloud of textured curls and wearing cat scrubs. "Ambrosia, we have an emergency here." Her voice is both urgent and calm, the tone of a professional who has experienced her share of emergencies. She swivels back to me, her compassion locking on my gaze. "What happened?"

"I don't know. She was like this when I found her in my living room."

Bailey and I are led to an exam room. The receptionist keeps Butterscotch with her, recognizing him as Troy's dog.

The next few minutes are spent in a whirl of questions about Bailey. What did she eat today? Could she have gotten into something she shouldn't have? Where has she been during the past twenty-four hours? My brain feels like it's filled with water. I can barely make out what they're asking me. And my body is shaking so badly, I'm surprised I can stand.

The nurse leads me to another waiting room and tells me she'll return once she has more information. The receptionist enters the room with Butterscotch and inquires if there's anything she can get me, or if there's someone she can call. I shake my head.

I lift Butterscotch onto my lap and fuss over him, thanking him for being here for me. He laps up the attention, but I can tell he's wondering where Bailey is. He's used to Bailey being by my side. I'm used to her being there too. I feel so naked and alone without her.

Maybe I should text Jenny and let her know what's going on. But what if she decides I don't deserve Bailey because I let this happen? I could text Zara, Emily, and Simone instead.

Or even Violet.

I brush the idea aside. I don't want to worry them. I'm not the only one who loves Bailey.

Fear and restlessness tighten my chest, turn my skin itchy. I push to my feet with Butterscotch in my arms and pace.

I've made a good start to creating a canyon to Australia when the vet comes into the room. He smiles at me. The smile isn't big, but it fits like a reassuring hug.

The tightness in my chest eases a little. "Is she okay?"

"She will be. She somehow ingested poison, but because you got her here so soon, we were able to prevent any long-term damage. I would like to keep her here for observation overnight, but she's young and will rebound quickly."

"Can I see her?" Hope lifts the pitch of my voice, loosens the tightness around my heart some more.

"For a few minutes. She's groggy right now and needs to rest."

Ambrosia takes Butterscotch back to the receptionist while the vet leads me to the room where Bailey is recovering. Rows of cages line one wall, and the tightness in my chest returns.

Breathe. In...two...three. Out...two...three. It will be okay. She'll be okay.

This isn't a prison, but even knowing that doesn't stop the flood of memories of my old prison cell. The emptiness, the cold starkness, the torment. I rub my arms, trying to rid my body of the chill creeping in.

Bailey is asleep on a dog bed in one cage, oblivious to my presence. I crouch to her level. The vet opens the door to let me stroke my puppy.

I run my hand over Bailey's thick golden hair. "I'm so sorry, Bailey." My voice is a low plea to the universe. "I have no idea how you managed to eat poison. But I'll make sure it never happens again. And as soon as you're healthy, you'll get to come home." Pressure builds in my throat, making it difficult to drag air into my lungs. "I love you."

The vet ushers me out so Bailey can rest, and I pay the breath-stealing fee at the desk. Butterscotch and I return to Troy's truck. But I can't go home yet. I'm too restless for that.

I could call my friends since I still haven't told them about Bailey, but I'm not ready for that either. I'll call them tonight. After I get back. I need to relax, to clear my head. *Hiking.* I really want to go hiking. And thanks to Troy, I have the means to do that.

I don't know Katherine, Troy's neighbor. Rose has offered to look after Bailey if I ever need to go somewhere that a service dog in training isn't allowed. I assume the offer applies to Butter-scotch too.

I take him to the truck. "I'm dropping you off at Rose's house. But I'll pick you up once I've returned. I'll only be gone a few hours."

We arrive at Rose's house. She opens the door and grins the warm grandmother smile that eases a tiny bit of my tension. "Hi, Jess." She looks down. "Hi, Butterscotch. Where's Bailey?"

I tell her what happened. Rose's face pales. "Oh, dear. The poor thing."

"The vet said she's going to be okay." I infuse my words with more reassurance than I feel. "Troy left for a search and rescue mission this morning. I'm looking after Butterscotch for him, but

I need to go somewhere for a few hours, and I was wondering if you could look after him until I get back."

"Of course!" Rose lets Butterscotch into her house.

I thank her and return home. A few minutes later, I'm in my hiking clothes—walking shorts and a T-shirt. My bag is packed, and I'm driving toward my favorite trail.

It's late afternoon and the parking lot isn't as busy as it might've been an hour or two earlier. This is the first time I've hiked on my own, but as long as I stick to the trail, I should be fine.

It's also the first time I've hiked without Bailey since she's come into my life. An ache spreads through my chest, but it's quickly doused, knowing she'll be okay. It's because of what Bailey has given me over the past two and a half months—a taste of my old strength and self-confidence—that I'm even able to hike on my own.

I pull on my backpack and walk to the trailhead, breathing in the clean mountain air, letting it wrap around the anxieties trying to push to the surface. I pick up my pace, needing to distract my thoughts from anything that doesn't involve hiking and photography. I focus on the rocks and the roots sticking out of the ground and the winding path that grows steadily steeper.

I focus on the wind against my cheeks, on the rustle of the leaves, on the call of the birds. I focus on the sounds and sights and smells and textures of freedom. Every so often, I stop and shoot frame after frame with my phone camera of whatever grabs my attention. The view. A chipmunk sitting on a rock. The hawk surfing on the wind.

Exploring the world through the lens relaxes me in a way I didn't think would be possible again. Not when I'd been sentenced to twenty-five years in prison. But even though I can take nice photos with my phone, I still miss the feel of a DSLR camera in my hand. I still miss what I was capable of achieving with my old one.

At the end of the trail, beyond the tree line, I slowly turn on the spot, taking in the view. The mountain ridge that continues from where I'm standing. The forest. The flat stretch of ranches and farmlands to the west.

It truly is breathtaking up here.

Breathtaking and extremely windy. Loose tendrils of hair whip in my face, and the force of the wind causes me to take a half step back.

I stand on the spot for a few more minutes, then remove my water from my pack. I drink some of it, snack on the small amount of food I brought with me, and start back down the trail. My phone battery is nearly dead because I've taken so many photos, and I don't have enough supplies to survive if I'm stuck up here. And I really don't want to become the next victim Troy and his crew need to rescue.

I carefully navigate my way down the hiking path, relieved to have the shelter of the pine trees once I'm in the forest again. I don't see anyone as I descend, and there aren't any vehicles in the parking lot when I arrive, other than Troy's truck. Dark clouds gather overhead, carrying with them the threat of a storm. The wind is now as strong here as it was on the ridge.

The rain starts coming down hard as I drive along the road leading to Maple Ridge. On the far side of the road, the shoulder is met by a steep embankment. A peaceful mix of forest and grass and wildflowers skirts the road on the passenger side. The road ahead and behind me is empty of cars. It's like I'm the only person out here.

A Pushing Limits song is playing on the radio. One of my favorite songs of theirs. I sing along with the lyrics.

A deer darts from out of nowhere, leaping over the railing separating the grass from the road, and lands in front of the truck.

I jerk the steering wheel hard to the left and slam my foot on the brake, trying to avoid the poor animal. But the road is now slick and there's not enough braking room between me and the far metal railing. Troy's truck crashes through it with a terrifying crunch and continues down the embankment.

Screams fill the cab. My screams. Loud and piercing. And never-ending. I'm jostled like a rag doll, and the truck flips onto its side. Airbags deploy. Something hits my head hard.

Troy's face flashes in my mind. His smile when he sees me. His kind and supportive words. The feel of his lips against mine.

And the world goes black.

DON'T MISS THE EXCITING CONTINUATION OF THE HIDDEN SECRETS TRILOGY WITH ONE MORE BETRAYAL.

YOUR BOOK CLUB READING GUIDE

A CONVERSATION WITH STINA LINDENBLATT

Please note that the following conversation and discussion questions contain some spoilers. I recommend not reading ahead if you want to be surprised.

What was your inspiration for writing Jessica and Troy's story?

When my kids were younger, one of them made friends with a boy while they were in the community soccer program. I got to know his mother, but it didn't take long for me to notice she had very low self-esteem. Plus, every time she did something (no matter how small), she would ask my approval. She didn't seem to trust her own judgement. At the time, I didn't understand why. It wasn't until she left her husband several years later that I learned he was emotionally abusive.

But she wasn't the only member of the family impacted by her ex-husband's actions. The boy, who at one point had been my child's best friend, became a bully, and my child was his favorite target. The father had taught his son by example that it was okay to pick on people he considered weaker than him. The bullying started in elementary school and continued through to high school. My child is on the autism spectrum and started to struggle from mental illness in part due to what happened.

Several kids belonging to friends of the mother witnessed some of the bullying and told the mother about it on more than one occasion. But the ex-husband shared joint custody of their children, and the father and son were close. The mother refused to get professional help for herself and her two children despite her friends trying to convince her to talk to someone. I wouldn't be

425

surprised if her son (now an adult) follows in his father's footsteps as an abuser.

As a result of what happened, my husband and I started donating to our local emergency women's shelter. We still donate to the organization (Fear Is Not Love), which has gone on to create many wonderful programs to help families in domestic crisis. And because I get their regular newsletters, it sparked the idea for Jessica and Troy's story.

As for the accident that led to Colton taking his own life, that was based on the Humboldt Bronco's tragedy in 2018. Sixteen people died and thirteen passengers were severely injured when a transport truck drove through a stop sign at a highway in Saskatchewan. Many of the victims were young hockey players, some whose families lived near my city. None of the adults on the bus survived. The loss of life and the horrendous aftermath of the collision had an impact on the mental health of the first responders and the witnesses who tended to the victims. I wanted to acknowledge the impact a tragedy like this has on first responders.

Why the outdoor mountain program for military vets of all ability levels?

When I started my kinesiology degree all those years ago, I was interested in adapted sports. Adapted sports involve the use of modified equipment (and/or rules) that allow individuals with a disability or chronic illness to participate in a sport or physical activity, which might not have otherwise been feasible.

During my MSc degree (in sports physiology), I had the opportunity one year to volunteer with the men's world wheelchair basketball championship. These men were high-caliber athletes who not only trained hard to be there, they did that while holding down full-time jobs in their home countries. I was the host for Team Great Britain. To get to one of the places the men needed to go, they had to take the escalator or elevator to the second floor. They chose the escalator. Escalators scare me. I get nervous standing on the narrow step while it moves. But that's nothing compared to going up it while in a wheelchair. That requires tremendous upper-body strength...and for you to be fearless.

I ended up going a different career route, but when I came up with the idea for the Carson Brothers series, I was excited to explore that part of my educational background again. There are several outdoor programs in the US similar to what the brothers created that are specifically designed for military vets.

Why did you decide to make Savannah Townsend's husband a police officer?

On May 25th, 2020, George Floyd was murdered by Derek Chauvin, a Minneapolis police officer. Soon after the incident, his wife filed for divorce. I wondered when the news was announced if she was a survivor of domestic abuse. I wondered if the disregard he showed for human life was something she had regularly witnessed at home. This led me to think about what would happen to a wife whose abusive husband was a police officer. How much harder would it be to escape him? Would she be able to escape him? Those questions became the backstory to Jessica's past.

One More Secret is a contemporary romance. What made you decide to include Angelique's story when a dual timeline like this is unusual in romance?

Over five years ago, I took an online Romance Writers of America workshop about the CIA. The first part of the workshop focused on the women of the SOE and OSS. The OSS was the American version of the SOE and the precursor to the CIA. I couldn't stop thinking about these brave women, many who didn't survived the war. They played a huge role in bringing the war to an end during a time when sexism was strong. Vera Atkin believed that women could make a difference in the war effort. Up until then, men were the ones sent to occupied countries, but they couldn't blend in the way women could. The men were supposed to be working during the day or in German prison camps.

Soon after taking the RWA workshop, I started reading historical fiction, a genre I never thought I would enjoy (unless it was a steamy historical romance). I fell in love with historical fiction set during the Second World War and began reading nonfiction books about the war and the numerous female spies sent to occupied countries. This led to the idea for Angelique's story. The idea for Jessica and Troy's story came to life soon after. The more I thought about the two stories, the more I realized they went perfectly together (as will become even more obvious in *One More Betrayal* and *One More Truth*).

When I started plotting the story, Russia's war on Ukraine hadn't yet begun. I didn't realize at the time that over a year later the world would be a different place, and we would witness the similarities between World War II and Putin's attack on Ukraine.

How much of the World War II story is based on truth and fiction?

The story is fictitious. All the characters, except for Vera Atkins and Major Maurice Buckmaster, are of my own creation. The *Carmen* network is also fictitious. However, several characters were inspired by real-life people or a combination of two real-life individuals. This includes Angelique and Johann. You'll have to wait until the end of the final book of the trilogy (*One More Truth*) to find out who the individuals were.

Even though the story is fictitious, many of the details are based on real life. *How to Become a Spy: The World War II SOE Training Manual* proved to be an indispensable resource when it came to Angelique's role in the war and her actions. It's the actual basic syllabus used at the SOE training schools, specifically Canada's secret training center in Ontario. I also used several other resources for researching and planning the World War II story.

I have taken some creative license to keep things simpler when it came to the number of characters mentioned in the story. And because of that, I have several individuals doing tasks they might not have done during the war when it comes to the SOE verses the local resistance circuits.

Do you have any personal experiences with the Second World War, including relatives who fought in it?

Yes, and this was part of the reason I felt so compelled to write Angelique's story. I was born in England, as was my father's side of the family. My father was born during the war, about sixteen months after the Blitz on Coventry, where his parents and brother lived. He was three years old at the end of the war and only remembers having green jelly (Jell-O) during a street party to celebrate V-Day.

My mother is from Finland and was born after the war. Her father was a Finnish soldier who fought in the war against the Russians. Finland defeated Russia and later sided with the Allies against the Nazis. I have photos of my grandfather in uniform while he was on the front lines.

My husband is Canadian, but his parents were both born in East Prussia (now part of Poland). My mother-in-law was born during the war. My father-in-law was five-years-old at the start of it. Their memories at the end of the war didn't involve green jelly or anything nearly as pleasant when the Soviets came into their towns. My husband doesn't know anything about his paternal grandfather (he died before my husband was born), but he knows that his maternal grandfather didn't support Hitler. He was forced to fight in the war even though he was too old. He was forced to fight in a war he didn't believe in.

In the story, Johann's sister is deaf. My two oldest kids would have been at risk like his sister if we were living in Germany during the war. Both are on the autism spectrum and deal with mental illness. They are high functioning, which at one point was referred to as Asperger's Syndrome. It was named after Dr. Asperger, a German scientist who during World War II came up with a system to determine who was neurodivergent. Those who were classified on the spectrum would be murdered or dealt with in another way. That's why the term is no longer used for people who are on the high end of the autism spectrum. All of this had me wondering what would have happened if we had lived in Germany during World War II. What would I have done to protect my two kids from the Nazis? And those questions led me to writing Johann's story.

DISCUSSION QUESTIONS

1. How does Troy help Jessica deal with her past trauma, even though he doesn't know what the traumatic event was? What emotions did you feel when he took all those steps to help her?

2. Jessica has faced several losses over the years. How do you feel that has shaped the person she is at the end of the book? How does that compare to who she was at the beginning?

3. Based on the information provided in *One More Secret*, what are some things Jessica's husband did that are part of the cycle of abuse?

4. How do you feel about Troy's reason for creating the fundraiser festival?

5. Why did Jessica give up her daughter for adoption to her brother-in-law and his wife? How do you feel about her wanting to be a part of Amelia's life again?

6. There are different beliefs when it comes to domestic abuse. Do you know anyone who you suspect is in an abusive relationship or has been in one? What are some of the signs that gave you pause about that relationship?

7. What emotions did you feel when you learned that Johann's sister is deaf and was hiding from the Gestapo? Did your emotions toward Johann change when you learned that and when you discovered he is hiding a Jewish family in Jacques Gauthier's barn?

8. Has your opinion of Johann, a German officer, changed from the time he moved into the farmhouse to the end of the book? How and why has it changed (or not changed)?

9. *One More Secret* is at the forefront a romance, but it is also historical fiction, women's fiction, and a story of empowerment. What parallels are there so far between the modern-day story and the World War II story?

10. Did you agree with Angelique's rationale for being on friendlier terms with Johann even though he is the enemy? Why did you feel that way?

11. The novel deals with Jessica's goal to start her life over again and how she hopes her daughter will eventually be part of it. Discuss how motherhood and her past have shaped Jessica's decisions and choices.

12. Successful romantic relationships require trust. In what ways was trust explored in the story? In what ways was the trust between Angelique and Johann reflected between Jessica and Troy?

ACKNOWLEDGMENTS

First of all, I would like to thank you, the reader, for giving *One More Secret* a chance. The story has been a passion project of mine for the past few years. One that required a lot of research for the two timeline stories, and one that required I plot the equivalent of four books (even though Hidden Secrets is a trilogy). I have loved every moment of it. But a passion project is even more meaningful when an author's words touch a reader's heart, and when readers fall in love with the characters as much as the author fell in love with them.

When I first came up with the idea of writing the Hidden Secrets Trilogy, I knew the editor I used for my romantic comedies wasn't the right person for Jessica and Troy's story. One of my favorite romance authors is Kennedy Ryan. Her novel, *Long Shot*, deals with domestic abuse in the most raw and honest way. I contacted her editor, Lauren Clarke, and told her about my plans for the trilogy. I am so thankful to Kennedy for linking her editor on the copyright page of *Long Shot*, and to Lauren for agreeing to be my editor. *One More Secret* is even better than I had originally planned thanks to Lauren's insight, wisdom, and sheer brilliance.

I would also like to thank Margie Lawson and my immersion sisters (Monica Corwin, Jenny Hansen, Lainey Cameron, Linda Dindzans, and Cassandra Shaw). Thank you for challenging me when it came to my writing and for making me laugh during our Zoom meetings.

Back when I was in the very early stages of brainstorming my story idea for the trilogy, I was lucky to get to talk to Nina Grinstead, the owner of Valentine PR. This was at the 2020 Romance Author Mastermind conference, which was online that year because we were in the midst of the pandemic. I had a Zoom appointment with her to discuss anything to do with promotion and the branding for my books. At the time, I had been nervous about writing a contemporary romance that included a dual timeline from World War II. While this format isn't uncommon in historical fiction, the contemporary timeline is usually women's-fiction focused. As far as I knew, a dual timeline like this was unheard of in contemporary romance. I told Nina what little I had figured out at that point for the trilogy. She loved the idea and encouraged me to write it. She suggested that I avoid mentioning the World War II storyline in the blurb because that might turn off some readers if historical fiction doesn't interest them. And then, low and behold, several months later, *The Things We Leave Unfinished* by Rebecca Yarros was released. Her book (which I loved) eventually became a TikTok favorite. This further encouraged me to keep writing Jessica and Troy's story, which I had already started before the release of Rebecca's book.

My teenage daughter has been seeing a therapist for over a year now to help her with an eating disorder and her anxieties. I usually sit in on the sessions and have learned so much from them. This includes some of the relaxation exercises that you will read about in the next two books. Her therapist also shared with me some insights into domestic abuse that fueled additional research on the topic so I could make the story as authentic as possible. One of my goals for the trilogy is to help bring additional awareness to the long-term ramifications of domestic violence.

And lastly, I would like to thank my husband and kids for their support and understanding of why I love disappearing into my story worlds. I especially would like to thank my daughter, Anja, whose name I borrowed for Johann's sister. She has been my biggest supporter from the very beginning. Although that might be because I told her when she was little that if I was ever published, we would get a cat. For years, whenever she blew out her birthday candles, she would make a wish that I would land a book deal just so she could finally have a cat. My family adopted a super shy rescue kitten after I signed a contract with a traditional publisher for my first book. Callie recently celebrated her ninth year as part of our family. I went on to name a heroine after her. A heroine from the Pushing Limits series.

ABOUT THE AUTHOR

Born in Brighton England, Stina Lindenblatt has lived in a number of countries, including England, the U.S., Finland, and Canada. This would explain her mixed up accent. She has a kinesiology degree and a MSc in sports biological sciences.

In addition to writing fiction, she loves photography, and currently lives in Calgary, Canada, with her husband and three kids.

For news about her books and to sign up for her newsletter, check out her website at stinalindenblattauthor.com.

facebook.com/StinaLindenblattAuthor
instagram.com/stinalindenblatt
bookbub.com/authors/stina-lindenblatt
tiktok.com/@stinalindenblattauthor

9 781990 177330